RAIDERS

Also by William B. McCloskey Jr.

Fiction:
    Warriors
    Breakers
    Highliners
    The Mallore Affair

Nonfiction:
    Their Fathers' Work: Casting Nets with the World's Fishermen
    Fish Decks: Seafarers of the North Atlantic

RAIDERS

A NOVEL

William B. McCloskey Jr.

Skyhorse Publishing

Skyhorse Publishing books may be purchased in bulk at special discounts
for sales promotion, corporate gifts, fund-raising, or educational purposes.
Special editions can also be created to specifications. For details, contact the
Special Sales Department, Skyhorse Publishing, 307 West 36th Street, 11th
Floor, New York, NY 10018 or info@skyhorsepublishing.com.

Skyhorse® and Skyhorse Publishing® are registered trademarks of Skyhorse
Publishing, Inc.®, a Delaware corporation.

Visit our website at www.skyhorsepublishing.com.

10 9 8 7 6 5 4 3 2 1

Library of Congress Cataloging-in-Publication Data is available on file.
ISBN: 978-1-62636-062-4

Printed in the United States of America

For my wife Ann
to whom all the Highliners books
are dedicated with love.

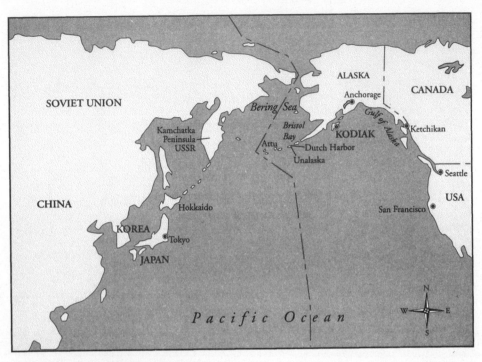

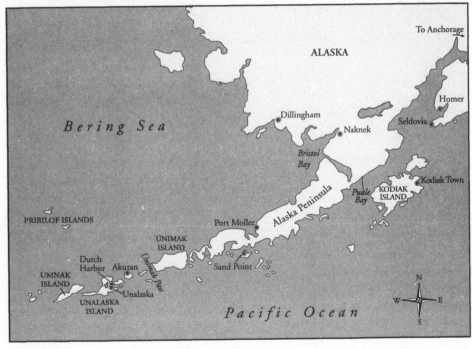

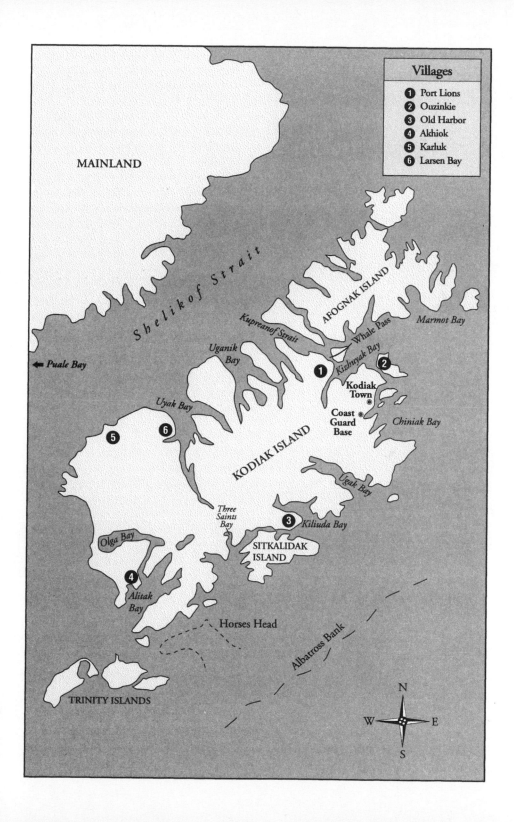

Villages

1. Port Lions
2. Ouzinkie
3. Old Harbor
4. Akhiok
5. Karluk
6. Larsen Bay

MAINLAND

Shelikof Strait

Puale Bay

Kupreanof Strait

AFOGNAK ISLAND

Marmot Bay

Whale Pass

Uganik Bay

Kizhuyak Bay

Uyak Bay

Kodiak Town

Coast Guard Base

Chiniak Bay

KODIAK ISLAND

Ugak Bay

Three Saints Bay

Kiliuda Bay

Olga Bay

SITKALIDAK ISLAND

Alitak Bay

Horses Head

Albatross Bank

TRINITY ISLANDS

N
W · E
S

Contents

PART I **THE SALMON TRADITION**
July–August 1982, Kodiak, Alaska   **1**

  1   Jones's Shadow   3
  2   Jumper's Song   19
  3   The Race   39
  4   Whale Passage   55
  5   Kodiak Talk   61
  6   The Beer Diplomats   71

PART II **RULES OF THE NEW GAME**
Mid-August to September 1982, Japan, Alaska   **87**

  7   Rising Sun   89
  8   "A Ruvrey Highriner"   99
  9   Bushido   111
10   The Suits   125
11   Halibut Buzz   147
12   Kodama   159
13   The Great Game Continues   167
14   Shakedown   185
15   Soakers   199

PART III The Wide World
October–December 1983, Alaska, Maryland, Alaska   217

16	Unfree	219
17	Moonjog	239
18	City Lights	251
19	Shaftsmanship	261
20	Honor	281
21	Splash	295

PART IV The Cold World
January–September 1984, Kodiak, Alaska   309

22	Shelikof	311
23	Overload	321
24	Ice	335
25	Fish Hold	357
26	Daylight	373
27	Epilogue: Sons	383

Acknowledgments

To set a novel in recent time and place, and thus to answer to those who were there, requires more than notebooks and personal recollection. I'm grateful to friends old and new, who shared their memories and insights while confirming or nixing my own. Others went out of their way to pull old reportage from basement files. While holding myself alone responsible for anything of questionable accuracy or focus, my deepest thanks to the following:

Thorvold Olsen, captain of the limit seiner *Viking Star,* who once tolerated me as a king crab crewman and on subsequent passenger rides has kept me alert with wheelhouse quizzes. (Thor, after answering pages of questions, even shipped me charts along with a piloting ruler and calipers to make sure I got things right by figuring them for myself.)

Alvin Burch, founder of the Alaska Draggers Association and a frequent negotiator on international fishery matters, who along with his late brother, Oral, set an early Kodiak standard for trawling aboard their twin vessels *Dawn* and *Dusk.*

Dave Milholland, engine guru and veteran of the Bristol Bay gilnetter fleet (he still fishes there each season, since, as he says, "I'm only eighty-three"), who in Anacortes with his wife, Dorothy, maintains a museum of working marine engines.

Robert Alverson, director of the Seattle-based Fishing Vessel Owners Association, who for decades has been a leader in charting a sane course to harvest the Alaska sea resources caught by longline.

Per Odegaard, captain of the traditional longline schooner *Vansee*, carried me aboard in 2001 during a run for black cod and halibut. Thanks also to his hospitable crewmen Carl Sebastian, Shawn McManus, Peter Erikson, Steve Thorkildsen, and Dewey Maletha.

Fishing captains Rudy Peterson, Kevin O'Leary, Dave Densmore, Leiv Loklingholm, and Mike Fitzgerald, as well as former fisherman and now-editor John van Amerongen, and the late respected Cap'n Lester of Chesapeake Bay, who took me shaft-tonging, were all willing to endure long taped interviews about their work and careers.

Tom Casey, advisor to Bering Sea crabbers, former fisherman, and long-term enthusiastic supporter of the Hank Crawford saga.

Alan MacNow and Jay Hastings, spokesmen for Japanese fishing interests, whose efforts to have me hosted in Japan fostered my appreciation of Japanese culture and the Japanese viewpoint. The isolated dark event narrated at the end of this book came not from their sphere but from official reports and media coverage.

Among those who searched out old documents or culled for arcane information: Gail Bendixen, staffer of the North Pacific Fishery Management Council in Anchorage; Peter Max and Judy Young of NERA in Washington, D.C.; and the always willing phone researchers at the Enoch Pratt Library in Baltimore. For medical information when I chose to injure a character, my daughter Dr. Karin McCloskey, therapist Bill Rhodes, and Dr. Richard Berg. And, for their guidance through the mysteries of contemporary art, J. Woodford ("Woody") Howard, collector, and professor emeritus at Johns Hopkins University.

Enrica Gadler, my editor at The Lyons Press, who has provided steady encouragement along with patience and insightful professional skill in guiding me through *Breakers* and now *Raiders*. Thanks also to publishers Nick Lyons and his son Tony Lyons, for supporting the "Highliners Trilogy" to its completion.

Final thanks to my family for their support and encouragement: my wife, Ann, always there for me, to whom this book is dedicated; my late parents, Bill and Evelyn, for the standards they once implanted; my children, Karin and Wynn, generous with advice in their areas of expertise; and now also my four-year-old grandson, Will, window into the future, who—stuffed into a lifejacket up to his ears—has already become a boat buddy.

PART I

The Salmon Tradition

JULY–AUGUST 1982
KODIAK, ALASKA

1

Jones's Shadow

ALASKA, KODIAK ISLAND, UGANIK BAY, LATE JULY 1982

Jones Henry was dead and that closed the book. Whether his ashes, soaked in scotch, had lured the humpies into the *Adele H*'s seine, or whether nature on its own had packed Uganik Bay with a greater storm of salmon than predicted, glistening silver fish thrashed the water to a boil inside the net.

It was "Yow!" all afternoon. And "Oh maa-an." No one aboard considered whether their shouts at the abundance covered grief for the recent past or came whole cloth from the present.

Hank Crawford, at the controls despite the cast on his shoulder, assumed the calm of command although his spirit whooped with the others. He guided brailer loads raised on the boom from water to hold. Fish bodies quivered against the tight meshes. When the big dip net opened, fish slurped out and thudded into the hold. Briny smells filled the air. Glassy wet covered metal and oilskins. Hank breathed the very heart of fishing again, at last. When it came time to harden the net and bring the remaining catch aboard, he leapt to grip web at the rail alongside his crew. They pulled arms-to-back as in the oldest times of fishermen, Hank as best he could. The bag of net upended to pour twisting fish around their legs.

"Yaa-hoo!"

So it went for set after set on the day they consigned Jones Henry's ashes to the water aboard Jones's own *Adele H.*

It was the culmination of two terrible weeks that had started for all of them, except Hank's wife Jody, within the salmon gill net fleet of Bristol Bay. Hank and his crew aboard his large *Jody Dawn* had been tendering fish received from smaller gill net boats, including Jones Henry's. During a storm, Jones's boat had lost power. When Hank didn't concentrate enough on present fishing, he could still see those waves smashing Jones's boat onto the mudflats that had been the graveyard for boats over the years. A helicopter from the cannery managed to lift Jones's single crewman Ham to safety. But during the hour before the chopper could return after refueling, the boat, with Jones aboard, began to break up. Thank God I went no matter how it turned out, Hank could tell himself now. He had risked his own life to launch a dinghy and row in to rescue Jones, and did indeed in the process smash part of his own *Jody Dawn,* but Jones had been his mentor and beloved friend. The shoulder he'd dislocated pulling Jones from the water was small price.

Then he'd done all he could to warm Jones under the frigid spray while he himself turned nearly too numb to function. Nobody's fault, the outcome. The helicopter had returned as soon as it could, and managed to tow the dinghy to safety, but even so Jones, a man in his sixties, had died of exposure.

Hank looked over the water at sights that had been a part of his friend. Oh Jones, he thought, picturing the man with all his stubble and spit. Back in Kodiak we gave you a proper church funeral, followed by an open bar aboard your beloved seiner that we're now riding in your honor. Even your new widow, Adele, agreed we did it right. But, Hank thought, somewhere now, Jones's caustic tongue must be summoning all the devils at the sight of Jody working on the deck where Jones had never allowed even Adele to set foot. And what would Jones say to Adele's calling the unbelievable from the pier as they left to bring Jones's ashes to his favorite fishing ground, inviting Jody to be the *Adele H*'s new skipper? It was just a joke, of course—Adele's jibe at all the men who held Jones's same superstition—but Hank doubted Jones would laugh. He stroked his beard. Admit it was funny, though, Jones: those startled male faces.

At least, thought Hank, Jones would have appreciated the way we gave his ashes to the water. All those boats in sight that stopped fishing to blow their whistles. And, then, Jones, you'd certainly understand that, since we'd traveled clear around Kodiak Island and the fishing was hot, we all then voted to stay and fish ourselves. Call that our own way to recover.

Hank looked around to ensure that nobody was watching, and pulled himself back into the present.

He cruised, looking for signs in the water. A breeze kicked along the surface. In the bright sun a glint could be fish-ripple or gust. His to figure, a hide-and-seek game reading the signs, requiring him to think like a predator half fish. Down swooped seabirds, looking also for their dinner. Their white wings merely quivered as they glided. This was the kind of fishing he wanted to do, in a boat big enough to keep elbows free of shipmates' ribs but small enough, at 58 feet, to allow him to smell the water. It didn't satisfy the power urge of his 108-foot *Jody Dawn* but . . . He glanced along a neat wooden panel, cleanly varnished except for the scuffs where binoculars dangling from a holder had bumped. Nice boat. She handled to his touch. Jones Henry's boat would have been no other way: Jones had kept her fit and had honed her performance. The creaks of her wooden hull were almost the voice of Jones.

Suppose he fished her the rest of the season while they repaired his *Jody Dawn?* It would give him some fresh air before resuming the hassle with the Japanese company he'd contracted to, back in the real world.

Around ten, however, with time before sunset for at least one more long set or a couple of roundhauls, Hank called halt. He joked about tender greenhorns and endured Seth's jibes, but in truth he himself had suddenly lost his juice. He wasn't that long out of the Anchorage hospital, and his shoulder ached in the cast. When they delivered to a cannery tender, he watched with rare detachment as his guys in the hold, waist-deep in dead fish, competed boisterously to see who could toss his quota into the brailer fastest. Jody, fatigued also at last, merely watched and egged them on. They anchored, hosed down, crammed in Mo's quick-fried hamburgers, draped wet socks above the galley stove, and slept within seconds of hitting the rack.

Hank declared he'd sleep on the wheelhouse couch to not disturb his wife in the narrow skipper's cabin. Jody understood. He still needed space and time. He woke around 2 AM and walked to deck. Jones had been laughing in his dream, not dryly as he had in life, but comfortably. Jones, you dear pisser, he'd told the dream, you never should have bought that extra boat you didn't need and gone to fish in places you didn't know.

Jones laughed again, this time with a Jones-like crackle: for once, Craw-ford, mebbe you got something right.

Hank stretched on deck with the satisfying ache of idled muscles bent again to purpose. Calm water reflected the lights of other sleeping seiners whose generators hummed. A piney odor drifted from shore. The pale sky of the new day silhouetted points of spruce atop low hills. Two nights before (or was it one?), under way from Kodiak with Jones's ashes, while fogs drifted and he lay on deck where now he stood, he'd dreamed of shipmates lost to the water. Now, even though this was Jones's beloved boat that the man had nursed and petted, Jones slipped into shadow with the others.

Dawn slowly invested the trees and boats with detail. Only weeks ago (or was it years?), he himself, gasping in spray and rising tide to save Jones, had escaped the same death by frigid water. And now clear light etched masts and branches in water that rippled smiling with: Me? Eat you? Never.

He relieved himself in a neat arc over the side. The splash broke the stillness. Then he washed his hands with dew from the rail. Something stung. A red blister bulged between softening callouses. Hands gone soft. And he still felt tired. Should go inside and sleep some more while nobody watched. He enjoyed an eagle's swoop as he stretched again. Muscles stiffer than they should be after a mere day of work that had been routine not long ago. Hurt shoulder, good excuse for a while. Jones Henry at more than sixty had pulled any weight he chose until his final few minutes, so his own age—thirty-five or whatever—wasn't old. (Nearly thirty-eight!)

Of course he was no longer that smooth-skinned kid from Baltimore who showed up on the Kodiak docks a few years ago, panting to get on a fishing boat (nineteen years ago!). Hired by Jones Henry, he'd been a kid jumping to please on his first boat, in the very Uganik Bay that now received his piss afresh. Now he was a highline skipper with his own boat, one bigger than any that Jones ever sailed (or wanted to—another story). And with his Jody, his three kids, a house overlooking the bay. All.

He leaned down to check current, looking into brown-green water smooth enough to reflect in the boat's lee. A face looked back, all beard, cheekbones firm, man in charge. The friendly water detailed none of the creases—not wrinkles—around the eyes that stared close-up from a mirror: creases from squinting into rain and sun. Seasoning. Badge of life on the water. Jones had been wiry, tough, acerbic, strong. How did Hank Crawford compare, now that he stood alone with his mentor dead? If he had ever pictured himself as he would become, he'd wanted it to be as a man strong and straight. Not acerbic. Anger, yes, real and large at times, although sometimes feigned to make a point. Not wiry. When he walked ashore his chest led the way and he felt muscles against the shirt. Bearded presence that filled a room. Gaze that firmed equally on man or woman. Jones hadn't laughed much. He himself laughed, whenever he felt like it, a rumble that his ear told him had deepened with time and authority. Everyone knew him to be a high-line skipper, no need to show it off any more than Jones had. A man at home in his time and place, able to handle anything on the water. Jody could bring him to earth, he could admit that, but it didn't happen often.

And this fatigue: just temporary.

A splash. He peered toward the sound. Suddenly a salmon leapt straight, silver against dark water. Hank strode inside and started the engine, then shouted below, "Mo or Ham. Anchor!" Seth appeared in the wheelhouse buttoning his pants.

Outside, a figure slighter than his solid crewmen climbed around to the bow. It wore short Terry's hooded jumper. "Honey," Hank called out, "let one of the guys do it."

Jody turned with mock gravity. "Your guys are still waking up. Do you want to fish or not?"

He started to ask if she was sure she could handle it, thought better and waved her on. She undogged the chain and kicked it loose as confidently as any man, but he at the controls still brought in the anchor as slowly as he could. Yet she had once worked on deck like a man, almost.

"You've got crew to do that," muttered Seth.

"Jody can handle it."

"Not the point."

The chain-in had barely begun before big Mo and bigger Ham hurried around the cabin. "Miz . . . Better let me . . ." said Mo.

Jody calmly cradled the shank of the anchor, flicked black mud from one of the flukes, and turned to give them her wide-mouthed smile. "Morning, boys."

"Morning, Miz . . . You didn't ought to . . ."

Hank ignored their discomfort but avoided looking at Seth beside him. "Keep it down out there," he muttered through the window. "Need to tell the fleet we're ready to buzz?"

Jody continued. She dogged the chain with a kick to finish the job, then grinned at Mo and Ham. "Who's making coffee?"

Hank in the wheelhouse caught Seth's sleeve. "Jumper off the starboard beam." As they watched, another fish splashed from the water.

"I'm on it." Seth headed below.

Hank leaned out the window to those on the bow. "Get fishing. Quietly."

"You got it, Boss," rumbled Mo in his best approximation of a whisper, and hurried aft. Hank heard gear clank almost immediately, and glanced through the back window to see Seth buckling the suspenders of his oilskins as he sprinted over the stacked net to the skiff. Good crew.

"Boss . . . " Ham, still on the bow, hesitated with the frown that Hank had begun to recognize meant his new man faced a problem. Jody gestured Ham ahead of her. He left obediently, but climbed at once to the wheelhouse.

Hank paced, eager to fish. "You're second skiff man, Ham. Better get out there."

Ham's head brushed the wheelhouse ceiling so that he hunched his thick shoulders automatically. It made him look as uncertain as his voice. "Boss . . . Sir . . . ?"

"What? What?"

"You know things better than I do, sir. But, other seasons at least . . . ?" He indicated the raised skipper's chair where the urn with Jones Henry's ashes had rested the day before and where Jones himself had sat peering ahead for years. "Captain Jones . . . No disrespect, sir . . . I'm really grateful you've took me in your crew, I mean, really . . . but Captain Jones made something of he'd never put out his net before six in the morning if it was a Monday, like right now. Don't ask me why. Like he'd sure never leave port on a Friday, so we'd wait until one minute after midnight into Saturday morning. I just thought you ought to know, being this is Captain Jones's boat. *Was* his. Sir. And what with adding a lady who works on deck—Captain Jones would never even let one on his boat. Not like I'm superstitious like the old-timers, sir, but . . ."

Hank wanted to laugh but found his throat tightening. To gain a moment, he said lightly, "Stop calling me sir. I'm not much older than you." Further sounds of preparation came from aft. Seth in the skiff and Terry, Mo, and Jody by the winch all looked up at the wheelhouse, waiting and ready. There to starboard leapt a jumper. Time to move, not talk. "Take it like this, Ham. You and I put Jones's ashes in that water yesterday. Now look at all the fish coming our way. Don't you think Jones down there's helping push them toward us? So I'd say he's okay with what we're doing. In the skiff if you're going."

"Yes, *sir!*"

Seconds to let Ham bound to the skiff. Another salmon leapt with a loud splash. "Ho!" Hank shouted. Mo's mallet hit the release, the hook clanged open, and the skiff glided off in the direction of Hank's arm. He wanted to dance, indeed, hopped in place. The net, with one end attached to the skiff, swished from deck to the bump of its corks, and payed out between skiff and boat with corks floating a beaded line. All of it was action that cleared the cobwebs.

His tight gaze stayed where he'd last seen the fish jump, while his arm directed the skiff and its lengthening line of corks. Like breath itself, the way his body felt the motions. From shoulder to knees he nudged the skiff. His hands held the unseen fish in place while he pictured the wall of net beneath the corks slowly encircling them.

Voices and clanks of skiff-launch came from other boats in the bay. The day's race had begun! Quick check on his own deck below: Terry straightened gear and shipshaped. Jody at the plunger smacked the cupped heavy shaft into the water with an expert touch, creating the noise and bubbles that scared fish into the net. Poor Mo stood beside her, hands out, wishing to take over the job. She pulled no rank as skipper's wife—no, she did, or Mo would have had the plunger. Determined to prove she could still crew her weight, and doing so. He enjoyed the sight of Jody reverted to the boatwise woman she'd been before they'd married.

A first touch of sunlight over the mountains spiked gleams on their yellow and green oilskins. Out in the skiff, Ham's arms pumped steadily at the plunger. Good man, but heavier and more eager than skilled. Instruct him later to pop that cup deliberately for max effect. (Spare him having Jody demonstrate.) Seth hunched at the tiller both calm and alert, an old hand at it like Hank, even though in recent years they'd worked pots together rather than a seine. He should wean Seth into his own command, he thought, not just Hank Crawford's deck boss and relief skipper.

Release him for his own good despite the need then to find a new mate whose sea-sense bent with his own. It was not the first time the thought had occurred.

Back on deck Jody had relinquished the plunger to Mo and stood with Terry. The little guy—no taller than Jody though he pulled full weight at work—was showing her how to coil. He spun an arm's length of line with his hand, flipped it into a natural circle, and dropped it symmetrically on top of the other coils. Made a cheerful joke when she did it clumsily, so that she laughed also and kept at it. Nice man. He alone didn't seem threatened by Jody's presence aboard.

Jumper again, farther from the boat. Whether a single fish or betrayer of a school, it was moving away. Hank circled his arm in the air for Seth to see, then called to deck: "Roundhaul! Coming in." Seth's skiff slowly pulled the cork line into a wide circle and headed with it back to the boat. Mo on deck thrust the plunger furiously, while Terry and Jody waited at the rail to receive the skiff's line.

The few sets yesterday after the spreading of Jones's ashes had honed them, and the operation progressed teamlike. Ham leapt from the skiff, where Seth remained, to join Terry on purse lines at the winch. Mo kept plunging. The taut circle of net still in the water had loosened into an uneven float of corks. Seth caught a line from the boat, and gunned his skiff to hold the boat free of entanglement in the seine. Jody first hosed some seaweed from deck, then waited to strap the net line over the power block when the time came. They were jobs that the others would have absorbed routinely, Hank knew as he watched. Jody was one hand more than needed.

Time to stack. As the net rose dripping through the power block overhead, Ham took center position to distribute web. Mo hurried to the corks so firmly after stowing the plunger that he must have feared Jody would grab his job again. Jody instead headed starboard to the rings, possessively, leaving Terry idle. He shrugged in good humor. Hank de-bated. The guy was smart enough to handle a boat, and needed experience. "Okay, Terry, you take over the controls here from me."

Hank retreated to the wheelhouse, odd man now himself, restlessly watching. But when the rings snagged on the shaft—routine problem— he jumped to deck for hands on rope and metal.

"Didn't you think I could handle that?" Jody's tone had the edge that Hank knew could take the matter in directions easy or tense.

"Gives the old man something to do, honey." (Why, after all, hadn't she stayed home with the kids?) He glanced casually. Had his guys caught that edge in her voice? Terry looked away discreetly: yes. Other boats circled nearby, all of them now geared for the day and scouting fish. Two boats hovered within earshot to assess the *Adele H*'s haul. From the bridge of the *Hinda Bee,* old Gus Rosvic, former buddy of Jones Henry, watched in silence, as did his crew on deck below. Did they see a skipper in charge, or a fellow run by his wife?

"Puttin' the old lady to work, eh, Hank?" called a man Hank's age and build from the bridge of the *Sleepthief Two.*

"Keeps her out of trouble."

"Haay Jody."

"Hi, Jeff." Jody continued placing net rings on the pole as they dangled free from the power block overhead. She grabbed each with the correct twist that lined them for the next set, keeping pace and rhythm.

"Rumor's all over the fleet, you know. About Jones Henry's widow? Now that she owns the boat you're on, the rumor is she's going to make Jody the skipper."

Hank laughed. "How rumors fly. From a joke yesterday, eh, honey? We were leaving the Kodiak dock to bring Jones's ashes over here, and there was discussion over Jody's coming along."

"Ohh, discussion; yes, we heard. Ol' Jones never let even his wife come aboard, did he?"

Jody grinned as she worked without losing pace. "Come back in a week or two, Jeff."

What's that mean? wondered Hank.

Watching them from the other boat, Gus Rosvic shook his head. Hank knew him well enough to know what he was thinking. An old-timer of the Slav generation from Anacortes. Face all scowl lines and leather under a faded Greek fisherman's cap. His *Hinda Bee,* painted mostly gray, looked well kept but as glum as its skipper and as stolid as the husky younger crewmen watching from deck. Gus had hung out with Jones Henry. The fleet joked over the two old skippers, both good at their game, bitching over beers about the Japs and everything else wrong in the world. Too bad, Hank decided. Let him stare. People would have to get used to a woman on deck.

"Hey, man," called Ham to one of the crew, Buddy or something. Bud muttered a return but looked away.

Whether Hank cared or not, he was glad when the *Hinda Bee* circled and left. Left, in fact, straight through other boats and out of sight. So be it, thought Hank. We'll keep distance between us if that helps.

The set came aboard. About a hundred fifty humpies, neither bad nor spectacular. "Ahh, now," called Jeff. "We made five-buck bets on Jody being aboard. Whether it meant you'd plug the net or water-haul. Nobody thought to bet for in between. Come on, Jody. My fin was for you."

"And which of you put five that I'd sink the boat?"

Jeff's crewmen around him laughed, but not as if it were out of the question. "Come on, Jody, we're not that superstitious." The *Sleepthief Two* moved off.

The encounters left Hank with a sudden feeling of malaise. He pretended to be hearty as he sent the others in for breakfast rather than set again at once. "After all, we're on vacation."

"You sick or something?" Seth called from the skiff. He tied astern and strode up over the net, then lowered the bill of his cap and threw back his head in a way that had become his gesture. "When did you start calling mealtimes when we're on the fish?"

"Gettin' old and lazy." In truth, he'd begun to shake from fatigue like the day before, although he concealed it. Still not recovered from the disaster. Jody watched him closely. "I'm going up and look at the charts," he muttered to cover. "Too many boats now crowding us here."

Jody followed him to the wheelhouse. "You look as spaced out as in the hospital. Lie down a while and let Seth—"

"No, no. I'm fine." He watched over the water to avoid facing her. The *Sleepthief Two*, not far away, had just released the skiff pulling its end of seine through the water. "Just give me a few minutes to myself, honey."

"Why don't you stop calling me honey." She said it lightly.

"Come on, you are my honey."

"Out here today I'm your crewman."

Ten years ago, when they had fished together, her name would have been Jody. Three years ago he'd have not seen her point, but now: "Got it. But . . . just give me a little space. Okay?"

She studied him, nodded. "Got it."

When she was gone he hurried to the captain's chair by the controls, put the clutch in neutral, and closed his eyes for only a minute. A comfortable buzz settled over him like a veil. He woke to the sound of laughs below and the smell of bacon. Close by in the water the *Sleepthief Two*'s net rose like a sail over the power block, dripping water over the guys stacking it. They'd made a full set, so at least a half hour must have passed, maybe more.

Boats were everywhere in various stages of seining. He eased the engine into gear and glided gently among them, avoiding their nets. Maybe below they hadn't noticed. Now, indeed, he needed to find uncrowded water.

Jody joined him, holding two mugs of coffee. "Awake now?"

He laughed, rose, hugged and held her. "Did I at least fool the others?"

"Mo and Ham for a while, I guess. They're so innocent and trusting, and Mo was busy doing breakfast. Seth knew right away. He's hot to fish like you are usually. Without me there, he'd have been up here shaking you." She lowered her voice. "Is Seth getting out of hand? I know he's always been scratchy."

"No problem. Leave that between Seth and me."

"Well, I'd say it's time for him to marry and get a boat of his own. He's beginning to challenge you too much."

Hank tried to lighten it. "Shall I tell him that?"

She ignored him, and settled on top of the cabinet by the captain's chair. "Terry, now, simply made a joke of the boss's nap. He's good to have around."

"Okay, hon . . . Jody. Okay." Shouldn't be talking about his guys with all of them just below.

"It's a nice boat. Do you think it handles well?"

Where was this leading?

"You know, Ham was Jones Henry's skiff man formerly." She seemed to speak casually. "Why don't you let him handle skiff?"

"And put my senior man Seth on plunger? Come on."

"No. Give Seth the wheel. He runs the *Jody Dawn* for you off season. Let him skipper this. You know you need a rest." A pause. "I'll go as Ham's skiff man. Learn new tricks."

Hank was glad that a clearing had opened in the water. It allowed him to gun the engine to a throb that precluded talk, and to peer ahead without facing her. Birds parted gracefully from his bow. The boat rounded a spit, past a beach with board-and-tin shacks. "Setnet camp," he said, glad for diversion. "Wonder who runs it?" She didn't answer. Farther along, two bears lumbered through a stream pawing fish. "Look. Bears. Competition." Silence.

He reached a cove removed from other boats that he remembered from working with Jones Henry, and reluctantly slowed the engine.

"Hank, you may as well hear me." Her voice was deliberate. "I'm going to take Adele Henry's invitation seriously. You go back to your big *Jody Dawn* and do whatever you promised the Japanese you'd do. I'll captain this boat. I want you to break me in."

He kept his back toward her to hide his expression, but said quietly, "What of three kids at home, Jody?"

Her voice remained reasonable. "Adele would love to take them for the summer. Now that Jones is gone, it'll give her purpose until she pulls her life together. And the salmon run slows in September in time for school, then stops until next June. Besides, Henny's nearly eight. He can ride aboard and—"

He faced her with no attempt to lower his voice or mask his agitation. "When my son's ready to fish, he's going with me! That's mine, my job. No harm for you to keep the kids in a fish camp earlier this summer before Jones died. I didn't like it much, but it was on land and you needed your freedom, you said. But when my son . . ."

They stared at each other. Her gathered battle expression that he knew well—wide mouth pursed and eyes cool—eased without losing direction. "All right, Hank. Got it." She took his face in her hands and her voice softened. "I understand. Our sons are yours to teach on the boat." She kissed him and turned away lightly. "But don't forget your daughter."

He relaxed, started to joke that Dawn could remain her mom's project, thought better of it.

"Now," continued Jody, businesslike, "that leaves breaking me in to skipper this boat for Adele."

"Hold on, I haven't—"

"Terry's already taken me down to the engine room and shown me—"

"Terry did that?"

"Terry even said he could crew with a lady skipper if it was me."

"Terry said that?"

"Don't worry, I wrung it out of him. Now, I know my way around boats but I'm rusty. And I've never taken command; there's always been you or somebody else in charge. One thing—I need to understand the skiff part of seining better. Come to think of it, I really ought to go out with Seth instead of Ham since Seth's the expert deck man."

"Like to see you wring him."

"Then, of course—especially—I'll need to spend time with you in the wheelhouse. But do you think Ham would come crew for me? Just for the rest of the summer, of course. It *is* the boat he knows since he worked for Jones. And I know you took him on out of kindness, extra man you don't need."

She won't be home to cook my meals, he thought. And what will the guys say all along the docks? He faced her, trim and determined, and saw the Jody he'd chased and married nine years ago. Be honest: he'd urged and pursued her. She had often refused because she didn't want to be tied down, the independent woman who crewed on boats as she chose and didn't want kids. Now she'd raised him three wonderful children, done it with love and care. "Well, hon . . . Jody. I guess we'd better work it out." He started to consider. Ham could go if he was willing—he was extra for the moment. But she needed somebody more alert than Ham to look out for her. What if he spared Terry for the rest of the summer? If Terry agreed, of course. Decent man with good judgment; he'd see she came to no harm. That would ensure that the engine didn't die under some green-horn and drift them onto rocks. "Poor guys in your crew, if you could ever slap one together."

"There's always kids on the dock. They'll know beforehand who's skip-per. And, incidentally, who says I won't hire women?"

Suddenly Hank was ready to laugh. "Poor Jones. He dies, and less than three weeks later the bitches—uh-oh, the witches—take over his boat." He held out his arms. "You're the witch for me."

"The bitch, too. Don't kid yourself." They hugged.

Her shoulders felt so slight beneath the heavy wool shirt! Impulsively, he shifted his good arm to her waist and started to dance. Instead of resist-ing she laid her head against his shoulder. They swayed.

"Hey, Boss," called Terry as he appeared up the ladder; then, "Whoa, sorry!" as he saw them. "Bet you haven't seen that Fish and Game boat heading to our stern." He kept a straight face but his eyes were merry. "Want me to dig up a jukebox?"

Hank released his wife, smiling. "Routine Fish and Game stuff. They'll just check our papers. Offer coffee; I'll be down. Stop staring, guy, scoot!" Terry gave a mock salute and started off. "Oh," Hank called after. "Might as well get out your licenses. Assume you brought 'em—deep shit if you didn't." As Terry's head disappeared, Jody gasped and cupped a hand over her mouth. Hank studied her. "Oh boy. You don't have a license, do you?"

"No."

Hank bounded down the ladder. The men were already around their bunks rummaging through seabags for papers. "Hear this! Jody's along only as a passenger. She hasn't handled gear, she's not fishing. No license. Got it?"

"Might have known," said Seth.

Mo and Ham exchanged puzzled glances, then understood. "Don't worry, Boss," soothed Mo, and Ham echoed with, "Sure, Boss, sure, we got it." Mo continued elaborately, caught up in the situation. "Your lady, Boss, she's just come along for the ride, that's exactly—we'll be cool about it. Whoever saw a lady like that work a plunger, huh? But can we say she makes coffee and stuff like that?"

Hank looked around for Terry as he muttered, "Coffee, does dishes, sure, sure, if anybody asks." Suddenly their enthusiasm warned him. "No. Don't say anything. Let Seth and me do the talking. Understand?"

He hurried astern, where Terry had just caught a line from the Fish and Game's rubber dinghy, and clapped Terry on the shoulder. "Jody's got no license," he whispered. "We say she's just along as a passenger. Understand?"

Terry squinted and frowned. Had he heard the words clearly? Hank wondered. Too late to repeat as the dinghy brushed alongside and two officers in khaki shirts with green insignia jumped aboard. Hank knew them. They all shook hands.

As Hank predicted, the inspection was a routine perusal of the boat's papers and fishing licenses, along with a look at the fish in their hold. Jody sauntered to deck smiling, and stretched as if she'd just come from bed. She had found some clean clothes not stained from fishing. "Heey-y, Jody," said one of the officers. "Life of leisure, eh?"

"Never slept so much in my life, Charlie. How's Edna?"

"There's a rumor back in town. We thought maybe you were already skipper here and telling Hank what to do."

"Got that one wrong," muttered Seth.

"You know about rumors, Charlie," said Jody easily, flashing her smile.

"Comes of a widow gotten kind of confused, eh? Suddenly gets crazy ideas. Poor old Adele, she needs time. Jones Henry wasn't that easy to live with, I hear. Best thing, she'll sell the boat."

Jody stretched like a cat. "Wouldn't be surprised at anything. But better not call Adele old to her face."

"Commit suicide? Not me." Officer Charlie drew Hank aside from the others. "I'm not asking unless she's got one, but does your good lady have a license?"

"Nope."

"Urge you call somebody in town, run 'em to Fish and Game and get her one fast. Anybody out here with binoculars knows Jody's working nets alongside your guys. I'll talk to the clerk by radio. With a guy, even you, I'd have to write a citation, but with a woman—"

"Appreciate that. Will do."

The officers left with a wave, and: "Jody, enjoy your sleep." They straightened back to official staunchness as soon as their dinghy headed for other inspections.

"I'll be damned," declared Jody. "They didn't even consider if I handled gear or had a license."

Hank shrugged in sympathy.

"Guess that settles it," said Seth, pleasant for once. "Your wife takes it easy till we get back to shore."

2

JUMPER'S SONG

UGANIK BAY, LATE JULY 1982

With the urgent radio call to buy Jody's license, Adele Henry, back in Kodiak, learned that Jody had decided to take up her invitation. "Oh, Jody, I can't believe it!" she exclaimed. "No—yes I can, yes I can! Poor Daddy, what he'd have thought, poor man. I'll just have to get over that. Now. Wait. Let me get something to write with. I'm excited as a baby."

So it happened. Mrs. Judith Sedwick Crawford would take command of the fifty-eight-foot limit seiner *Adele H* to fish salmon around Kodiak Island for the rest of the summer. To see it through safely, Hank recruited half of his own deck—Terry and Ham—to crew for her. When the word spread in town it amused some, wives and husbands both, but appalled others.

The once-unthinkable to Hank became his concentrated project for the next several days: to hone his deckwise wife to the mysteries of spotting and capturing humpie salmon from the viewpoint of the wheelhouse. He took on the job in orderly military fashion, as befitted even a one-hitch naval officer with a year of Vietnam service. She paid attention soberly, although sometimes the enormity of the new venture troubled her enough to escape into lighter talk than he thought appropriate.

Seth O'Malley, age thirty-two, Hank's second and his fishing companion for more than a decade, watched glumly. Despite coming from southern California where anything went (and where he'd spent a restless year as a freshman at UCal Berkeley), he'd acquired an opposite outlook in Alaska. For him, the whole process of letting a woman run a boat undermined a man's position in town. (Unless she failed.) If he was ever dumb enough to marry, Seth told himself, it wouldn't be to a woman who jerked him around like that. His woman would keep house, raise kids, and come no closer to the boat than to wave good-bye. Jones Henry had that one right. Maybe the old pisser was right in a lot more ways than anybody ever gave him credit for. Seth's face, in the old days puplike—as had once been his nature—behind a shaggy beard, was now shaved and square, weathered brown around eyes known for their glare. Given his height and shoulder breadth and his deep voice, he had become a presence, and knew it. His nature in the process had grown brusque, or, as he saw it, responsible. "When you know firsthand like I do the tricks the ocean can play," he'd say gravely if twitted, "you don't laugh at nothing about catching fish." Thus, he seldom joked, never felt like joking in light of how the world banged you down if you let it.

Big Mo Wheeler, age twenty-seven, Seth's shadow for years since Seth as deck boss had trained him, felt obliged to echo Seth's disapproval when the two talked—or rather, when Seth sounded off in private. But Mo's loyalty to Hank as boss, held in awe, kept him ready to cooperate. Mo was not, in any case, a man of independent opinion. He worked hard and well, and had mastered all fishing-boat skills that required practical reflexes. He did as he was told with consistent good humor—glad enough not to still be on that Iowa farm and expected to go to Methodist this and Methodist that after long days of work—happy to be on a high-line boat under one of the best captains around, and therefore, a man respected on the Kodiak docks.

Ham Davis, also twenty-seven, was Mo's buddy and carbon copy in both build and obliging temperament. He, too, had escaped from the fields, although he remembered his Idaho farmboy days with greater warmth than Mo. Now they even had girlfriends ashore who looked alike. But Ham came to the crew with different loyalties than Mo. Circumstance had shunted him from crew to crew. Originally, he had been Tolly Smith's man aboard the *Star Wars*, but that meant nothing when the king crab stocks collapsed in 1981 and Tolly lost his boat to the bank. Hank, Tolly's old friend, had persuaded Jones Henry to take Ham aboard. Now, after the way it had all happened like a nightmare, Ham would revere the

memory of Captain Jones forever; would choke with tears whenever he
remembered that Captain Jones might still be alive—still bossing him
sharply, which would have been fine, fine—but for the disaster, when
he'd forgotten his survival suit and Captain Jones made him take his own,
leading to Captain's freezing to death in the water. Never forget it. If Captain Hank's wife was going to run the boat for Captain Jones's poor
widow, and they wanted him aboard, that's all there was to it, no matter
that he'd rather work under Boss in a crew with Mo. It might even be his
rightful punishment. The main thing: He hoped guys ashore wouldn't
make fun of him for having a lady skipper. Fights were a lot of trouble and
sometimes hurt your knuckles.

Terry Bricks, twenty-five, from Oregon, watched it all as lightly as a
grasshopper on a weed. However this wind blew would be all right. He
owed nothing to Jones Henry's memory but a chuckle over how things
were turning out with Jody and all, Captain Jones being such a lady-
hater—at least on the boats. That Jody was something, holding out like
she did. Boss had his hands full with such a lady, but he was plenty lucky.
If he himself had been so lucky, he wouldn't now be divorced and lonely
each time they came to port. At least he'd finished with saying yes to a
woman who'd complained right after the wedding that his clothes smelled
fishy, and started in on him right away to be some gas pumper or shoe
salesman ashore so he'd be home nights. When Boss himself asked if he'd
crew for Jody and make sure the engine stayed running, it was easy to say
sure and mean it. Jody wasn't like some ordinary broad anyhow. Maybe
you'd never agree to call her Boss, but the way she looked you in the eye,
you knew she could take charge. And for once he'd be with somebody as
short as he was—maybe not when on deck with big Ham and all, but in
the wheelhouse and around. He and Ham together, they'd protect Boss's
lady and make sure she did all right.

One evening Hank pulled them into the Uganik cannery and delivered
pierside to give Jody docking experience. He accompanied her from frame
building to building along the boardwalks, suddenly nostalgic. Unlike the
dozen canneries in Kodiak town itself, seasonal canneries in remote places
like Uganik Bay on Kodiak Island were self-sufficient villages, and Hank
enjoyed them as such. Little but the paint had changed since his greenhorn days here stapling boxes and forking fish from hopper to slime line.
In the long warehouselike processing station, it could have been the same

Filipino men as two decades ago who stood shoulder to shoulder in long green oilskin coats. They lined the conveyor belt leading from the iron chink that lopped fish heads and tails. Their same lined faces—or duplicates of a next generation—stayed frozen in the same scowls while their hands, with factory regularity, cut fish carcasses or hosed and scraped them. "Just think of it," he muttered. "Thousands and thousands of humpies through their hands, their lifetime summer after summer."

"So?" Jody shrugged. "Then they can pay their bills and be home with their kids winter after winter."

Farther on, clattering machinery stamped cans into shape and pushed them along overhead racks to belts where chattering native women filled the cans with fish. Odors in the warehouse building progressed from brassy slime to heavy fish steam down by the retorts that cooked the sealed cans. Nothing had changed. Hank started to explain the operation.

"You don't think I've worked in a salmon cannery?" said Jody dryly. "Just not this one where you say you came of age."

"Every smell takes me back," said Hank, unabashed.

"You can play wistful, but you wouldn't want to be back here any more than I would."

"But . . . we were so free."

"Speak for yourself. No foreman ever tried to paw you."

Across the ramp leading to the piers, another building housed a newer operation to freeze the fish. Along these belts stood kids of a college brightness. They giggled and kidded above a blast of rock music while their hands, in heavy rubber gloves, scraped the usual fish guts and blood. The girls wore kerchiefs and the men white paper caps, but they all looked fresh from the campus.

Just how I started, thought Hank. Summer adventure from Johns Hopkins U with never a thought of staying. Then Jones Henry took me on his boat. The cycle of years with Jones, first as mentor, then partner, then rival and antagonist, made his throat tighten. He needed to turn away.

"The girls may be dressed for sloppy work," observed Jody, "but most have sneaked a little lipstick, I see. Just like we did." With hands on hips, she added, "As for the boys, not a bad crop of young studs there, beneath those oilskins. The lipstick might just pay off."

Hank disliked remembering that part of Jody's life before she took him seriously. But okay, he'd play her game. "Yup. I remember once putting on a slimy wetsuit to dive beneath floating offal and free some clogged scupper. Volunteered in fact, to impress some sweet little—successfully impressed, I might add." She merely raised an eyebrow. He should have kept quiet. "Oh man, we were young!" he added quickly.

"Speak for yourself."

They separated. Jody went to the little cannery store for toothpaste and for work clothes to replace the borrowings she had been wearing. As Hank headed to the machine shop to grind down a winch guard that chafed, he continued to enjoy memories. Some of the steamy odors might have been miserable throughout those fourteen-hour days sliming fish, but now they evoked younger times. On the boardwalk, a short Japanese in a hurry nearly bumped him as they passed. The man's crisp brown cap and shirt each bore a round Japanese insignia. That had changed! How freely they'd once talked of distant Japs who "raped the resource." Now, he was in their debt (although friendly enough), and on automatic to not even think the word Jap.

In the machine shop they loaned him goggles to use the grinder. He had finished and turned off the machine when a voice behind him growled, "Surprised she's not doing that for you."

Hank turned to face Gus Rosvic of the *Hinda Bee*. He braced for a showdown. "Hello, Gus. You have a problem?"

"Only with the memory of poor Jones Henry." Up close the man's lined face didn't seem hard, only troubled. What showed of his hair beneath the worn cap was more gray than brown, and turned white at the shaggy sideburns. Rumor had it he'd passed seventy. A slight bend of shoulders didn't keep him from standing erect.

Hank eased. "I loved him too, Gus. But he's dead. I've got other things to consider." A burst of metal hammering drowned Gus's reply. Hank motioned him outside, using the time to choose his words. "I respect you, sir. But sometimes old ways don't work in new times. I'm sorry."

"I heard it at Jones's funeral, all the talk. How you tried to save him. Good for you. And I see that shoulder's still in a cast." Gus looked up at him with clear eyes surrounded by wrinkles. "But son—let a woman on poor Jones's boat, and now they say she's going to run it? That ain't right."

Hank had no answer since nothing was going to alter. "I'll do this. I'll see that Jody keeps Jones's boat away from yours as much as possible. Two of my best guys are with her. They'll keep her out of your hair."

"However you do, it ain't right. And I think you know it." Gus started away, then turned back. "And son, I know it ain't my business. But all this going to Japan that Jones told me you do. You're too young for Pearl Harbor, that's the trouble. Or you'd never have anything to do with those little yellow killers. You ain't in their pocket now, are you?"

"Take it easy, Gus." Hank left him quickly.

He headed toward the mess hall where the crew was to meet for an off-the-boat lunch that he'd arranged at the cannery office. Just put Japan out of mind today, he told himself. Time soon enough to face it. He looked around him. So little had changed—same net lockers, dorms, laundry shack—except in himself. Near the mess hall a circle had gathered. Seth's unmistakable voice roared, "Break it up!" Hank hurried over.

Inside the circle Ham and the *Hinda Bee*'s crewman, Buddy, glared at each other, fists clenched, blood on each of their faces. Seth stood between them, glaring around. "Nothing here for you," he barked at a knot of curious cannery workers. "Go back to cuttin' up our fish or whatever you do." His tone backed them off: pale kids in floppy landsman boots with heads in paper caps and kerchiefs. Seth gripped Ham and Bud by their shirts and pulled them one on each side toward the back of the building. They followed docilely under his authority, trailed by fellow crewmen of both boats. Seth appeared enough in charge that Hank felt no need to intervene.

"You want to fight, now you got it," Seth continued. "But you take on all of us." His glance included Mo and Terry, who stepped forward gravely, while the men of the *Hinda Bee* nodded in turn. "Me, I'd rather save my hands for the nets, and settle it next winter in Kodiak."

Zack of the *Hinda* spoke up. "First time somebody's made sense."

"Okay," said Ham. "But Seth, you tell 'em to stop mouthin' off like that."

"We'll fuckin' do it like we please," said Bud. He was not as big as Ham, but probably just as strong. "Our skipper says it's only days or even hours before she screws up, and we're making it interesting is all."

Terry sauntered up. Although he was shorter than the others, they knew him enough to listen. He held up two twenty-dollar bills. "It's all I got here in my pocket, but call each one of these things witch's dough, each a hundred bucks. It says that, starting today through the rest of this opening—since both our boats are empty now, we can count from zero—we highline you guys out of the water. Out of your pants! End of opening, we

Back on the boat, Jody's shakedown continued.

The opening lasted more than a week and they fished all of it. Since they had come from Kodiak merely to scatter Jones Henry's ashes, no one had packed chow for more than overnight. The cannery had steaks enough for workers but only basic food to sell to boats. Seth hung strips of salmon to dry, and the leathery odor joined the odors of fresh fish and engines. Mo alternated salmon boiled in seawater with salmon fried in bacon grease until Ham and Terry groaned. The previous crew on Jones's boat had left cans of baked beans and tuna, which helped, while the tender to which they delivered sold them coffee, bread, cheese, macaroni, and onions. The men yearned for meat.

"This chow seems good enough to me," declared Jody with hands on hips. "What more do you need to stay fishing?"

Hank glanced at the anxious faces of her two designated crewmen and laughed. "Maybe salt beef and hardtack's the great tradition, but not when you're close to town and making money. When you're skipper you'd better keep Terry and Ham happier than that. And whoever else you pick up."

"Meat and fresh stuff," said Terry confidently when asked what should be ordered. "Green stuff and, like, carrots and apples. Oh. Don't forget peanut butter. And candy bars, things with nuts. But mainly steak."

From Ham: "Just give me meat. And ice cream. And bug juice? Raspberry bug juice is best. Best in ice cream's chocolate fudge. Meat, well . . . you know . . ." He grinned, unsure how far he could go. "Prime rib?"

There were also deck and engine supplies. Adele Henry, in Kodiak, copied the list by radio, with only an occasional gasp at its extent. "You'd think the boat was left untended for years instead of a few weeks since Daddy left for Bristol Bay. However! Shackles? Does Sutliff's have them?" Hank advised her on stores and establishing credit, and offered himself as reference in case there was a question. "You mean poor Daddy's name isn't enough after all these years?" Before Hank could answer diplomatically, she continued, "My God, I'm busier than when Daddy was alive! But don't worry, the children are fine. Dawn makes friends everywhere and Henny tags along like a little man. Pete's my baby, he still keeps me company. Now Jody? Are you there? Jody, listen to me. Don't let those men get so full of themselves that—wait. Somebody's banging on the door with no consideration. I'm coming! Oh. It's one of Dawn's little friends. What was I saying? Never mind. Jody, you take care, and remember—

Pete! That's not clean, honey. I'm going. Yes, of course I've got the list. Good-bye."

"Are we putting too much on her?" Hank wondered. "She's only a . . ." he checked himself.

"A poor widow? You wait."

Hank, in teaching Jody, found his wisdom challenged. "Why do you always work nets to starboard?" she demanded. "Why not be flexible?"

"Everybody does it that way."

"That's a big man's answer."

Hank remained patient. "The gear and controls are set that way, by the starboard rail. Look, you wanted to learn. I'm telling you how everybody sets their seines. If you want to do it backward, go ahead—find out the hard way."

"Find out what? That another way might work better?"

"Look! These things have been worked out with experience."

He said it with such exasperation that she patted his cheek. "You're so serious, it's fun to tease you." A splash and they both turned to watch a choppy stretch of water. A minute later a fish leapt dark against the light.

"Now, Captain," said Hank, back to business, "that a humpie or a chum?"

"Straight up and then down in the same place? That's a humpie. Straight out of the water and down again."

"Good. How would you tell a chum? Remember, he's worth more than a humpie."

"Bigger. Jumps not as high. Wiggles his tail, that's important. And maybe he'll just fin instead of jump."

"You could have a humpie finner too."

"Well then, I'll just set on either and catch 'em all."

In the wheelhouse, with voices crackling on separate frequencies left open, Hank checked her out on radios. "The CB there monitors boats close by, the ones fishing around us."

"I know that, Hank."

"Anyhow—then the VHF over there covers us within about thirty miles. We keep that on emergency frequency at all times. Then the single sideband, that's for farther away—for weather reports, all that. We did sideband in Puale Bay when Adele stood by as your matron of honor over radio from Kodiak, remember? But we had CB for Jones Henry's boat alongside us. On that good day." The memory sent his arm around her, of riding out a storm while Jones as captain read the ceremony that married them. His hands started to move further.

She kissed his cheek but gently pushed him away. "We're working, mister." She unrolled a chart of the bay. "Get to your schoolmarm pitch on this if you have to. But I've read charts before, you know."

"Well. Yes. Always check first to see if soundings are in feet or fathoms. You know a fathom's six feet?" Her look told him she knew. He drew a breath, annoyed at her self-assurance. "Each degree of latitude on the chart divides into sixty minutes, each minute a mile—a nautical mile, longer than a land mile—but never mind that."

She took up calipers to show that she knew, and began to measure spaces along the bottom of the chart.

"No. He stayed patient while glad he'd found her mistake. "You measure that along the sides."

"Oh. Yes." She worked correctly, and announced Uganik Bay to be five miles wide and about fifteen miles into the arms.

He had started to explain magnetic deviation when a voice on the CB radio said, "Boats fishing South Arm or East Arm, this is *Sleepthief Two* off Mink Point. Little engine problem here. We think it's a faulty fuel injector if anybody's got a standard Jimmy-engine spare."

"Yo, Terry," Hank called. "Check if Jones kept an extra."

Jody frowned. "What if we need one ourselves? That's why we'd carry it." Hank brushed her off.

Other voices on the CB began to give advice in case the trouble was something different. By the time Terry called up with the part and Hank started to offer it, two other boats had logged in and the *Lady West* was en route to deliver one.

Jody laughed. "Wasn't it the skippers of *Lady West* and *Sleepthief* who had that fight in Tony's last spring and landed in jail? Something about their wives?"

"That's different. You'd better learn the difference."

Jody alternated wheelhouse observation with crew jobs, even those a skipper traditionally did not perform. Terry showed her how to troubleshoot in the noisy engine room, to check RPM's, battery water, and oil and water temperatures, while assuring her he'd do it all. But, methodically, she wanted to know what to expect. When it came time to pitch fish at delivery, she pulled on oversized hip boots left by a previous crewman and climbed into the hold with the others while Mo fixed dinner.

The sight made Seth snort. "Hey," said Hank diplomatically, "Why don't you stay topside and check scale on the tender? Three in the hold's enough."

Seth continued to descend the ladder. "Without me it'd be more like two and a half today."

To Jody in the hold, the brassy smell of salmon dead no more than a day evoked memories of independent bachelor days when she had worked on boats, usually as cook in the galley, never called on to pitch fish except in an emergency. Not a bad smell down here, she decided. Terry quickly made a joke of how he and Jody were so short they sometimes got too buried in fish to move anything but arms. Cold fish carcasses soon chilled her legs through the boots. Indeed, in the low space where they needed to crouch, the rigid, slimy fish held her fast. When the loaded brailer rose over their heads bulging with a few hundred pounds of fish, it was hard work to back under the deck boards and avoid the dripping slime.

After they had pitched some thousand fish into the brailer for loads that Hank lowered and raised from the controls above them (which earlier she herself had handled beside him), she could move more freely. She found sorting by type of salmon easy since the smallest, the humpies, dominated the catch. Only occasional chums had appeared in the seine, and they were larger, to be set aside for separate delivery. Her hands soon worked automatically, and her main concern was to keep up with the others.

Each person, counting silently, was to throw fifty fish into the brailer to make a load whose weight could be approximated. Her hands gripped slippery tails, but often fish slipped free of her slickened gloves to bounce short of the brailer rim and back into the pile. The air of the hold, at first frosty enough to show their breaths, soon turned steamy. Sweat trickled into her eyes; she had nothing not fishy to wipe them with. Try as she would, Seth, Terry, and Ham reached their fifty fish before she had tossed thirty—Seth at a deliberate pace, the other two competing. Seth waited with hands on hips, but Terry would say gaily, "Ten each more, Ham, race you buddy," to catch her up.

Seth, standing opposite her, broke his pace and leaned into the brailer to pull out a fish she had thrown in.

"Baby chum?" asked Jody.

"Early coho. You better learn those things." Without further explanation, he intercepted others.

When they had climbed from the hold and hosed down, Terry drew her aside. He had laid out three salmon on a board. "Now, here you got a humpie—people also call it a pink—about a two-pounder. It's the littlest salmon, and he's got that sort of a hump on his back, which is why we call him humpie, so he's easy to tell, mostly. The middle one's a chum—also call him a dog salmon, four- or five-pounder. It's easy to sort when there's only those two kinds. But . . ."

Terry paused for emphasis, then held up the fish on the end. "This here's a silver, also call him coho; maybe this one's only three pounds, which is why you confused it with a hump, but they get a lot bigger. Look at their tails first. Humpie tails is spotted and the others have stripes. Chum's stripes are milkylike, cohos more clear. See? And chum has a thinner tail. Now, we don't get silvers generally for another month, but that's nothin' to count on, like Seth showed, and silvers bring a better price than chums, which of course are worth more than humpies, so you want to keep them sorted. Now, see the chum—he's got no spots up here on his body. A silver now, he's got these little spots, see? Whereas a humpie has bigger ones even though he's a littler fish. And a thicker tail." He looked at her earnestly. "It's easy once you get to know it. Couple of years since I've salmon fished. But once you get it . . ."

Jody nodded with tightened mouth. Did I ever know all this? she wondered. Suddenly she lost confidence. What am I trying to do? she thought.

"Later, in September," Terry continued, "maybe you'll see a king or two, people also call them chinooks. Best way to remember, they're usually bigger than the others and they got black inside their mouths. Now reds, sockeyes, the fifth kind of salmon—you know them from Bristol Bay, little reddish inside the gills sometimes? Silvery tail stripes? Stuff like that? Sockeye runs hit Kodiak Island on the Shelikof side—but they're over for the year. Anyhow, skippers don't have to sort. You see how Boss just runs the brailer? Don't worry, Ham and me are good at sorting. All you got to remember when you're skipper is, that each kind of salmon brings a different price. Silvers bring higher than chums and chums is higher than humps."

"Thank you, Terry."

"Sure. Me and Ham, we'll see you through. Don't you worry."

Worry she did. Memory of days spent carefree on boats had deceived her. She'd steered boats and felt their reaction against currents, but with somebody else in ultimate charge to help or take over. And every boat had a different feel. What if somebody fell overboard in rough water where it was hard to maneuver? Steering in open water was easy—but what of docking with everybody watching to see if she'd bang the pier just like a woman? Radio bands: which for calling ashore and which for the Coast Guard if trouble hit? The life raft tied over the cabin—did anybody know how it worked? The fish ticket the tender gave after delivery—what if they'd cheated on weights when she wasn't looking? My God, she should be home making sure her children didn't come to harm! Not too late to call it off. Make it a joke. They'd kid, everybody would, then all would be forgotten. Adele might be disappointed, but then she'd just sell the boat, take the money, and go on back to San Diego or whatever. Or find a man to run the boat.

While she worried, Jody continued to press and make herself learn. She compiled lists of questions, more than she wanted to admit she needed to know. She asked Terry some of the questions first, casually in other forms since he needed little prompting, so that Hank wouldn't realize the extent of her ignorance. Questions even of Mo and Ham. As for Seth . . . he belonged to Hank and would soon be off the boat. Her boat. She smiled. Then the big sour grumbler would need her permission to come aboard.

Hank, once committed, watched his men to make sure they did right by his wife. Asking Terry and Ham to crew for her had been easier than expected, so easy that he jealously wondered for a moment. But, as Terry said without being asked, "She's our family too, Boss. Don't you worry." It wasn't going to be easy for two strutting men to crew for a woman. He knew they'd be teased ashore, even tormented. Nice guys.

As for Seth, deck boss and relief skipper of the *Jody Dawn,* his biggest problem beyond resistance to any new idea was losing his best deck man, Terry. Loss of the newcomer Ham mattered less but was still an annoyance. Hank soon realized that "consulting" Seth had been only pro forma since Terry had already said yes. Wrong strategy, Hank concluded, except that negative Seth might have changed Terry's mind, while Jody needed a good engine man above all else for safety. Seth was becoming as scratchy as Jones Henry at only half Jones's age, and his temper blew increasingly. On deck he couldn't be bettered for knowledge and reflexes. Their careers had run together for too many years to consider parting. He'd saved Seth's life at least once, and Seth probably his by solving problems before they became emergencies. But what of Seth's reaction two weeks ago, when Hank stepped into the life raft to rescue Jones and Seth, trying to stop him, had cried: "You're all I got!" It troubled Hank whenever he remembered. Seth's dependency had become a burden.

Hank watched Jody take hold with reluctant admiration. Part of him kept hoping that she'd give it a try for a few days, then change her mind, and they'd conclude the thing as casually as it began. She had their children to raise! And once she hired crew it would be all the harder to back out. But he didn't want to see her fail. In the wheelhouse, after two days, he let her scout and decide where to set with only an occasional comment. She took the controls, maneuvered, and directed the sets with driving energy. Hank watched with a mixture of concern, even irritation, but also pride and love as she ran from wheelhouse to deck shouting, sometimes laughing, the ponytail tucked inside her shirt to avoid machinery tangle, a baseball cap squared on her head, all business. (And all business at night after he'd followed behind for hours, his wife too keyed up and too weary for more than a good-night peck on the cheek.)

Her instincts were good, while her alert mind absorbed facts that she needed to cram. She became confident. Too confident, he felt. "Wrong water here," he observed once. "You ought to be closer to shore, especially with the tide going out."

"This still looks good to me," she declared, and shouted *Ho!* astern for the skiff to go. It turned out to be the best haul of the day. All but he and Seth exclaimed and congratulated. Her bounce and grin didn't help. During the next set Hank saw clearly that the net was going to encircle short of the fish, but said nothing. An hour's tow brought in three fish. He shrugged and felt justified, but also ashamed.

By now Ham occupied the skiff full-time since he would be Jody's skiff man, with Mo and Terry alternating second position. Jody rode as his second once or twice daily, working the plunger, then leaping back to the main deck after the seine had encircled the catch. Seth watched her restlessly. One day as they readied a new set, he entered the skiff. "This trip's mine," he told Ham. "Go back on deck." Ham, used to obeying, obeyed.

Jody had already taken position. Seth appeared to ignored her. Terry hit the release hook and the skiff pulled free of the boat dragging out the seine. "What you want," Seth began impersonally, his gaze straight ahead, "is to fix in your mind the way the fish act." Step by step he instructed, gradually warming. While he accepted command signals from Hank on the bridge, he maneuvered on his own and explained each move, then explained why Hank had given the signal from the boat's viewpoint. "You got to leave some initiative to your skiff man if he knows what he's doing. But with Ham, you got to take charge more than with me. See that tide rip? Worth going a little wider to suck in what may be riding it. Now you plunge—not there, out as far as you can while I'm trying to pull toward 'em. Hit it! Think of herding cows—maybe there's one going to get away if you don't scare him back. Plunge!"

Jody plunged, and listened, and strove to absorb. Her ignorance was increasing! When Ham ran the skiff they had followed Hank's signals from the boat. This was different—a fisherman's mind at work creatively.

Seth became impersonal again. When the set was completed and they returned to the boat, she thanked him. "You got it," he said abruptly, and started off. Then he stopped and faced her. "Everything you do, it's got ways to do it. Not just skiff. All kinds of stuff you can't learn in two days."

"I hear you." It increased her unease.

Fish and Game extended the opening day by day into the second week. By now Hank had moved into the skipper's cabin with Jody. One morning Jody rose unrested from the narrow bunk below Hank's. She had lain awake in the dark trying to picture the flow of hydraulic lines from Terry's sketches. Suddenly the steady hum of the generator had changed. What's wrong? If wrong, what to do? The hum returned. So much not understood, that in the old boat days others had simply handled while she thought she knew it all. Not ready. July had passed to August and the days were peeling off. Soon they'd be back in town, Hank and his men to return to their own boat and then he to Japan for his mysterious deal, she for supplies and for extra crew if she chose. Then, back to Uganik Bay or elsewhere around the island. If she chose. On her own.

Decision: time to call it off. Announce with firm, good-natured cheer. She dressed with elbow-tight movements in the close quarters, quietly to not wake Hank. Take coffee before facing anybody.

Hank coughed to show he was awake, but remained in his bunk. "Boat's all yours today, captain," he said quietly. "Get out there and fish."

Good. Face it. "Since you're awake I've got something to admit, Hank. I'm not—"

"Can't hear you." Hank rolled over and covered his head. "Wake me for lunch."

"It's not working."

"Shut the door when you leave."

It was so final that she started out. Coffee first. But damn his arrogance!

As she left, Hank declared evenly, "You've come this far, Jody, and you're doing fine. Run the whole show today before you decide. I love you. Go!"

She shivered despite his words—they blocked an easy escape, however grateful she was for them—shivered despite the heat in the galley. The place was deserted, and quiet except for the puff of the propane stove left on low during the night. She turned up the burner and readied the coffeepot, then straightened cups on the hooks, wiped the condiments in the rack, shuffled fish delivery tickets that had already been sorted and logged. Each mechanical step postponed serious thought.

On deck she breathed the wet morning air and shivered again despite a thick hot mug of coffee she held in both hands. She felt so numb and alone! Mist rolled among the nearby boats at anchor, showing some with a full spread of nets and corks heaped on deck and skiff bobbing astern, hiding others except for a tip of mast or top half of suspended power block. Anchor lights reflected on patches of water, and dimmed or glowed through curtains of fog. The sight soothed, then suddenly panicked her. Barge into this intact society of boats and fishermen? Men who answered to the water and had adapted to its conditions while she lived ashore and raised children?

Not yet 4 AM by the galley clock. All crews still slept except for a kid on one stern relieving himself. He noticed her, and quickly turned away although she tried to act as if she hadn't seen him. The trouble with a woman in the fleet. The poor men needed to think before they even pissed, no matter how like a guy the woman made herself to be. There was no way around some things. Who'd want to see a woman squat on deck just to prove equality? It remained a brotherhood. If she failed, any husky teenage boy with two weeks on the plunger could echo Seth's inevitable "Could'a told you."

A gust of wind swirled the mist while it jerked the boat at anchor and rattled the rigging. She enjoyed the sound, rocked comfortably with the feel. "But I damn well *am* part of this," she muttered. Entered it at scrub level all those years ago, broken free from Army brathood and come to Alaska for the hell of it. Survived. "No man's squeeze unless I chose." She smiled. How to tell your kids that one? Worked ashore at canneries and that diner destroyed in the earthquake. Cooked chow on boats and helped on deck, salty-tongued and untouchable. "Unless I chose. I'm as much a damn part of this as any man!"

Independence had been her pride and reputation. Now the mirror, when she used it, reflected a tamer face. The very fact that she now needed a mirror to put on lipstick or brush her hair proved the taming. In the old days such things fell in place or not. Giving in step by step. Give in on this with the *Adele H,* and farewell altogether to the old image of Jody.

She'd probably loved Hank from the time they'd met. No, not when he was that drip-eared college boy nursing pennies over diner coffee while he tried to find a boat job, and she was the waitress who poured it impatiently. Only a year or so later during the cleanup after the '64 earthquake had she begun to feel interest despite her conscious detachment. His eyes trailing her—she might have acknowledged sooner except that her growing attraction to him might have endangered independence. It had been her own decision, finally, to crawl together into the same sleeping bag after a rough day cleaning earthquake debris, that night on Jones Henry's boat where by then he crewed. It didn't mean marriage. But he always returned after she'd reluctantly shaken him free. Even later when they lived together, she hadn't meant it to be marriage.

Then she married him in spite of it. By then enough years had passed that he skippered his own boat. She loved him deeply, and he'd forced her to admit it. Bearded, earnest Hank, grown from green kid into able and intelligent man, insistent and decent. All of it now settled years ago and three children to prove the settlement.

Until his trick with that woman in Japan last spring. Would she have known if he hadn't confessed? Damn right! He wasn't a good deceiver. She'd let her hurt run its course in anger, but she'd meant it when she'd kicked him out of the house. Be true or go. She'd seen enough of mate-swapping in Kodiak, and slimy excuses from both sexes of long separation on boats. She could go alone again if need be, even with the children. But thank God he'd faced it honestly, and convinced her it had been the only time, never to happen again. In the wake of reconciliation she'd buried her resentment over his letting the Japanese take their house as security on his boat. But damn Japan! They'd had troubles before that, but never betrayal.

A stomp, and Terry appeared yawning from the galley, unzipping his fly. He stopped when he saw her, and his hands automatically covered himself. "Oh. Hey—sorry. Didn't know—"

"Don't worry, I'm turning my back."

"I'll go inside or something."

"No need. Just don't expect me to go in either. I'm busy looking at the water. We're on this boat together."

"Well . . . here goes, but it won't feel right." A light splash ran its course. "I might have known you was up since coffee's made and Mo's still snoring. Want more coffee? I'll bring it."

"I can get my own, thanks. You don't need to treat me like a woman."

"You think Boss gets his own coffee if he's studying the water?"

She started to insist that she was no skipper yet, but instead changed the subject. "The generator. Does it sometimes skip? Last night I thought . . . ?"

"Shifted, maybe. Nothin' to worry 'bout."

"But our engine. Does it need some kind of overhaul?"

"Naah. Engine's good. Good. These Jimmy engines, some young guys call 'em old-fashioned and got to have the latest Cat or Volvo, but they hold up good. Ol' Jones Henry never let anything go bad on his boat. He was professional."

"Terry . . . I asked you this once before, but what do you . . . what does Ham think about working for a woman? If I should take over the boat?"

"If? I thought you was." A pause. "Ham's okay with it. Don't worry. And don't let Seth scare you. What you don't know is, he's been driving Ham and me crazy with instructions about what we'd better be sure to do after he's gone. To not fuck—not screw—not make dumb mistakes. You know?"

"You mean Seth assumes I'm taking over?"

"Sure. We all do."

A fish jumped. Another leapt from the water, wriggled its tail for the instant it remained suspended, then splashed back. "Chum jumpers," said Jody, not bothering to ask for Terry's confirmation. Suddenly she felt able. "Get the others up. Let's fish!"

"You got it!"

As Terry hurried off, she added with a grin, "But let Hank sleep. Old bosses need their rest."

Terry looked at her, startled, then laughed.

3

THE RACE

UGANIK BAY, EARLY AUGUST 1982

"Hit it!" called Jody. Her voice had sharpened in the space of hours after taking command the day before.

"Ya-hoo!" cried Ham, and entered the skiff so heartily his big frame bounced the craft. Mo followed with a yell and equal leap.

Terry led it all with running jokes that Jody didn't seem to mind about working for a dame. When Charlie of Fish and Game glided up in his motor dinghy, and with a wink handed Jody an envelope with her license, Terry entered a new round of speculation on how they'd all escaped being jailbirds.

Hank watched, glad enough for their spirits but wary of the sudden festive atmosphere among all but Seth. His men never frolicked like that under him. Making a game of it? Why not, so long as they did their jobs. He himself, having declared he'd stay apart and having already pushed his injured shoulder too hard so that it ached, now wandered idle unless he chose to stack rings, wash dishes, or do some other light job. Does you good, he told himself.

His own concern needed to be the Japanese and how they planned to convert his *Jody Dawn* to longline. He certainly wasn't in their pocket as Gus Rosvic had disturbed him by hinting, but did he yet grasp all he'd committed to? It was going to require new tricks of him and new grounds—that would be good, exciting. But what of all the new fish politics that until now he'd scorned and dodged?

During the past few days of happy old-style fishing, he'd managed to forget for hours at a time that somebody else, and Japanese at that, controlled the boat of his heart. Director Tsurifune and his son Shoji of Tsurifune Suisan Ltd. seemed honorable. But what good was the 51 percent of *Jody Dawn* that they'd let him keep officially when they held her papers as security, along with those for his house? Jody was being understanding about the house after her initial explosion, and given the wide-open abundance of black cod he'd catch for the Japanese he'd soon bail them out—but a lien on their home?

They'd already jerked him around once by forcing him to tender his *Jody Dawn* for salmon in Bristol Bay under an altered boat name that, to his embarrassment (humiliation!), enabled secret deals with strikebreakers; they'd forced him, however velvet the glove. At night, his loss of freedom kept him awake. How could he have let it happen?

Then, in daylight, either gradually or in a burst, the project's opportunities and adventures took over. Japan rode the wave, and they'd pulled him up to share the crest. Prosperities as vivid as that Kabuki he'd enjoyed in Tokyo lay ahead. If the world insisted on sweeping along, you either watched and lost out, or joined. Jones Henry hadn't understood, and the pain of that would grind forever. Nor did old Gus understand—but looking ahead wasn't for the old. Or the dead.

The Tsurifune deal made sense and hurt nobody. They needed him to supply them the black cod they called sablefish, and he needed them to relieve his debt. He would deliver the fish, frozen, directly to a Japanese cargo ship, having caught it as an American with access to a virtually unlimited quota, that eroded nothing from the Japanese's tight and diminishing quota negotiated annually with the U.S. State Department. The Tsurifunes thus ensured that they'd receive a steady supply of sablefish no matter what happened within international fish politics.

Nature had changed things by making the crabs disappear and leaving him vulnerable and in debt. His move now was to change and thwart Nature—no, to follow where Nature led. If the little yellow men, as Jones would have called them (or worse) wanted to bail him out, why lose his boat like Tolly and so many others? For a price, of course, the way of the world, but not a permanent price if he kept his head.

In truth, he could reassure himself, he was merely taking steps for the future and the good of his family, and was lucky to have the chance. Shoji/

Mike Tsurifune and his dad, the old director, had hinted of future boats in his name if this first arrangement panned out. Potentially, the deal could start him on a path to greater possession than he'd ever dreamed. Riding on top of that Japanese crest could offer a mighty view.

Thus Hank pondered midday in the stuffy skipper's cabin, self-sequestered to let Jody test her authority without his presence. He tilted back in the single chair with his feet propped on the bunk rail, making notes and lists for the forthcoming trip to Japan. When the others bounced into the galley on the other side of the metal bulkhead, banging objects and laughing, he tried to ignore their lively talk. It included him not at all. Behind a closed door he was out-of-mind. Even Seth forgot him, calculating in gruff good humor the number of chums in the catch and the price they'd bring. Smell of bacon, crack of eggs, signs of comfort between sets, and he was not even missed. Jody's talk, though clipped and authoritative, had a buoyancy to it that she seldom used around him anymore. Reverting to her freedom days before they married. Nice to see, but who was going to be home for the final wash and iron when he left for Japan, much less the good-bye hug, kiss, and wave?

Seth offered to show Jody something on the wheelhouse charts. "I guess you know I've been reading charts for a lot of years," he said expansively.

"I know, I know," Jody declared with vixen warmth as their voices receded.

"Shucks," from Mo, presumably to Ham and Terry after the others had left. "Wish I could crew aboard here, too. You guys are going to have a ball."

Hank started to throw open the door and declare that nobody had better go slack working for his wife when Terry said: "We're makin' a ball of this, but you think there ain't problems? Things about the boat she don't know and hasn't learned? Even Seth—everybody knows what he thinks of a lady skipper—even he watches and tells us things we'd better remember to make things go smooth, since Boss is pretending to look the other way. Our Jody's going to highline because we'll bust ass to make sure of just that. We've made what you call a pack on that, Ham and me."

"That's it," said Mo. "That's what I mean. And those two-hundred-buck bets. I ought to put down money somewhere too." He lowered his voice, as ineffective as damping a kettledrum. "Two guys ashore? I don't know from what boat, but loud enough I could hear. They were saying Boss lost it after Jones Henry died, to let his old lady run Jones's boat. I

turned and got ready to take 'em on. They got embarrassed and walked
away like little babies."

Terry laughed. "We've got us a situation. But no reason we can't have
some fun with it."

"Like I said, man." Mo's voice turned wistful again. "Wish I was with
you."

Hank brushed sweat from his eyes in the stuffy room. Always take care of
these guys in future. Might have known. No way out of it now but straight
ahead, while training Jody to the utmost. Give her Mo with the others? But
the *Jody Dawn* should be repaired by now, ready for conversion and facing
what the Japanese expected. Seth needed at least one deck ape he could trust.

Fish runs throughout Uganik Bay turned so strong that the single cannery began to choke with more pinks than it could process. First, it put all
boats on a quota, then stopped buying from boats like the *Adele H* that
had not contracted in advance. Floating cash buyers took up the slack.
Usually they paid higher than the cannery to lure contracted boats, but
now in a buyer's market they offered less. Meanwhile, in Kodiak several
canneries were paying a nickel a pound more than Uganik for fish brought
dockside, while one of them in code offered Hank two cents further under
the table. When Fish and Game declared the opening would end the next
day, Hank decided. Rather than moor at the cannery and fly home, they'd
fill the hold to a safe level—take less chance than he might without Jody to
watch and learn—and steam to Kodiak. Keep training her on the way.

On the final morning they pulled aboard such a load that they plugged
the hold and needed to pile the extra fish on deck. It was too tempting not
to continue, but it opened a tricky choice. Deliver to the cash buyer, selling low, then fish like hell for the rest of the day and hope they'd have a
catch to deliver in Kodiak, or leave for town at once? If they sold here they
might need to line up for a couple of hours, a delay that might force them
to compete through the narrow Whale Passage with other boats of the
fleet returning to Kodiak. During the course of the action Hank had
missed the morning's weather forecast, but the sky was clear. Carrying the
deckload would probably pose no problem. Hank included Jody and the
others in the decision, although he considered himself still in authority.

"Shag ass, I say," observed Seth, "or all kinds of fuckers'll beat us to
town and we'll wait in line there, then watch, or they'll likely cut the price
while we wait."

Hank turned to Jody. "Go?"

"Go!"

"Amen," cried Terry.

Soon everyone was on the run. They boarded off a bin amidships for the fish on deck and covered them with tarps. The seine lay aft of this in a hill of web flanked by orderly snakes of cork line. Under Seth's bark they winched aboard the skiff on top of the web.

Jody joined Hank in the wheelhouse to study charts. "We'll go around outside by Shelikof," he stated.

"You're kidding! We're so deep into the bay we'd lose at least an hour." Jody tapped her pencil on a narrow strip of waterway. "East Passage on a calm day? I've been through this shortcut before."

"Not for years and not as a skipper. I don't want you taking chances."

"You don't want? Well, it's the difference between making Whale Passage on high slack or hitting the flood." She paused to enjoy his surprise. "I just did the homework."

Hank was impressed but shook his head. "Rocks. Tricky bars and shoals. No. We'll steam the long way and still make it."

Shouts from below and Seth's head appeared from the ladder. "You see what the *Hinda Bee*'s doing over there?" Hank grabbed binoculars. The men on the *Hinda*'s deck were also building a pen around fish on deck while preparing to haul aboard their skiff. "We go now or old Gus and all our bucks—or old Gus beats us to Kodiak."

Jody's wide mouth twitched at the sides in her old way, close to a grin. Before Hank could speak she declared, "Not likely!" and became animated. "Our anchor's up and skiff's aboard, right? Then here we go. Yes. Let's go!" Within moments Seth's voice barked orders below. Jody turned to Hank and said firmly, "I'm ready to be in charge, and I'm taking the shortcut."

Hank acquiesced, impressed again. Better she did it with him, since if she returned alone he'd have no way to stop her. "Rocks on that eastern bank, some hidden," he pointed. "Always give it a wide berth even at high tide. Submerged spit there, then shoal, shoal, shoal." He found a red pen and circled the symbols.

"Don't you think I can read danger marks on a chart?"

"Just the same. Now, here . . ." She had already gone to the controls. "Other boats around us have nets in the water, Jody. Go easy."

"Yes, yes." She frowned at the water, then eased the engine into forward gear. From deck came *Yo!*'s of approval. Ahead to port the *Lady West* had begun a set and its skiff was pulling the seine into a semicircle. Farther off to starboard the *Hinda Bee* was still getting ready.

The *Adele H* glided smoothly under Jody's hand. She's in control—not bad, thought Hank, and dismissed the thought that she might have consulted him further. Suddenly Jody gave a whoop like Mo or Ham and throttled full ahead toward open water. The boat shuddered. Objects clattered and the chart slipped from the table. Startled, she jerked the rudder switch in the wrong direction and they surged directly toward the *Lady West*'s skiff. With a full hold they moved like a battering ram. Hank pushed Jody aside and grabbed the controls in time to veer. The skiff disappeared under their bow to cries everywhere. When Hank circled back, the skiff was rocking from their waves while the two men aboard struggled to hold down gear, but they had not been swamped. Both shouted angrily.

Jody hurried to the wing, and called: "Sorry—I'm so sorry!"

One of the skiff men, Nick, calmed at the sight of her. "That was you, Jody?" He grinned. "I thought it was your old man should know better. Hey. You owe me a new cap like I just lost overboard."

"Easy man, easy," called Mo from the *Adele*'s stern. He leaned over the rail with a pole while Ham held his legs. The pole end dipped from sight and emerged with a soggy red cloth. Hank maneuvered in reverse until the pole reached the skiff.

Nick picked off the dripping cap and slapped it on his head. "Baptized by Jody!" Everybody shouted and laughed.

When Jody returned to the wheelhouse, Hank kept his voice low even though he wanted to shout. "You're part of a community. Don't ever cowboy like that again."

He expected her to blaze and he prepared to blaze back. Instead, voice small, she said, "You're right. Stupid. Never again. I don't know what came over me."

"And incidentally, skippers don't usually apologize. You wait until you can stand them drinks or something."

"Well, I don't think that makes sense. But it won't happen again." Her hand trembled when she took back the controls. She now moved cautiously around other boats and nets. "I mean it. Not again."

He kept his voice grim for emphasis. "Be sure of that."

Terry's head appeared from the ladder. "Whew. Before you gun her like that, give me time to stand back. I figured we was still on a mosey kind of speed and I'm just checkin' the batteries when *voom!*"

"I'm really sorry."

Hank had been watching the *Hinda Bee*, now distant, through binoculars. Her skiff was still in the water although it nosed against the stern. Maybe they weren't racing to town after all. At least their *Adele H* had a good head start. He relaxed as did the others when they saw. His mood lightened. "Hey, Jody. Want to try it from the flying bridge?" She nodded, switched to neutral for the change of controls—did all the steps correctly, he noted—and tucked back a strand of hair in passing.

It was a good afternoon to cruise: mirror water that left a wake like pencil lines, hazy sun that rested the eyes. After frantic hose-downs and tie-downs, with all gear secured, Ham and Mo jumped and boxed like puppies on the crowded deck while Seth and Terry converged topside as they usually did under way.

"My men make you nervous?" Hank whispered to Jody. "While you're learning?"

"Make yourselves comfortable, guys," was her reply.

Relax with it, Hank told himself. He could see how much she liked her new role. Tucked back her hair, did she? A woman after all when she's on display at the open wheel.

They glided past the *Sleepthief Two*. Its crew had just emptied their seine and were preparing for another set. "Hey, man," called Mo's bearlike voice to a friend aboard the *Thief*. "Five cents a pound, maybe more in Kodiak—you think we're stayin' here?"

Hank sent Terry to bring up Mo and Ham. "He ought to know by now that we tell nobody our plans. Set him straight, Seth."

"Thought I had. Mo needs telling only once for anything to do with gear, but for ideas, ten times won't do it. Jody, you'd better know that Ham's the same."

"I'll keep Ham straight," said Terry calmly. "Don't worry."

They next passed a setnet site where half a dozen plyboard shacks blended with the scrub. In addition, two tents were staked precariously into the sand. Smoke lazed up from chimneys—no wind at all—but everyone was down at the water. Men and women waded waist-deep around a net that enclosed a frenzy of fish.

"There's Madge Farley!" Jody declared. She called, and a woman muddy in waders with hair in a knot looked up without loosening her grip on the communal net.

"Jody! Look at you. We've heard. Way to go!"

Jody held herself straight. "Nice haul there, I see."

"How're you doing?"

"Deckload and riding low in the water. Guess that says it."

Like a braggy kid, thought Hank, and wanted to sweep her up and dance. Instead, he stepped back to make it clear that Jody held the wheel. Terry grinned, and kept his position behind her with legs apart. Seth eased to the opposite rail out of sight, followed slowly by Mo, then even more slowly by Ham.

When they had passed beyond earshot, Jody said carelessly, "That was Madge's husband beside her. They're both at the high school. Madge and I sat across from each other for two years on city council. Don't ask how seldom we agreed. But together we blocked that proposal to set aside half the seiner slips for party boats. Even an English teacher understood that one."

"They say you raised some hell to council and back," said Terry appreciatively. "Even guys in the bars talked about it."

Hank smiled to himself. A banker in town had actually offered him special credit if he'd curb his wife. He watched her with a surge of love and pride. Let her come to no harm in this new business.

They entered alone into the waterway around the back of Uganik Island toward Viekoda Bay. If sour old Gus Rosvic chose to follow, at least they had a head start. The land closed in with odors of evergreen and mud. Glistening humps of rock rose out of the water like half-submerged hippos. The trees that hemmed the banks were too close for sight of the Kodiak mountains. No breeze twitched even the top branches, and the air hung damp and warm.

"Spooky," murmured Terry. He left the edge of the rail and settled on a storage chest near Hank and Jody. Seth yawned and went below, declaring that people had better sleep when they could. Mo and Ham followed.

Hank felt absorbed by the land, but watched it, detached. Tree shadows so blackened the smooth water that the shoreline appeared to extend to their keel. When they passed bluffs the thrum of the engine reverberated, a sound he heard so automatically that it seemed they cruised in silence.

They'd make good way even riding loaded, and would be home not too long after midnight. Leave the guys aboard to deliver. The kids were safe with Adele. Grab private time with Jody before the hassles began.

"Easy cruisin'," declared Jody. She stood at the wheel with legs apart, clearly enjoying herself. When Terry offered to steer, her answer was a toss of the head.

"Shoal over there," said Hank. "And watch for logs, always watch for logs around all this timber."

"I'm watching, Hank."

When next, he wondered, will I ever seine salmon again in friendly bays? His shoulder still ached, but the pain decreased each day, and he even felt less fatigued. He was healing. This episode had helped. The disaster and Jones Henry's death would always be part of memory and nightmare, but the heartache had already begun to dull. Pressures waited. The Japanese would demand. Life would become a push. Soon, he'd be ready. If only it could be both ways.

On deck Mo and Ham grabbed chunks of bologna from the galley, cracked down their boot tops, and lay back like pashas on the hill of web under the skiff, their feet propped on the boards of the fish bin.

Seth, with work done, went to his bunk. Hanging around a wheelhouse where Hank's woman took the helm didn't feel right. It's what came from letting marriage run your life. He covered his eyes with a T-shirt and the musty old-sweat smell became part of the comfortable dark. Just as well little what's-her-name, Mary—no, Marion—married a damn storekeeper named John instead of Mr. Seth, although she'd never have run his life like Jody. He and Hank were supposed to be the team at sea. At least Jody was going to run her own separate boat and he didn't wish her harm. Nice girl when she wasn't bossing. With luck she'd not screw up, so long as she stuck to fishing inside water. Let the real team get back to normal. He rolled a blanket around his legs and chest to enclose himself further. Sure, he was a skipper too, a good one when Hank gave him the *Jody Dawn* off-season. Don't ever admit the personal cost. Sour stomach and sleepless, day and night, until Hank came back and took over. The Japan business would be new stuff but interesting—so long as Hank kept control. Why couldn't it always stay like that? Hank was Boss. He adjusted the blanket further until it covered him feet to head. With his fisherman's clock set to sleep when he could, he soon fell asleep.

Terry stayed topside with Hank and Jody. He enjoyed them. They
didn't rub in the lovey-doo in front of a guy divorced and wishing for
a lady of his own. The three of them chatted in good cheer, pointing to
wildlife ashore when they saw it.

Suddenly Terry exclaimed, "Lookit!" Behind an outcrop of rocks astern
glided the top of a mast. At a bend the bow of a boat emerged. Terry
grabbed binoculars. "I'll bet, I'll bet . . . I'm right, *Hinda Bee,* grumpy Gus!"

"Make bets against me!" Jody declared. "I'll show 'em!"

Terry turned, surprised. "Who told you?"

"Think I'm deaf? Stop protecting me." To Hank: "You do know this
water best. Can we gun her?"

Hank had also caught the spirit. "Stick to that east bank and gun her."

Terry continued looking through the binoculars. "He's riding low like
us. Even match, but we're ahead. Boss! See he don't beat us. I mean, Jody,
don't let him."

"Beat us?" exclaimed Jody. "Like hell!"

They entered Viekoda Bay and wide water while the *Hinda* still picked
through the last of the narrows. Jody throttled full ahead. After the shelter
of trees and banks, a breeze hit them. It rattled the chart she had spread on
a box and swept ripples across water previously glassy.

"She'll never catch us," said Terry. "We're too good for that, right?"
The breeze had cleared the general haze. Snowy mountains showed on the
mainland across Shelikof Strait thirty miles away, whitecapped even in
August, glowing against sudden gray sky. "You sure don't forget winter
for long up here. Whew—is it me, or has it gotten colder?"

Blowing easterly, Hank judged. Hard to tell the force since they'd travel
in the same direction until Kupreanof Strait. Should have caught the
morning weather report. By the time *Hinda Bee* had cleared the last of the
rocks, the breeze had strengthened to build chops in the water. Both boats
churned steadily. Only two miles separated them. Sometimes one seemed
to gain, then the other. Hank checked to make sure Jody held full throttle. We might take water on deck after all, he noted. A chance to judge
Jody's reactions while he could still advise, whether she accepted or not.
In an emergency, she'd better.

The chart began to flap. Jody gathered it. "Let's go below," she said to
Hank. "Terry, take the wheel until I click in." Down in the wheelhouse
she turned to Hank seriously. "When we round the point into Kupreanof

Strait, won't we be heading right into this?" He nodded. "Terry," she called. "You and the guys strap the tarps tighter on those deck fish, anything else you see that needs—"

"Gotcha," Terry shouted down. "We have already, but I'll look at everything again. Now we're spinnin'!" He bounced down the outside ladder with a *Yah-hoo!*

Seth appeared. Bushes of hair beaded with water popped like wires from the sides of the wool cap slapped hastily on his head. "Don't worry. I've checked."

"I knew you would," said Jody calmly. "But since my guys are Terry and Ham after you leave, let's make them do it again."

Seth's voice remained gruff, but he said, "Good idea."

He's with her, thought Hank gladly.

They rounded the rocks and steep slope of Outlet Cape. Whitecaps surged across the water they faced, bearing straight from the direction in which they needed to head. They turned. The *Adele H* shuddered and her bow veered as they hit wind and sea. Instantly their motion changed from easy roll to pitch and thud. The weighted boat slowly rose on swells. Then its bow plunged heavily to slice the water into fans of spray.

Whoops from below, and Terry stomped up exuberant and dripping, followed by Mo and Ham. "All's on deck tight as a witch's ass," Terry announced, then caught himself. "Sorry, things just all tight, Jody."

"Witch's ass it is," said Jody.

"Wow, that spray and all caught me and Ham asleep under the skiff," crowed Mo. "Good thing Terry woke us. Won't need another bath for a month."

A spit of land hid the *Hinda Bee* for a while. Then Terry announced, "She's comin' round." The *Hinda* hit the waves head-on just as they had, moving at full throttle to judge by the sudden buck of her bow.

The wind continued to increase. An hour later, spray from the *Adele H*'s bow arched higher than before, over the wheelhouse, while seas slapped across the afterdeck. The seas laced harmlessly into the mound of web held secure under the skiff, but gushes of water tugged at the edges of the tarp covering the fish. By now Hank had roused Kodiak by radio to learn that a sudden storm was moving in from the southeast across the Gulf of Alaska.

"I might need to decide something you won't like," he said quietly to Jody.

"We'll beat the storm." She said it without altering her concentration ahead or relinquishing the controls. "I'm not letting Ham and Terry lose their bets."

"If it's not safe you will."

"We're a long way from that."

Spray splatted against the windows and dissipated in rivulets that obscured the view. Terry, Mo, and Ham exclaimed with each barrage as they peered ahead at rocky banks misted by the spray. When they looked astern they jeered happily at the thrashing *Hinda Bee*. Like kids, Hank mused. Rough weather still turns them on, so long as they trust their skipper and feel safe. Long gone for me. Too bad.

"Keep her comin', Jody!" called Terry, always the boldest of the three and becoming bolder. Meanwhile Seth, beginning to think like a skipper, soberly blocked their position on the chart and checked the Fathometer, while still as deck boss watching the lines that secured gear on the afterdeck.

Hank outlined the situation. "I'd hoped to reach Whale Passage in time for high slack, but with this wind we'll miss it by an hour or more. So we'll buck into the first of the flood running in the same direction as the wind."

"No sweat," said Terry. "We've got a strong engine."

"Ho for Terry!" from Jody.

"I'd rather be on the other side of Whale before the storm hits," Hank continued. "So I'd as soon keep going. However—"

Seth broke in. "To keep going's good if we can. What it means is, old Gus is two miles behind us—that's a whole hour's advantage for us the way this is building. So he'll buck through Whale at even stronger flood, which slows him further and puts us more ahead. And you know these old farts. Maybe he's chicken. Maybe he'll wait for next slack."

"The old farts survive to tell about it," snapped Hank.

His concern grew. The wind had shifted enough that sidewise waves slapped the bow off course and the rudder corrected only sluggishly. Blame the fish under the tarp. The load weighted the hull too deeply to maneuver, and lowered the rail so that water churned freely onto deck, pushing the boat farther down.

Mo became expansive. "We're sure to beat 'em now. With that deckload out there of fish? She's piled higher than the one on *Hinda Bee*. We'll wait pierside, take their lines, say 'pay up the bet, we beat you.' Right, Seth?"

"Chee, can't you keep anything quiet?" muttered Seth and turned away.

"You guys didn't make new bets?" said Terry.

"Oh yeah? Seth and me, we've each got our own two hundreds riding on the biggest single delivery this opening, which better be this one right here. We did it in the cannery mess hall that day, after you guys bet yours." He added proudly, "Kept it a secret until now."

"That's sweet, you guys," said Jody from the helm. "I'd come hug you each if I wasn't working so hard here. Boat keeps wanting to go to starboard, stubborn as a horse that sees grass where you don't want him to go."

Hank half listened, sorry that he alone hadn't staked faith-money on his wife. But he watched astern with growing unease. Their weighted boat had turned sluggish, and the *Hinda Bee* was gaining on them. At last he decided reluctantly, and announced: "Dump the deckload."

"Boss! That's our money!"

"I'm sorry, Mo."

"I think this is supposed to be my boat," Jody began.

"Seth. See to it." By his tone Hank took command. "I'll slow to reduce deckwash. Call when you're ready. Be careful in this sea." Automatically Seth beckoned the others and they hurried below, even though it meant losing his own bet.

Hank patted Jody's shoulder, eased her from the controls, and reduced speed. "Are you crazy?" she flared. "We'll drift right back even with the damn *Hinda.*"

"Unless Gus is stupid he'll unload the same. Don't you feel our drag? We need to ride lighter, need more freeboard to maneuver in this. Besides, we're top-heavy, off balance, perfect condition for capsizing." He hesitated, then said bluntly: "If you can't feel it when your boat talks to you, Jody . . ."

With the boat slowed they indeed closed toward the *Hinda Bee.* On deck Mo pointed and groaned. The sight activated them all. At Hank's signal they flung aside the tarp and bin boards to get it over quickly. The hill of fish slipped apart like wet soap. Furiously Mo and Ham kicked carcasses through the scuppers while water washed some back to swirl around their boots. Seth cursed steadily. He and Terry grabbed shovels and slung fish into the lee wind that carried them clear.

Jody turned quiet. "That sight makes me sick."

By now they had lost enough way to be within earshot of the *Hinda's* crew exuberantly ranged on deck. Their rivals' grinning faces, framed by oilskin hoods, showed as blotches of eyebrows and beards through the spray. Old Gus scowled from the wheelhouse window, with jaw squared and black cap pulled close to his eyes.

"Chickened out!" called Bud. "Countin' my two hundred!"

Zack, beside him, waved a rope. "Hook on, fellahs. Free tow!"

"Hope to hell you know what you're doing," muttered Jody. "You've lost your guys' bets. Now they're being humiliated."

"It . . . ain't . . . over," Hank said grimly.

By the time the deck was clear they had slipped first alongside and then astern the *Hinda Bee*. But at last their boat, relieved of weight and imbalance, pitched higher and responded with greater life. Within minutes they had overtaken the *Hinda* and looked across rail to rail.

Terry picked up a fish still sloshing on deck. "Hey, you turkeys! Charity!" He tossed it by the tail toward the other boat. Bud reached out in good humor but it slipped past his fingers. Mo and Ham jeered as Terry continued, "Poor turkeys can't even catch a humpie." He threw another fish but the wind blew it short. The *Hinda*'s turn to catcall at a poor weak kid who thought he could throw.

Hank, listening from the open window in the wheelhouse, noted that the taunts didn't touch on Terry's size. Good guys; they didn't hit below the belt.

"All right. I feel the difference," Jody conceded. "You're right. But now that we've dumped our deckload, Seth and Mo lose their bet on biggest delivery. Then Terry and Ham—what was their bet?"

"Biggest total catch the entire opening, from the day they made the bet." Hank knew that his action had probably also cost this bet. From Jody's expression, she realized it too.

The *Adele H*, now livelier than the *Hinda Bee*, began to pull ahead. Jody laid her hand on his arm. "Just keep abreast for a minute." She called down to Seth and he appeared. "Listen. See if they'll take another bet. Two hundred of my own money says we'll make it first to Kodiak today. But don't use my name; spread it, say, fifty from each of you." She considered. "I'll double that if they give you a hard time!"

Seth laughed. "You're on."

"Can I believe this?" Hank cried. "Since when did you approve of bets?" He turned to find them watching him detachedly, as if he didn't matter. Initiative was slipping from his hands. "Lay down another fifty each from me right off. So we've covered the four of you for another hundred each."

When Seth shouted over the proposed bets, Gus Rosvic studied him from the wheelhouse window. The old man shook his head, then shrugged.

The bets were accepted from the other rail with appropriate calls and insults, but not before Seth had been goaded jovially into doubling them.

4

WHALE PASSAGE

Hank knew, as did every other fisherman who worked the fish-filled bays around Kodiak Island, that Whale Passage was the shortest route by miles between Kodiak town and the west side of the island. He and the others also knew Whale to be potentially dangerous. Nature had created here, between mountains, a mere slit of a trench to connect two bodies of fiercely tidal water. Worse, the slit was booby-trapped with hidden shoals that generated turbulence. "Eddies may cause vessels to veer toward danger," warns the *United States Coast Pilot.* Fishermen needed to keep all this in mind while hugging a ribbon of safe channel.

Upon each rise and fall of tide, water sucked through the Whale Passage slit at speeds reaching six to seven knots, equal to the total power of some boats if they also bucked a headwind. Moving thus against the flow could be like pushing a barge of bricks. A boat traveling with the flow, on the other hand, could be swept recklessly over speed and lose control.

Hank seldom traversed Whale Passage without remembering the horror during his greenhorn salad days. Back then, in 1963, the Whale had churned down his buddy Pete and all the rest of the salmon tender *Billy Two* to which he'd just helped deliver fish a few hours before, leaving intact only a shard of scale and the red beard of a decaying corpse.

He stirred and put it from his mind. No time this trip to dwell on drowned shipmates. The boat approached Whale Passage with the wind gusting at their face and the head-on flood tide already strong enough to nudge against the bow. It's stupid, he knew, to hate anything of Nature. But respect this place? Always. Far ahead rose the whalelike hump of Whale Island, flanked by another low mountain. The hilly slopes dipped into a narrow cut of water blocked in the center by a rock mound. Through binoculars he could see no whitecaps against the gray horizon, a reassuring sign.

The *Hinda Bee* churned alongside, not falling behind as he'd expected. It moved through the water like a truck, accepting deckwash. His own *Adele H* pitched lighter and responded with more life, but gained no headway in what had become a race. Jody and the others watched in silence. No one said it, but they all saw that the tarps on *Hinda*'s deckload of fish held tight. Busy seas had neither swept it away nor destabilized the boat. But indeed it was a smaller pile than they had needed to throw overboard, and that might have made the difference.

The shorelines of rocks and green slopes that led into the actual Whale Island Passage began to narrow. Jody became tense. "Can't we do anything to pick up speed?"

"Only stupid things to lighten," Hank muttered, "like dump gear we'd need to replace." He pressed the throttle uselessly. Every response had already been milked.

"*Hinda*'s got more power than us, that's for sure," mourned Terry. "This engine of Jones Henry's a good ol' Jimmy, and I know Gus has a Jimmy too. None of the old-timers like to change from what they know. But maybe Gus got him an upgrade. Bet that's what Gus has."

The *Hinda*'s whistle blasted a volley of toots and the boat edged ahead. A few feet across the water Captain Gus regarded them from his wheelhouse window. His face had lost its furrows, and his eyes flashed like a man's in full prime. With a grin no more than a slit, he nodded toward Jody and tipped his cap.

"Oh, damn him!" Jody exclaimed.

The *Hinda Bee* spurted farther, inches ahead. They could hear its stronger engine throb above their own. From another of the *Hinda*'s windows, crewman Bud solemnly waved a fistful of dollars, then kissed them.

Mo and Ham groaned with a simultaneous "Oh man, oh shit."

"That old Gus," muttered Hank half in admiration. He kept his boat moving abreast of the *Hinda*, but they now stared at the back edge of its cabin as Gus continued to gain. Opposing wind and current were making it more difficult to steer a straight line without veering.

By the time they reached the Whale's first kicking swirls the *Hinda* had eased enough ahead that her battened tarp astern rose by the *Adele's* wheelhouse forward. They looked down on it glumly. Water chopped against the tarp and trickled in glistening rivulets down its slope. It remained firm and unthreatened over the solid hill of fish that would win the bet against Seth and Mo.

Gradually, they entered Whale's enclosure. Churning bubbles began to boil into circles. The wind, channeled through the gap between mountains, gained momentum. It whined around the stays and pocked spurts of prestorm hail against the windows. Their boat's speed became a crawl past the light to starboard on the rocky hump called Koniuji. Wind flattened high grass around the light's structure. Current stretched the kelp below it into ribbons. The current kept trying to buck them toward the kelp and the shoals beneath. Hank anticipated, and successfully corrected even though this was not the boat of his experience. The *Hinda* ahead of them, riding heavier with its deckload, responded more slowly both to current and to correction, but with no difficulty. Gus Rosvic obviously knew his boat and how far he could push her.

"Always stick close to the north side," Hank instructed Jody. "But not too close. Stay a hundred feet off. Shoals closer in."

White birds careened and swooped around the gray rock that loomed above them to port. "I could lob a stone over there easy," muttered Ham. "Could hit, say, that seaweed stuff in that little shelf. Easy."

"But for the wind you could," said Mo. Neither left the wheelhouse to try.

The swirls in the water multiplied around them like busy creatures. They passed a buoy that the current had begun to drag toward a slant. Off to starboard a whirlpool among rocks had captured a broken branch. The vortex sucked in the stem, pivoted the leaves like a bouquet in a vase, then slowly released its hold so that the whole branch swirled in a circle.

"We'll beat those guys after we get through this, won't we, Boss?"

"Haven't given up, Ham. We'll be the ones riding lighter."

"I knew you had a plan."

Wish it were so, thought Hank.

Suddenly the *Hinda Bee* ahead of them slowed and started tooting short blasts. Hank raised the radio volume to hear if Gus had a message.

"Yeah. *Adele H,*" came Gus's voice. "Got trouble."

"I read, *Hinda*. How can we help?"

"Losing power. Engine smoke. Oil pressure's dropped. No way we can turn around. We'll drift back, hope to clear back the way we came, out of the passage. Give as much space to our port as you can."

Hank turned to Seth who had already motioned the others and started below. "Fenders on our starboard. Then get the longest, strongest towline you can find. Do nothing unless I call. Be careful."

"Got it." Seth and the others were gone.

"What can you do?" asked Jody.

"He might drift back okay if he keeps power. If power goes he could hit rocks and smash. We might too if he hits us."

Hank slowed to keep pace with the *Hinda*. Doing so made his stern edge toward water he knew was shoal. Without strong forward motion his rudder provided less control.

"Power's gone!" exclaimed Gus on CB. His voice remained steady over shouts in the background. "Stay clear." The *Hinda*'s hull began to waver and thrash in the water, then to drift back askew. Her crew had pulled loose the tarps and were desperately kicking and shoveling overboard their deckload of fish.

"Tell Seth," Hank barked to Jody. "Throw 'em line as they pass. We'll tow if we can." She hurried out and her voice rose over the wind. On radio Hank snapped, "Gus! Send your guys to grab line. We'll tow."

"Don't wreck yourself with us."

"Grab line." He glanced at the rack of survival suits in orange bags by the ladder. Good they'd brought them.

Hank throttled enough to regain way and control. He peered back through rain-splatted glass at his men astern. They'd had no time to put on oilskins. Terry crawled over the mound of web to carry the line clear of the skiff. Seth stood with legs apart by the starboard rail, gripping the end of line coiled to throw.

When Jody returned, Hank ordered her to loosen the orange survival suit bags. Within moments the *Hinda* wallowed past. Hank pulled his whistle. Seth's line flew over as they passed rails. Wind blew it into the water. Hank slowed to drift back again alongside the *Hinda* as Seth and Mo feverishly retrieved the dripping line.

This time Mo threw the line.

"They caught it," said Jody. "They're pulling it to the bow."

"How much slack?"

"Two boat lengths, a little more. They've got it on a chock now. Wrapping it down."

"Call everybody stand clear. Warn me before the line tightens."

The rocks seemed slowly to move ahead as the boats drifted back. "Now!" called Jody. A jolt shuddered the *Adele*'s very seams despite his effort. *Hinda* was connected.

"My God, that line's stretching," she exclaimed.

"Danger it'll part. Keep your head inside. Whiplash if it snaps."

A deadweight drag on the *Adele* told him they held. Slowly he advanced the throttle. At first the *Adele* wavered in the water like a sluggish fish hooked tight. Then gradually the rocks seemed to stop moving forward and steadied alongside the rail. Under his full throttle the *Adele* with her tow ground ahead a foot at a time. Slowly they again overtook the current-tilted buoy they had passed earlier before backing. It now dragged at such a slant that its sides rippled eddies in the water. They had reached about the halfway point of the two-and-a-half-mile narrows. With the tidal current increasing against them, they'd be lucky to stop dead and merely hold way if they didn't soon get through. Rain so dimmed Ilkognak Rock a mile farther ahead that Hank could make out only the skeleton tower, not the white daymark.

A shout from outside and Jody relayed the message. "Seth says he's standing by with ax to chop line if *Hinda* drags us."

"I want Seth the fuck clear of whiplash! Get 'em all back up here where I can keep an eye!"

On CB from the *Hinda*: "Not bad, *Adele H.*"

"Any time, Gus."

"Looks like water in our fuel line. We're on it."

Seth stomped up the steps. "Now she's dumped her deckload, at least we're even again." Mo, Ham, and Terry trailed behind him. Without oilskins their clothes dripped water but all were in high spirits. Mo and Ham declared they'd stand still and the one who left the biggest puddle won— let Terry measure.

Hank countermanded curtly. "One at a time below into dry clothes. Terry go first, check the engine too. Others stay ready. Not sure what's ahead, so check your survival suits there." It silenced them all. Terry quickly left.

Seth watched astern. "That nylon line's a rubber band the way pull stretches it. Should be longer to absorb shock, but best we could grab. If he starts to drag us with him, you going to let him?" Hank didn't answer. They strained forward by the yard.

One by one the crew changed into dry clothes. They gathered in the warm wheelhouse, keeping oilskins handy for a rush to deck. (Ham chose to wear his, although it soon made him sweat.) Each man identified his survival suit bag reluctantly as if the mere look would trigger a need for use. Hank returned the helm to Jody but stayed close. She needed to feel the force and knock of the Whale's current for herself. After allowing it to push aside the bow once or twice, she learned to anticipate. The boat and its tow gained way slowly. Despite the threat of crisis they settled into routine. Terry soon recovered enough of his lightheartedness that even Seth smiled.

On CB: "*Hinda* to *Adele*. Changed filters, she's running again. Will make slack and send back your towline."

Hank remained cool. "To *Hinda*. Read that and good news. Do you want to ride tow a few minutes more to make sure of your engine?"

"No on that. Drained sediment tank, won't happen again. We'll cast loose when you're ready."

"He might at least thank us," said Jody.

The *Adele*'s men hustled back their line when the *Hinda*'s men released it, pulling fast to keep it from entangling their own screw.

"Hey, man," shouted Bud from the *Hinda*'s bow. His face glowed ruddy and grinning. "Bets still on?"

"Yeah. Yeah," called Ham.

"Fuckin'-A yeah!" added Seth.

Slowly the two boats made it the rest of the way through Whale Passage. Both had passed Ilkognak Rock at the far end and entered wide Marmot Bay when the full storm hit.

5

KODIAK TALK

KODIAK ISLAND, EARLY AUGUST 1982

As the *Adele H* beat through rough water her crew's widespread legs bent with the motion. Shifting wind had turned the sea erratic. When the boat dipped into troughs a slanting horizon of whitecaps coasted past their eye level. When the bow upheaved and plunged, everything in the wheelhouse rattled, from cups in wooden holders to hinges on the overhead chart rack. Waves gushed across deck to knock against the battened skiff and make it quiver. Steady water dripped from the rigging. A wave hit broadside, the boat shuddered throughout, and something in the galley below broke loose and clattered. Mo raced down but returned unconcerned. Empty metal pot had jumped the rail on the stove, should have been stowed in a drawer.

It was the damned *Hinda Bee* thrashing alongside that held their attention. Now that she had lightened to an equal weight with the *Adele* and had regained her superior engine power, the *Adele*'s advantage of being first through Whale Passage lasted only minutes. In open water the *Hinda* pulled ahead. Hank and the others watched glumly.

"And not even a thanks," Jody repeated.

"Thanks isn't Gus's style," said Hank.

Spray arched a fan over the *Hinda*'s bow. The boat pranced and dipped as did their own. When its hull hit a trough, scudding crests blocked all but the cabin top from view. There from the wheelhouse windows gazed

Bud and the other crewmen. They seemed detached. "Already countin' our money," muttered Ham. Gradually the *Hinda* increased its lead so that those aboard the *Adele* faced its aft quarter and then its stern.

When they entered the narrows leading to Kodiak, hilly islands blocked the wind, taming the worst of the seas. By now the gray evening sky, normally light beyond ten at this time of year, had darkened to black. Mist blurred house lights along the shore, but bolder lights from canneries reflected in the choppy water. Hank had ascertained their best price by radio and coded words, and they headed past town to the APS cannery. At the King Crab plant en route, the *Hinda* lay moored. Her men on deck had already opened the hold and were climbing down to pitch fish. Up on the pier forklift trucks brought pallets, and the crane operator had settled into his seat.

"That's your bets lost, Boss," said Mo. "They've beat us here and gone to unload."

Jody shook her head. "I still can't believe what they've done."

"Just witch dough," said Terry. "Don't worry. Ham and me, we'll make it up with our bet for best of the season. And look, until we see both tickets it's still anybody's biggest load this trip to win Seth and Mo's bet."

"If that old fart don't put his finger on the scale," muttered Seth.

"Yeah," echoed Mo. "That's just the sort of thing they'd do. Wouldn't it?"

Hank coached Jody on docking. She brought the *Adele H* alongside the pier with only a bump against the pilings that fenders absorbed. The tide remained high enough to place their rail close to the top of the pier.

Even though it was close to Saturday midnight the cannery was in full operation, and there stood Adele Henry, hands on hips, silhouetted against the work lights. The translucent plastic of her kerchief and raincoat glowed like a halo around her middle-aged bulk. When Ham jumped over to secure their lines, Adele took his arm and said crisply, "Best put your forward line on that cleat there."

"Yes ma'am." He was grateful that it was the cleat Jody had already told him to use.

"Now give me a hand, dear." Adele started to step aboard.

"Wait until we've finished tying," barked Seth from deck, and tossed Ham the stern line.

"Oh!" Adele strode back and forth, then called to the wheelhouse, "And how's my boat doing? How's my Captain Jody doing?"

"No wonder Jones never let her aboard," muttered Hank. He continued to instruct Jody in shutting-down procedure.

With mooring completed, Adele held Ham's hand from the pier while Terry in the boat leaned out and gripped her arm. Her raincoat stuck against the sides of calf-high rubber boots and she stumbled with a "Whoops!" then recovered to fall into Terry's arms. Although he was nearly a head shorter, he caught her firmly. She straightened, thanked him, smoothed her clothes, and looked around. "Well! Good trip? Everything shipshape?"

"Real good, ma'am."

"I trust you boys caught your share of fish?"

"Lots, ma'am."

"Oh, for heaven's sake, you needn't call me ma'am like an old lady. Just call me . . . Mrs. Henry, I suppose. Now. Take me to Jody."

Hank had been watching with Jody from the wheelhouse. "Adele's a grand gal, but . . ."

"Did she just come down and leave the children alone?" Jody fretted. "I need to see them before anything else. I'll use her car if she wants to stay."

"Adele wouldn't do that. You know they're safe. First, do your shake-down properly, then your business at the office. That's what skippers need to do."

Adele's high, confident voice came up from the galley. "That coffee urn! I told my late husband repeatedly it shouldn't be right by the door where any sleeve could hook."

"Makes it easy to reach in from deck for a mug-up, Miz Henry. We're careful."

"That's not the point when you could scald yourself, Terry. Men never listen. We'll see." Her tread was heavy on the steps to the wheelhouse. Near the top she stopped for breath, then called businesslike: "Your hand, Hank dear, pull me up the rest of the way." Hank duly complied, pecked her on the cheek, and asked about the children. "All dears, asleep now like angels, though I must say little Pete's in his devil stage. A neighbor's in the living room while I'm here, of course. Help me off with this coat, please."

She ignored Hank further. "Where is she? Where's my captain? There!" She threw out her arms and advanced to Jody. "I'm so proud of you." Her voice turned husky. "Oh, I'm so proud!" They hugged. "All by yourself catching those fish and bringing them in. Oh! We're going to show them!"

"Thank Hank for showing me."

"Yes, yes, I'm sure he was helpful. You said on radio that you're keeping Terry and Ham for crew. Good choice instead of Seth, since that Seth's manners aren't very . . . Let me look at you. Yes!"

Hank listened restlessly, then said that he and Jody needed to go to the office. "Sign papers and talk price a bit."

"At this time of night?" Adele gathered back her coat. "Well, I should see how it's done."

"It's generally a one-on-one process, Adele. Jody's going because after this she'll need to do it by herself."

Adele's hands went to her hips. The sags of her cheeks drew down to the pug-dog expression she assumed when challenged. "And I take it you don't think I'm part of this operation? Well, I have a few things to say about what they pay for my fish, and this is as good a time as any. Jody! Tell him!"

Jody had resumed stowing the charts. "I think tonight had better be just Hank and me."

Pause. "Well, Jody. If you say so." Pause. "Now, you're all expected back at the house, of course. I've made up the couch, and Hank can sleep on the floor. It's late, so don't be long."

Jody took Hank's arm. "We'd better hang around the boat if you'll handle the kids just one more night. We're really grateful. But I should learn everything about delivering to the cannery."

Pause. "Yes, well, I suppose you must. I'll see you for breakfast. Seven thirty, that's when I'll have it all hot, so don't be late."

Jody tightened her grip on Hank's arm as he started to object. "We'll be there."

Up in the office Hank confirmed the coded price he'd been offered: two cents a pound above the published rate. With easy banter he tried for two cents more.

The manager laid thick-lensed glasses on the table, his sign that he'd finished. "I paid extra, Hank, only because you're first at the dock, that's why. And maybe because what the hell, everybody's talking about Jody taking over. Somebody from the *Mirror* asked around yesterday who you'd deliver to. Said they'd want photos and a story. But there's a whole fleet from Uganik at the other side of Whale Pass slowed by the storm. By tomorrow morning boats'll be more like paying me to take their fish."

Jody smiled her wide smile. "Bob, we understand. By the way, did you know that my crewmen are Terry Bricks and Ham Davis? They're already competing to highline for me, so you can count on fish. Since I have no commitment to other buyers the way Hank and his buddies have, you might just lock me in when things get scarce and you want to keep the plant going." The smile continued wickedly. "With all that publicity, my fish could make you famous."

She gained them another cent a pound.

In the old days at most canneries there would have been a handshake to seal the bargain, followed by a bottle, shot glasses, and chaser at least for the lady. Jody's signature on paper did it here.

Hank put his arm around her as they descended back stairs into the washed fish-ammonia odors and gunning noise of the plant warehouse. "How about this?" he murmured close to her ear. "Get a room at the K-I tonight, tell nobody, have you to myself. No crew, no Adele, no little ones, *nyet*. The way it never happens any more."

"I thought a skipper stayed with his boat."

"I wasn't being that honest with poor Adele. After the unloading starts, if the skipper has a good man on deck he can trust . . . "

"You had me fooled."

"Well, I meant it about duty to the boat. The boat comes first. But—"

"Not your family?" Her voice took on the edge he knew signaled beware.

"As long as you know the family's safe, boat first."

"You'd better mean that."

"I do."

She lightened and her head brushed his cheek. "Kodiak Inn sounds nice." The concrete floor was slippery from hosing. They stepped aside at the beep of a forklift, and she lost her balance, perhaps deliberately, to fall more closely against him. He gladly took advantage to hold her.

In a long room adjacent to the warehouse, people in floppy yellow oil-skins stood arm to arm at a long sliming table. They had none of the young jaunt of the college kids at the remote Uganik Bay plant. Most were copper-skinned. All were intent. The women wore kerchiefs. Some of the men had thick black mustaches and Latino faces.

"When I worked those lines a dozen years ago there wasn't a single Viet-namese or Mexican or anybody else foreign," said Jody. "Just Americans drifting through. These guys look so permanent. Not even music while they work. The Vietnamese crowd a big family into a room or two and save to bring more family. In counseling we have to deal with conditions for their kids. It's so different. Faces in town are different. I didn't expect to speak of days gone by so soon."

"Don't forget that some of us drifters stayed," said Hank. "Call us the newest pioneers."

"No, it's strange, I mean it. All that time in our lives that's slipped by. Not that I'd go back, but—"

"All that freedom. Now we sneak half a night with a little lie, but have to report for duty again by seven thirty."

When they returned to the boat, Mo and Ham were opening the hatch while Seth called up to the crane operator. A worker in oilskins already stood inside the hopper that would receive the fish and channel them along chutes to the processing bins inside.

Hank stood by Jody to direct her at the controls. He also called up Terry from the hold. "You're deck boss here now. I'll check you out too." Halfway through the unloading he touched her shoulder. "You've got the hang. So does Terry. He can take over. Let's go up the hill."

"Nope." She grinned wickedly. "Boat first."

When the last brailerload had been swung across the pier and emptied into the hopper, Seth left to check the *Jody Dawn* at the boatyard, and Jody finally declared, "Terry! Scrubdown's yours. See you tomorrow."

"You got it. Say, is anybody going to check what the *Hinda Bee* delivered? You guys going over there now?"

"That's yours too," Jody continued. "See you tomorrow. We'll need to take on two new crew, so talk around."

"I'm on it, skipper."

Like I didn't exist, thought Hank. But their confidence reassured him.

As they left a figure approached them from shadows on the pier. Despite alternating drizzle and rain he wore only cotton sweats with a hood. "Excuse me, sir, is that your boat?" His wet hair was slapped onto a thin forehead.

"Hers," Hank said. Now see how Jody handled a potential crewman.

"Oh, a woman? Whew." The kid started away, then turned back. "Excuse me again. You wouldn't need an extra hand—ma'am?"

"Not right now." Jody looked him over quickly and impersonally. "Any experience? If I hear of something."

"I'm a fast learner. You'd see."

"Name? Where from?"

"Joel. New York. Joel Schneweiss, means white snow, not Snow White. I've been up here four weeks now, about gone broke."

"The canneries are hiring."

"Yeah, but I came up here to be on a fishing boat. Anyhow, canneries? I just got off a ten-hour shift down the road. But I ask at any boat when I see one come in, even if it's midnight."

"Shift doing what?"

"Just now the halibut line."

"And you do what?"

"Lift them from the bin, slime 'em, stuff like that. Not brain surgery."

"Those fish are heavy."

"You tell me. Especially since I came up here to be on a fishing boat."

Hank became interested, and amused. "Don't you think you'd bust your ass on a fishing boat?"

"But that would be different."

Right answer, Hank thought. But the kid still didn't look strong enough to hold out. He wouldn't have hired him.

Jody nevertheless pointed to her boat and told the kid to check with Terry on deck. Climbing the hill, alone again with Hank, she said, "Probably stumbles over his feet. But a bird in the hand."

"That's the kind of scrapings you'll find this late in the season."

"Sticking out halibut shifts says something. Terry can sound him out."

He kissed her. "Tomorrow's problem, not now."

The men of the *Adele H* had scrubbed the hold with disinfectant and were hosing gurry from each others' backs when the kid named Joel called down to Terry. The tide had lowered so that Terry needed to squint up against pier lights to see the hooded figure. He had other things on his mind but said, "Climb down for a minute if you want." He nudged Ham who was about to follow the others inside. "Help check him out. You and me are the ones got to work with anybody gets hired."

The two watched the newcomer coolly. He wasn't husky, and his climb rung by rung down the slippery ladder was cautious. Wet in more ways than his clothes, thought Terry. "So like, uh, what boats you been on?" asked Ham. No boat.

"Can you cook?"

"Sure, why not?"

At midday they might in charity have invited him to the galley for coffee before sending him off. At this hour Terry merely told him to drop back tomorrow if he wanted. The kid wouldn't leave. "It must be funny, working for a woman. But I'm ready to take anything."

"Suit yourself. But we're likely full."

"The fellows on the *Hinda Bee,* just unloading at my cannery, said you needed crew."

"*Hinda,* huh? How'd they do?"

"It looked like lots of fish. But I was on halibut line, not salmon. It's just that I ask at every boat. I came up here to be on a fishing boat."

"What did they act like, those guys on the *Hinda?*"

"I don't know. Busy. Didn't say much."

They watched the kid climb awkwardly back up the slippery metal ladder. "Good-bye to him," muttered Ham.

"Except there might not be much damn choice."

"Think we ought to go check out those pricks on the *Hinda?* See how much they delivered?"

Terry took time to consider, although the thought had been his also. He checked around deck as he'd often done before, but now uneasily. Different being deck boss instead of a mere ape in the crew, especially since Jody above him might need watching to not screw up as skipper. It was more responsibility than he'd known. Or even wanted, likely. Ham stood waiting. "Might not hurt to check. After they played that trick on us. Knowing they had more engine and all."

Both looked around to make sure nobody watched, then did a few push-ups and stretches just in case.

The gravel road between fish plants was dark. "Those pricks on the *Hinda,*" muttered Ham as they hurried. "Some nerve after what we done for them. That Bud, I used to think he was okay. He better not try anything." He stumbled in a pothole, cursed without venom, and did more push-ups before rising.

Same words as on my mind, thought Terry. But now he was deck boss. "We'll see." He tried to make it sound wise.

The pier space at the cannery where the *Hinda Bee* had delivered was empty. The shore gang stood ready to receive another boat—from a distance it looked like the *Lucky Sue* coming in—while a set of red and green running lights moving away toward the harbor could have been the *Hinda*. The crane operator wouldn't tell them how many brailerloads the *Hinda* had delivered. "Go to the office for that," he said. Terry looked up at the white fluorescent tubes on the ceiling of the second-floor office. A man with papers, wearing a necktie, moved near the window. Not a place to venture.

Lights stretched in a crescent from south cannery row, where they stood, through town to plants on the north facing the narrows. Boat lights glided from the narrows, dim through drizzle and fog. "Now they're all coming in," observed Ham. "But we beat that whole bunch to town, didn't we?"

"You've already forgot the *Hinda Bee?*"

"Yeah. Shit." Suddenly: "Only five minutes to town if we run. Maybe in time to grab those pricks' lines, talk 'em over a little."

Terry considered. A deck boss needed to keep his dignity. But a deck boss had to stand up to things. "Race you."

6

THE BEER DIPLOMATS

KODIAK, EARLY AUGUST 1982

Adele Henry, new owner of the *Adele H* by inheritance, found herself an object of attention as never before when she'd been just another fisherman's wife. Boat-to-shore radio with Jones had been, "Exactly what time are you coming to dinner, Daddy?"—gruff annoyed evasions, and then henpeckish clucks from other men on the frequency when they thought she'd signed off. Now she was talking business. She positively strutted to the stores with Jody's order for groceries and specific new parts.

In just the week that her boat had left for Uganik Bay to scatter her husband's ashes, then stayed to fish under her patronage, people had suddenly begun to solicit Adele's opinions instead of glancing at their watches. Her opinions soared accordingly. "I'll tell you this," she soon started declaring, and followed with whatever crossed her mind, from the subject of Pastor Hall's sermon to the unavailability of the proper shackles at Sutliff's Hardware.

Her pantsuits, once lime green, then brown for as close to mourning as her wardrobe allowed, had become bright red by the time the *Adele H* came back to town. Red might not go with the long beige coat bought during the last trip to Paris France, but it didn't matter since she knew who she was in Kodiak. Nevertheless, it hurt nothing to have her hair styled for the first time ever, and in the process to have the creeps of gray eased back to brown.

Adele's new importance did not compromise her stewardship of the Crawford children. She loved them. Loved them more, she knew, than the adopted Russ and Mark, long gone from the nest and so estranged by Jones's attitudes that the relationships would probably never recover. Her imagination still hugged close darling Amy, the only birth child God had ever permitted but then cruelly taken back after barely a year. Doctors did better with meningitis now, they said, for what little good it would ever do Adele Henry. On every April 19 she bought a cake, and added one more candle year by year as she pictured Amy the first grader, the graduate, the bride with full wedding preparation—finally, the mother producing grandchildren to gladden the house. Adele the realist would have denied it, but in her heart the children of Amy were Dawn, Henny, and Pete Crawford.

On the morning after the midnight return to port of the *Adele H*, Adele was awake before six for coffee by the window overlooking the harbor. There might have been a cigarette except that they now said smoke was bad for children, so of course the pack went out of sight under the linen whenever they stayed. Her boat was tied to its berth on the floats. Thank God she'd put her foot down long ago with poor Jones, and insisted that the boat's papers include her name as co-owner. The way men thought a woman's only role on a boat was her name on the bow! And now such plans that had opened! To move that coffee urn was the least of them. Jody would do things that people had never permitted Adele Johnson Henry even to think of doing, and she, Adele, now had the power to make it happen.

Six-year-old Dawn was first up as always. She bounced in to hug Auntie Adele and meant it. (Not like reticent Henny, a year older and already guarding his male behavior: it was ominous to watch how even the youngest of them geared to call the shots. Thank goodness little Pete's mind was still uncluttered by more than his approaching fourth birthday party, still a month away.) "You can get out the bacon, sweetie. We'll need more than two slices each this morning, so we'll use the big pan."

She plaited Dawn's pigtails, while the child arranged bacon strips like soldiers in the cold pan and chattered about the things she'd tell Mommy as soon as she came.

By the time Hank and Jody arrived—at seven fifty, hardly on the dot! and looking more tired than necessary after a night's sleep—Dawn had put on her party dress for the occasion and Henny had at least wriggled into jeans. Sleepyhead Pete remained in pajamas, the last to wake. His engine would start soon enough.

Hank kissed her heartily and joked in his fine deep voice. Adele wanted to focus on Jody, even ignore this man to keep him in place. But Hank's presence filled the room whenever he entered. Tall, confident, hips lean as a bottle, shoulders muscled against a black sweater, face weathered like a man's should be but not hard. Jones had stood like that in the early days, an erect Marine just back from defeating the Japs, back when his opinions had vigorous charm and had not yet become slaps in the face.

"The eggs have dried in the pan I'm afraid, ready a half hour ago, but sit, sit." It didn't seem to bother them. Lucky Jody, hair pulled back without a thought to how she looked and thus beautiful even in an old shirt and no makeup. "Well my dear, we've got a world of business ahead, so eat up and then we'll talk."

Hank gladly escaped from Adele's house with his children to let the women make their plans, but he couldn't help thinking that they'd have profited from his advice had they asked. Pete held tight to his hand while Dawn skipped ahead and Henny walked at his side. The pickup truck waited by Fisherman's Hall where he'd left it two weeks before, expecting to be back within a day. That's how things happened.

He drove to the boatyard to check on his *Jody Dawn*. There she stood, still on the ways facing the harbor. A patch was welded smoothly where the boat had struck an object during the rescue of Jones Henry, and it appeared that the metal needed only paint to finish the job. Out of water his boat became less his own, a creature of land. Its bow loomed above him like a skyscraper and its hull spread beneath as wide as a house. Office locked, only a Sunday watchman, no one to consult. He wanted to climb over the scaffolding and check inside the boat, but not with young children in tow.

"Petey," chirped Dawn. "That's Daddy's boat. See Daddy's boat?"

"He can't help but see it," observed Henny. His voice was deep for a child's, and solemn. "You always act like a schoolteacher."

Dawn ignored her older brother. "Petey. Say 'Daddy's boat!' Say '*Jody Dawn!*'" Jody and Dawn, that's Mommy and me. Nobody names boats after boys. Ask Daddy. Isn't that right, Daddy?"

"Seems so." He bent to pick her up with a hug. A quick intense return hug and she squirmed away. Pete, released from Hank's grip, ran up and down the slope leading to the water. Dawn followed, telling him to be careful.

"Girls sure try to run things," said Henny. "Girls are a pain in the . . . ass."

Hank wanted to laugh but said, "Hey, watch your language."

"Everybody else says things like that."

"Not at your age, fellah." He loved the clear-eyed look of his son, smooth towhead face turned up to him. Without thinking further: "Tell you what. I won't say it anymore if you don't."

"All the bad words, Dad?"

"Oh boy." The kids were going to pick up his easy tongue if he didn't watch. How the hell would he keep such a bargain? Keep it! At least till the kids were older. (At least in their presence, he amended to himself. Be realistic.) "You're on. Shake." The small hand in his big one was soft, but it squeezed firmly. (No, he amended again. At least *try* to honor a son's bargain all the way.)

Next Hank drove to the floats, built to rise and fall with the tide. The seiner fleet was in. Seen from the road above, their masts crowded against each other like wireworks. Skiffs, piled atop web and corks, were reflected in the strips of water separating arms of the boardwalk. The walks were deserted. He'd have been sleeping in too, back late night from a week or two on the grounds and it not yet ten on a Sunday morning. With Jody's new commitment, Adele Henry was proving to be a package, however grand a gal.

The *Adele H* lay in her slip, brought over safely from the cannery by either Terry or Seth. The rival *Hinda Bee* lay only two boat slips away. Would Gus Rosvic really be the supreme asshole (don't voice the word) and let his men collect their bets? He debated banging on the *Hinda*'s door to find out, decided not with the kids. Let it happen by itself.

At the far end of the floats, by the breakwater, lay the halibut fleet moored apart from the seiners and crabbers. The boats now longlined also for black cod, they said. He'd soon be competing with them, and on behalf of the Japanese at that—something unthinkable only months ago. Best not go over. The sight of the wooden schooners, ultimate fishing craft older than any other boats around, solid and graceful, with their venerable sharp white bows lined in a row as orderly as the old Norwegians aboard, still stirred him as they had since his greenhorn days. There among the familiar names were *Vansee, Grant, Republic, Thor, Northern, Polaris,* and the *Lincoln,* aboard which a halibut had broken his arm. How long ago? Dozen years. Since Jones's death, time's passage and its changes dogged him everywhere.

He clattered down the ramp with his army of children. At the bottom
Pete suddenly broke into a run toward the far end of the walk. Hank
started after, ready to jump in the water if Pete veered and fell, although it
seemed unlikely since the child ran a straight line on such fine sturdy legs.
When Pete saw he was being pursued his voice rose high and gleeful and
he ran faster. By the time Hank caught up they had reached the end arm
of the floats by the breakwater. Pete flopped down laughing, and held up
his arms to be carried.

Hank tousled him. "Say it, you buzzard. What do you want?"

"He still won't talk much, Daddy," said Dawn. "Go on, Petey, say what
you want. Say 'Carry me, Daddy.'"

The arms remained outstretched and the happy laugh continued, but
Pete said nothing. Hank lifted him. The weight pained his shoulder under
the cast, but he controlled a grimace and straddled the kicking legs around
his head. These would be the last little legs until grandchildren, probably.
Enjoy 'em. A clean soap-and-child smell went with the burden. Madam
Adele might be a pain, but she cared for those she loved.

"He'll never talk if you do what he wants all the time without it, Daddy.
That's what Auntie Adele says. And he never minds."

"He talks all right if you leave him alone," said Henny. "It's just girls he
won't talk to and mind. People who try and make him."

They now stood among the high wooden bows of the halibut fleet,
right by the *Lincoln* herself. Hank stared. Yes, he remembered: broken
arm at the start of a second three-week trip as an apprentice Norwegian
style, excited by every breath of the fishing game (especially here). The
very boat still smelled of sweat and traditional ways. In presence he felt
like the kid inbreaker again, yes to anything they barked him to do but
nearly choked with pride at having been accepted aboard. He'd barely
seen the men afterward, since they seldom tarried in town. Other fisheries of his involve-ment followed different cycles, but those old Norwegian shipmates' names remained vivid. Whatever the circumstance, it
would be good to handle fish on long baited lines again, gaffing them
aboard nose to nose.

The cabin door opened, and a lean leathery man in city clothes came on
deck with a valise. He climbed carefully over the rail to the float, and
stopped at the sight of Hank.

"Trygve!" Hank wondered if he'd be recognized. "Trygve Jensen."

"Ja." The voice was slow and mild. "You come back to inbreak again, or you bring kids to do it for you?"

"Either way. Either way. Henny, Dawn, Pete, shake hands with a great fisherman who hired Daddy once."

"Oh, it ver Igvar who hired, he is captain. So, inbreaker, you don't fish no more I guess."

Hank started to correct, then shrugged. They really kept to themselves, these guys. Not only didn't remember his name . . . He himself could still enjoy the memory. Trygve's face was older by only a little. Straw-yellow hair that had poked from a work cap seemed dimmer slicked into shape beneath a wool traveling cap, and his manner was even soberer (if that was possible), but he still could have been patiently teaching greenhorn Hank to coil and bait to the boat's exact standard. "How's halibut fishing these days?"

"Too many boats, only."

"And black cod now too?"

"Jaaa. Except the fucking Japs and Koreans t'ink dey own it." Each answer came slowly. Hank asked of the others by name. Igvar was still captain, sure, and Olaf still was cook. (Olaf of the lean horse face, possessive of his stove, Hank remembered.) Sverre and Ralph, ja. Only Sven no longer fished. "Has apartment houses in Ballard, doing good. Sven's boy is now half-share man. Vell, got to catch plane to Seattle. Got to go."

Hank asked if the others were around, learned that they'd already gone to the airport and that Trygve had just locked the boat. He offered to drive Trygve.

"Taxicab is vaiting." Trygve walked off, friendly but detached as ever, then stopped and turned. "Nice kids you got, Hank. You treat them good, maybe they'll be fishermen."

"I will. I will, Trygve. Thanks." The recognition after all left him smiling.

He walked his brood back along the boats to the *Adele H* among the seiners. Mo sat in the galley alone. He rose anxiously. "Whew! Seth found you, I guess. That's sure a relief. Are Terry and Ham okay, Boss?"

"What do you mean?"

On the night before, Terry and Ham, having stretched and flexed just in case, trotted down the gravel road from the canneries to the floating piers. By the time they had located their target among the seiners moving in to moor for the weekend, the *Hinda Bee* was locked and deserted.

"I guess we don't need a map to figure where they've gone," said Terry. "It's just do they like the noisy bars or the quiet ones? Old Gus, figure him for one with cobwebs."

"Bud, now," said Ham. "He hangs out—I think I've seen him either at Tony's or Solly's, one or the other."

The amplified thrum of rock at Tony's drew them from across the square. Inside, surrounded by familiar noise, smoke, and the pleasant smell of beer, they waited for their eyes to adjust. None of the faces etched by neon around the square center bar was *Hinda Bee.* Maybe in the dark corners.

"I'll buy first," said Terry. Guys they knew made room for them at the bar.

Their bottles had barely arrived over the counter when Rob from the *Lucky Sue* leaned across Ham as if he didn't exist, and called to Terry above the noise: "Caught Jody fishing without a license, they say."

"Nothing to speak of. Little mistake was all."

"Ho ho, yeah. A woman, and being she's Hank Crawford's old lady didn't hurt. Like to see me caught without a license, like to see what happens."

"That ain't your business, fellah," growled Ham.

Terry stopped Ham with a hand on his shoulder. "Shit, Robbie, you're so fuckin' ugly I'd do it myself—throw a bag over your head and dump your ass in jail."

"What say? Talk louder, man."

Terry's face crinkled into its monkey grin. He leaned over nose to nose and repeated.

Rob studied him, then laughed. "That's what would happen, man. Just that." He returned unperturbed to his drink.

"You sure get away with jokes," muttered Ham.

Terry shrugged. "I know him. He's just talk. Short guys like me need to rely on their mouths."

Joe Pone from the *Lady West* leaned in from Terry's elbow and called across: "Robbie! You don't know the half! Jody's now skipper, and you're looking at her new crew. First thing she done, she run down our skiff man, Nick." He needed to repeat at a shout above the music. Suddenly the music stopped between numbers, and, loud throughout the room: "Jody, she run down Nick in the skiff!"

Faces all around the bar, and both bartenders themselves, turned. "Hey, lay off it," called a voice in good humor from the bar opposite. It was Nick himself. "Nobody got hurt. Give Jody a break."

"Sure, sure if you say, man," Pone continued, and faced Terry and Ham with boozy, half-closed eyes. "How about it, you two? What's it like, orders from a woman?" Ham started up in his seat, but Terry raised his arm in an elaborate yawn and eased him back. Pone edged closer. "She got you yet to put doilies on the winch and perfume in the hold?"

Terry drank from the bottle, keeping his grip on the neck, and cleared his throat. "Don't forget we wind daisies through the web."

A few *Heyyy's*, and some bottles waved in their direction. The music started to blast again, and Pone returned to his drink.

Terry sent a beer over to Nick, and paid up. "*Hinda Bee* ain't here. Let's cruise."

But the bartender banged two wet-beaded bottles in front of them. "Compliments of your buddies over there." Some hands waved to them in the dim light. Terry acknowledged with a "Yo," and Ham followed suit, although neither recognized the faces through the smoke.

They drank up, left a large tip, and moved out with a backslap and thanks to the buyers as they passed. It was the *Sleepthief* crew from the Uganik grounds who called merrily, "You birds going to need charity, fishin' under a dame."

Ham stiffened. Terry pushed him along, and called back lightly: "You're the ones going to need the luck. We're hot." Outside, he muttered, "Pricks. Shouldn't've drunk their beer."

The air was sweet after the smoky bar. They both stretched and drew breaths. A single dark figure stumbled across the square facing the harbormaster's office and the boats, and entered one of the other bars among darkened shops. "I don't know," mused Terry. "We might look into Solly's, I guess." As he thought about it, just what *was* their gripe with the *Hinda Bee?* "Saturday night after a week's fishing and it's already near morning? By now everybody's too shitfaced to talk sense even if we find them."

A boat, traced by its lights, was moving from the canneries and around the breakwater to the floats. Terry cupped his hands like binoculars and peered. "Yeah, that's our *Adele H*. I thought we'd parked over there for the night but Seth or Hank must have decided—or Jody. We'd better go catch her lines."

"Forget *Hindu Bee?*"

"Find 'em tomorrow."

A taxicab careened to a stop and three men whooped out to head past them toward Solly's. They staggered enough to bump against Terry and Ham. The tallest muttered, "Sorry," and the shortest, "Who moved the fuckin' phone pole?" It was Bud, Zack, and Alec of the *Hinda Bee.*

Ham, on eye level with Zack, the tallest, blocked the entrance. "Wanna talk to you guys."

Alec—the shortest, but built like a table—halted swaying and adjusted the bill of his cap. "Heyyy. Company. This calls for a drink."

"Who are you guys?" Bud flopped his chin over Alec's shoulder and winked. "Feelin' rich, don't know why. Maybe 'cause we won a bet today and got money to burn." He giggled. "Do we know you?"

"Why's because you cheated," growled Ham.

"Ohhh, now I rek'nize you," continued Bud, his chin still on the shoulder. "Sore losers. Work for some lady."

"Watch it, fellah," said Ham.

"Cheat? Where?" Zack looked around elaborately as he eased in front of his two crewmates. "Let me handle this, since I did law school almost a whole year once in Florida." He walked ceremoniously around Ham, shook Terry's hand, and, in a voice rolling and formal, declared: "We thank you." He was slim, but Terry had seen him working out and knew a bed of muscles lay beneath the jacket. He also knew Zack to be an easy guy who liked to play-act for fun. Zack now sounded like a lawyer in some movie. "What you did for us today, harrumph, yesterday, maybe— how time flies—was pretty good, and done even with a woman in charge at that. So I'm here to tell you tonight that the bet you lost—call it wager to jack it up—you can take your time to pay it. Harrumph."

Terry wanted to laugh. It was a good act.

"You making fun of us?" Ham advanced.

"Take you on any day," declared Bud, waving his arms but with chin still on Alec's shoulder. Alec, legs planted firmly, swayed as he nodded agreement.

"Easy, easy," said both Terry and Zack separately.

Ham held his ground. "We saved your ass and then you beat us to town. Which you wouldn't've done if we hadn't saved your ass. That's what we need to settle here."

Zack went to Ham and shook his hand. "We owe you. But we'd have done the same, thrown you a line." He returned to Terry. "Then, when we left Whale Pass, we started even again. And we beat you fair since we were faster. That's one bet down for us whether you pay or not. Tomorrow we compare fish tickets, and who delivered most wins bet number two. Bet three hangs loose till our skippers count tickets for the whole opening. Do you see cheating anywhere there?"

Terry nodded and tried to appear wise. In truth, he realized, all he'd wanted was a thanks. "Sure, we're going to pay. It's okay, Ham. Let's go to the boat."

Zack's hand pounded his shoulder. "Not until we buy your ass a drink! Yo! Inside!"

There was nothing for it but to follow. Solly's was brighter than Tony's, and less smoky, with a dining room removed from the bar. The jukebox, though loud, blasted at a lower decibel level than at Tony's, so conversation was possible. Full bar. They crowded around a table against the wall.

"Double scotch all around," called Zack, and the bartender acknowledged.

Terry didn't want it but he shrugged.

When the drinks arrived, Zack held up his glass. "To women. In bed, or in the wheelhouse."

Ham glanced at Terry, uncertain. Terry debated quickly, then said, "I guess we'll drink to that."

With friends and booze it was soon easy to go mellow. Even jokes about a lady skipper were acceptable among friends. After Bud told of how old Gus got so excited he had to take a pill when the net wound in the prop, Terry volunteered that Jody sometimes got carried away. The incident of nearly running down the *Lady West*'s skiff became hilarious. "You'd like to seen Hank's face. I thought he'd explode." They all laughed and laughed.

Terry, to preserve the reputation of the *Adele H,* ordered another double round even though the stuff had begun to taste like brass in his mouth.

Much later, light hurt Terry's eyes, and memory was hazy, but "tastes like dog shit" defined the mess in his mouth. Somewhere along the way another crew—*Lady West* maybe, or *Sleepthief,* maybe both?—had started ragging about a woman skipper. What did it was when one of them called Jody a cunt, that much was remembered. All at once chairs were swinging in defense of Jody. Image of Ham's fist socko into some face. Now this floor was concrete and cool. Had nothing to do with chairs. Was that his own puke smell or somebody else's?

"Up, men, up." A foot prodded his leg. "Time for the judge or you stay to Monday. Wash over there if you want." It was the big cop Randy, had kids and a garden on the edge of town, standing over him tall as a pole. Now that Terry needed to open his eyes, he recognized from talk the long bare room they called the tank or something.

"Ohhh, Mother o' God, I'm sick," moaned a voice; Bud's, it sounded like.

Funny, thought Terry. Can't remember whether I'm supposed to be pissed or good with Bud. The picture of last night cleared only in patches, like the ocean in fog. Hadn't maybe Bud stopped something coming toward them, chair or something? That's right. Bud and the other *Hinda Bee* guys, pricks maybe once about something—oh, the bets, they shouldn't have taken advantage after Whale Pass—but the *Hinda Bee* guys had helped defend Jody's honor. That's right. Side by side. Really too bad then if Bud felt sick.

"Terry, you alive, man?" came Ham's gruff, anxious voice.

He found his own voice speaking for him, but each word took effort. "Yeah. I guess. But . . . dog shit."

A while later—time went on and on while dying would have been nice—they muttered and wiped and leaned on each other, *Adele H* and *Hinda Bee* men together, keeping apart from the *Sleepthief* and *Lady West* men as much as possible, though all crowded around the same washbasin. Then Officer Randy marched the lot of them into a room, this one not concrete but wood. Benches, high desk, flag. Terry straightened and nudged Ham to do the same. There sat Hank, he saw with a rush of gratitude. And old Gus of the *Hinda Bee* sternly beside him. No Jody, glad of that.

The judge hurried in, dressed in black like for an execution. Somebody whispered he'd come straight from church. "A sorry sight," he declared of them all as he adjusted his glasses.

Randy the cop testified that around 4 AM his car had received a call of a disturbance, and he drove straight to the square to join other policemen on duty. "There was plenty of noise, Your Honor. These three . . ."—he indicated Ham and two of the *Sleepthief* crewmen—"were punching it out on the sidewalk outside Solly's. It was two against the big guy, but he was holding his own when we stopped it. Inside it was mostly chairs thrown and yelling. This man . . ."—he indicated Terry—"was on top of this man . . ."—he pointed to Joe Pone of the *Lady West*—"and had him down. We broke it up without much trouble, Your Honor. They were all pretty drunk."

The judge asked if the defendants had anything to say. Zack, the one-year lawyer from the *Hinda Bee,* raised his hand and stepped forward. He brushed a shock of black hair from his eyes, straightened, looked around, then lost his nerve.

"Yes? Speak up, speak up. Our dinner's waiting at home."

"Nothing, Your Honor." Zack stepped back into the security of the group.

The bar owner testified that four hundred dollars' worth of glassware and two chairs had been broken. "But the boys are all good customers. I don't need to press charges."

"Yes, yes, yes," snapped the judge. He divided damages evenly "among the participants," added individual fines and court costs, and was about to gavel a finish, when the back door flew open and banged against the wall.

"John! Two of those men are mine and I need them for my boat, so don't you dare send them to jail!" It was Adele Henry.

"You're interrupting this court, madam. Sit down and be silent or you'll be escorted out. Sit down, Adele. And shut up."

She sat with a thump.

It took a while to sort out the fines and charges. The crews of the four boats were left standing together. Now that they knew the worst that would happen, they settled into a graveyard kind of cheer. Soon they began to compare notes on the fight, combatant to combatant without heat, and to examine the cuts and bruises they had inflicted on each other.

Hank had encountered Gus Rosvic as they entered the police building, after he had delivered the children to Jody. The two men nodded, then looked away, but they walked together since neither would have delayed and trailed the other. The courtroom was still locked, so they needed to stand together. Hank determined on silence. This was no place to start an argument.

"Your boys in trouble too?" Gus ventured at last.

"Appears so."

"Wish I never had to make town during season. Always trouble." After another silence, "Who was in charge yesterday at Whale, you or your wife?"

"She was," he lied.

"Then tell her thanks."

Hank debated saying "Tell her yourself," and settled for "I will."

"And tell her if she needs anything out on the grounds, call me."

"I'll do that. Thanks." On impulse he started to slap Gus's back.

Gus's eyes flashed up. "But tell your wife never to set foot on my boat." Hank stayed his arm. "And saying I'm there to help don't mean it's right for her to run Jones Henry's boat or any other. You ought to know better, Hank, to let it happen. Jones Henry's legs must be rolled off in his grave by now, to watch what that woman of his is doing to the boat that was his blood and bones."

"It's happened, Gus. Live with it." Hank tried to say it mildly, but his voice had an edge.

Gus flared. "You'll see when she gets into trouble. And don't think your men is going to win any of the bets with my men if I can help it, because that would make it seem right, which it ain't. None of this is right. If you don't see it you're not as savvy as they say you are."

"Our guys have one bet finished now," said Hank coldly. "Don't worry. Yours won, mine'll pay up. And after this court business we'll compare fish tickets and settle the next."

The courtroom door opened. Hank and Rosvic looked toward separate sides of the small room but, neither willing to deviate, grimly moved in a straight line and sat together.

Try once more, thought Hank. "If bets are what our men were fighting each other about, we'd better be sensible and damp it down or we'll both lose the season."

"That's one piece of sense."

They both leaned forward when the dog-eared fighters shuffled in. Eleven in all, more than just their own. None seemed in worse condition than shaggy hangovers. Hank quickly noted a purple swelling on Terry's cheek and a cut on Ham's mouth, but as best he could see, knuckles were only reddened—not swollen—so their hands were not damaged for work. With his own men assessed, he could be relaxed over the injuries to others. Plenty of purple, some cuts. Gus's man Bud had a fat lip, probably served him right. Confusing, though, that Terry and Ham seemed to hang together with the *Hinda Bee* men as if they were buddies.

When Randy the cop described the fight the sides became clear, but still not the motive. Adele Henry came in mouthing off. Hank hunched and lowered his head, ashamed but hoping she wouldn't see him and sit alongside. He glanced and wanted to laugh. Gus at his elbow was doing the same.

But the calculation of charges took time and left the few spectators free to move. Adele Henry plumped down beside him. "They ought to be ashamed of themselves," she declared. "I won't have scrapping hooligans on my boat, although I certainly intend to see that Terry and Ham don't go to jail. But they're going to get the lecture of their lives. And did you hear how John Flaxen treated me just now? As if he wasn't a neighbor whom I see every day! Judges get a swelled head, I think." She leaned across Hank to Rosvic. "Gus! I'm shocked at your boys. You and my dear late Jones were such devoted friends, and since Daddy never permitted his men to carry on when they had to fish and stay healthy, I'd have thought that you, too—"

Gus edged away as best he could. "Not the place here, Adele. I uh . . . Hope you're staying well."

"Of course I'm well, as much as a grieving widow can be."

"Sorry. I mean, glad to hear it."

Jeff Mathews, skipper of the *Sleepthief Two*, sauntered over. "Seems our guys were in this together, Hank. Can you figure it?"

Hank and Rosvic both welcomed the interruption. "Not a clue," said Hank.

"You can be sure we will find out," snapped Adele.

The fines and costs totaled seventy-one dollars per man. Adele elaborately peeled off three fifty-dollar bills and demanded a receipt along with change. "This is going to be collected, boys," she told Terry and Ham sternly. "And we're going home this minute to have quite a talk."

"Yes, ma'am."

Only the skipper of the *Lady West* had not come to bail out his men. Hank wrote a check to cover their fines.

Nick the skiff man pumped his hand. "Don't worry, we'll pay you back."

"Forget it. We don't run over your skiff every day."

"Ahhh . . . Nobody hurt."

"All right, you birds," said Jeff of the *Sleepthief.* "What happened?" One of his men started to speak.

"Nothing," interrupted Terry firmly. "Nothin' we didn't handle among ourselves." He looked at Ham and the others sternly.

"'Nothing' is not going to do it when we get to the house, young man," declared Adele.

Leave it alone, woman, thought Hank. No wonder Jones turned crabby. He told Adele, "I need to take them right away, back to the *Jody Dawn.* We've got all kinds of work, after the time we took off to set up your boat, before I can release them." Sleep was what they needed. And their privacy. Terry and Ham both regarded him gratefully.

Joe Pone of the *Lady West,* who had a black eye, went up to Terry and shook his hand. "You made your point, man. Nobody rags you anymore, about working for a woman. From here on, Jody's okay."

"Oh my God, so that was it," exclaimed Adele. She hugged Terry, then Ham, and burst into tears.

PART II

Rules of the New Game

MID-AUGUST TO SEPTEMBER 1982
JAPAN, ALASKA

7

RISING SUN

KODIAK, MID-AUGUST 1982

It turned out that the men of the *Hinda Bee* won all three sets of wagers. They spent much of the winnings on a steak and booze bash with their new buddies on the *Adele H,* all to ritual insults given and taken. None of this, of course, affected their now-sworn rivalry on the grounds.

Hank yearned more than ever to keep seining for salmon in Kodiak bays under snow-draped mountains with Jody at hand and the kids safely close in town. But such an oasis was a mirage now that the Japanese waited. Their money had enabled him to keep the *Jody Dawn* after crabbing collapsed and other skippers lost million-plus-dollar boats to the banks. If the Japanese now held him truly in their pocket, as Jones Henry had accused, then he needed to face them and accommodate them until he could find a way out. If they were giving him the opportunity of his life, then it was time to grab and benefit from it.

The days ticked on to the time when the *Jody Dawn* would be fit for the trip to Seattle and gear conversion to longlining. (If Jody hadn't tied herself to the damned *Adele H,* Hank fretted, Seattle could have been an all-family vacation.) At least the delay allowed them time in Kodiak. Once the cast was removed from Hank's shoulder, Jody massaged it often, easing the ache and restoring mobility. Her skill had been acquired from living among men in an injury-prone occupation. Hank pretended jealousy over this, Jody teased, and it became a tender time together. When the children were elsewhere they ended up in bed laughing, with Hank's Jody no longer a skipper barking orders.

And daily he stood beside his sleek-hulled *Jody Dawn,* now dry and vulnerable on the shipyard ways. He'd even helped rivet her, planned her inch by inch until the very groan of her metal was part of him. The boat's design was adapted to many of the sea's changing fortunes, but not gracefully, he fretted, to this conversion the Japanese felt they needed. The Tsurifunes, father and son, had money enough. But judgment? The *Jody Dawn*'s work deck lay astern for crab pots or trawl, while longline needed a work deck forward where the skipper, at the controls, could watch down directly and maneuver. He'd told them. Not the boat for longline without moving the whole cabin structure and desecrating the boat's integrity. They were impervious to all but getting his boat online before the bureaucrats locked boundaries and quotas. Understood. It was an exciting game of opportunity. Yet, whenever immediate action stopped to leave time for thought, Jones Henry's disapproving shadow invaded his mind.

It was a glum sunny morning when, with a new salmon opening announced, Hank hugged Jody and (suddenly terrified for what he could lose) admonished her not to take chances. He virtually crushed Terry's hand first and then Ham's to exact their promise yet again to look after her, then fixed a stern eye on Joel and the other dubious kid hired to fill out the crew, to reaffirm to them that they'd account to him if anything happened to Jody.

The lines of the *Adele H* slipped through his hands until at last he tossed each aboard the departing boat. The gap widened. He was still shouting last-thought instructions when she waved gaily, blew him a kiss, then pointed to her ears and shook her head. Now he couldn't reach her! This should be experienced only by his three children and Adele Henry beside him waving good luck. No fisherman should have to see off from dockside a boat bearing his love.

Adele's busty cheer didn't help, busy everywhere in bulging red pants and giving only lip service to her husband dead a mere month. Why couldn't she have played the widow poor Jones might have expected: sold the boat, gone to France or whatever, honored Jones's hang-ups, if only for his memory? Adele now had them dependent and beholden. Yet, what would he and Jody do without her as the trusted (and loved!) caretaker of their children?

Adele hugged him. "Hank, dear, they'll be just fine. Don't look so worried. Jody's a true heart—she'll make us all so proud. I'm simply . . . overflowing."

He returned the hug, wishing she'd leave him alone but touched by her sincerity, then hugged a second time and meant it. After dinner tonight, though, what a relief it was going to be to take the kids to their home surrounded by woods and water, miles from Adele. Hole up with them for a few days, ignoring town. Precious time to know each other.

"Now come along," Adele continued. "If we hurry we can drive to Spruce Cape and wave to the boat again. Hurry." She included Hank.

"Sorry, need to go back to the boatyard. But remember, I'm taking you all to dinner, say, seven thirty."

"I should think more like six, or at the most six thirty. Not for myself, though Daddy and I always ate early. I like to feed the children at six sharp and give them regular habits. And then there's certainly no reason for you to drive all that way out in the country to your house with Jody not there. We'll all settle down for a nice quiet evening at my house."

"Generator needs work at the house, sorry," he lied. "But okay on six thirty." Now he needed to rush to his radios on the *Jody Dawn* in the boatyard, to stay in touch with Jody at least through Whale Passage. She'd rejected his wish to see them beyond Whale and fly back from Port Bailey, rejected it with impatience. She'd firmly become Captain Jody. Indeed, the weather was calm, she'd be hitting the right tide, and there trailing her were the *Hinda Bee* with good old crabby Gus and Jeff Mathews's *Sleepthief Two*. Maybe they wanted her to fail, but they wouldn't see her come to harm. (In truth, wouldn't a safe, face-saving failure return his Jody home? One, of course, that would leave her content knowing she'd tried?)

As he trotted on the road, glad for the exercise, he heard a voice from a car exclaim, "Hank! Well, that's something at least, your shoulder cast's gone. Good. Get in." It was John Gains, returned from Bristol Bay. Even in plaid shirt and baseball cap the man looked pressed and combed for the office.

"In a hurry, John," Hank snapped, and kept moving.

"Not so fast. I've come looking for you. Important we talk." When Hank gave his reason for speed, John assured him the cannery had plenty of radios. "You can monitor Jody from my office while we talk." Hank acquiesced and entered the car, since in any event John's company radio might have a stronger signal than the boat's.

Hank instinctively kept his talk in the car to a minimum. Gains, his former crewman and his junior by a decade, but already a hustling company executive for the Tsurifune interests, always made him restless. The man never stopped acting like a schoolmarm. A glance in the car confirmed that, as usual, John's full black hair was no more rumpled than his clothes. Did he get that way just from pushing so hard that he needed to stay on guard? He was the son of a Kansas plumber, he'd once admitted, as if it was something to be ashamed of.

Hank never felt comfortable with the man, even though he knew John had grit for all his office primness. He'd been a boxer in college, as he'd proven by knocking Hank down in the ring during that informal Fourth of July bout in Kodiak four years back. And he'd placed himself in danger during the storm and failed rescue of Jones Henry, volunteer-crewing on the helicopter that had towed the raft with Hank and Jones aboard to safety. Hank owed him and knew it. But John understood—give him that also, Hank conceded—that grateful payback would come with an emergency, not in casual exchange. For the rest, John had become a company man for the Japanese, and maybe their spy.

Gains's office indeed had ample radio equipment. Hank talked to Jody throughout Whale Passage, although she didn't seem to need him. Gus had taken his *Hinda Bee* ahead to lead the way and she followed close, while Jeff's *Sleepthief* trailed. Her tone was light. Gravity would have better reassured him. Her "Ease up, Hank—don't worry" didn't help.

After Jody had signed off, John Gains said reproachfully, "Tsurifune in Tokyo's been trying to reach you. Why haven't you stayed in touch?"

"Well, John, I figured Tsurifune could find me when he wanted. Are we talking the young Tsurifune or the old man?"

"Shoji, of course—young Mike. Not his father the director for day to day. Expect to see Director Kiyoshi Tsurifune only on special occasions if my experience serves. You were privileged last spring." John's face was calm and serious, with the confidence of being in charge. "Frankly, Hank, I don't think it's wise to be heard calling the director an old man even if he is in his seventies. He wouldn't like it."

Hank grinned. "Does he still buy those paintings of nothing but splashes? And pay the price of a large boat for 'em?"

"Not the sort of thing the director would confide in me."

John's reclining executive chair might as well have been rigid for the straight-backed way he occupied it. With clasped hands on the shining-clear desk, and with a sunny window behind him that cast glare in a visitor's eyes, he appeared faceless and solid. "Now, Hank. It's already eleven in the evening Tokyo time since it's taken me so long to find you, but Shoji Tsurifune told me he'd receive your call at his home. My secretary's putting it through as we speak. You should have stayed in touch. If I hadn't been off in Bristol Bay . . . What's this about fishing with your wife when you should have been in town seeing to your boat? And recovering from your injuries so you'd be fit for your part of the bargain? Tsurifune father and son might not be that amused if they heard, though they won't from me. Your boat's their investment now, remember. And you are, besides."

"Remembered all too well, John. What's so urgent?"

"I believe they want you over there."

Indeed, over the phone Mike Tsurifune was succinct. Leave the *Jody Dawn* in Kodiak for whatever repairs were necessary, he said with his usual cool, Harvard-educated confidence, but plans had been canceled for the Seattle retrofit to longline. "We considered your advice, Hank. Very good advisement, Father himself agrees. We must use your vessel *Jody Dawn*—*our* vessel together *Jody Dawn,* ha-ha—for other purpose and prepare a different vessel for longline. Now, soonest plane here please, Hank. Seat reserved for you tomorrow on United hop from Anchorage that leaves at noon, Narita 1:30 PM next day, eight-and-half hours later, driver will meet you. Your visa's still good from last spring, yes? Or I'll arrange."

"You've sure thought it through, Mike. But I've got—"

"Good, then all arranged. See you tomorrow; no, day after."

Hank held out for one further day in a tone that warned Mike to acquiesce. It gave him another night to cuddle and read to his children before delivering them back to Aunt Adele, and time to make sure by radio that Jody reached her fishing grounds safely and was settled in.

Her voice, cheerful and businesslike, changed when she heard the news. "Japan again. I see."

Hank had anticipated this. "Listen. You're my love. What happened there before won't happen again. Believe me, Jody."

After a pause: "I believe you, Hank."

Hank caught his breath after the conversation ended. So much had happened since his visit to Japan three months ago that he'd dismissed Helene Foster from his mind until now, except when thinking about the near-wreck of his marriage when he'd confessed to Jody. On this trip, he told himself, don't even go near the Tokyo Kabuki theater where Helene studied.

On the flight from Anchorage to Tokyo, he enjoyed the flyover view of Mount McKinley, then had a scotch, and dismissed again all thoughts of Helene as he pictured his Jody.

Members of the fishery agency waited at Narita airport to greet him, as had happened on his first visit to Japan. There was limp-handed, smiling Teruo Hayashi, and the aggressive fellow named Kodama. Hayashi had relaxed with him during their travels to fishing towns, and Hank assumed the informality remained. "Yashi-san!" he declared, and threw out his arms in a bear hug.

Hayashi backed away, startled. "Mr. Crawford. You are welcomed."

"Mr. Hayashi," Hank corrected. "Nice to see you again."

Kodama, beside him, frowned, and offered a curt but firm handshake. Not even a bow. Hank knew Kodama less well since he'd been one of many at meetings, but he had noted him above the others as sturdier and more direct. Gym bag with smiling cartoon animals, wasn't it? Ran or something. "Do you still run, Mr. Kodama?"

"Of course."

Hayashi explained that although Hank was now connected with the Tsurifune company, Mr. Shoji Tsurifune, son of the director, had requested that the agency first show him more of important Japanese fisheries.

"I didn't come over here to be a tourist again, whatever Mike Tsurifune requested."

"However, Mr. Tsurifune gives his driver to transport us all, but sends regrets in this letter. He is called on emergency and asks you be patient. You must enjoy interesting time in Japan until he can return. Very soon, Mr. Crawford, very soon."

The letter, scrawled in black ink, was on heavy paper with a letterhead in elegant Japanese characters:

Dear Hank,

Shit and all that, but family business suddenly calling. Don't worry, everything paid and fair emolument to you besides for time loss. I've arranged for you to visit an interesting part of Japan where we have investments. Happily please enjoy yourself and learn more about the importance of fish to Japanese.

Shoji/Mike Tsurifune cordially.

PS: Ancestral fact to interest you. Family name Tsurifune from long time before myself or Father. "Tsuri" means to fish (like line and pole old-fashioned way), and "fune" means ship or vessel. How convenient is such a name, eh? And how can go wrong?

Will soon return.
Mike.

Hank controlled his resentment at being hustled from Kodiak only to wait. Go home? Would probably need to pay for that himself and possibly lose everything. He decided to call the delay part of business and make the best of it, but to be firm. "Last time I was here, I wanted to meet fishermen and go out with them on their boats, but all we did was sit in meetings and drink green tea. This time, I need to have more to do with fishing boats."

"Oh, naturally, Mr. Crawford," said Hayashi. "Fishing boats."

"I mean, meet fishermen and go out on a fishing boat. Is that understood?"

A pause. "Yes, yes, Mr. Tsurifune arranges everything, Mr. Crawford."

"All has been arranged, Mr. Carford," added Kodama in a deeper voice. "Boat, of course." His confidence was reassuring. Hank decided that he liked him. In contrast to Hayashi, whose slight build suggested nothing more physical than racing an elevator door and who voiced a thought only after consideration, Kodama was vigorous and direct. His eyes glinted with energy. His presence seemed to promise fewer deadly meetings at the least.

During a dinner of seafood, raw and cooked, both guides were constrained. They conversed gravely in Japanese (undoubtedly, Hayashi explained life with his difficult American) and spoke in English only for courtesies or when Hank initiated a subject.

It turned out that Yukihiro Kodama was to be his guide and interpreter this time, since Hayashi had been promoted to supervisor. Indeed, next day the gym bag with cartoon faces came to the train as part of Kodama's luggage. Despite Hayashi's limp handshake, Hank suddenly regretted leaving such a comfortable presence. The guy had been concerned and gracious. His receding forehead framed by silky hair looked vulnerable beside Kodama's crew cut, thick as grass.

The train sped them for hours through hilly countryside, past tile-roofed towns and occasional bizarre sights like a giant gilded Buddha on a hill. "Kanazawa is ancient and beautiful," declared Kodama sternly, as if Hank might contradict. They arrived late afternoon in heavy rain. Kodama opened his umbrella and announced: "Now sightseeing. Come!" Except for a dark castle of gloomy stone facing a vast formal garden park that dripped green without bright colors, and a damp old temple that a caretaker needed to open, Hank saw little except ugly buildings sur-rounded by loud traffic. "Certainly interesting," was the best compliment he could muster.

"Of course."

"What's for tomorrow?"

"Fishing cooperative. Important."

"Go on boats?"

"No. Fishing cooperative."

They ate in the hotel. Hank, still tired from the long flight and switched time zones, looked forward to an early night and sleep. Worry about boats in the morning. But, "Come, take coat," ordered Kodama.

A taxi continued for miles along dimly lighted streets and roads to a busy waterfront. Through the cab window drifted familiar smells of grease, rust, and fish. "Hey, Mr. Kodama!" Hank exclaimed. "Are you actually going to show me fishing?" Steel boats some ninety feet long scraped sluggishly against fenders. Nets lay aft of open holds. A human chain of crewmen in towel headbands handed white containers dripping ice from hold to pier where another chain lifted them into trucks.

At once Kodama's sternness disappeared. He joked with the men, some-times roughly, although he sidestepped Hank's requests for translations. Following banter with a tired-eyed man standing on one of the bows, he told Hank, "Is Captain Maruyama. His boat Number Fifteen, *Chosei-Maru,* meaning Long Life Vessel. We have fished together on far seas, but now Americans have taken the grounds and he must stay near shore. You wish to speak him questions?"

"Hey, you've been a fisherman? You didn't say."

"Of course. Captain Maruyama busy, Mr. Carford. Will go to his business if you do not wish to speak him."

The translated conversation was polite but impersonal despite Hank's attempts at warmth between fellow fishermen. The captain, middle-aged with an anxious face sunburned the color of earth, said that they had just delivered sixty-three boxes of shrimp, and also several species of fish. His crew numbered six including himself. The boat would leave again soon after midnight to reach the grounds by daylight, then would fish all day and return as now to deliver between nine and ten in the dark. (Perfect! thought Hank. Daily commitment so that when Tsurifune returns I'm not long at sea.) The captain kept glancing at his wheelhouse while a crewman beside him restlessly jiggled a mooring line untied from its cleat.

"Further question quickly, please, Mr. Carford."

Hank turned to Kodama. "Ask if I can go on his boat tonight, out fishing tomorrow. Say I won't be in the way. Just one fisherman to another, to observe his gear. I have my own boots and skins. It's not raining anymore. I'll sleep on deck."

"Impossible. Very important cooperative tomorrow."

"Then the day after."

"There is schedule."

Not the place to argue it, Hank decided. The boat would come in every night. "Thank the captain and please say I wish him good sleep now and good catch tomorrow." At once the man hurried to his wheelhouse. Hank released the line from the bollard by his legs, then hurried to cast off the line aft. The simple scratch of rope in his hands felt right. Long-Life-Fifteen moved off and another boat took its place at once.

Next, they entered a long, brightly illuminated building. Boxes of iced seafood stood in clusters, while trucks delivered more. Fresh brine odors filled the air. Shrimps appeared to be as bright red and fish as silvery or green as the moment they had come from the sea. A knot of attentive people with notebooks moved from one cluster to another. They trailed a barking auctioneer who thrust down his arm at each completed sale like a baseball umpire declaring man out. Unlike the bigger auctions in Tokyo that he'd seen on his previous trip, Hank noted, here the buyers included women. Their short white boots stood the wet floor as firmly as the men's. In further contrast to the intensely driven Tokyo Tsukiji Market, the bidding sometimes exploded into jokes. Even the auctioneer laughed.

Nice people, Hank decided. Kodama was okay as well. When you got them out of their offices.

8

"A Ruvrey Highriner"

KANAZAWA, JAPAN, MID-AUGUST 1982

Hank woke next morning at six thirty when Kodama entered the room with his fiercely tight face streaming sweat. "Hey, why didn't you wake me to run with you?"

"Need sleep more than run, Mr. Carford. Important day, now we must hurry."

A bus took them along a peninsula facing the Sea of Japan. Through pines and sand brush the sun sparkled on blue water and gleamed over the reds and blacks of high-prowed fishing boats trailing nets. This was country Hank could understand. A car waited by a stop in the road. After courtesies the driver took them into a hillside village. Men with nets worked beside boats on a quay below, but the car parked by a solid building far from the water. Inside, a woman rose from her typewriter and a dignified, white-haired man hurried to conduct them to a hall whose windows faced rooftops. Kodama and the man, Mr. Nagao, bowed and exchanged cards.

"The boats below," Hank ventured. "Will they fish today?"

"Of course."

"Let's have a look before they go."

"Later. Here is provided the information."

"I'll get important information by seeing how you build your boats and set your gear."

"Mr. Nagao has pictures of the vessels and equipment. I will ask."

"I mean the real boats, down there. And real fishermen."

"Of course. If time."

Both Japanese lit cigarettes and conversed in Japanese as the secretary brought a pot of green tea. Hank considered walking out and down to the boats, but decided to continue the game. A shrine mounted on the wall contained a paper boat and pieces of rope and net. A shelf below it held a vase, a dish, a doll, and a ceramic mask. He walked over to study them.

"Mr. Carford, you must come sit for information."

"My name's Crawford, and since you're not speaking English, what the hell?"

"Carford, hai, of course. Come sit I must asking."

Mr. Nagao slowly unrolled a chart and attached it to a screen pulled from the ceiling. He pointed like a lecturer to line by line of Japanese characters as Kodama translated. Forty seiners of four to fourteen tons fished a few miles from shore for *iwashi* and mackerel. The search through a dictionary the secretary brought concluded that iwashi were sardines. Annual catch 500, 1.3 million yen. Some iwashi were kept in cold storage for bait and shipped elsewhere, but most were salted.

"So this is the fleet here? Let's go have a look."

Neither Japanese acknowledged the interruption. The presentation went on to cover gill-net vessels that fished sixteen to thirty miles offshore around seamounts and along a two-hundred-meter depth curve. They caught rockfish (another dictionary search) as well as bream and cod. Then there were boats that directed strong lights in the water to attract squid and a fish they called saury in English. Then there was yellowtail, grown in ponds. Mr. Nagao read from a paper the quantity of each species caught for each of the past six years, and Kodama translated them one by one.

To be polite Hank asked about yellowtail aquaculture. No aquaculture, replied Nagao, since hills on the peninsula went straight into the sea and thus no land existed for farming or aquaculture. "But you said yellowtail ponds . . . ?" Hank asked.

"Please hear the further information, Mr. Carford. Therefore, Mr. Nagao informs, all here must be fishermen not farmer. Many many once fished far seas. But since America sent fishing ships from water where Japanese fishermen for long time caught fish Americans do not catch or eat—"

"I get the point. Why don't we see the boats?"

"Important further information."

The secretary brought in two neat boxes of sushi and cold tempura wrapped in cellophane. Hank and Kodama lunched while Nagao lovingly rerolled the poster, then attached another to the screen. This one had rectangles connected by lines, like a family tree. It showed facilities.

At last the three men entered a waiting car to drive around "for observation." Mr. Nagao stopped first at several oil tanks, gestured at them from the car, and explained the capacity of each. Next they stopped at a long building to view two hundred sixty boxes in freezer storage awaiting shipment, and to see trays of squid in flash-freeze compartments that would soon be transferred to shipping containers. Mr. Nagao read them the writing stenciled on the boxes.

They then reentered the car to drive the hundred yards to a portable machine for sucking sardines from a hold, then drove another short distance to a low building of water pens with stuffy brine and seaweed odors. Dark flatfish swam in the water. "It is here, you see, Mr. Carford, that yellowtail is grown. Not in farming ponds unfortunately impossible, you did not listen. Mr. Nagao now explains."

Shadows outside had begun to lengthen when they left the yellowtail building. "We must soon to the bus return Kanazawa, but first Mr. Nagao will show us fish-drying racks, fish filet line, and water cleaner. And most important, ice-making machinery. Please hurry, Mr. Carford."

Hank strode in a straight line toward the boats.

"There is not time, Mr. Carford! Return to us immediately."

Clean wooden boats, the kind it would be a pleasure to work aboard. Fishermen stood mending seine. In universal fashion they passed the nets through raised blocks, so that tents of web were stretched along the quay. The men wore baggy sweat clothes stained only a little. Hank towered a head taller than most of them. A hearty "hi" drew only puzzled or impersonal glances. He noted that his own web-mending procedure was no different. A spare flat needle lay on the concrete. He picked it up and entered a group, but found no rip in the net free of a man mending it. Everyone watched, but no one offered him a place. "Howdy, *konichi-wa*. My language is English. This is net in English. Net. See? This needle. This web." The men exchanged amused murmurs but only increased their concentration. He was dressed like a tourist, not one of them.

The car pulled alongside. Nagao and Kodama took position, facing him silently. The car doors remained open and an automatic signal dinged relentlessly.

"Kodama-san. Explain that I'm a fisherman too."

"We must go."

Hank considered, laid down the needle, followed to the car, and quietly endured the remaining lecture. Back in the office Nagao held out a guest book that contained page-long entries, some in English with sappy praise. "Nice facilities," Hank scribbled, and walked away.

"Mr. Nagao hopes you writing more of good impression."

Hank added, "In good repair."

Back on the main road he bowed cool acknowledgment when Mr. Nagao expressed ritual pleasure to have entertained such an important visitor, and pocketed a keepsake medallion with no more than a nod.

"Mr. Nagao wishes to know your best impression."

"All very interesting."

"Mr. Nagao wishes to know, if you now understand? How his village is . . . " Kodama consulted a paper from his pocket. "Self-sufficiency. To this and other villages nearby. Taking fish very careful, for market."

Hank forced himself to cool down. He bowed to Nagao, who now appeared sincere and dignified rather than a mere bore. "Impressive, sir. Thank you. *Domo gozaimas.*" Suddenly he felt ashamed, regretted not having been more generous in the guest book. "That ice plant was amazing, please tell him. I've never seen anything more . . . efficient."

Mr. Nagao appeared pleased. And relieved. He and Kodama left Hank alone after that and conversed in Japanese for the fifteen minutes before the bus appeared on schedule and stopped at their hail.

Hank glumly watched water and boats at work pass by the window. Yes, impressive. Had he acted like a brat? But when they treated him like a doll trophy in a case . . . Good old limp but flexible Hayashi. At length he ventured, "We'll be back in time to go to that wharf and ask your friend to take me out with his crew tonight."

"Not on schedule. Important meetings tomorrow."

"Next day, then."

"Fishing machinery dangerous."

"I'm a goddamn fisherman! I know machinery. Didn't anybody tell you?"

Kodama suddenly scowled. It was the first time Hank had seen anger among the careful Japanese. "You do not understand, Mr. Carford."

"Then explain it."

"Duty is not explain."

"Why didn't you help when I tried to meet those fishermen?"

"Common fisher folk. Mr. Nagao important, waiting."

"Start here, then. You let it drop last night that you'd been a fisherman yourself." Hank grinned to break tension. "Nothing common about you."

"Fishing master. On high seas."

"Like a captain, right? Okay then, good for you, Captain. Me too, fishing captain. I like boats, all kinds. I like fishermen, all kinds, not just captains. Want to understand Japanese fishermen." Kodama's expression remained tight. "Tell me about yourself."

"Busy fishing. Then *pfft*. Now office. My duty to give you information." A pause. "Your duty, Mr. Carford, listen to information. Mr. Nagao giving important information to show self-reliance in village far from city."

"Well, it was good information. But understand. Part of my work is to see boats and fishermen. To understand."

"Fishermen in village are only innocent."

"Didn't you yourself start as a fisherman, pulling nets or lines on deck?"

"Fishing academy. Very high grades."

Heavy rain started again. It did not help that the hotel had kept a reservation for Hank alone—single bed in small room—so that, in the pouring dark, Kodama needed to search out a lesser room in town. Nor that Kodama's umbrella, when he returned for dinner, disappeared from the common receptacle by the hotel door where patrons' umbrellas were left as a matter of course. Hank would have cursed routinely, but Kodama's explosive spat-out fury unbalanced the world.

Although Kodama regained composure before grimly stalking into the rain, he did not join Hank for breakfast next morning and barely spoke when he collected him for meetings. Instead of hailing a taxi he strode the slick streets with Hank trailing. During introductions he glowered the Japanese courtesies. The meeting droned. Clearly, Hank decided, he'd never see a boat with Kodama.

At lunchtime Hank phoned Hayashi in Tokyo. "We are in important meeting, Mr. Carford. You are happy your visit?"

Hank declared that after today he'd attended all the meetings he'd stomach, and that there was a good fishing boat right in Kanazawa that could take him to sea for a while.

He could hear Hayashi talking to others, then: "Oh, Mr. Crawford, this will not be necessary. Very dangerous. All information can be furnished to you in the offices, where those in charge will gladly to answer all questions. The fishermen are not educated. And besides, there is no time on the ske-jure."

"Then we'd better rewrite the schedule."

"But ske-jure is . . . ske-jure!"

"Then ship me back home."

Silence. Hayashi excused himself, saying he would call back quickly. As they waited, Kodama sat with arms folded, scowling.

The phone rang. It was John Gains in Seattle. "Jesus, Hank, it's past midnight and I've got an early plane to D.C. Don't you know the Japan games by now? What did you say to make them so upset?"

"Just said I wanted to go out with fishermen. Tsurifune's stuck me here killing time and they have me back in twenty-four hours of meetings."

"That's how the Japanese do things."

"They promised me a boat. All this 'yes' shit. Then when the time comes it's a blank wall."

"Hank, don't you ever listen? Last spring I briefed you. Asians don't say no, especially Japanese. They think it's offensive. So they say maybe to save everybody's face. 'Maybe' or 'perhaps' both mean forget it. 'Yes' means only maybe. Drink some sake and roll with it."

"They're wasting my time. I've got a wife I want to be near back home. And kids. At least I could be learning something about their boats."

"Don't you have a life besides fishing boats? Look. Forget this boat crap. You're their guest and they don't want anything to happen to you. Roll with it. Don't mess this up for me."

"*You?*"

With the conversation over he did feel like a brat. Had asshole John put himself on the line? Sake toasts at lunch made him feel it more. They were nice people. (Nice when they weren't torturing American prisoners during Jones Henry's war. That's where the Kodama scowl fitted.) He remained docile for the rest of the day. On impulse he found a secretary who spoke enough English to understand that he wanted to buy an umbrella. With a self-conscious giggle she undertook the job. The price shocked him. Japan was expensive; the purchase cleaned the major yen bills from his wallet. But when Kodama accepted the gift, he bowed to Hank for the first time, and the scowl softened to merely a frown.

Next morning they ran together.

After another day of meetings that Hank forced himself to accept with grace, Kodama declared abruptly: "You have *kappa*, Mr. Carford? *Nagagutsu?* I do not know words in English. Rubber clothing? Come. We must hurry."

It happened in a rush. Kodama snapped directions to a taxi driver and they sped through the dark streets. Rain and sun had been intermittent. Now it rained heavily. They reached the delivery pier around midnight. There stood Captain Maruyama, calling in rough good humor from the wheelhouse of his Number Fifteen Long-Life Ship. Hank jumped aboard. He nearly fell on the slippery rail, dodging solicitous crewmen who blocked his way to steady him. No way but to land in their arms. "*Konichi-wa*, howdy," he laughed, out of breath, and they laughed back.

Kodama in his running clothes followed behind, stepped over the rail gingerly with new umbrella raised, and made for the wheelhouse. Hank called an amiable excuse when Kodama gestured him to follow. He donned oilskins and remained on deck while the men unmoored.

A crewman with a calm face long as a horse's pulled a fish from a side bin and presented it gleaming in the rain for inspection. "Beautiful!" said Hank, patting a black band on the skin, and elicited the name, *ishidai*. The man gestured toward the housing. Hank followed with barely a wave toward Kodama frowning from a wheelhouse window. He stooped to enter the cabin but still bumped his head. Inside he could barely stand erect without scraping back his cap. It made for pantomime joking. He peeled oilskins with the others and hung them on pegs in a sheltered passageway, cheerfully brushing elbows in the cramped space.

The cabin centered around a charcoal stove. Beyond stretched a low space divided into rectangular pens. One of the men crawled barefoot into a pen, stretched full length, and pulled a sheet over his face. The other four crewmen invited Hank to a bench. The man with the fish knelt at a board to deftly skin and filet it, then sliced it into strips. Chopsticks were produced along with bowls, brown sauce, and chopped green horseradish, and the men passed strips of the fish. Hank knew to swirl the brown and green together, and had mastered chopsticks enough to grasp a strip of fish and dip it in the mix. The ishidai had firm red meat with a mild, sweet taste.

Kodama appeared with grave demeanor. "Go now sleeping, Mr. Carford. Choice for you. Sleep up with captain who invites you very kind, or . . ." The voice took on an edge of disapproval. "Or sleep with workers."

"With workers be good," said Hank firmly. "Thanks." Kodama nodded and left.

Although the men included him and cooperated with friendly sign language, they soon turned back to themselves. Hank considered visiting the wheelhouse for a quick check of charts and electronics, but decided that if Kodama was leaving him alone he'd better not push his luck. He'd check the skippering part later.

At length the man with the horse face yawned. He tossed a ragged futon into an empty compartment and motioned Hank to use it, then settled with his remaining blanket. Hank thanked him in Japanese. The boards of the pen rose around him a foot high. The enclosure was little more than shoulder width, its length an inch or two short for western size. Cozy coffin. He crooked legs and rested knees on the sides, folded hands on chest, and lay enjoying the boat's roll and musty fishing smells.

A few hours later the engine slowed and he popped awake. The others were crawling from their compartments. Someone shook his foot. Rain pounded on the roof of the passageway as they pulled on foul-weather gear. His oilskins were stiff plastic, theirs rubber thick as inner tubing.

On deck it was still dark. The rain fell straight. It dimmed the lights of other boats that swooped and bobbed, some close enough for voices to carry. Within minutes the skipper called down and the men heaved over the trawl bags on each side of the boat. They trailed out of sight, submerging in the water as the boat gunned ahead. Hank watched without helping so he could see their division of labor. Another call and the paravane doors splashed down. The rig was for side trawl, which raised the catch up over the rail instead of sliding it more safely up a ramp astern— gear that Hank had worked a dozen years before but that had now become obsolete on all but the smallest Alaskan draggers.

Since the tow would last a couple of hours, the men returned to their compartments to sleep. Hank climbed at last to the wheelhouse.

"You must leave all rubber clothing and feetwear outside," commanded Kodama as Hank started to enter. In complying, Hank's head bumped the overhang and a sudden wind gust sprayed him before he could enter.

Kodama's profile was etched by green electronic light. He stood with chin jutted and legs apart, gripping the wide spokes of an old-fashioned steering wheel as if he were a crewman. The shadow of the captain hovered over an array of dim lights and dials. Hank recognized conventional radar and loran. The depth sounder read 470 meters. Its signal appeared to be clearer than that on his own *Jody Dawn*—a sign of the latest equipment.

"Rocky bottom? Mud bottom?"

"Of course."

"Which?"

"Mud on top. Rock under. You are now happy fishing, Mr. Carford?"

"Very, thanks." The overhead was an inch shorter than his height. He needed to slump on the rail or stand with head bowed or knees bent. "The guys below, the fishermen, they've been very kind."

"Of course."

Outside, early gray light showed choppy water and the outlines of other boats. "Regular fleet out there," Hank said to make conversation.

"Too many vessels. Fishermen who can no more on high seas, therefore crowding."

The captain spoke to Kodama, apparently about course and speed, then retired into a raised crawl space. He patted the edge and motioned Hank over. "Captain Maruyama says regret low ceiling and invites you." Hank thanked him and went over. The space was fitted with bedding, and with comforts that included a small color television. He and the captain exchanged smiles and nods. A crewman delivered a bowl of steamed shrimp fresh from the sea, which they all peeled and ate with gusto.

"Americans growing tall," muttered Kodama. "Because always eating, eating."

Hank smiled, taking it as banter. "You sure stuff it down yourself, Kodama-san."

A pause, then curtly, "This so not always."

"Sorry. You grew up poor?"

The edge continued. "As boy no food. Thusly not grow tall. Every Japanese depriving."

"Oh." Caution. "After the war?"

"Of course. Americans have dropped atomic bombs on innocent Japanese, and so conquer heroic Japanese soldiers who are fighting for homeland. All nations in hate for Nippon. Very jealous. So thusly, Americans drop atomic bombs. And thusly, everybody going hungry."

"I'm sorry for the hunger," Hank said quietly. "You've got the rest wrong."

"The rest of course you say, is how American propaganda! Of course. And more lately, Japanese people building ships to catch fish so not going hungry. But Americans say go home, there is fish we do not want, do not catch, but Japanese must not have fish because we are in hate for Nippon."

"Oh, bullshit! What screwed-up history do they teach you people?" Hank caught himself and softened his tone. "Come on, Kodama. Mr. Kodama. Where to start?" He summarized Japanese 1940s aggression with a veneer of diplomacy (certainly compared to how Jones Henry would have snapped it!).

Kodama interrupted angrily. "Japanese trying to liberate all Asia from greedy colonial nations of America and Europe. Then atomic bomb. This is truth and history, Mr. Carford. Nippon is great Bushido people. Other nations jer'us."

"Other nations what?"

"Jer'us! Jer'us!"

"Oh. Jealous." Hank shook his head. "Come on, Kodama-san. You really believe that?"

"Of course." Suddenly it was a snarl.

Hank studied splats and snakes of rain on the windows. Go on with this? No purpose unless the guy cooled enough to listen. They'd be rid of each other in a few days. Without further comment he returned outside and dressed for deck.

When the first tow came aboard he helped strap in the net and pull it bulging with fish and shrimp beyond the rail. Good feel, the dripping bag's heft, even the slime globs. Better yet, when his long-faced friend pulled the cord that opened the money bag, was the mass of sea creatures that gushed around their legs.

The haul had targeted shrimp. Fish bycatch included the thick, flat, black-striped ishidai they had eaten raw, and a rounded red-snapper type. Pink squids wrapped their tentacles around the web and needed to be pried loose. (Squids had personality. Hank shut his mind to it.)

The pace now went steadily since, after they set the trawl again, there was catch to be sorted and iced. Hank entered the work pattern step by step. Soon he knew their names. Junzo, the long face, coached him on the Japanese words for the varieties of fish. Round Hajime showed him how to distinguish two nearly identical fish he'd never seen in American waters. Words and instructions became their game. The net was *teichi-ami,* sometimes just *ami.* The boat was *gyosen* and they were *gyomin.* When he mispronounced, they chuckled, but their biggest laughs came from mouthing American words themselves. Hank invented "lovely little highliner" for the boat itself, to play with the l's. The effort that produced "ruvrey ritter highriner" sent Haji-san rolling on the deck.

The sea, not cold by Alaskan standards, still chilled Hank as hours passed. Thermals had not been part of his travel pack, nor gloves, and he missed them. Sorting fish and strapping a net lacked the action of working seines or crab pots. He glanced at the wheelhouse. Kodama watched, but turned away at his look. Warm up there. The day would end eventually. When it came time to ice the shrimp he followed into the dank hold despite their polite objections, and grabbed one of the three shovels before someone else could take it. Shoveling ice restored his heat.

At last there came a break and everyone went inside. Up in the wheelhouse Kodama's set face watched Hank follow the others. They hung rubber jackets outside but, with another tow coming soon, merely peeled pants to their boots as they bunched around the stove. The man who served as cook brought out a panful of squids he had gathered from the nets. The creatures' tentacles moved as they crackled on the grill. Still alive! Hank held back at first, then shrugged and, following the others' example, picked them off with chopsticks. Chewy and sweet when picked off at once, charred and crisp when left over the coals for a while.

Junzo showed Hank photos of his family. Hank passed around photos of Jody and the children. Hajimi in turn displayed his naked pinups. They had started another round of "ruvrey ritter highriner" with high-pitched laughs when Kodama appeared. He watched with a puzzled scowl, regarded sideways by Hank but ignored by the others.

At length Kodama cleared his throat to attract attention. "Mr. Carford, you are having good time?"

"Very good time, K-san."

"Yes, I think it. You are having good time. I will therefore stay and make you translations."

Hank glanced at the intrusively authoritative face. The man would change everything. "Thanks, Mr. Kodama. But not necessary."

"Ah."

Hajime pushed the last squid on the grill toward Hank and gestured for him to take it. "Ruvrey ritter highriner," he declared, delighted afresh.

Kodama studied Hank. He seemed to struggle with half a smile before he turned abruptly and left. A moment later a bell rang from the bridge to signal haul-in, and everyone scrambled back to deck.

9

BUSHIDO

JAPAN: KUSHIRO AND TOKYO, LATE AUGUST 1982

At last Shoji Tsurifune—Mike to his western contacts and by either name heir apparent to Tsurifune Suisan Fishing Co., Ltd.—arrived back in Tokyo and flew with Hank north to Kushiro to see the ship that the company had prepared for Hank's captaincy.

As he had three months before, Mike alternated between being the structured young Harvard-educated executive, and the bright connoisseur of Japanese pleasures who had insisted last spring on entertaining Hank every night with lavish food and attentive individual waitresses. Hank remembered his occasional unsure laugh, and his sudden quiet in the presence of his father, the director, but otherwise Mike appeared to be a man totally comfortable in his two cultures.

On the plane Mike spoke gaily of his favorite restaurant in Kushiro and the quality there of the serving girls—"You'll see tonight for yourself, Hank-san"—but then snapped arrogantly at the stewardess to remove their lunch trays. He pulled papers from his briefcase. "Specs of your vessel. Study them closely, please," he said, all business. It was a longliner already geared, four years old, 135 feet long, named something-*Maru* but to be repainted with an American name. "Now it's your choice, Hank. Japanese crew to sail her to Kodiak or Seattle discreetly and then flown back, or your own Yanks flown here to take over at once. Naturally, in any case you'll need a Japanese processing master to ensure quality product."

Hank had avoided the thought of foreigners aboard his boat. He'd hoped there would be some way around it when the time came. "I already have capable men, so I don't need a Japanese boss on the payroll. It might cause friction. Believe me, I know how to process fish."

"Nonnegotiable, I'm afraid. Absolutely necessary to have one person aboard knowing Japanese market requirement. Especially the proper way to cut black cod for us, J-cut only, very tricky. Understand, Hank—Japan is the market. We do recognize the difference of personalities, so I'll have you meet four of our processing masters and leave you to pick."

When they reached the Kushiro shipyard, there it stood, scraped and huge on the ways. Hank surveyed it with mixed emotions. It was a ship that would require a large crew, rather than a comfortably sized boat that a handful of men could work as buddies. That would take some adjusting to. But—captain of a ship! He climbed aboard, determined to be positive. It felt wrong, however, the second he entered the housing and bumped his head. The overheads were built for short Japanese. Dream's end. He wanted to sit and cover his face to think.

"Don't let the rust bother you, Hank," said Mike. "She'll shine by the time our people have her reflagged and ready to fish American."

"Won't work. The overheads. We can't run stooped all day. I'd never keep a crew."

"Ai!" Mike's smooth Japanese face lost its composure for an instant, then became impassive again. "Let's consider." He remained quiet until they left the ship. In the car back to town: "Forget fishing vessels for to-night. Serious party with local friends who wish to know you. Men you'll need to do business with. And, of course, girls, like last spring, one that might attract you yet."

Hank remembered the disturbing temptations of the last visit. "Well, Mike . . . food sounds great, but leave off on the pretty hostesses."

"Disappoint local friends? Come on, Hank-san. I've told them you're a tiger."

The toasts were many, as usual. Once he'd decided to let himself go, it was easy to progress with the others from polite good humor to boisterous conviviality. Delicious seafood came in volleys, all of it delicately presented. And despite his protestations, what harm to have his own charming lady ready to refill a sake cup or feed him if he'd let her? He knew now that it had no more expectation than casual male ego stroking. Maybe the

Japan venture wasn't going to work after all, but he might as well enjoy a banquet night. It led to nothing dangerous.

Next morning over abundant coffee at an otherwise Japanese breakfast, Mike said calmly, "I talked to Father. You're right. We must have American headroom, western vessel. It's a shock to us, this idle fleet we'd hoped to use." As offhandedly as he had been ordering breakfast, he added, "Must now seek credit ourselves, buy or build with western headroom."

"You mean the deal's not off?"

"It's sink or survive, Hank."

"I don't have money of my own for this, you know."

"No, no. We shall buy the vessel outright, and then, just as done for vessel *Jody Dawn*, shall assign you fifty-one percent ownership on paper. Formality, as our lawyer explained to you last spring when we assumed your debts. Naturally, vessel *Jody Dawn* remains Tsurifune property for security, as does your house, until debt is paid."

Hank's mouth tightened but he nodded. Whenever the terms were stated it chilled him as if they'd been spoken for the first time, even though he'd agreed and signed.

"This is only business, Hank. Mere formality among friends, I assure you. Soon you will earn such money aboard the new longline vessel that you'll pay off all obligation, also own new vessel, and be rich. And will happily continue by contract for six more years to deliver exclusively to Tsurifune. But, ha-ha, we hope of course deliver for longer among grateful friends."

Hank nodded again.

He met two processing masters from Tsurifune ships. Both tried hard to please him, and they probably needed the job, but he felt comfortable with neither. Once committed, they'd be hard to send back. He knew that it was a position of authority on Japanese ships, one that could rival his own if accepted in the Japanese pattern. Not going to be that way. Two other candidates remained to be interviewed in Tokyo.

During the flight back to Tokyo, Hank wore jeans to save the suit he had brought, but Mike—Shoji Tsurifune, heir to a distinguished fishing company—was crisp in a dark suit and tie. Mike's conversation shunted with ease between chatty informality and blunt business. He talked of a forthcoming tennis tournament and his own chances for the trophy, then of his undergraduate days at Harvard. "Miss it, Hank. Miss Cambridge and all the fellows. Part of me, you see, has adjusted American." Then, all business: "By the way, the director expects you for lunch tomorrow in his office. A driver will pick you up at twelve fifteen from wherever you are. I believe we have you interviewing processing masters. You know, you made more impression on Father last spring than most who meet him these days."

"I like your dad. Glad he's still friendly after what I told him during that long meeting with interpreters. John Gains figured it was the end between us."

"John Gains? The fellow kisses ass, as you'd say. He's useful to us and efficient, thus he has future here so long as . . . But we don't take John to special places. Oh, yes. Remembered well, how you tried to give the director Japanese guilt for the war. Told Father perhaps he'd be in prison except for merciful American conquerors. Ho ho. Nobody had ever dared to say that before. It gave the rest of us breathless moments until Father decided to laugh. I suppose we had been pushing you for a while over wicked Americans now taking our fish."

"Four long goddamned hours at least."

"But Father laughed! He liked your straightforwardness. Between us, Hank, in reality, we've wondered why America has taken so long to claim possession of fish off your coasts."

"If you and the Russians hadn't been so greedy with your hundreds of boats fishing straight over American gear, including mine, you'd probably still be there pulling your share of crabs and pollack."

"Oh my, say *that* next to my poor pater. And you'd get away with it! You remind him, he tells me, of the vigor in his valued American abstract expressionists."

Hank was glad to change the subject. "Those paintings your dad showed me. Do you really think they're good? I don't understand 'em, so I'll lay off if you do. No offense."

Mike leaned forward, his eyes suddenly merry. "They're quite valuable, Hank."

"Come on. It looks like you could just flip paint around on a brush and do the same. And get the price of a good boat for it, that's what bugs me."

"Then go flipping and astonish us all!" Mike settled back and rolled his martini like an old brandy. "Boats wear old, you see, while abstract expressionists are rising in world price slowly. Little bit higher now than just last May. You'd be wise to understand and start buying while they still cost just a little boat. Other Japanese now pay price of a ship for Van Gogh's

Sunflowers, while Father looks ahead with his Rothko and Pollock bought now for mere thousands instead of future millions."

"Crazy."

Mike shifted in his seat to make sure he had Hank's attention. "Good luck that Dad loves his paintings since so much is invested." His tone lost its easy bounce although he kept it casual. "Bad luck, of course, if he ever needs to say good-bye and sell. Many fishermen and fish-factory workers now unemployed. We need raw product to keep our vessels going."

They're running scared! Hank realized. It hadn't occurred to him before.

Back in Tokyo the two other potential processing masters proved as troublesome to Hank as the first ones. They all were committed company men, probably ready, if things weren't going Japanese enough, to overbear and complain, even tattle back home. He'd seen it happen in Bristol Bay on the Japan-funded processors. And what if they *were* running scared?

Hank expected the meeting with the old man—Director Kiyoshi Tsuri-fune himself—to be a resumption of the grind over the American draw-down of fish quotas to the Japanese, and he'd steadied himself to fend off accusations without losing his temper as before. Instead, the meeting was informal to the point of friendliness. Hank had thought ahead despite having been summoned to Japan on short notice, and had bought the best Kodiak souvenir cup he could find. He presented it with, "Nothing much, sir." Nothing much indeed, compared to some of the other gifts in the glass case he'd remembered, but the director placed it ceremoniously among fans, dolls, and other cups from American senators and admirals.

The senior Tsurifune's smile stretched over his teeth. Short and wiry, with tight yellowing skin over a shiny bald head, he still moved erect although he was in his seventies. He reached a hand up to grip Hank's shoulder and led him through the door cut in the office paneling, into the private gallery. When Hank had seen the gallery back in May, it had been brightly illuminated, and some two dozen modern paintings had lined the walls. Now, in subdued light, there were only seven or eight. Each had a ceiling beam directed on it.

"As you see, Mr. Crawford, new Jasper Johns on that wall, purchased since you came before. The perfectly nice Sam Francis and other small good artists now removed to back room, so that here we have only most famous Americans, Jackson Pollock, Mark Rothko, and Jasper Johns. You are continued amazed I am sure, to find such distinguished collection in the office of Japanese fishing company."

"Amazed as ever, sir." And impressed, as before, by the director's ease with English even though, months before during official meetings, he had spoken only in Japanese through an interpreter and pretended to understand nothing in English.

After they had stopped by each painting in turn, Mr. T (as Hank had begun to term the director affectionately to himself) placed a firm hand on his shoulder again to guide him back to the office. "Now, Mr. Crawford. Before eating must please tell me of American events and your impressions. The aggressive Mr. Alexander Haig of State Department. Is it true that President Ronald Reagan now decides nothing without him? And there are reports of building an American vessel with American crew for catching and processing groundfish in the Bering Sea. I am told ship is called Golden . . . Golden what? Now please tell me how this can succeed. Very, very risky for investors. I wish you to please warn Mr. Haig, that American fishermen too restless to stay long months at sea on catcher processor vessel. This is work where Japanese fishermen are very good and very successful, please speak him seriously."

Hank glanced around. In a sunny adjacent room, bare except for tatami mats and a polished table inches from the floor, women were arranging lacquered dishes. It was going to be a long meal, and with not even Mike to help absorb conversation. Maybe he could divert back to the big messy paintings and ask questions. At least then he could merely listen.

But the director eased off himself when they settled cross-legged at the table, facing each other across dishes of prawns and sea urchins arranged with delicate flowers. His conversation centered on American museums and American baseball. Hank held his own on the latter subject, and at least remembered enough from school trips back home to mention a painting of worn work shoes by Van Gogh at the Baltimore Art Museum, and of the battle scenes on a Roman sarcophagus in the Walters Art Gallery.

"I have not seen these," mused Mr. T, impressed. "And so close to Washington, D.C., where I have visited influential senators. You go often to see the famous Old Shoes?"

"My parents live in Baltimore. That's where I grew up and went to college." Hank did not bother to admit that visits back home never included museum trips.

Mike arrived to take charge of Hank once again. It was agreed that, after several scheduled meetings and a trip to Kawasaki shipyards to look at vessels that might have American headroom, Hank would return to the States until a new longliner had been found.

Mike addressed his father in Japanese, using a deferential tone Hank had not heard him use with others, then turned to Hank, smiling. "No banquet tonight, Hank. Business business. However, Father has instructed since he remembers your strange fascination with Kabuki drama." He produced a ticket. "Good time for you. First-class seat for Kabuki. Starting four in afternoon the writing says—I don't attend these things, but so it says here—so you'd better hurry."

"But I don't . . ." Hank started, then checked himself. No way to explain that a woman might be there he didn't want to meet, didn't want even to be seen with. He accepted the ticket and made a courtesy bow to the director. "Really nice of you, sir. Thanks." What indeed were the chances in a whole theater crowd of encountering a single person?

An hour later he approached the fluted entrance to Kabuki-Za with a stirring of pleasure. Several women in the busy lobby wore the traditional kimono and obi; the place was like Japan in books. For a man who seldom went even to a movie unless it was John Wayne or if Jody wanted to, he'd been sucked in by the wildness of this Japanese theater. The color, yes. And it reminded him, maybe, of wind and weather with its long calms broken by violence. Helene had taken him to Kabuki-Za for the first time after they'd met by chance at that yakitori café, but it no longer needed to be tied to her . . . apple perfume. He joined the Japanese bustle, holding his ticket in anticipation.

"Well, I declare. It's Cousin Herbert back in town, great shaggy-dog beard and all!"

And there stood Helene Foster, the woman who had almost cost him his marriage. She was as lively and feminine as ever, in a crisp outfit with a signature scarf over her shoulder. "Well . . . hi," he said. "Uh, nice to see you."

"And you, and you." They shook hands. "My goodness gracious. You're back."

She waited, expectant but at ease. And at once playing the little country-cousin game they'd invented, which inevitably had led them twice to bed. He needed to keep it sober. "You're still here studying Kabuki, I guess," he ventured.

"Generous Fulbright, yes indeed."

"That's . . . great."

"But not many big fishermen come through, and Japanese men aren't exactly . . . One does get homesick for you woolly bears." Her face had all the lights and expressions he'd remembered, so that anything she said sounded amusing and agreeable. "My, isn't it hot! You're lucky Kabuki's running this week with special performances. A traveling company. They're normally closed all summer, you know."

"Well. Lucky!" He looked around. Fortunately, people were hurrying toward the auditorium. He held up his ticket. "I'm really snowed with business this trip. Meetings day and night. Didn't plan to visit Kabuki here, but friends bought me this as a gift. Bad Japanese manners to refuse."

Her eyes rested merrily on his face. "Certainly not. It would have been impolite."

"Well . . . Guess I'd better find my seat. It's sure nice to see you again."

"Sure nice." She flashed her saucy smile. Was she making fun of his discomfort? (He had firmly broken off with her back then.) And did he now detect that light, applelike scent that had somehow turned him on, or was his imagination doing tricks? She held out her hand, and said evenly, "So good to see you again, Cousin Herbert. Good-bye."

The finality of it relaxed him enough to reply with the play name he'd given her. "Me too, Daisy Mae. You take care."

She squeezed his hand spontaneously. "You remembered! I do declare!" Instead of parting she took his arm. "Just for that, Cousin Herbert, you can walk me to my seat so the folks who see me here all the time will know I have connections."

Nothing but to go with it. "Sure. Glad to." He began to construct the details of a fish conference that would force him to leave at first intermission.

She examined his ticket and exclaimed, "My stars! Your friends are some influential. It's a house seat just like mine." Indeed, he was located directly behind her.

The performance began with all the elements of Kabuki he'd liked. Snarling warriors stomped down a ramp waving swords, their elaborate costumes swaying with each violent movement. The actors' faces, painted in garishly colored lines, contorted with expressions larger than life, while their voices lept from gravelly growls to high-pitched whines. But he enjoyed little of it.

There she was in his vision coolly inescapable, wearing indeed that aphrodisiac perfume that wafted back. The easy scarf in silhouette would be

carrying the odor same as her hair. He couldn't help reacting. And thinking. If he'd been free as in old fisherman days there'd be no question. For
that matter, as he considered, not one of the fisheries people who might
recognize him would be attending an afternoon performance on an office
day. No one would see, no one need know. She was so quick and vivacious.
Lively in bed. Fun. Such a light touch. None of . . . other women's seriousness—party-dampening seriousness at times. The perfume brought it
all back so potently that he needed to keep shifting in his seat.

The performance droned on. An interminable scene with two players
seated, immobile, singsonging at each other, ended at last, but not before
he wondered what the hell he'd ever seen in this stuff. At last the lights
came up for an intermission. Helene rose and faced him.

He stood with resolve and stretched. "Hey, let me buy you a drink, or
ice cream, or something."

"Lovely!"

Her arm brushed his as they walked up the crowded aisle. Outside the
auditorium a gallery of kiosks offered everything from sake to sushi to
souvenir dolls. Hank waved his arm. "Take your pick."

"I think a drink would be nice."

They clinked whiskeys and sipped. She smiled. "This is nice, Hank."

"Nice seeing you again, Helene."

"Dare I hope this is a new start?"

He allowed his sight to travel over her face and trim body once more.
"No. A second good-bye. After we've toasted I'm leaving."

She took it as gracefully as he'd hoped she would. "I like you, Hank.
Good luck."

"I like you too, Helene."

As once before, she took his face in her hands to turn it to her. He closed his eyes. Her perfume seemed overpowering. "All the woolly bears,"
she murmured. "They do climb that male tree and pull up the ladder,
don't they?"

"Seems so, Helene." He touched her cheek. "Guess it's good-bye now."

"'Bye, Hank." He started to say he was sorry, but she kissed him lightly,
and walked away. It left him free to watch her. She had style. He hurried
from the theater.

On the afternoon following his lunch with the director, Hank called
on the fishery agency. He now moved there as a creature of importance.

Principal supervisors—their level apparent by the isolation of their desks from others crowded together—came to shake his hand (their own hands all limp). Lesser employees who had been friendly during meetings in the spring looked up bashfully and leapt to their feet when Hank came over. Hayashi, now a low-level supervisor, who months before on the road had become "Yashi-san," greeted him with careful reserve from his desk at the head of a long table. Kodama alone, seated at the table below Hayashi where he worked elbow to elbow among others, nodded vigorously with the trace of a smile.

Hank had spent a restless night with his body awake from the Helene encounter. He craved exercise to keep his mind on Jody. After he had conducted his business with an official three desks higher than Hayashi, he approached Kodama. "Do you run after work? I'll join you."

"Only in morning, of course."

"Good. What time and where?"

"No. Two hours away, doing before train to office."

"You commute that far?"

"Of course. All here coming train. Having family apartment in Tokyo impossible for mere office worker."

"Too bad. I need the exercise."

Twitch of the mouth, Kodama's ultimate expression of humor. "I go to Kodo-kan after office. You do judo?"

"Sure! I mean, wouldn't mind learning."

"Ha. Years of discipline." He appraised Hank. "You come, I shall introduce."

"Done."

"It shall make you very fatigue."

"Good!"

"Maybe . . . painful." Kodama gestured at his leg, then his back.

"Okay. Today?"

They reached the establishment called Kodo-kan by subway, packed like fish in a net. It was a large building with the statue of its founder outside. "Jigoro Kano," said Kodama, bowing low to the figure. "Other Bushido is very ancient. However, judo started hundred years ago, only." Inside they climbed to a balcony. Below in a wide gymnasium, pairs of men in loose pajamalike garments fiercely tumbled each other. Their shouts echoed. Hank had seen Bruce Lee movies of fantasy violence, but here it was real. "You do that?"

"Of course."

Hank felt an uneasy thrill. "You're taking me out there?"

"*No,* of course. Small room, thick mat, for beginner."

Kodama tossed Hank an extra roll of the rough pants and shirt from his locker. "*Ghee,* first judo word." In the exercise room he started Hank with slow stretches, but soon was barking him into trots and push-ups. Sweat blurred Hank's eyes. Kodama did it fiercely, with zest.

"Now you will practice fall. Quick lesson only. Do more today than sensible, but, however, since only today you come." He showed Hank how to roll to the mat in a ball bracing himself with a curved, supple arm—over and over as Hank panted, wished for a break.

A man looked through the doorway and Kodama called him in. "My partner sometimes." They spoke in Japanese. When Hank paused to listen Kodama barked: "Go! Go! Thirty more push-up, go!" Hank heard their low laughs as he obeyed.

"Okay, you rest," commanded Kodama offhandedly, at last. With a sigh Hank started to lie back. "Up! Up!"

Hank watched Kodama and his partner exchange curt bows, then circle snarling as they grabbed for each other. Sudden grip and shout from one, hard thud to the mat for the other. Like lions in their intensity but over and over, like business. When the partners separated, they bowed cheerfully.

Kodama summoned Hank. "You wish now attack, Mr. Carford?"

Hank knew the outcome, but: "Sure!"

The mat was mercifully soft, but the throw was hard enough that Hank felt the floor beneath. He rose and attacked again. Floor harder. He made himself rise again.

Kodama stopped him with outthrust palm. "Now demonstrating one throw, given only to Japanese beginner after month, two month." He placed Hank's grip on the shoulder of his own ghee and Hank's leg behind his own ankle, coached a circular sweep of the arm, and allowed himself to be thrown to the mat. The mechanics had amazing logic.

Hank was exhausted and beginning to hurt, but said, "Okay, now I'll attack you again!"

"No. Finished." Kodama directed him to exchange bows. And, unexpected from Kodama, grins.

The aches began in earnest before Hank's cab reached the hotel. They increased until he felt he'd discovered all the wires that held his body together. A hot soak helped. He phoned Mike and for once feigned illness to cancel a night at the microphones of a karaoke bar. Instead, he took a quiet stroll (more like a limp!) past the Ginza, walking several blocks out of the way to avoid Kabuki-Za. In May the air had been pleasant, but now it was steamy.

Next morning he felt like the rusted Tin Man until another hot soak eased his joints. He met with company lawyers through lunch, then with company accountants. In late afternoon he quietly left a conference to phone Kodama at the fishery agency. "Judo again tonight, Kodama-san?"

"Ha. Not cripple? You wish again?"

"I'm leaving soon. Learn while I can."

"Ha. Tonight I had expected with family. Okay. Judo."

Hank made excuses to Mike. "Rappongi's really nice. But I need to think about what your accountants told me."

"Some tiger!"

Kodama allowed him no more ease than the day before. As Hank panted and sweated, judo seemed more the essence of Japan than anything else he'd encountered: his personal Kabuki. When they finished, the ultimate compliment: "Too bad you go home, Mr. Carford." Hank persuaded Kodama to join him for dinner. They ate at an inexpensive place that displayed plastic replicas of the dishes served inside.

"When you were a far-seas fisherman, Kodama-san, did you work on longliners?"

"Hai. Longliner." (He pronounced it "rong-riner.") "Gulf Alaska. Six years. Before Americans drove away." He made the statement now as matter-of-fact, without the earlier anger. Hank asked him questions about gear and fish preparation. He answered knowledgeably, with curt authority.

An idea began to grow. Next day Hank asked Mike Tsurifune if he knew Kodama's qualifications as a fisherman. "Just thinking out loud. If I must have a Japanese aboard to ensure Japan quality, what of Mr. Kodama?"

"No, no. He's not our company man, merely a fisheries employee."

"Then hire him. We work well together."

"We have many of our own."

The more Hank thought of it, the firmer he became. At length Mike sighed. "I'll inquire about his qualifications."

Next day Mike declared, "Very well, Hank. My source informs that this Kodama was a longline master during his final years of fishing. He came home only because a single-ship company owned the vessel." Mike raised his eyebrows and pursed his mouth significantly. "Loss of Alaska quota made the company bankrupt. The vessel delivered sablefish in good quality, however. So, very well—Kodama, if you wish."

Hank considered it all day. Could Kodama answer to him as captain, or had his own judo submission to Kodama imprinted a different relationship? It was Friday, with departure home booked for Sunday, following a final Saturday night banquet. "Dinner now, Kodama-san?"

"No." It was positive. "Tonight with family. I must good-bye until you come again." Hank had seen photos of a respectful wife and three smiling children, reluctantly produced at Hank's urging when they had toured.

"Can I visit you tomorrow?"

"Fishery office closed."

"I mean at your home."

Wary unease. "Home very . . . not special."

"You said two hours' train from Tokyo. Tell me which train to take. I invite you and your family to lunch near your home."

Head to side, eyes narrowed, mouth twitching. "Home very not special." Hank assured him it didn't matter. "Then, therefore . . ."

Next morning, on his own, Hank found helpful train officials who nodded at the Japanese characters of Kodama's instructions and passed him person by person to the correct platform. En route to the station he bought some little dolls with round wooden faces and a paper bird on a stick, the only things other than food packages at an open stall. The ride took him through accumulations of ugly concrete structures with virtually no countryside between.

Kodama waited at the stop, stiffly. He was not wearing office clothes, but his pants and open shirt were crisp.

The Kodamas lived on the seventh floor of a concrete apartment building. Kodama strode past the elevator and led the way up the stairs two at a time. At the fifth landing Hank laughed and slowed. Kodama returned, grinning, to urge him on, and for the first time called him "Carford-san" rather than "Mister."

Waiting at the apartment door was his wife in modified traditional dress. When introduced she bowed, holding a hand close to her mouth. Behind her stood two bashful but curious boys and a very bashful girl, all dressed for show. Hank realized he'd put them to trouble. More so when it became clear that he was not taking them to lunch but being served. The foolish gifts, gratefully received, were embarrassing compensation.

He and Kodama faced each other cross-legged around a low table while the wife brought plates of sushi and dips. Occasional titters came from the children, who watched by the edge of a screen. "Eh!" commanded Kodama to the oldest boy, about ten, and gestured him over. The child, straight and grave, came at once. Kodama put an arm around his legs and introduced him. Low bow. Next came the girl, reluctantly, then the younger boy with a bounce. In the dimness of an inner room stood an old woman in traditional dress. When Hank noticed her, she bowed low.

Hank's negotiation, when it came, went swiftly. "Do you like working in the Tokyo office, Kodama-san?"

"Pshh!"

"Rather be a fisherman?"

"Of course. When I am a fisherman, all live in house in village—wife, mother, children. Now . . ." He flicked his hand toward a window that opened to concrete structures. "But I am lucky. Many from the boats that America makes go home must now do like pulling cart in the market."

"I guess I'm lucky too. Do you know that I'm to be captain of a long-liner?"

"Of course."

"Would you consider coming to be . . . sort of my mate in charge of the factory?"

It did surprise Kodama. For a moment his face actually softened. Then the eyes flashed. "Of course!"

"You understand that I'm the boss. Captain on an American boat is the boss."

"Yes, Mr. Carford."

That evening, as he had the previous spring, Director Tsurifune himself attended the farewell banquet. He and Hank sat in double seats of honor and filled each other's sake cups. As before, a company photographer snapped the two together arm to shoulder while Mike, less easy in his father's presence, stayed discreetly aside.

During the long flight home across the Pacific, Hank's head ached from the toasts while his body hurt from the judo. They were realities of what otherwise still seemed a dream. Some of the dream he'd finished. What of it lay ahead?

10

THE SUITS

KODIAK AND ANCHORAGE, LATE AUGUST 1982

Within the cycles of nature, the seasonal runs of pink/humpie salmon around Kodiak Island reach a climax every mid-August. By then most of the red/sockeye salmon have completed their similar natural instructions. Both species (like all Pacific salmons) must swim in from the ocean where they have matured in order to spawn in their birth streams. They run a predator gauntlet, including fishermen and hungry bears. The survivors lay fertilized eggs in the gravel, then die. Water and land creatures then feed on their carcasses and fulfill different cycles.

By mid-August around Kodiak, others of the five Pacific salmons native to North America begin to appear in force to mix with pinks: first the larger chum/dogs and then the coho/silvers. A fisherman needs more and more of an eye to sort them since, say, chums bring a better price than pinks and cohos more than chums. By September the local runs usually diminish to spotty appearances that also include a few of the grand king/chinooks. Other parts of Alaska see salmon runs in different distributions.

The natural patterns repeat year after year with abundance or scarcity dictated by the health of the year-classes and the condition of the waters that sustain them. In the human pattern, at least in Alaska, state biologists count the migrating salmons as best they can and regulate in favor of the fish, to ensure that enough escape the gauntlet to breed future generations before man competes for the rest.

For Captain Jody of the *Adele H* and for other seiner skippers working
the Kodiak bays, the movements of salmon led fishermen around the
island and that was all that mattered. From Uganik Bay on the western
side Jody followed the drift of the fleet south to Uyak Bay, then down past
Karluk (once the site of the world's largest sockeye runs but overfished to
depletion by the early 1900s, before state controls) to Alitak and Dead-
man Bay, then around up the east side into Kiliuda Bay and back to the
town itself. In the process Jody turned alert as never before when someone
else held command.

Terry, as Jody's deck boss, grew in stature with the responsibility. Big,
obedient Ham remained Terry's right hand so long as he received directions. Together they kept the two greenhorn crewmen from snagging the
gear or hurting themselves, barked them, in fact, into being useful.

As for competition with the *Hinda Bee,* Gus Rosvic's men now had new
bets with Jody's crew, although on a more modest scale—and sometimes
more exotic. One bet hinged merely on the capture of the season's first
salmon over twenty pounds, with a buck a pound at stake. The two boats
sometimes shared the same grounds. They did so less and less after skipper
Gus decided that the woman wasn't going to sink the boat of his former
buddy and wouldn't need his rescue. (Not that he condoned a female's
presence in the wheelhouse any more than before.) When the two boats
fished within sight of each other, both crews remembered their wager and
noisily worked nets as hard as they could, shouting appropriate insults
across the water—even the greenhorns who had no stake in the settlement
but had caught the spirit. When the boats were separated, Jody and her
men often forgot the wagers in the drive to capture fish.

When Hank returned from Japan, Adele and the children met him at
the airport. He looked around while holding Pete and hugging Dawn and
Henny, glad for them but restless for Jody.

"Out fishing, of course, and doing quite well I'd say, from all reports,"
declared Adele. "I can't believe how it's turning out. Now Hank, get your
bags, we do expect to have dinner at six to keep the children on schedule,
and the plane from Anchorage has already come in late."

"Thought I'd take you all to dinner tonight, after I've showered."

"With a roast in the oven? Hurry, children."

He talked to Jody by radio. Indeed she sounded happy and vigorous.
Glad he was home safe, but: "Ham's bringing in the skiff, I just waved

him in, talk to you later. Hank, you wouldn't believe the fish! We're practically roundhauling in a patch all to ourselves so I have to pay attention. I miss you too, dear, but . . ." Suddenly her voice raised and sharpened. "Joel! Get your ass moving there, plunge! Don't you goddamn see those fish slipping out?" Back in regular voice: "Damn dreamer kid, you were right, never should have hired him. Got to go, Hank.'Bye."

She didn't even ask for advice. Settled in, with tongue turned salty as any skipper on the fish. Out there doing what he wanted to do, and he the expert.

Next day he took over the children, hearing first a lecture from Adele on food they should eat and books they should be reading. "And make sure you give them little jobs, it builds character. And be sure they wear socks and that their shoes don't get wet. Make them change underclothes at least every second day." She handed him a bag of clean clothes. "After a while you'll need to start washing them yourself. Leave time for them to dry if you wash way out in the country instead of in town at a laundromat. Children can catch cold in damp underwear. Men don't understand these things. And, now, let me see . . ." She handed him a list.

The house echoed bleak without Jody, lonesome even when Pete crawled over him or when Dawn noisily made them all Jell-O. He read to them but nobody really paid attention. They picked at meals from cans. There was always plenty of repair or construction waiting around the house that he'd half built himself, and dead trees to cut for firewood. Henny waited by tools since it was his job to hand them to his dad, but Hank had no urge for hammer or saw. Even the view of town lights over the water from the picture window had lost its pleasure, as had drinking a scotch in the armchair by the window after the children were asleep. All of it lacked the seasoning of Jody's presence. Instead of the solitude he treasured by living an hour's drive from town, he wanted friends—Jody more than any—to talk out his feared growing dependence on the Japanese—or to talk over it.

"Daddy, when are we going to town?" demanded Dawn. Younger than her brother but by nature the forward one, she stood in front of Henny and Pete and presumably spoke for them all. "Melissa, my very best friend in all the world, is in town. And poor little Petey misses Aunt Adele, and Henny . . ."

"I like it here with you, Dad," said Henny, trying to make his voice deep.

"Well, you can just say that," snapped Dawn. "But you know you miss all kinds of things we have at Auntie Adele's. We didn't even bring ice cream."

Adele over the phone laughed, but to Hank it wasn't nice. "I could have told you. Of course, come back if you don't mind sleeping on the sofa. I have the children so packed into their own little rooms that it would be cruel to move them."

Hank instead slept aboard his *Jody Dawn*, now back in the water at the shipyard awaiting orders. His men had flown home in his absence, Seth to California and Mo to the Midwest. Neither seemed refreshed by the experience. Both had returned to Kodiak sooner than planned.

Seth had encountered the Marion he'd almost married, and she appeared to be the better without him, even cheerful. There she was wheeling a grocery cart with one child in the basket straddling juice cartons and a smaller one in the seat waving its little arms. Hell of a lot prettier woman three years ago, he consoled himself. Now she had messy hair. And weight. He wouldn't have minded holding the kids, but she didn't offer.

Mo's mom and sisters let no hour go by without some hint that he ought to call up Alice, who still wasn't married either, or how sad it was for a man already twenty-seven not to have a family. Although he pitched in, both his younger brother (maybe stuck at home because he'd left) and his dad, implied that he'd deserted responsibility for the easy life. "Catching things that don't need to be plowed, planted, or mucked," his father put it. "You know Sundays right here at the pond, you can catch all the fish you want. After milking and church and dinner. All afternoon to your heart's content."

They reunited over fried halibut at Solly's that evening. The place was nearly deserted. "Everybody's off fishing somewhere but us," muttered Seth. "So the Japs treated you nice as usual. The *Jody Dawn*'s good in the water again, but nothing's happening. When do we fish?"

Hank explained the change of plans and the forthcoming new ship specifically adapted for longlining. "My contract with the Japanese saves the *Jody Dawn* as long as we can keep her productive." He gulped beer without savor. "You guys have an option. As long as I can keep the *Jody Dawn*, you run her if that's your choice. Seth stays skipper, you've got her all to yourselves. There are possibilities. They say there's still king crab around Adak."

"Weather there's even more shitty than the Bering," said Seth. "Not that it matters."

"Or, maybe . . ." At his tone both Seth and Mo frowned, and listened. "Or . . . I could bring in somebody else to run the *Jody Dawn*—Tolly Smith's without a boat just now—and we'll hang together on this new longliner. New kind of fishing. Different for any of us. Bigger crew." Mo groaned. "Seth as mate. Then you, Mo, and Terry after Jody's salmon ends, as deck bosses spelling each other, two shifts clockaround." Hank decided to make it a challenge. "That is, assuming everybody can learn the gear."

"Since when can't we learn new gear?" snapped Seth. It brought him to life. "And since when have you and me been separate?"

"Yeah, Boss," echoed Mo. "But I don't know about in charge of crew. You just let me work under Seth like before."

"We'll figure something." At last he could drain his glass and enjoy it. They were with him. He waved for another round. Next hurdle: "A catcher-freezer ship's a different game. The processing line's separate. I . . . have a Japanese who's going to be boss there. His name's Kodama, and he might be scratchy. But what he says below decks goes. You've got to know that. Topside, of course, Seth's in authority. But you'll be sharing some apes be-tween deck and factory depending on workload. You'll have to get along."

In the silence John Lennon and Yoko Ono sang from the jukebox. "What are you doing to us, Hank?" said Seth softly. "A Jap?"

Hurdle passed. No fury. "Kodama's our kind. You'll see."

But Seth looked away. His face was no longer the boyish open one of a dozen years before, when he and Hank had buddied and crewed together. Scratchy as Kodama, each with hang-ups. What have I bought for myself? Hank wondered. And, worse than crew disruption, what of this new long-line regimen with factory at sea? He'd never done it himself at any level, and now to be in charge?

They slathered tartar sauce across the halibut steaks and ate in glum silence.

The bartender called Hank to the phone. It was Jody from Alitak on the south end of Kodiak Island. Her voice was brisk and concise. "Adele guessed you'd be there. Boozing it up? Now listen. We just brought in a good load, waiting to deliver. A few days' closure coming up. Leaving Terry and Ham to mind the boat. I'll fly in tomorrow morning."

"Hey. No. Send home Terry and Ham. I'll fly down there instead. Then it'll be just you and me."

"You're forgetting our children. I miss *them* too." Her voice lightened. "But if you pick me up at the airport all by yourself . . . No need to tell anybody for a few hours."

"I'll be there!"

Hank had barely returned to the table when the bartender called him again. It was John Gains at the cannery, his asshole manner as perfunctory as usual. "Why does it always take a day to find you? Now there's no time. Pack your bags tonight. Black cod quotas suddenly coming to a head at the North Pacific Fishery Management Council in Anchorage. Shoji Tsurifune's flying in. Pack for several days. We might need to go on to D.C. Our driver can pick you up tomorrow morning at nine fifteen if you don't want to park at the airport."

"Can't do it, John. Made other commitments. Since you seem to be talking to Tsurifune, tell him sorry and wish him luck."

"I don't think you understand your commitments."

"They bought my boat, not me."

"Shoji wants you there. You'd better read the contracts you've signed."

In the end, controlling anger as best he could, Hank stood in the airport next morning dressed in a suit, able to see the arriving Jody only minutes before his own plane took off. He watched her bounce from the small plane, the image of her old self, hair tied back in a ponytail, wool shirttails flapping against jeans, and ran to greet her as she sashayed across the tarmac.

Her arms went around him, and they held each other. She smelled of fish and other boat odors with barely a scent left of Jody herself, but still he was stimulated at once.

"Hank wearing a suit? Who's died?"

He explained. She turned indignant at his giving in, until she saw his own frustration.

"But, now," he said. "This flight to Anchorage is full, I checked. But I've got you reserved on the afternoon one."

She laughed. "My God you men. I'm filthy, I'll need ten hot baths and all kinds of laundry before I'd feel right for the city. And, I haven't seen our children in two weeks." John called urgently to board the Anchorage plane. She kissed him again. "I'll come tomorrow."

Hank hurried off in better spirits knowing he'd hold her soon again. It was a blue-sky day for the flight up Cook Inlet. Hank could now relax. He spoke more easily than before to John Gains beside him, and watched the water catching sparkles. By the time the plane swept up the tidal mudflats that led to the scatter of high square buildings that was the city, he'd managed to be agreeable.

At the big Anchorage hotel there were the usual serious faces that now peopled Council meetings. Hank had grown to recognize most of them. They bustled between sessions or conferred in knots with their heads bent inward. The men wore suits, the women business costume close to suits. Only a single halibut crew's shoulders bulged from plaid shirts. Standing apart from the rest, short Asians huddled in bunches.

Council meetings had changed greatly in the five years since they had been established under the national act that claimed for Americans the fish within two hundred miles of their coasts. At first, fishermen came in clean boat clothes to state their cases, and the few lawyers and many fishery bureaucrats who listened all tried to dress like fishermen. Now the lawyers had multiplied enough to dominate the scene, so that the bureaucrats dressed like lawyers, and fishermen felt they needed to dress the same to be heard.

The elevator closed to carry Hank and John Gains up to floors with windows overlooking mountains snow streaked even in late August. Before they parted to their separate rooms, Gains reminded him: "We're having lunch with Tsurifune in his suite. You might want to make notes."

"Gotcha," he said in good humor. Play the game today, he'd decided. Then to hell with anything but Jody tomorrow.

At the Tsurifune suite, a Japanese Hank didn't know admitted them. Shoji Tsurifune, impeccably trim, strode over to greet them smoothly. He merely nodded to Gains, but shook Hank's hand. "Glad you could make it," he said, as earnestly as if he himself had not ordered it.

Other Japanese stood around in the room, and hotel employees bustled about, laying platters at a long table. Hank gestured pointedly toward the mountains through a window. "Welcome to *my* country, Michael."

Shoji became for a moment the easy, westernized Mike. "After four years at Harvard I call it second home myself." He reverted to his role as company heir and introduced Hank to several Japanese all in the same dark suits. Hank remembered meeting some of them in Japan. Each man bowed and presented his card. Hank had brought only five, packed in haste. It made for mild apologies and pleasantries. John Gains pressed in to meet them also, but plainly Mike did not give him the same priority as Hank. John held exactly enough cards to exchange. He produced more when others arrived.

Hank drew Mike aside: "We've got to talk about this business of making me—"

"Later, later. Good news. We've found you a ship with western headroom. It arrived in Kushiro two days ago and went straight into shipyard for refit. Talk about it later." Mike eased quickly into a conversation in Japanese.

John Gains came over. "You should be learning some Japanese, more than just the little courtesies. I started by attending classes."

"Impressive, John."

Two senior Japanese arrived with younger ones in tow. All in the room treated them with deference. One was old and paper-frail. The other Hank remembered—oh boy, the thick gruff fellow with the red face, who'd been so insulting in a meeting last May that Hank had been triggered into telling off the assembled group. The guy's thick glasses caught the light. Name? The man greeted him with curt good humor and Hank returned it.

"You remember Mr. Satoh, Hank. Say back konichi-wa and bow a little."

Hank complied. At least John was good for something.

Everything remained informal until a door opened, and in strode Director Kiyoshi Tsurifune. He exchanged bows with the older men, then accepted deeper bows from the others. His look darted, and fixed on Hank. "Ah. Mr. Crawford, famous American fisherman." Apparently he said the same phrase in Japanese since several of the others turned to Hank with new interest.

When the director spoke to his son, Shoji answered in English. "The other American's not here yet, Father. Or the lawyer."

The old man came over, raised his hand to pat Hank's shoulder, and smiled up with a gleam of gold teeth. "You will be astonished, Mr. Crawford. Jasper Johns painting which I bought last May while we talked of fishery, I have just received offer paying ten thousand more. Ten thousand dollar, naturally."

Hank grinned in spite of himself. "Did you take it, sir?"

"Ah, ha-ha, naturally not. Reason one, my private excitement this painting. Reason two, it will become valuable more and more." Another pat on Hank's shoulder, then Mr. T gestured abruptly toward the table and led the way.

Suddenly a familiar voice behind Hank declared, "Hey man, now I'm on the bandwagon too." Hank wheeled to face Tolly Smith. Hank had never seen him in a suit before. He hardly seemed the same man with his hair trimmed, no beard, and a neat sandy mustache. Gold earring gone.

Hank wanted to yell with relief that he wasn't alone, but also to mourn.

"You will sit there, please," said Mike to the Americans, and pointed to the far end of the long table. The director took his place in the center, flanked by the two other seniors. Another American hurried in apologizing: an overweight lawyer named Rider whom Hank had met briefly at other times. A seat had been saved for him among the Japanese. Hank had never liked the man—he seemed arrogant—but he gave him a cool nod that was returned coolly.

For the next half hour, while hotel employees served, the entire conversation flowed in Japanese.

"So, you know the language. What are they saying?" Hank asked John Gains.

"Too fast for me, I admit."

Hank turned his attention to Tolly. "How are you hooked into this?"

"Oh, man. It happened so fast after somebody in Uganik passed the word I was looking. I thought maybe it was you?" Hank shook his head. "Anyhow, they're fitting me out with a limit seiner converted to longline. I'll own fifty-one percent. All I've got to do is deliver black cod to them."

Hank felt a chill. "What security?"

"Nothing as important as having my own boat again, buddy. Life insurance policy. Little house down in Washington that Jennie inherited. Nothing I can't buy back, the way they say black cod's running and the price it gets."

"Shh." John Gains nudged him. Several of the Japanese were frowning in their direction.

The meeting in Japanese had turned energetic. Gruff Satoh's face reddened and he pounded the table to emphasize whatever he said. Several around the table scribbled notes. Most of the food remained untouched.

Shoji Tsurifune began to speak, gripping the papers he held, in a voice that sounded even and reasonable. His father interrupted with a question, then waved him to continue. Satoh muttered and glared, then began to exclaim again.

"Something's sure got 'em pissed," muttered Tolly.

An interpreter had stayed close to the American lawyer's ear, but when the discussion became heated his raised voice allowed Hank and the others to hear occasional phrases: "Japan market control . . . demand that they . . . force them . . . yes, possible . . . greedy . . ." Suddenly Director Tsurifune snapped something and talk stopped. Mike rose at once and ushered the remaining hotel employees from the room. Faces turned toward Hank, Tolly, and Gains. "But they should stay and hear," said Mike in English.

"Stay and listen, *hai,*" said the director. "Go. Proceed." The discussion resumed with audible translation in English.

Mr. Satoh glared toward Hank. The overhead gleam on his thick glasses blanked out his eyes. His voice was gruff, although the translator's voice delivered the words at an incongruously high nervous pitch. "I will repeat what I have said. This sablefish—what you Americans call black cod. It is common knowledge that no American wishes to eat this fish and no American captures it. Exactly why, therefore—?"

Director Tsurifune interrupted calmly in Japanese.

Satoh's tone modified. "I shall explain. Like in case, when my company first caught king crabs in Bering Sea and no American cared. Then all at once, Americans saw our success and expensive market for king crabs. Thus, Americans forced us to stop capture of king crab because they wish to take it all. Here is history. Then it was that my company, visiting Sitka after king crab was lost to us, have discovered great mass of sablefish in Gulf of Alaska that no American wishes to eat or capture. Therefore, at great cost, my company changes all vessels, good-bye king crab, welcome sablefish."

Satoh's face reddened again and his hands banged the table. "And now, Americans see our success with sablefish and are greedy to take it from us." He sprang from his seat with a fist in the air. Several around the table rose also. The director frowned and snapped something that sent Satoh abruptly back down, followed by the others. Satoh continued in a milder voice. "I mean to say, it is time to announce: back off Americans! Stop being greedy. Only Japanese eat sablefish. Therefore should only Japanese capture them." The director muttered something. "Yes, yes," Satoh replied, as translated, "and few from South Korea who are merely pirates stealing from Japanese technology. We must this afternoon tell American Fishery Council that Japanese will not buy sablefish caught by Americans.

And we further will not any more buy their salmon"—fist bang on each main word—"or roe, or groundfish, or crab."

Several of those around the table murmured approval. It gave Satoh the confidence to draw himself up and declare, "Without Japanese yen purchase, American fisheries will clearly collapse."

Shoji Tsurifune leaned forward and spoke in Japanese to Satoh, in a voice both deferential and urgent. The interpreter translated it for the lawyer, too softly for Hank to hear.

Rider, the American lawyer, held up his hand. When he spoke in English, the interpreter reversed to Japanese. "Please listen to Mike, uh, Mr. Shoji Tsurifune. It's what I've tried to tell you. Let me be blunt . . . no . . ." To the interpreter, "Make that forthright—no, make it sincere." He waited, a man calmly self-possessed. "I wish to tell you sincerely. Japan may be strong, but you are in a vulnerable position—a not strong position here. It would be bad public relations to Americans if you were to follow Mr. Satoh's advice." Satoh started to rise. "Even though I understand the pain and anger that Mr. Satoh feels." Satoh harrumphed, mollified.

"To the American mind, Japan presents several problems." The lawyer held up fingers one by one. "Point: Japanese whaling that America disapproves of—problem. Point: Japanese trade imbalance that affects American economy—problem. Point: long Japanese fishing lines in the water that tangle American fishing gear—problem. Point: the memory of Japanese catching too much fish off America—problem." He hesitated. "And point—excuse me, but you pay me to be . . . sincere—unfortunately, older Americans still remember a very big problem: the not good events of wartime long ago."

Satoh and some of the others muttered angrily when they heard the final translation. Hank could decipher the words *Hiroshima* and *Nagasaki*. The director, unsmiling, waved his colleagues to silence and gestured for Rider to continue. Whether Hank disliked the lawyer or not, he began to admire his diplomatic objectivity.

"Excuse my bluntness, but all this is a reality. Americans are your friends, basically. You need each other. They want to be friends and cooperate. However, Americans have no great concern that Japan loses fish on American fishing grounds because they have many problems of their own. And American fishermen must fish also to feed their families. This is only natural."

After a pause, "My son and I understand," said Director Tsurifune in English. "Your advisement, please."

"Accept what you cannot change, sir. Plan for the inevitable future. Use strategy. I see the Japanese use strategy in other fisheries. For example, we both know that representatives for the Japanese are now talking to American congressmen and officials in Washington. They're lobbying for large Bering Sea groundfish quotas for vessels that deliver to shore plants where the Japanese have investment, even while other Japanese here with us today insist that groundfish can only be processed successfully at sea with Japanese technology. This is wise strategy for what Americans would call 'hedging your bets.' To plan for all possibilities. In the same way, with sablefish in the Gulf of Alaska . . ."

Some of the men at the table had begun to look at each other and mutter in consternation. "This is not to speak of!" snapped the director. "Information you should not know!"

The lawyer seemed unperturbed. "You're paying me to watch everything, sir, and to advise you."

Tsurifune muttered in Japanese to his son. Mike hurried over to Hank and the other Americans. "We'd asked you in to hear our problems. Thanks for listening. But you don't need to be bored with us anymore."

Hank smiled. "I'm not bored."

Mike returned the smile. "Father doesn't wish you to be bored anymore." He gestured toward the door. "Please."

As they left, the lawyer was saying: "My advice, respectfully, is to sacrifice something here to keep American good will. Do it for what we call the long run."

Outside in the hotel lobby, knots of people dressed for Council chatted or read papers. All seats were filled at an open-terrace restaurant. A boat crew just arrived called to Hank from one of the tables. Big men, they pressed against their chairs but assured Hank heartily that they'd make room. He waved no thanks, although that was where he wanted to be.

Tolly stretched beside him. "Was gettin' antsy in there, all that blah blah in Jap. Nice chow. The rest was bullshit, what I could follow, but I know this—they've got no right to our fish unless I catch it for 'em. After a while I stopped listening."

"Good thinking," said John Gains. It wasn't a compliment. To Hank he said, "They'd have let me stay if I'd been alone, you know."

"Yup," said Hank. Gains had changed again before his eyes. Once a game but incompetent young crewman, then a self-possessed office climber who seemed headed for the top with the Japanese, he was now an insecure cog in their machine. Danger. It could happen to Henry Crawford.

"Americans are never going to run successful factory ships," Gains continued. "It's not in our nature. Scut work at sea for three months at a time? We ought to be glad to cooperate and just deliver to the Japanese, now they've agreed to joint ventures with us. And now it's sablefish. Good Lord, Americans don't eat it and it's a Japanese market, so what right have we to take it from them?"

"You've sure bought their line," said Tolly bluntly.

"I see where the future lies, if that's what you mean."

Tolly shrugged in good humor. "Suit yourself."

Nels Tormulsen and his crew from the halibut longliner *Karmoy* passed, and stopped to say hi to Hank and Tolly. They ignored John Gains, who looked away disinterested, or feigned it.

"Hey, fresh air," exclaimed Tolly. "Nels, my man! I hear a beer calling! Follow me."

"Council time, you horse," said Nels Tormulsen in a voice as deep as his chest. He was lean, shaggy-haired, and muscular, in his mid-thirties, a man reserved although he wrapped a playful arm around Tolly's neck and squeezed.

Tolly rabbit-punched lightly to free himself. "It's just talk in there. You'd hear better after a couple brews."

Nels regarded him seriously. "We tied up the boat to be here. And our hired gun costs a hundred-plus an hour. Name your booze if we win. But the vote in there now means banknotes."

Tread lightly, Tolly, thought Hank. He knew the issue at Council and where it might lead. If Nels's side succeeded in pushing what had come to be called ITQs, Individual Transferable Quotas, it would mean private rights to the halibut, favoring those like Nels who had longlined the big fish for decades. They could shut out the new competition that was crowding the water. And after that, Nels's traditional halibut schooner guys were also the ones best able to take over sablefish/black cod from the Japanese, since they fished the same longline gear in waters they knew. He himself and Tolly would soon be their competition.

"And how's your dad?" Hank asked to change the subject. "What does a famous old squarehead halibut skipper do when he retires?"

"Ohh . . . Arthritis. Bullheaded. Manages his apartment houses in Ballard. A good Norwegian puts his money in solid stuff. Keeps him busy, out of my mother's hair. In my wife's hair a little. He comes into our kitchen even when I'm off fishing. Tells her how I should be running his boat. Don't matter I've bought it from him share by share, now owned it for five years." Even when joking with a trace of a smile Nels sounded deliberate. Hank knew him of the steady Norwegian type that seldom laughed or even smiled despite his vigor and second-generation freedom from old-country ways. "Dad doesn't understand us paying some lawyer to speak for us at Council. He thinks we could still shout the other fellows down. Or that we've had to get political. Well, I never thought political when I started baiting hooks on the old man's boat. Back then a bottle on the table at the cannery was the politics, while you bargained price."

And back then together we all hated the intruding overfishing Russians and Koreans . . . and Japs, thought Hank wistfully. No disputes back then between ourselves. "Yup. Now we've become the old-timers, I guess."

Nels shrugged. "I'm probably old in ways you don't know. We're still so traditional on that boat that you wouldn't recognize the fishing."

"Oh, wouldn't I?" Hank laughed, savoring the memory. "After once aboard the *Lincoln,* when Igvar Rasmussen hired me as inbreaker?"

"Mr. Rasmussen? Old Igvar? The devil he did! I remember talk in the fleet, some inbreaker he'd hired off the dock not from the families. Broke his arm when a soaker banged it. Was that you?" Hank nodded. "Well, I remember Igvar said once in Dad's living room, that was a good kid and he'd have kept him on, if it makes you feel any better."

"It does. It does." Should I tell him, Hank wondered, that I'm headed back out to longline, but now as a skipper and without any further experience? "I wouldn't mind going back to face down those big halibuts. This time gut 'em without breaking my arm." He hesitated. "And now black cod, too."

"Any time, Hank. We've got an inbreaker opening you'd fill just right." The rest of the crew shared the joke. Nels stretched and cracked his knuckles. "Well, Council time. Lucky the old man was smart enough to make me do U of Washington before I came with him full-time. It helps kick my way through some of this bullshit." He glanced at John Gains.

"Next round: we'll boot the foreigners off the black cod. And take back the rest of what's ours. The foreigners have raided us long enough."

"If you want to argue foreign raiders," said John evenly, "you might consider where your dad was born. Across another ocean, wasn't it?" He drew himself up and jutted his chin. Hank remembered John's past as a college varsity boxer. All this education in the circle around him, and all of it now directed at chasing fish!

Nels surveyed Gains without rancor. "Different. Norwegians aren't Orientals." He looked at his watch and started off. "Council time. Take care."

"Narrow minds," muttered Gains when Nels left. Hank said nothing.

Tolly pulled from habit on the ear that once bore his gold earring. "What's this sound I hear? Why it's brew calling. Comin', baby. Hank buddy, save me a seat in case I come back." And he too was gone. Hank watched him stride with a bounce. Solid man at sea, but still light as a leaf on land while others changed. It made Hank wistful again. Tolly had been his first buddy in Alaska. Greenhorns together working the cannery lines and cannery girls. Then together grown into deckhands, finally skippers full of themselves. Now Tolly was in bed with the Japanese like himself. But still a breeze, unlike himself.

The Japanese, with their private meeting apparently over, now knotted to one side of the lobby around their American lawyer. Mike Tsurifune caught his eye. It would be the honest thing to join them, Hank realized. Instead he headed in the opposite direction toward a group he knew. They opened their circle to include him.

"Meet our visitors from Norway," said Steve Bunt, a steady former fisherman who now headed a boat owners' organization.

Hank shook hands and they exchanged pleasantries. The newcomers were dressed as conservatively as the Japanese—a different kind of Norwegian than Nels's dad or even Nels. Their English was confident. Indeed, Hank thought dispassionately, when fishing money beckoned, people who probably never baited a hook came raiding from over the world.

When the Norwegians left for the meeting, Hank observed, "Thought I'd read in the *Kodiak Mirror* that your visitors came from Denmark."

"That was last year." Steve lowered his voice. "You don't think only Japanese want a share of the pie? Only how they get it's the difference. The Japs want quota for their ships and for the Alaska shore plants they mostly own. The Scandinavians expect to get their piece by providing the trawlers we'll need to take the fish we now control."

Hank absorbed the information reluctantly. Not what I committed for, he thought. All he'd wanted to do was have his boat and fish. But he needed to stay abreast, and to show it. "Didn't I hear that some of you guys flew somewhere in Russia for talks? How did you manage that with the State Department?"

"Never heard it from me." Steve slapped his shoulder and headed away. "But like I said. Everybody."

When he phoned Jody in Kodiak, she answered with "Oh! The things to untangle after just a couple of weeks away! You men back from your boat never have that with wives at home. But I'm on a noon flight tomorrow. You just stay busy with your meetings. I haven't been shopping in a city for ages. All of a sudden I'm looking forward to a few days of city life before I go back to the boat." Her voice lowered to a throaty purr. "But save me dinner and every evening, mister."

The prospect sent Hank back to the afternoon Council session with a lively step. The room was jammed to the doors and people stood along the sides. The fifteen Council members took places by name cards around long tables that formed a semisquare. Witnesses faced the Council from a chair and table. Within the audience the Japanese stayed in a bloc and listened solemnly to a translation through headphones.

Those who would benefit or lose by the imposition of individual halibut quotas voiced their stands so strongly that the Council postponed votes for a later meeting. It left Nels and his buddies, seated behind Hank, muttering about overpaid lawyers and lost fishing time.

The scheduled topics moved to the remaining foreign fishing effort still allowed off the Alaskan coasts under the two hundred-mile law of 1976.

A staff member reported on the program called Joint Ventures, only a couple of years old, between U.S. and foreign vessels. The JVs negotiated so far allowed Americans, who lacked ships to process masses of fish at sea, to catch and deliver to factory ships from Korea, the Soviet Union, Taiwan, and now Japan. The staff man noted that the Japanese, the newest to agree to the program after great reluctance—since they wanted to retain the catching privilege also for themselves—were now being cooperative.

Nels leaned forward with a hand on Hank's shoulder. "You know it. They agreed after Ronnie's State Department told the Japs: no JV co-op, no fish. Finally we've got Republicans back in D.C., people who get the picture. Fuckin' finally."

A Coast Guard enforcement officer reported that its patrol planes had counted more than four hundred Japanese vessels in Alaskan waters during the period, plus a few of other nationalities. All were fishing legally negotiated quotas.

"A pathetic four hundred," whispered John Gains beside Hank. "Compare that to two *thousand* four hundred Japanese boats out there in 1976 just half a dozen years ago, and you see their problem. Think of the personal disaster in that cutback, whatever the American interest. Not to mention more than a thousand Russian boats back then, plus the Koreans and Taiwanese. All those fishermen gone home hungry. And we have more fish here than we can catch."

"Tough," said Hank. "They were greedy, or more of 'em might still be there."

Gains nodded back toward the halibut crew. "Hark up behind us if you want to hear greed."

The Coast Guard officer listed citations issued to foreign vessels during the period since the last Council meeting. Infractions concerned mainly catch log irregularities but included, on a Soviet trawler, "failure to stop immediately to facilitate an authorized boarding" and "failure to provide a safe boarding ladder for the authorized boarding party."

"Nab the cheaters however you can," muttered Nels.

During a five-minute break to stretch, someone said, "Hello, Hank. Is this seat taken?" It was Odds Anderson, his voice quiet and his words slowly chosen as always. He wore the sober clothing of spokesman for one of the native corporations formed with Native Claims Act money. They shook hands, and Hank removed his coat from the seat he'd saved for Tolly. Odds settled beside him with knees straight ahead and large hands clasped on his lap.

John Gains on his other side coughed expectantly. Hank introduced his two former crewmen from different periods. "Oddmund Anderson now makes the wheels turn at the native—"

"Not Anderson anymore," interrupted Odds. "I went to court and changed to my mother's name. I'm Nikolai. A native name. Because maybe I'm part Norwegian, but more important, I'm Aleut. I wanted to change Oddmund too. But people told me I'd better not, even my wife. Because they wouldn't remember that so easy."

"Interesting," said Gains, all business. "Your corporations are acquiring properties, I hear. Even trying to outbid the Japanese, they say. What are you working on?"

"Oh. We've got plans." Odds nodded. "There's lots happening."

"Like what?"

"Lots. Wise investments. We're doing real good." With that the conversation died, since Odds volunteered nothing further. Hank listened, half interested since Odds had clammed up. Ask again another time without Gains around, he decided. "So, Odds. Are you still fixing up the old Russian Orthodox churches?"

"The one in Kodiak's doing good. Lots of good people there give some money. And the church in Ouzinki village, it just needed some paint. It's the other village churches. The one in Karluk's real bad. Near as bad as the church I helped fix in Unalaska when I was on your boat."

"You didn't help fix it, Odds. You fixed it by yourself whenever we hit port. Have you been out there recently?" Odds shook his head. "Well, those onion domes are still the first good sight coming in from a rough week in the Bering, and now thanks to you, they're all blue and shiny." Odds appeared pleased, so Hank added, not sure it was true, "People around there clear over to Dutch Harbor thank you for it."

"People there thank me? That's nice." Odds's smooth Aleut face changed expression no more than his voice, but the compliment brought a light to his eyes. "I only did what God told me to. But I'm glad people like it. Important thing now—do they come to church regular?"

"Sure they do." (Whether true or not.)

The meeting resumed. One by one, representatives of American fishing groups took the witness chair facing the Council. The testimony concerned possible new restrictions on sablefishing in the Gulf of Alaska. Speakers couched their statements in formal terms, using so many acronyms that for Hank they talked a half-foreign language. But clearly all those representing American interests opposed further allotments to foreign vessels since the foreigners crowded the grounds. ("Even though," muttered John Gains, "American boats can't begin to catch all the sustainable yield the biologists state is out there.") On the table indeed was one proposal to eliminate any further foreign quotas, and a tougher one to cancel even those quotas already granted to foreign boats for the remainder of the current year.

Hank shifted his legs on the narrow chair and tried to appear neutral. Where's my loyalty here? he fretted. He envied Tolly's freedom at some bar.

"Under this approach," droned a staff member reading from a paper, "The OY for Area 3-A west of one hundred forty degrees west would be set equal to seventy-five percent of EY. DAH would be determined so that the unsatisfied domestic needs in southeast, and in east of one hundred forty west, would be met. TALFF in the area would equal OY slash DAH. The SSC heard public testimony which suggested . . ."

"How in hell does this shit make sense?" muttered Hank.

"Do your homework, that's how," said Gains. He scribbed for a few minutes and handed Hank the paper. "Partial list, but this should do it for you here."

—NMFS or "Nimfs" of course = National Marine Fishery Service
—ADF&G = Alaska Dept. of Fish & Game.
—FMP = Fishery Management Plan
—FCZ = Fishery Conservation Zone
—JV of course is Joint Ventures
—TALFF = Total Allowable Foreign Fishing
—OY = Optimum Yield
—EY = Equilibrium Yield
—DAH = Domestic Annual Harvest
—DAP = Domestic Available Processing
—ABC = Acceptable Biological Catch
—AIC = Allowable Incidental Catch
—PMT = Plan Maintenance Team
—EIS = Environmental Impact Statement

Within the Council:

—SSC = Scientific and Statistical Committee
—AP = Advisory Panel

Hank sighed. "Thanks."

After intense whispering within the Japanese bloc, their overweight American lawyer took the chair. His manner was earnest and sincere. "We wish to offer this in the spirit of cooperation with American fishermen," he began. His voice stayed cool as he leaned his elbows on the table in front of him and read a statement. It named the large area west of Yakutat in the Gulf of Alaska, and declared that the Japanese would refrain from fishing there until October despite any previous agreements or negotiated quotas.

Silence followed the statement. "Boy, oh boy," muttered Nels. "Look that one over for holes."

"We also wish to offer technical assistance to any American fishermen who need it in those areas where Japanese boats do fish. We'll share catch information, and alert boats to any high concentrations of fish we encounter. Again, this is in the spirit of cooperation."

Hank glanced back at the Japanese. Some listened to the headphone translation so intently that they leaned forward. The oldest senior had fallen asleep. Satoh's face was angrily red. Tsurifune father and son, without headphones, might have been watching an interesting movie for their calm demeanors. Mike Tsurifune's eyes caught Hank's and an eyebrow twitched.

The chairman, a man with graying reddish hair who was normally outspoken, even aggressive, conferred with staff members beside him and suppressed a smile. Some members passed him notes, and two came up to bend over and confer. At length, he said, "Do we understand that Japanese boats have offered to leave the Yakutat West area immediately?"

"Yes, sir."

"That's . . . mighty interesting. Let's hear from members first, and then I expect we'll have input from the audience."

Many commended the Japanese, even some of those who had spoken most strongly against them. Although others, including Nels's spokesman, still urged an immediate end to all foreign quotas, the Japanese proposal had dampened their drive. By a near-unanimous vote the Council agreed to postpone action on foreign quotas until a committee had examined the new proposal and could report at the next session in two months.

"They got away with it this time, but fuckin' something's up their sleeve," commented Nels. "See you at the bar, Hank."

"Sure. Later." Hank kneaded his neck to occupy his hands.

After the session, Hank took a different elevator to avoid passing the hotel bar, and returned to his room. He had begun to hang up clothes bunched on the bed, keeping things neat for Jody tomorrow, when Mike Tsurifune found him there by phone. "Well," said Mike with brisk smoothness, "that strategy saved us from the killer vote, at least. But there's no time to lose, Hank. Not going to D.C., as I'd originally planned. We need you back in Japan. Must get you out there fishing for us. As I said, we have your long-liner with western headroom, but it's still rigged for trawl. You'll like it. I've booked you back with us to Tokyo tomorrow. On to Hokkaido the next day."

"Now, wait!"

"You'll probably want to fly back to Kodiak tonight for passport and packing, then back here first flight in the morning. We've made those reservations for you. Paid by the company, of course."

Hank controlled his impulse to let loose. Instead he said firmly, "Sorry, Mike. Made other plans with my wife. I can join you in three or four days."

"I don't believe you understand, Hank. Father and I've decided we want you in Japan. This is business, not personal pleasure. Your good wife will accept when you tell her."

"Four days, Mike."

"Father the director will be displeased at this."

"Too bad." Hank hung up.

11

HALIBUT BUZZ

JAPAN, EARLY SEPTEMBER 1982

A few days later, on the layover night in Tokyo between Alaska and Hokkaido, Hank waited for Mike's inevitable banquet or party invitation. None came. If Shoji was pissed at his delayed arrival, too bad. It allowed him a stroll through the neon Ginza, and then freedom from a hangover when he made a 5 AM return to the frenetic, structured Tsukiji auctions. The abundance of sea creatures that were offered and passionately presented amazed him afresh.

Mike sent word that he needed to stay in the city, so Hank flew north alone to Kushiro where the ship stood in drydock. Kodama met him at the airport. The man no longer wore an office coat and tie. His chest and shoulders, freed to press against a crisp sport shirt, seemed to have gained inches. Kodama had left the fishery agency—cut himself loose, on faith, Hank knew—and committed to the Tsurifune payroll as technical advisor on converting the trawler to longline gear. The fierce expression now allowed a certain humor. "You looking fat from eating eating, Mr. Carford!"

At the shipyard Kodama held out his arms. "See, Mr. Carford. Your vessel!" The ship was five years old, built to western headroom. Refitting was already under way. Hank gazed. Should feel excited, he thought. Why did 130 feet of hull appear twice as long as the *Jody Dawn*'s 108 feet? This boat would hardly take waves with the same bounce. Nothing merry about it like his *Jody Dawn*. To what had he committed?

Once aboard and on deck for a while, however, he began to accept possession. He crawled into every hold and space, and pored over specs and blueprints. He examined rivets in the plates; strode the wide wheelhouse inspecting grander electronics than ever he'd needed before; examined the crews' four-bunk staterooms, supervisors' two-bunk quarters, and officers' singles; fingered double stoves in the big galley; wandered an engine room the size of a small seiner, idly wiping spots of oil from glistening valves as he studied a capacity of marine power new to him.

Most of the metal nameplates over the hatches were in Japanese; some remained in Spanish from the earliest owner. "I want all these pulled off, or painted over completely, Kodama-san."

"I am seeing done, Mr. Carford."

"Call me Hank." He grinned. "I give you permission."

"Phooo . . . " Serious face. "Not right."

"After all, when you can throw me in judo . . ."

Flash of amusement, but, "Different," Kodama said.

"At least get the Crawford part straight."

"Mr. Carford, of course."

While in Kushiro Hank traversed other working Japanese longliners, ducking perpetually low overheads as he quizzed Kodama on gear and placement. Kodama's knowledge was reassuring. Hank had begun to feel possessive enough to call his new ship informally "*Jody Maru.*" The real name, he settled with the Tsurifunes (who insisted it was entirely his choice, while suggesting names like "American Enterprise," "Victory," or "Fortitude") would be *Puale Bay.* The name should please Jody; it was their wedding site nine years ago in remote wilderness, aboard the old *Nestor* pulled in from an ice storm.

His calls home to Kodiak were restless affairs. Usually it was Adele he reached. Only once did Jody pick up the phone from the house, in from fishing for three days and full of anecdotes. "Oh, I'm bushed! We hit a jackpot jag of chums and cohos in Kiliuda Bay, set right on top of them. Call it luck, or my good eye. And Terry's eye, of course. Then Ham's quick maneuver in the skiff. Those two are great, and you'd better not have hired anybody to take their place."

"Don't worry. Just give 'em back in one piece."

"Well, the other two we hired aren't worth much, but without Terry they'd be near zero."

"I told you midseason all the good ones would be taken." He enjoyed being right.

"Yes, yes." She barely noticed the small victory as she continued. "Well, that big jag we set on? Wait." Her voice sharpened although it went out of range. "Pete! Get off there! You want my hand? Dawn, you're supposed to be watching your little brother. Well, see to it." She returned to the phone. "Adele's spoiled them, although I couldn't be more grateful. Anyhow, that big jag? We must have set on all the fish in the bay since none of the other boats caught much. If they'd sounded I might have lost the boat. The tender came right alongside and we brailed straight into her. For hours! Old Gus in his wheelhouse, the whole *Hinda Bee* crew on deck, they'd come alongside now and then just to watch and kibitz. It was wonderful! They weren't catching anything! Terry and Ham nearly hopped from their skins ragging them. It meant that finally my guys won a bet."

"Ah. Wish I'd been there." He tried not to sound as wistful as he felt. Remaining casual, he told her he'd named his new boat *Puale Bay*.

After a silence, Jody said quietly, "That's nice, Hank." But soon she began again to talk of her own fishing excitement.

A few days later it was Adele who phoned him. "Hank! Don't worry, everybody's fine, no emergency—even though imagine me calling all the way to Japan! Your children are even better than fine, I'd say. I love 'em, but they're a package. Lord knows I've never phoned Japan before on my own. Poor Daddy would have had a fit, although once he did call home from Paris France, when I dragged him over there for a little culture, and he read of a tidal wave scare in Kodiak, years after the big one you and he survived. Where was I?"

"It's your dime," said Hank gently. "I'm glad everybody's fine. I miss you all."

"Oh. Yes. Hank! Jody's on the way home for good this year. That one big amazing run she found in Kiliuda Bay seems to be the end of it, nobody's catching much anymore. I'm so proud of her. And I hope you are too. But I think a mother shouldn't be away from her children for too long, much as I love them."

Amen to that, thought Hank.

"Now. You know, Hank, now that I'm an owner, people have been advising me. Many of the boats my size around here, they tell me—as if I don't know after forty years a fisherman's wife stuck in Kodiak. People up here seined for salmon all summer, then used to convert to crab pots in the fall. Nobody needs to tell *you* what's happened to the crab, of course—they're gone. At least for a while. But they say halibut's now everywhere in the water. Do you suppose those big halibut ate all the crabs? That's what some people say."

"Maybe, Adele. Nobody knows."

"So, do you know what I'm thinking? There's a halibut opening just next Friday, one week from today. It may be for as much as a week, but definitely for several days. The biologists still haven't decided. They count and count and I do think waste our good taxpayers' money, but! Definitely the final one this year after that couple days each last May and June. Halibut's all the rage. Everybody's going, because there's so much money to be made."

"Adele, halibut needs an entirely different gear than salmon."

"Exactly! And that's why Elwood Stevens at his boatyard has offered me—El loved poor Daddy, you know—the dear man's giving me a nice price at fifteen thousand on credit to fix up my *Adele H* for longline. Secondhand roller and gurdy—that's what they're called—but good condition."

"I guess El wouldn't cheat you, but I'd advise caution."

"Too late, my dear. I decided yesterday. El's converting my boat as we speak. Now to the point. I need a crew."

And how I'd love to do it, thought Hank. Hands-on steamroller fishing straight from the sea like none other. "But with such a short opening, a crew needs to start on the run and be a crack team."

"Exactly! So I've asked myself, who do I know who has a crack team? Hank, dear, those big fish bring over a dollar a pound! It's money from the sky! Don't tell me you and Jody don't need . . . And one lucky halibut load could easily pay my conversion—easily!—and then I'm set. Lord knows salmon aren't fetching much all of a sudden with that awful botulism scare. I pity those Englishmen who died, of course, but couldn't they have been more careful? Everybody over there eats canned salmon, they say, and nobody else ever . . . Of course in Paris France you wouldn't find them eating things from a can since they do all their foods fresh, and you can't imagine how delicious! . . . Where was I? Oh. Hank. What a crack team like yours could catch in a week! And it's west of Kodiak only, not on the old traditional Albatross and Portlock banks where the old-timers know every inch. New ground for everybody. They say the water's black with halibut. Don't let's lose out. I'll even pay your airfare. Bring your boys, and crew for me."

"We've got other commitments, Adele."

After a silence: "Oh, Hank. Things used to be so much simpler."

How well he knew. But that ended it.

Then, amazingly, when he mentioned the conversation casually to Tsurifune father and son, they exchanged glances and spoke together rapidly in Japanese. The old man chuckled, and Mike declared, "Why not? Good entry longline for you and fishing master." In any case, the shipyard had just detected some weak hull plates on the *Puale Bay* and consequent water damage. It would delay the final launching.

Mike Tsurifune buzzed for his secretary and snapped orders in Japanese. Then to Hank: "Excuse me, now I must use influence quickly for Kodama-visa USA. Go hurry tell him—no, I shall tell and instruct, please hurry now yourself and prepare." He buzzed the secretary again to summon Kodama.

Seth's reaction when Hank phoned with a list of things to be done was: "Fuckin' time we got back into the real stuff. I guess you don't know anymore what it's like to just sit around with a finger up your ass while everybody else hits the fish. And halibut is *the* deal, everybody's gearing. Boats are taking six or seven crew for max in the few days. We're only five. Not many apes left not hired, but I'll scout the docks."

"Hold off on that." Hank hesitated. "I've got one new man."

"Who?"

"I've mentioned him before. Kodama."

Silence, then, "That Jap?"

"You'll like him. He's a good man. I've got to go."

"What are you doing to us?"

It'll work out, Hank reassured himself.

Shoji Tsurifune himself saw them off two days later on a plane leaving Narita. In his presence Kodama turned stiff as a soldier, and his normally stern expression darkened further when the two conversed in Japanese.

No democracy here, Hank concluded as he pretended not to watch. Nothing wrong with management instructing an employee to go out and produce for the company, but he was surprised to see Kodama made so uneasy.

Kodama's discomfort continued throughout the hours of the Tokyo–Anchorage flight. He sat like a ramrod most of the time with hands clasped on his lap, and spoke only to give monosyllabic answers. He barely touched food, and refused alcohol.

Hank suddenly doubted his decision now that it was too late. Maybe Kodama wasn't going to fit in, uptight as he was. How indeed would he make out on deck if he was the expert but Seth was the established boss? Seth now echoed Jones Henry's anti-Japanese hostility more and more. Had Jones by dying passed him the sword? Hank found his own hands seeking each other on his lap.

After clearing customs at the Anchorage airport Hank said, "Come on, Kodama-san. We've got two hours before the Kodiak flight. Let's loosen up. Buy you a drink."

"No alcohol."

"Coke, then. Come on."

People with suitcases hurried by them in the corridor. Kodama instinctively edged so close to Hank that their shoulders touched. "Hoo. Americans are very large."

"You've seen this before. Haven't you fished in Alaska, and Canada, even Argentina and the Caribbean?"

"Never go ashore. Sometimes in for fuel, of course. But always pier and office." Suddenly three men with knapsacks and rifle cases strode by talking loudly. Their smudged clothing and unshaven faces made them seem more aggressive than they probably were. Kodama nearly knocked Hank over to crowd against him. "Guns!" he whispered.

"Just hunters. Back from a few days in the bush, probably."

"Everyone in America necessary must have guns. Oh, I have read this."

"Come on. Where's my gun? Do you see any?"

"Not needed in Japan, of course. Here you must have gun to protect. Quickly I must buy gun also."

Hank laughed it off.

Kodama reluctantly accepted a Coke with a dash of rum when Hank told him this was very American. It did not relax him. He sat tight and silent in the lounge. A voice over the speaker announced that fog in Kodiak would delay the flight. Hank looked around for some diversion. There sat Oddmund Anderson in a dark corner. They nodded. Good. Start Kodama meeting people with an easy one. Hank urged Odds over.

The Aleut and the Japanese shook hands cautiously.

"Odds, Mr. Kodama's my good friend from Japan. He's a fisherman. Very skilled in longline. A fishing master, in fact." No reaction. Hank chattered on, although the two men stared at each other without expression. "And, Kodama-san . . . Odds here, Mr. Oddmund Anderson . . ." Odds started to correct. "Oh, yeah, Nikolai, right?" Odds nodded. "This gentleman's also a good friend. He too is a fisherman. Once a valuable member of my crew, catching king crab in the Bering Sea. Same waters you once fished. Now he's an important member of the Kodiak—of one of the Alaska native corporations, directing how to spend native money on things like, uh, fisheries."

Oddmund cleared his throat. "Longline's very important now," he stated in his flat, earnest voice. "Everybody's going out next week to catch halibut. Longline's the best way. Everybody who can get on a boat. Since I stopped fishing to work for the corporation, all my brothers and cousins, they've filled their boats without me." A pause. "I'd go too."

Why not? thought Hank. But he'd first assess manpower with Seth, give Seth the choice. Give Seth something after forcing Kodama down his throat. "Hey, let me order another round." He regretted as soon as he spoke. Odds had been a problem on the boat when he drank. On the other hand, a test of the present Odds.

"I don't need more root beer," said Odds. "This is plenty here in my glass. You go booze all you like if that's what you want." His manner implied no judgment.

Kodama also waved aside a refill.

They both seemed content to sit without speaking. Hank excused himself and went to the bar for another scotch. He took as long as he could, and drained most of it while bantering with the bartender, but finally returned to the table. It appeared that neither of the two had spoken, although Kodama seemed finally relaxed.

"Well, Odds. Your work at the native corporation must be pretty interesting. You guys are busy investing, aren't you? Did I read you'd bought into one of the canneries?"

"Buying?" The serious face turned graver. "I guess you didn't hear. Somebody in a far-off place got sick with a thing called botulism. Got sick and died. People say from a can of salmon from Alaska. It's a bad time for canneries. Stores all over don't want canned salmon."

"Hey." Hank made it light. "Good time to buy canneries cheap." Odds didn't pick up on the tone. (Why indeed try to joke with sober ol' Odds?) He tried to assess Odds's physical condition through the suit. Had an office left him too soft for heavy fishing? "Do you work out at all? Shoot hoops? Go to the gym?"

"No time for that sort of thing, Hank. I'm very busy."

"Ever tried judo, Odds? Kodama here could show you a thing or two."

"Fighting's violent. Almost as bad as drinking booze."

"Come on," Hank eased. "Weren't Aleut people famous fighters long ago? Tough as hell, I've heard!"

"If you studied enough, Hank, you'd read that the Haida People and Tlingit People further south, they always made war. My people, well, maybe we'd fight a little over sealing grounds. My people, the Aleut People, we survived in bad weather. On the ocean, in little skin boats, in cold, terrible weather. That's how we were tough." Odds sipped his root beer. "Then, two hundred years ago, the Russian fur traders came to the Aleut villages. They gave presents and we trusted them. And then they made us slaves, easy, because they had guns. It wasn't right. All this country was ours. Then Americans bought Aleut land from the Russians that wasn't Russians' to sell. Or Americans' to buy. That wasn't right, either."

Hank regretted what he'd started. He deferred it with, "At least the Russians gave you those beautiful churches."

It left Odds silent for a minute. Then, "It was God's way to save my people. But the rest was wrong."

Suddenly Kodama laughed and drained his glass. "Yes!" he said when Hank offered to bring him another. As Hank left for the bar, Kodama was addressing Odds for the first time: "*Hai*, injustice. Do they also take away your fish?"

"All the fish used to belong to my people."

"Oh, boy. Make it stiff," Hank told the bartender. When he returned, Odds and Kodama had entered an intense conversation. Hank wondered whether to laugh or be annoyed. The Japanese and the Aleut were telling each other how Americans had deprived them of their entitled fish.

By the time the plane was ready—after further delays for bad weather in Kodiak—the rum in Kodama's drink had not relaxed him as Hank intended, but had instead emboldened him. When the three walked together over the tarmac to the plane, Kodama and Odds continued to talk intensely, ignoring Hank. The Japanese fiercely shook the Aleut's hand in parting, then joined Hank with an angry look.

Should he tell Kodama to goddamn lighten up, or leave it to circumstance? Hank decided to play it easy. "Soon you're going to meet the guys you'll crew with. My crew. They're good men. And I've told them you're a good man. They'll be your friends." He studied the lines that had hardened around Kodama's mouth. "But it's important to start by being, uh, positive. Friendly."

"Of course," Kodama snapped. His expression still could have faced down an opponent on the judo mat.

Should have kept Kodama sober. One thing for certain, Hank decided. Forget Odds in the halibut crew. There'd be enough friction with sorehead Seth. As the plane circled the hazed Kodiak mountains and bumped to a landing, he braced for the first meeting.

They walked through rain from the plane to the airport terminal. Oddmund drew alongside Hank. "Your friend says you're going to longline this halibut opening. If you need more crew, Hank . . . I've got a meeting tomorrow morning but after that . . . Native corporation don't pay all that good with three kids and my wife talking college for them all of a sudden, so I've thought about also fishing again."

"I'll sure keep it in mind, Odds."

Instead of the crew he'd expected, Jody and the kids met them waving. He'd seldom seen her so clear eyed and confident. It was like old times with her hair neatly back in a ponytail (that couldn't be a white strand among the brown?) and her wide mouth in a smile. As their kiss and embrace continued little Pete wrapped arms around his leg. Dawn held his hand and looked up to tell everything that had happened since he'd left, while Henny stood gravely apart waiting to be greeted. Hank hugged them each in turn, and kept tousling Henny's hair.

Hank introduced his new man. Jody greeted Kodama with a spontaneous light kiss. It startled him. He backed away instinctively.

"Your boys are nearly snowed getting ready, but they've come to life," she said gaily. "All those tubs of line and hooks! And Adele everywhere making suggestions, they're even rolling with that."

"Even Seth?"

"Seth's gotten good at being polite while he still does what he's decided to do. He might make a husband after all." They strolled across the slippery floor where attendants wheeled in dripping baggage and boxes from the plane.

Hank had paid no attention to others around him until a familiar voice near them grated, "I count seven. Where's the rest? And the new crankshaft, where's that?"

"Crankshaft, sir, Joey grabbed it right from the plane and took it to the truck. The peanut butter, you only ordered seven of the big cans. It says right here."

Hank turned to see Swede Scorden in coveralls with a clipboard, surrounded by crates, boxes, and a new motor scooter. The bill of a red baseball cap shaded his eyes even indoors, and his chin jutted beneath it as always, now with a graying stubble that once had been black. Hank had last seen him in a rare suit and tie at Jones Henry's funeral.

"Put on glasses. That's seven*teen* in my order. Look like a seven to you?"

"Oh. That little stick of a one in front of the seven, it's all blurred. Shit. Sorry, sir."

"Sorry enough when those birds gobble their peanut butter and yell for more. Think we're going to feed 'em fresh crab legs instead? And what kind of grease is that all over my new boat fenders there?"

"I don't know, sir."

"Clean those things before they go on the truck. Use your own shirt if you have to, but wipe it."

"Right, sir."

"Swede, you pisser," called Hank.

"Crawford. Back from Japan." Swede Scorden barely looked up as he spoke. "I want to see you. Soon. At the office." To his assistant: "See to it." Swede pushed up the bill of his cap, and his face eased as he walked toward them.

Jody gave Swede another of her light kisses. "Why are you so mean to your kids?"

"Breaks 'em in." To Kodama: "I've heard about you. Scorden here." He offered his hand. The two men exchanged direct looks. They evidently approved of each other since the handshake, started curtly, ended with (could that be Swede?) clipped ceremonial bows. Swede turned to Hank. "You're going for halibut. Delivering to me?"

"Depends. You going to cheat me on price?"

"As much as I can."

"Then I might trust the thief I know."

"Then come by the office like I said. But keep Adele Henry away from me."

"Oh? She's on your tail?"

"No more I guess than on anybody else from canneries and boats." Swede waved his hand. "Or shipyard, hardware store, gear shed from what I hear. Fishery office, harbormaster's, town council even. Since Jones died the woman can't shut up. Ask Jody." He turned to Kodama with another handshake. "Good luck." Then he resumed checking his shipments.

After Swede had left, "He's stopped drinking, you know," said Jody. "All that boozy haze is gone. I'm so glad."

Hank started to say that maybe he'd found a way to stop the Japs from screwing him, checked himself in front of Kodama. "Is Adele that bad?"

Jody shrugged in good humor.

On the drive to town, piers they passed swarmed with men carrying boxes of groceries and gear to the boats. Deck lights glistened on wet orange and yellow oilskins. The activity looked even busier than it did during the start of the salmon runs. "Oh, yes," Jody confirmed. "Everybody has dollar signs for eyes these days."

At the yard, Hank's *Jody Dawn* rode in the water rather than dry on the ways, the repairs to her hull completed. His boat bobbed there deserted. Rails and superstructure showed the scuffs of Bristol Bay, inflicted weeks before when he'd left her abruptly after the storm and Jones's death. He started toward her at once.

Jody followed and caught his arm. "I know your thinking. But you'll lose yourself over there. You've got short time, and a new man to settle in."

Hank continued toward the *Jody Dawn* but called back, "Just for a minute, honey. Kodama-san! Follow me. Come see my boat."

"Hank! You'll disappear once you go aboard." Her voice hardened. "Your crew's waiting on a different boat."

He started to brush her off with a joke but thought better of it and retraced his steps. She was right. He'd want to check every inch of his *Jody Dawn* and he could lose himself there.

Kodama watched, shocked. Under the drive of the rain he took a thick black rubber jacket from his bag. The coat added to the darkness of his frown.

The *Adele H*'s deck was as busy as the *Jody Dawn*'s had been empty. Seth, peeled to the waist with a red cloth looped around his forehead, leaned into the windlass bracing a wrench. The short, grease-caked figure half hidden in the same machinery would be Terry. Up on the mast Mo braced himself with locked knees as he rigged a block. Ham serviced him by rope from the deck below. They all worked despite the rain.

And there beside Ham stood Adele Henry. She wore bulging oilskin pants and a hooded slicker jacket. A bandanna locked down most of her hair. "I think a little bit higher, Mo dear," she called.

Seth looked up, scanned the mast, met Mo's glance, and turned down his thumb.

"Yes, ma'am," said Mo. He shimmied slightly farther up the mast and seemed to place the block a few inches higher, then imperceptibly slipped back to his original position as he readied the brace.

"Yes," said Adele. "That's better." She returned to scrubbing what looked like an old bait box that was white scuffed to gray.

Hank pointed out each crew member to Kodama. "And the lady is Mrs. Henry. She owns the boat."

Kodama frowned. "You have told me boat is yours."

"Not this one. My boat's the one over there that I almost went aboard."

"Boat which wife said do not go?"

Hank's turn to frown. "Well, something like that." He announced, "Hey, everybody. Over here when you get a chance."

Adele barely glanced up. "Just come aboard, Hank dear. As you see, we're all busy."

Instead of the encounter for which Hank had braced, everyone merely called hi to Kodama and then continued their work.

12

KODAMA

A fulfilled samurai, of course, served a master worthy of the blood he was prepared to shed. No such master had ever entered the life of Yukihiro Kodama. Fishing masters under whom he'd worked before becoming one himself invariably betrayed weakness, and no self-inflated fishery official had ever proven worthy. It left him a modern *ronen*—samurai for hire without a master.

Kodama often daydreamed of his samurai ancestors and the authority they'd held over their world. An engraved sword hung in the apartment beyond the reach of all but his oldest son, but close enough for all to gaze up and see the inscriptions and absorb their meaning. It was the household's treasure. To lie wasn't his nature, but he never announced that he'd bought the sword in bachelor youth with his first money as a fisherman. Since the sword hung close to the tidy shrine with a photo of his father and a ceremonial cup, all assumed that the hands of Kodama ancestors had once gripped the hilt.

His own father had been a noble fisherman—a fishing master, of course—after serving the Emperor as a destroyer captain in the Imperial Navy during the war of American aggression. In modern peacetime, even those of samurai tradition needed to make a commoner's living, since Japan was unfairly prevented by victor nations led by America from keeping the military profession. And since the ocean had finally claimed his honored father after what was surely a heroic battle pitted against the unconquerable Bering Sea, fishing vessels were acceptable to the warrior tradition. Thus so, like this, he too had cast his lot.

Captain Henry Carford was a few years his junior, but he had about him the confidence of leadership. He wasn't weak—he'd bravely stood up to judo knocks when clearly he had no defense against being injured, and he'd been firm in demanding his way among Japanese fishery officials, however unseemly his actions—but how strong *was* he? His wife appeared stronger. No Japanese wife would stop her husband from boarding his own vessel, certainly not in front of others. (And imagine such a bold kiss in public to a stranger, from surely an otherwise respectable woman. Any pleasure it gave was immaterial. Would she do such a thing to him again? Surely not in front of other Japanese?)

Captain Carford had shown himself reassuringly knowledgeable in the Kushiro shipyard, although so childish in his desire to pull nets that he offended Mr. Nagao of the fishing cooperative who had prepared a hospitable day of information. And then he foolishly descended to the net-pulling level aboard the Kanazawa boat where he'd been invited to observe as an honored official. Immaterial that the fishermen themselves enjoyed his behavior, and had announced in Japanese that if Americans were like this, they were perhaps not barbarians.

Americans had always put him on guard. Of course they were powerful and selfish. It came with successful aggression. They had even removed the rights of their own Indian fishermen. But they *were* bold. The man named Swede. Straightforward. Appraising eye strangely warm. In spite of himself Kodama liked Americans. And he felt excitement to be among them.

It would be necessary to guard against foolish enthusiasm for America in the reports he needed to send back to Director Tsurifune via the son, Shoji. To make reports bothered him less now that he'd thought it over. The task—which Subdirector Shoji Tsurifune named a requirement for his being hired—could be done with honor by reporting only simple facts that everyone knew.

It was the sealed envelope that made him uneasy. "To be shown to no one, and opened only if you are instructed," the Subdirector had said when handing it to him in private before he boarded the plane in Tokyo. He then had added lightly: "Don't worry, it's written in Japanese, for nobody to read but us. Probably you'll never be told to open it, but rather to burn it."

Thus Kodama surveyed the boat that was to be his first American bat-tleground, and its seamen who would be either colleagues or adversaries. The boat was smaller than he'd expected, although it appeared sturdy and well maintained. But an elderly woman, the owner, in fact, performing labor on deck? Nothing in this country respected proprieties.

Captain Carford's wife informed him that he'd stay the night in their house since it was too late to worry about settling on the boat, and now she herself drove the car. The captain rode as a mere passenger. May the home be cleaner than the car, Kodama hoped, and brushed grit from the seat. They traveled into wilderness over a road eventually full of holes. He sat in the center row of seats with the youngest boy, while the older boy and girl sprawled in the back section with luggage and boxes. After crawl-ing for a while, intoning *voom, voom,* the child curled up with his boots against Kodama's thigh. Kodama squeezed against the side of the car and looked toward the parents up front for a reprimand. They paid no atten-tion. What kind of discipline was this? The legs unlimbered further to fill the gap he'd left. Nothing for it but to grip the small ankles to keep the boots from touching him. Sturdy young bones. Like his own children, now far away.

"Stay on your side," said the girl in back. "You're wet."

"I *am* on my side," the boy said calmly. "That's the line right there. And so are you wet."

"Oh. Well, stay there." Soon all three children were asleep.

Kodama wished for his own children.

They drove mile after mile in a direction away from town, on a road with holes so wide that the wife sometimes slowed to swerve around them. The warmth from the car heater had relieved his chill, but it intensified odors of oil and fish he hadn't smelled this close up for years. Rain pelted against the roof. His feet remained wet. A dim daylight persisted. Gloomy mists enclosed the countryside. The occasional house they passed stood desolate on rocks or engulfed darkly in vegetation. One stream they crossed gushed against their wheels with a force that shook the car. What if it rose further and prevented their return?

His head jiggled with the car's bounce and he began to feel ill. A handle that might have lowered the window to give him air wouldn't turn. The trip continued on and on. So far from town! At one point the road skirted a bay. Sinister high rocks rose from the water. Huge tombs surrounded by fogs.

Ghostly. A place to encounter ancestors. It both repelled and attracted. "This is your home?"

"Gettin' close."

At length high trees formed a wall on both sides of the road. Enough light remained to see green mosses that clung along the trunks. The wife pulled from the road onto a bare rise in the forest darkness. "Pete," she said in a voice of easy command, "Hurry in and move your toys and pajamas. Mr. Kodama's sleeping in your room, and you'll go with Henny. Hen, give him a hand before you start your homework."

"Okay," said the boy without rancor. His child brother evidently liked the idea because he gave a happy whoop. "But look here, brat," said the eldest. "One fart and you're on the floor."

Kodama left the car slowly. A chill engulfed him at once. Water dripped from the trees, and the vegetation smelled of wetness. In American movies this would be a place for mystery and murder. A low house of dark wood lay lightless ahead. Captain pulled Kodama's bags from the back and carried them himself along with his own. "Here it is, Kodama-san. Welcome. Hope you've packed better shoes than those."

They entered the house through a damp vestibule where, seen by flashlight, chopped wood stood on one side and shelves of cans on the other. Suddenly a dog and a cat brushed his legs. He leapt aside. Humiliating, that the captain laughed and the others joined. These people did not understand. Entering the house, now angry, Kodama braced himself for a continued chill. Instead it was warm with a mellow odor of burning wood. Captain explained in the dark that the generator must need gas, and everyone busily lighted oil lamps and candles. By flickering light he could see unwashed pots in a sink on the left, but otherwise the kitchen appeared neat.

"Shoes by the door, please, Mr. Kodama," said the wife, pointing to the line of boots and heavy shoes left by the others. She started dropping pieces of wood into a stove by the sink. Soon a flame licked up through a circular opening. To the right, inviting him, lay a carpeted room with stuffed chairs and wood paneling. Through a large window, lights from the town glinted far away over water.

"His feet are wet," said Captain. "Henny, in my top drawer, bring Mr. Kodama a pair of boot socks." The boy went obediently. In Japan, people said that American children did not respect or obey their parents. This at least appeared not to be so.

In truth they all showed him great kindness. Soon the generator was working and they had electricity although it was dim and flickering. But then he needed to use the toilet. "Here we go," said Captain with strange cheer. "You'll need better shoes than those." He produced rubber boots too large even with two layers of thick socks. Captain called the animals, now all outside, and locked them away, then led him with a flashlight through dripping trees to a bare wooden shack. Inside, there was only a hole in a board, and beside it a roll of paper over which a spider crawled. What safe home high from the ground had he left for this?

"Want me to wait for you, Kodama-san?"

He felt hollow and desolate. Be brave. "Not necessary."

"See you back at the house."

Alone, with only a flashlight to connect him to civilization, he squatted above the hole and looked out through black branches at the distant lights. Barbarians lived like this. Suddenly he laughed to himself and relaxed. So had lived every ancestor. Thus, it was good.

Next morning the sun sparkled on water seen through the large window. They ate fried eggs. The children obediently cleaned the dishes while Captain and his wife (by now she had told him more than once to call her Jody, but this was not proper) packed boxes into the vehicle. Kodama stood, not sure where he could help but feeling he should. Soon they were returning to the town and the wife again drove. The trees now looked less sinister. The mountains were green. One had snow on top, very like Japan although rougher. (Everything was rougher. Expect it of America!)

After delivering the children to school they returned to the fishing vessel. The others were already there working, even the elderly owner-woman who now was painting the box she had cleaned.

He surveyed the machinery. Through fervent study during the past month, after Captain Carford rescued him from the hated office and placed him in the shipyard, he had reeducated himself in longline equipment, especially that developed since his own experience and that suited for smaller vessels than he'd known. The most vital part of it on this vessel, the ridged wheel that would grip the line and pull it from the sea, appeared sturdily mounted by the starboard rail. Its black hydraulic hoses seemed connected in the right places. They had erected bins properly along the cramped deck space, wide enough to contain large fish. But where did they expect to cut baits and place them on hundreds of hooks?

From that table in the center against the hatch, where it interfered with bringing aboard the line? He followed Captain aboard.

"Hey, everybody. Meet your new shipmate," announced Captain Carford. "Hi" and "Yo" they called, but only one of them stopped work to come over. "Kodama-san, meet Seth O'Malley, my mate," said Captain. "Seth, this is Yukihiro Kodama, traditional longline man." He left for some other business.

"Right," said the large, hairy man named Seth. "How're you doing?" He glanced at his hand, then held it out. The hand was streaked with grease.

Kodama considered, controlled resentment, and took hold of the hand. It squeezed his slowly until he wanted to jump from the pain, but he kept his face impassive. Too late to harden his own hand against the crush. He remembered now that Americans made a contest of their handshakes. But this pressure was purposeful. When at last it ended, his hand had lost feeling. He glanced at it, black-matted and limp.

"Oh. Grease. Too bad. Rag over there."

No regret in the voice. Nor with the face, set in unsmiling lines even though the mouth stretched in something like a grin. Greasy red cap clapped down on random hair that showed no care for appearance. The appraising eyes had no warmth. Kodama took care to return the gaze with equal chill. A thick-boned American who'd never lacked food to feed his bearlike size. They would be enemies. And this was the only one who had even bothered to come greet him.

"Kodama-san's going to show us how to prepare for the Japanese market," Captain called across deck.

"I figure we already know how," said the man named Seth.

The two men's eyes continued the duel until Seth shrugged and walked away.

"Well, how do you do, sir?" It was the woman in trousers who owned the boat. She looked him over in such a frank and friendly manner that he felt confused. Easier to identify an outright enemy. She offered her hand.

He held up his own and backed away. "Not clean, madam."

"I should say it isn't. Don't get that on your clothes. Seth dear, fetch him a rag."

It was satisfying to see the reluctance with which the Seth man obeyed. This was the second strong American woman today, and the only two he'd ever met. He liked them both. (But please, madam, do not kiss me.)

To his relief she merely asked about his family and said she hoped he'd enjoy his stay.

"But now tell me," she continued. "I'm serving the boys steak tomorrow tonight for bon voyage as the French say, good trip. Animal protein for strength, and nothing but the best. Do Japanese eat meat, or should I pull you some fish from the freezer? And then you must tell me whether you want it raw or cooked."

Captain Carford laughed.

Kodama followed her talk enough to say: "Steak very nice, madam. And yes, cooked, also very nice."

"Good, good." She patted his arm and didn't seem to notice how he edged away. "See? You're already becoming one of us. And you may call me Adele."

"Yes, madam."

Kodama's perspective kept him in good humor even when Captain Carford next conducted him down a ladder with his gear into a dark compartment of bunks, and he realized there existed no space to separate authorities from crew. Even though he'd prepared himself to work side by side with ordinary fishermen as if he were back to being a student, he'd assumed that Captain had means to separate those he relied upon for expert advice. Captain helped place his bags on a bunk among all the others. An upper bunk at that, requiring him to climb with feet balanced first against the rail of a crewman in the more privileged bunk below.

As he unpacked, the thick envelope from Shoji Tsurifune fell to deck from among tightly folded clothes where he had slipped it. Papers forgotten in the excitement of everything else! He tensed.

"Dropped something," said Captain, and handed it to him.

Kodama restrained his impulse to snatch it back, and received the thing with a steady hand. Captain paid it no further attention.

Best to forget this envelope again, Kodama told himself. As the Subdirector said, it would probably never be opened but eventually burned. He placed it carefully at the bottom of his bag, and turned to the disagreeable high bunk that would be his quarters. Remember: better this, all of this— even the envelope that was surely of no importance—than a life spent sitting shoulder to shoulder at a table checking papers, supervised by an office weakling who trembled before his superiors.

"Think you'll be shipshape here, K-san?"

"Of course."

13

THE GREAT GAME CONTINUES

KODIAK, MID-SEPTEMBER 1982

Hank gave himself barely enough time to introduce Kodama and settle him in. There was an entire new set of gear to face. At least his friend appeared to be be adjusting. First hurdle passed with Seth. Even though Seth was snappish, he and Kodama seemed to have shaken hands warmly, judging by how their grips had lingered. The others would fall in behind Seth.

The sight of longline gear stirred old memories. But back then he'd been merely a bright-eyed kid with more muscle and energy than sense, jumping to Norwegian orders at beginner level. He might remember, after fifteen years, how to gut and ice a halibut, but he'd never been in charge of stalking them. It suddenly hit him close to panic. Only another day before they needed to leave for the grounds, with no way to learn by trial and error before getting into the thick of it. Adele's money was at stake. And his own reputation.

The floats around them clattered with activity. Crews thumped boxes from carts to decks and checked out noisy gear. But missing were the usual shouts and high-flown jokes before boats set out. The men all seemed grimly intent. He didn't recognize many of them, strangers to the regular fleets probably recruited in expedience: kids with big dangling hands, standing unsure of what to do. In command he was going to be nearly as greenhorn as the dumbest of them.

Jody stood dockside. He gestured her aboard but she shook her head. "Only when I'm crew. I'd be in the way now."

It meant he needed to lean over the rail. He tried to keep his voice down. "Go to Fish and Game, would you? But act like you're checking for your own info, not mine. About halibut. What depths do you find them? Any regs to the number of lines? Where's the best grounds west of here? And bait. Herring and squid, that was bait in the old days. And hooks. Somebody said they even have a different kind of hook these days, so maybe also different bait. Look for some booklet, or printouts."

Seth glared up from the windlass that he and Terry were fixing. "Try asking me. Think maybe I'd've asked around? Like, they find these fish down forty to a hundred fathom give or take, if you want to know. And up in the wheelhouse I've got a chart all marked with places. I've stood for drinks and found out all about places. And we got a hundred boxes of herring and squid waiting in the freeze locker. And incidentally, since this boat don't have freezers, we need ice—but for your information there's more boats this trip than ice to go around. But Jake at the icehouse, I shoot hoops with him nights at the high school since we've been on the beach. You can be glad I do."

"Wow," Hank cajoled, relieved. "You've seen to it all. Good job!"

"And maybe you'll notice we've got half the old-style hooks shaped like a J, but also partly the new hooks shaped in more of a circle that they say holds the fish tighter. Couldn't get more than a few hundred circle jobs from any one place because everybody's suddenly crazy for them."

"Good. Good for you. I'm impressed as hell."

"Yeah." Seth seemed mollified. "You just might've asked me, that's all. We don't need picture books to do this."

"Hey!" called Terry's good-humored voice from the depths of the windlass. "Stop your bitchin' and hold that flashlight steady."

"And we don't need imported experts, either," Seth added as his head returned to the machinery. The head popped out again. "Incidentally, boats our size are going out with seven crew for these pushes. I count we've got five of our own to do the work, and this one expert. With beefed-up crew on every boat in town, any spare dock rat worth hiring's taken. Odds came by last week before he went to some meeting in Anchorage, and I told him to come by again if he wanted. At least we know Odds, assuming he's not gone soft."

"Don't count on his not." Gone soft, Hank decided, could be the way out of hiring Odds if he really didn't want him.

Kodama emerged from below, planted legs apart, and circled his gaze. He had changed from traveling clothes into olive fatigues and a low, flat brown cap. The altered clothing seemed to have restored his old judolike confidence. But good Lord, thought Hank, it also made the man look like a classic Jap from old war movies. And those short boots barely above his shins would ship a sea-sweep in seconds. The guy must never have gone on deck in his days as fishing master.

Mo, who had finished work on the mast, came over to greet Kodama. Ham followed. All three were large men on the same eye level. It seemed friendly, although, Hank thought, Kodama might have managed a less superior air. As he started over to lighten the meeting, Kodama declared, "Bait table in wrong location. You move from there to here, please." He pointed, but clearly didn't intend to help.

Hank joined them quickly. "You think the bench here's in the wrong place?"

"Of course. Line will come in over machinery, coming in straight direction so. So therefore line must be coiled into basket. But table is where basket must locate. Table for cutting bait and securing bait onto hooks must locate somewhere else, but somewhere also away from place where entrails removed from fish." His hand swept the area. "This vessel is very small, thusly crowded. Therefore," he pointed far astern, "must carry table over there."

"Good," said Hank, taking one side of the bench. He made his voice firm and looked straight at the Japanese. "Grab your end, Kodama-san."

The head jerked back and the mouth tightened with a flash of judo combat. Hank held his gaze. With a curt *phhh,* Kodama placed hands under the bench and lifted. It was heavy even for two strong men. Automatically Mo and Ham lifted also.

"Good advice, Kodama-san. That's just where the baiting table belongs."

"Of course."

Tell Kodama flat out that he was only an equal among equals? Hank wondered. Or hope he got the message.

Adele drew Hank aside. "Your friend. Look at those silly little boots. He'll be wet in a minute. Send him up to Sutliff's for proper ones and put it on my account. Poor Jones would die to see a Japanese on his boat, but he wouldn't want him to suffer. Well, maybe he would, but never mind; Daddy's dead, rest him, and I'm in charge now."

Hank caught up with Jody on the dock. "Look, besides Fish and Game, will you take Kodama up to the store? At least find him something other than that Jap army cap, something with a tractor on it, maybe. And denims. And the right kind of boots. Adele says pay for the boots on her account."

"He does look kind of . . . Jap. But we'll pay. Adele thinks she owns everything she buys these days. She's being wonderful, but we should watch it."

It was unexpected how reluctant Kodama was to go with Jody. He insisted on riding in back of the wagon. Hank watched them off. Strange guy in ways not anticipated. Afraid of women? Or just women drivers?

Hank left to call on Swede Scorden and settle plans for delivery. He strode down the floating piers among the shouts and engine whirrs of preparation. Black exhaust spurted from tailpipes, then cleared, as engines were tested. Men swarmed over decks, more to each boat than usual for seining. They bent knees and grunted up frosty, dripping boxes of bait, or clanged new attachments into place. One crew was removing its seine to make room for longline, hand by hand over the power block into a wide-beamed skiff. Did the whole damned salmon fleet expect to hit the halibut?

When he passed the *Hinda Bee,* one of the guys saw him and waved. So did Gus Rosvic watching calmly from a chair crowded against the back of the wheelhouse. Hank returned both waves with a "Yo!" While his own men under Seth's bark were doing everything right, this crew seemed to mesh without instruction. Indeed, their baiting table was located astern where Kodama had ordered theirs. They'd longlined before and had it together.

"Wait up, Hank," called Gus. He climbed carefully down the ladder, then passed from his deck to the pier deliberately with his seat on the rail and legs lifted over rather than with the bounce and jump of younger men. Hank lessened his stride when Gus joined him, but the adjustment was not as great as he'd expected.

"You're going to spin for the halibut, eh?" Gus's words drawled in a comfortable voice that took its time.

Hank relaxed. "Joining the crowd, Gus."

"Nothing wrong with that." Pause. "Can't help but think yes and no, about seeing Jones Henry's boat fish without him. But it still pays his lady's bills. He'd be glad of that." They stepped aside to let a man pass wheeling a hand truck piled with gear. Bananas and waterproof gloves drooped over the rim of the top box. "Boat paid all right with your lady running her. Got to admit, Jody done all right out there."

"She'll appreciate your saying."

"Now, Jones's lady. That woman meddling much?"

Hank grinned. "As we speak, she's painting the fuckin' bait box yellow."

Gus halted and slapped his knees. "Ah hahaha! You don't say? Oh my. Somebody'd better park a truck over Jones's grave so it don't explode. Yellow, you say?"

"I'd hoped it might be some new kind of primer, but no such."

"Curtains and geraniums yet at the wheelhouse windows?"

Hank hesitated. He hadn't meant to make Adele a public joke. "She's just finding her way."

"Well, Adele's a fine girl. No weepy widow, I admire that. But Lord keep her out of my way! She ain't going to sea with you?"

"Not likely." (What if she ever got such a notion? He'd be firm.)

They had reached the road, and Gus was headed toward town instead of the fish plants. He held out his hand. It was big, and softened by years of water, but firm. "Good fishing to you out there, Hank." His clear eyes were calm beneath shaggy brows. "You maybe saved me some trouble in Whale Pass last month. Not that I couldn't have handled things on my own. Nothing to talk about, but I know it. I'm there if you ever need me. That goes for your lady too."

"I thank you, Gus."

The eyes squinted as they scanned Hank from head to knees and back again. "It's just a shame how much more fish my boys is going to catch than your poor displaced crab-pluckers."

Hank felt his energy revive. "You Anacortes Slavs would bet on your grandma's wedding night!"

"Now Hank, that's not nice."

"How much did you have in mind?"

"Same as last time wouldn't hurt nobody."

"Done." Another handshake.

The gravel road leading from the docks to the fish plants was pocked with holes that held water from one rain to the next. Hank automatically dodged water from trucks that hit the potholes. As he approached the plants, the prevailing odors changed from boat oils and fish from the net to a mash of steamed fish and ammonia.

The cannery in town that Swede Scorden managed, Pacific Future—which was now controlled by Tsurifune Suisan Ltd.—had a corrugated front visible halfway down the line of low buildings crowded close together. Hank chose to ignore a door cut in the metal, where steps led up directly to the office, in favor of the delivery wharves and bays in back where he could judge activity.

He heard shouts above the usual hums and grinds of machinery. Rounding the corner he saw people clustered rather than working, while a forklift with a pallet of fish stood unattended.

"All you had to do was fuckin' look where you was going!" shouted a voice. It came from a beefy young man in denims with a cap pushed back on curly hair.

"You try run me over!" The Asian facing him was thin and a head shorter. He wore the floppy yellow rain gear of the fish-handling gang.

"Back in Vietnam, don't they teach you to look where you're going?"

"You try all the time run me over."

A half dozen other Asian men watched without speaking. From inside the building several Asian women in hairnets and aprons came out cautiously.

"Somebody's got to teach you people to stay clear." The American jumped into the forklift seat and gunned the motor. The Asian folded his arms and remained in front of it. "Get out of my way or I'll fuckin' ram you!"

"Come on, stop this, back to work," called Gillis the dock foreman as he hurried over. He was a now-overweight man in his late thirties with whom Hank had slimed big halibut a dozen years before, a drifter from hippie times who'd stayed. "Go on now, go!" The women retreated toward the building and the men backed off, but the two contestants ignored him.

The American jerked his forklift into gear and advanced until the pallet board in front touched the Asian's knees. "You don't think I mean it? I mean it!" When the Asian didn't move he leapt from his seat and pushed the man aside. The Asian crouched and drew a knife. The American ran to a stack of pallets and grabbed a crowbar. He started swinging it like a baseball bat at all the Asians.

Foreman Gillis stayed clear. "Knock it off, knock it off!" he cried without effect.

Hank's voice, added to Gillis's, was lost in the general noise. He picked up a board, and decided to thrust it between the two if they closed on each other, but not to endanger himself further.

"*Halt!*" Loud, cold voice. The two men stopped. The group of Asians parted. There stood Swede Scorden. He strode to the American by the forklift and, being shorter, looked up at him. The man backed away. "Robbins. Go to the paymaster, then off."

"For the day, Swede. Right? Sir?"

"Fired. Move. Gillis, go with him and make sure. Call security if you have trouble. Robbins, you got warned twice about smoking that shit on the job."

"Swede, I only had a puff. These Vietnams, they get in the way like, like fuckin' ants. I'm just trying to keep 'em clear."

"I've watched from the windows. Some day with a pea-brain dizzy head you might succeed in running one down. But not on my wharf." Swede faced the Asian, who had quickly put away the knife and backed off. "Knife again and you're gone with your whole family, Tong. Understand?"

"Yes, Mr. Swede."

"All of you, to work!"

They scattered to their jobs. "Sir," cried Robbins. "Who's gonna operate forklift without me? I done it all summer."

In reply Swede climbed into the forklift seat. He circled the vehicle to stop by Hank long enough to mutter, "Fifteen minutes up in the office, make yourself at home," then drove into the shipping well.

Hank lingered instead. He looked down at the seiner that was delivering and chatted with its crew, then walked inside to the conveyor belts and watched gutted salmon flow past the women's brushes and scrapers. A half hour passed before he walked up the slippery back stairs to the cannery office. The unappetizing odor of steamed fish meat followed.

Dolores, at the front by the barrier ledge, knew him well enough to say, "He's back, all right," and to click open the gate without his asking. He walked past others waiting in chairs against the wall.

Swede Scorden sat with elbows on desk, calmly checking invoices as if nothing had happened. Glasses on his nose, a new addition to the man, tamed the scowl and set jaw of minutes before. "Yes, Crawford, come in and shut the door." Hank entered, and wondered if Swede was back to bringing a bottle from the drawer.

"Sit down." No bottle.

Hank settled into the single scuffed chair in front of the desk. Here was the man who had probably saved his life even though Jones Henry died in the same rescue, when Swede boldly drove a chopper through the storm to tow their life raft to safety. How should I thank him? Hank wondered.

Swede swiveled back and raised the visor of his signature red baseball cap. His square chin was shaved bare, revealing wrinkles and small blotches. Crisp gaze, starched shirt. This was the town-Swede on good behavior. Hank's Swede remained in the old days, lord of a remote cannery with a bottle of scotch always handy to lubricate negotiations, barking different radio messages at once to a half dozen seiners and tenders, uncanny in his ability to see through walls from his window overlooking the boardwalks and hold everything in motion. The red cap hadn't changed, but back then Swede had been all stubble and wire.

Hank cleared his throat. "Did I ever thank you for that wet tow from your chopper?"

"I trust not. We have enough soft heads."

"Where did you ever learn to pilot? You lowered that basket to our raft like a pro."

"Know the conditions. Then make it up as you go along. You think daily life's any different?" The voice sharpened. "I assume you're still taking out Jones Henry's boat and plan to deliver here?"

Hank grinned. "Since gratitude and business don't mix, it depends on what you're paying."

Swede adjusted his glasses and surveyed some papers. "For you, I'd say ninety cents for halibut up to forty pounds, a buck for those up to sixty, and a buck twenty for bigger."

"Wow. A cracked record. That's what everybody else quotes. What happened to three years ago when—I wasn't there, but I checked the records—you paid over two bucks?"

"You figure. More fish now. More boats. Back then halibut was still scarce. Now you could row out to Marmot Bay and shoot one for supper." He opened a drawer and produced a bottle of scotch and a single shot glass. He held out the glass. "Yes?"

"What about you?"

Swede merely filled the glass, passed it to Hank, and returned the bottle to the drawer. "Bring me quality iced, Crawford, and we might adjust a penny here and there. And by the way, cod has its price too, so don't use 'em for bait."

"You mean sablefish, what they're calling black cod? Or the cod with a little string from his jaw?"

"I mean the second, the straight New England cod. Black cod has black skin and oily meat—not bad, but it's not true cod whoever named it."

"We'd see one in the crab pots now and then but not enough to matter."

"Look sharper now. Your crab-pot world has changed. Crab's gone and true cod's taken its place. The one eats the young of the other, so if you clean out crab and weaken the stocks, look for fins in your net. That shouldn't be news to you, after all the opinions on why crab's disappeared." A buzz and he flipped on a speaker. "Yes, Dolores?"

"Joe Gillis is here. Should I tell him later?"

"I want him now."

The foreman entered, nervously brushing the bib of his coveralls. "I did what you said, Swede, but—"

"I smelled marijuana smoke this morning, just around the corner from the forklift well. Chased it. Your boy thought he'd gotten away. I've warned before. No potheads around machinery. Accidents close processing lines. And accidents bring lawsuits, now that everything's your brother's fault."

"But Swede, we're shorthanded. All the other young bodies went back to school. What about these big halibut deliveries coming up? The new Vietnamese you shipped in don't know enough to fill the gap. Besides, Robbie's a good worker. Knows the forklift. He's trying to save money so he planned to stay."

"He might have been a dead Robbie. Make do. No potheads."

"I *mean* we're shorthanded. Guys with not much more than a kicker engine now think they're too good for cannery work, that they'll go west for halibut. So there's nobody to pull in off the street. Some other plant gone short is sure to hire him. But Robbie's settled in here and we work good together."

Swede rubbed his chin. The zips of an office duplicator and clanks of machinery below filled the silence. "Take him back, then. Say you begged me as a special favor. No pot on the job, leave the foreign workers alone, one more chance. I'll be watching."

"Swede, you've gone soft," muttered Hank when the foreman had left.

Swede turned away, annoyed. "I meant that he might have been *dead*. Tong was once with Special Forces over there, and I imagine he's sliced a few throats for the U.S. Army. I've committed to helping some of these people who committed to helping us in Vietnam."

"Side of you I didn't know."

"Side of me you'd best forget. To anybody but Jody; I'm realistic about husbands and wives and she doesn't blab."

Hank remained thoughtful. "I was so glad to be done with my Navy hitch in 'Nam and get back to fishing that it's only now and then that I think of the people who helped us."

"You're not alone."

The foreman had left the door open. Craig Stevens of Fish and Game rapped on the frame. Hank knew the biologist from encounters and consultations; a bureaucrat to the bone, short hair, tie and all, but outdoorsman enough that his lean face had as much leather from sun and wind as any fisherman's.

"Have you people made up your mind?" growled Swede.

"Every time we check, we see more boats gearing up. Give me a final boat count, and I'll tell you how many days it'll take to fish up three million pounds. That's my quota." He shrugged. "Fact is, it'll probably be a full week."

Swede locked hands behind his head, a sign that he had relaxed. "You number crunchers. Why don't you stay in your office and phone if you don't have better answers than that?"

The biologist remained serious. "I like to keep moving."

"Not surprised. Keeps you harder to shoot."

"Considering the threats I get, that's not funny."

"Crawford here—you know each other?" Swede continued smoothly.

Craig glanced at the glass in Hank's hand. "The Japanese still treating you right, Hank?"

"Not bad, Craig." He didn't like the tone.

"Cushy deal, eh?"

"Has its points." Hank rose to leave and terminate the questions, but the biologist suddenly changed his tone.

"Uncle Swede," said Craig with a frown. "You're close to all this with the Japanese. With black cod in the Gulf, why at the Council a couple weeks ago did they get so reasonable all of a sudden? Some say they're going to lead us Americans into black cod and seem to cooperate to hell and gone. Then they'll slash price, shut down the market, and let us go broke so they—the Japs, I mean—can fish it all again for themselves?"

"Seems reasonable to me. That's how I'd play it."

"I wasn't joking, Swede."

"Nor was I."

The biologist left as stiffly as he had come. Hank began to look around for a reason to leave also. He had sipped the scotch for old times' sake, but booze no longer sat well in the middle of the day.

Swede, however, had cranked up and wanted to continue. "You're getting closer with the Japanese all the time, Crawford, so you'd better keep alert. What they're doing for you is definitely part of a plan."

"You know it. A damn game."

"So be realistic. These people have to maneuver. You yourself have helped squeeze them off more fishing grounds each year. For a while after we took over our two hundred miles, they panicked and paid well for other peoples' catch. But they've wised up. They hold the trump since they buy more seafood than anybody else, and sometimes their warehouses haven't emptied as fast as predicted. So they pay less, and the world price drops accordingly." Swede slapped papers on the desk. "You're right, it's a game. I've called it the Great Game before. The loser is whoever blinks first. Join where you can or fall behind."

"Then is Craig right? Was that just a game I watched at the Council last month? When the Japanese announced they'd close their black cod fishery in Three-A and help Americans get a toehold?"

"They know how to be graceful when they see they're losing. It'll probably let them keep more than otherwise, so call it survival strategy. Craig's probably right, though he wouldn't know why, and . . . I didn't feel like helping him out today. I think he'd expected to cry on my shoulder if he'd found me alone, since those quota-setters take flak all the time. Sure, the Japanese hope to hell Americans try for black cod and fail. Then with everybody mollified that they cooperated, they'll get back whatever quota they want. But in case that fails, they're getting American quota from people like you and Tolly Smith. They won't lose all the way in any case."

And I'm in their hands, thought Hank. It made him finger the shot glass and wish for another.

Swede echoed his thought. "You've fallen into their hands whether you admit it or not. I've been there longer than you. Sometimes I feel they've cut my balls off. But cheer up. They'll hold the rope loose as long as you deliver."

"What's become of us, Swede?"

Swede pulled open the drawer and thumped the bottle on the table. "We've crossed the ocean, Hank. That's what." He appeared older and tired as he poured a drink.

Hank returned to the boat with heavy feet, but at the sight of deck activity he brightened. Adele's friends had installed the new gear in the right places, if old memory served. Cramped indeed, all of it crowded onto a boat smaller than the old halibut schooners, but how good it all looked, prepared for action! He tapped the graceful curve of the chute that would guide the line overboard, now bolted where the seine skiff would have nosed. The metal gave back a satisfying *bong*.

Piece by piece he remembered. Boards on deck had to be fitted to form bins—checkers, they called them—that would receive and hold the fish until they could be dressed and sent below to be iced. And the gurdy, secured to the starboard rail where the rollerman would stand to gaff aboard the fish. He gripped the vertical gurdy wheel and shook it to test its stability. Next, he ran a finger in the ridge around the wheel's circumference where the line would be gripped, then patted the wheel and wiped a smudge on the shiny surface left by his hand. Neat piece of engineering.

Behind the gurdy stood the arrangement of cylindrical rollers that would press the line tight to continue moving it and to knock off any fish not removed by the rollerman's gaff. What had they used to call that thing? Hangman? Executioner? Chopper? "Oh, yeah, crucifier," he muttered aloud. And then there were slanted boards placed below the crucifier to catch the fish and slide them into the checkers.

But the biggest adjustment: the wheelhouses of the old schooners designed specifically to longline stood aft facing the work deck. This wheelhouse was located forward so that, to maneuver, he'd need constantly to look over his shoulder through the back door. He calculated his distribution of manpower. One man in the wheelhouse—himself or Seth. One at the roller, one or two to gut depending on volume, one below to ice, one or two to bait. They were six including Kodama, whose ability to pull his weight on deck was unknown. A seventh man would dilute the crew share, but if fish stormed in as rumored, the seventh would pay for himself.

As if in answer to his thoughts, Oddmund appeared alongside the rail. At least Odds wasn't wearing a suit. He'd come dressed for work.

"Yo, man!" exclaimed Mo when he saw him.

"You're comin' with us?" exclaimed Terry. Both seemed happy with the idea.

"Hello, Terry. Hello, Mo." Odds's voice, face, and manner were as sober as ever.

Hank studied him. As crewman once, Odds had pulled his weight and gotten along, and he seemed still sturdy despite his new office career at the native corporation. They shook hands. "So, Odds. Had a good meeting?"

"Our meetings are all good, Hank. Very important. But like I asked at the airport yesterday: Do you need an extra man this trip?"

Hank decided that on a short, pressured trip, Odds and Kodama would have little chance to continue their gripe about cruel white men. "Get your gear. Come aboard soon as you can. One bunk left below. You'll need to clear stuff off it."

"That's nice, Hank. Thanks. I've got everything in the truck. Office work is very important, but I miss boats."

Mo and Terry quickly absorbed their former shipmate into the work, and introduced Ham who had replaced him. Terry gleefully pretended to boss him around like a greenhorn, at which Odds smiled without taking offense.

When Kodama returned from shopping with Jody, he hovered between dignity and a new kid's excitement. Poking from the top of one bag were the shiny rims of new rubber boots, and from another a pair of work gloves on top of new foul-weather gear. A yellow cap with the name of a marine engine company nestled into his hair, and he wore stiff new jeans and a denim shirt. A red bandanna encircled his neck. On his feet were soft leather deck slippers of the kind the others wore.

"Now that's more like it!" exclaimed Adele. She had just cleaned her paintbrush and was preparing to leave. "No man on my boat should ever look anything but Amer—When you come to dinner tomorrow night, Yukihiro dear—you see, I've studied your name and already gotten it straight—I'll just throw those ironlike new dungarees into the laundry and have them dry and limber before you leave. So bring them in a bag and wear other pants and shirt."

Kodama's free hand touched the stiff denim ridge of a pocket possessively. "New pants are . . . ex'erent so thusly, madam."

"Yes, yes. Wear your clothes from the airplane, though, not those . . . army things. Now." She turned to Hank. "Three plants have approached me to buy my fish. I've told them each—"

"We're delivering to Swede."

"You've certainly taken hold! He's not one of the three." She drew herself up, then relaxed. "Well, I suppose that saves confusion for a poor widowed . . . Mr. Scorden could take a lesson in politeness from the French, but so could have Daddy, rest his soul." She pointed toward the bait storage box she had just painted. "Sunburst yellow. It certainly brightens things, don't you agree? What do you think? Be honest."

Hank decided to take her at her word. "Adele, it doesn't. We'd all hoped that was just an undercoat."

"Well now, no need to be *that* honest!" Her face with its aging folds drew down in what had become a pug-dog expression. "You men. Afraid of a little brightening up! Well." She sighed, and her face returned to its authoritative set. "Just like Daddy. I suppose this is still his boat, however much I . . . Do what you want, Hank."

"Thanks, Adele." When she had gone at last, Hank turned to his Japanese friend. "You're lookin' sharp, Kodama-san."

"Very American. And Madam Carford also bought new *nagagutsu,* what name here? Not thick rubber clothing but soft plastic, very strong." Kodama grinned in spite of himself. "And not black. Yerro!"

"Yellow, eh? Great. We call them oilskins, or just 'skins."

Kodama started to protest that he saw no oil on the clothing. Hank escaped toward the tubs of coiled line and bundles of line still unopened, and beckoned him to follow.

Seth called from the wheelhouse: "We still got miles of line to put hooks on, but make sure you know what you're doing there."

"Yeah, yeah, yeah," chirped Terry. He was cleaning his hands with a kerosene rag. When Hank passed he confided, "Ol' Seth's been on a dance ever since you called us to go fish. Plain buzzed." His face expanded with his grin to the ears. "Never seen him so buzzed. Everywhere! Sleep? We'd sleep, and there he's still looking over the charts by flashlight. Seth's been too long from real fishing. So don't mind him."

"Thanks for telling me."

Hank started to introduce Kodama, but Terry's hand was already wiped and extended. "Didn't have a chance last night. I'm Terry Bricks, and you're goin' to be fine here."

Terry's goodwill was so obvious that Kodama grasped his hand at once. "Yes, good. Thank you. Brick."

Hank explained the western use of first names. "So you'd call him Terry just as I've told you to call me Hank." Kodama frowned and listened, as he had done at least twice before, and trailed to the bundles of line as he insisted: "Hai. But, saying name is Brick."

"Work it out later. Now, there's all this line and all these hooks to attach. It might be different on big Japanese longliners. Do you see how it's done?"

Kodama frowned again. It seemed a struggle before he declared, "Of course."

"Then that's a good thing for you to start on. Oh. Maybe here's a new word for you. We call that monofilament string that separates the hook from the line a gangion."

Another pause, then, "Of course."

Seth had come up behind. "I'll stand by at first to make sure you get it right," he said with elaborate cordiality. "Can't afford to screw it up."

Odds joined them. Since he had worked gangions before, he attached them correctly. Soon Kodama had learned the trick (or knew it already). It relieved Seth of his pleasure.

But then, as Hank had feared, Kodama and Odds began to talk earnestly while their hands attached hooks on gangions to the main line. Starting already. Hank looked around to see Mo heading off for groceries with his sidekick, Ham. "Hey," he called. "I need Ham for something here. Take Kodama-san with you instead."

Mo's wide face dropped. He'd probably planned a quick beer with his buddy. Too bad. "It'll let Kodama see another part of town, and an American supermarket."

When they returned, Kodama was carrying a box as heavy as Mo's. Maybe he'd learned.

Mo drew Hank aside. "You should have seen it, Boss. They had hot popcorn in the store, with lots of butter, you know? You'd never seen anything like the way ol' Kodo plowed into it. Never seen popcorn before! So I got us a big box of popcorn to pop."

"That's nice of you. But where'd you get that name Kodo?"

"Seth, I guess. It's easy to say."

"He may not like it. Japanese are pretty sensitive about some things."

"When I called him that he didn't say nothing. Just kept hittin' the popcorn."

Activity became progressively more hectic next day, the final one before departure. Fish and Game confirmed that the opening would run from Friday noon to the next Friday noon. The rules were clear: no gear permitted in the water before the starting noon signal, and all gear back on deck by the closing signal. Strictly enforced. ("Enforced over four, five hundred miles of ocean?" scoffed Seth as he listened to the announcement. "Good luck on that one.")

Adele Henry made her own terms clear that afternoon before she left to prepare dinner. "Six sharp, boys. We're always informal, but you know the rules."

Adele's dinner featured masses of steak flowing with juice. There were seconds for everyone, since, as she stated, "I believe in protein for a happy crew." She served it all herself, insisting that even Jody stay seated, "since captains have better things to do," while wearing an apron decorated with green rolling pins and yellow spoons and phrases in French. If the red wine, "à la français" as she called it, wasn't as good as cold beers to anyone except Hank and Jody, it had everybody mellow following the household's single-stiff-scotch-each before dinner. "I know you boys like your booze first, just like poor Daddy when he was alive," Adele had declared earlier. "And we don't stint on a single drink. But there's a limit when French wine's to follow."

Hank had raised his highball glass, and winked aside to Jody. "To Jones it is!"

With the wine, Adele herself lifted the first glass. "I want you boys to drink to our Captain Jody. I'm so proud of her and so should you be. This last summer, she's done all womanhood proud."

"Give it a yo for Captain Jody," seconded Terry. "That's a lady who's gotten to be some fish-killer out there."

Kodama turned to Hank. His eyes had widened in near horror. "Your wife is fishing captain?"

"She's that."

Kodama's unconcealed shock unleashed gleeful shouts and further Jody-toasts around the table.

"That ought to tell you something, Kodo," said Seth with a thin smile.

Jody raised her own glass. "Here's to our new friend Kodama-san. We hope your stay with us will be just wonderful." Her sharp look around the room brought up even Seth's glass.

Kodama's hand went to his mouth. Then he pulled it away, to admit openly the pleasure he felt.

Dessert was pecan pie with mounds of ice cream. Adele brought in also a bottle of orange liqueur and a tray of small glasses. "Now this is how the French do it, and I shouldn't have to tell you how civilized they are in everything they do. Of course you just sip it for the flavor. And inhale it for the bouquet, as they say. It's a lovely custom."

The crewmen murmured cautiously over how nice this was.

Mo, usually bashful in company, had by now drunk enough to wave his little glass. He started to stand up, almost tipping his chair, thought better of it, and spoke from his seat. "Seth? Think we better drink to our new bet with the *Hinda Bee* guys?"

Jody laughed. "You didn't!"

Seth gathered their attention and leaned back, enjoying it. All scowl had left his face so that, framed by the signature tumble of straw-blond hair, he looked like a friendly Viking. "Sure we did. *Hinda Bee*'s geared for long-line too. So Mo and me bet 'em three hundred each of us on biggest delivery this opening."

After general shouts, Ham said, "You ain't the only ones. Terry, tell 'em about us."

Terry stood. "Well, after Ham and me ended in jail last time fighting over our own bets with *Hinda Bee,* and got to be buddies with them and all? There's no way we didn't put something down too, me and Ham. So, I guess, the only people don't have bets riding on this trip are our skippers, and Odds, since he'd call it a sin or something, and Mr. Kodo here, who I guess nobody asked."

"And who asked *me,* I'd like to know!" exclaimed Adele. She stood with the apron just removed and hands on hips. "Heaven knows I'm no gambler, but I'm good for another three hundred, right at that Gustav Rosvic himself when I see him. Thank God for such tigers in my crew! Some bets might be a sin, I suppose, but not when it's for our very honor."

Hank cleared his throat. "Well, a couple of hours ago Gus and I shook hands on a bet."

Jody's eyes narrowed. "How much?"

"Uh, what was our bet in Uganik, honey?"

"Too much! What's that have to do with it?"

"We just said, same bet as before."

"You know we've got three children to send to college?" She glanced at the others at the table, and pulled herself together. "You boys had better fish your hearts out!"

"We will!" said Ham earnestly, and Mo echoed it.

Kodama watched it all, understanding some, confused by the rest, but somehow included and captured within the group's energy. Was this something that Director Tsurifune expected him to report?

Next morning the men unmoored to the good-bye waves of Jody and the kids and to Adele's admonitions to keep safe but bring back tons of fish. Other craft of all sizes were leaving also. By now Adele had marched herself to the rail of the *Hinda Bee*, called out to skipper Gus, and challenged him three hundred dollars on his crew's catch against hers. She said it in such a loud voice that he could only pull at the hairs of his white sideburns, look around at other crews listening and at his own men's expectant faces, and say, "All right, woman, you asked for it." He glanced again at his crew. "Afraid to make it four hundred?"

"Four? I'm not afraid to make it five!"

"Five it is!" he said, echoed by *Yo!*s from his crew.

Hank took ice at a further pier, where, thanks to Seth's preparation, they went to a side bay instead of a queue behind other boats. Hank steered them through the buoys toward the open horizon, squinting into the sun. The water sparkled. Leaving harbor at last, the deck began to breathe and roll beneath their feet. After the turn west at Cape Chiniak they hit a thirty-knot southeaster nearly head-on. Sea gurgled through the scuppers. They joined a flotilla on the march, one of many boats bucking swells that raised bows and plunged them into spray.

Kodama regarded the others' whoops and loud jokes with curiosity. Even Odds swayed smiling to the vessel's motion. Water splatted against the wheelhouse windows. It did feel like going into battle. His own mouth stretched wide in spite of himself.

14

SHAKEDOWN

GULF OF ALASKA, MID-SEPTEMBER 1982

It was a good thing they had radar. Visibility often fell to a few feet of rough water on every side. Hank could only keep track of boats around them, unseen in foggy rain, by their green electronic blips on the screen. Yet however he adjusted the gain, seafoam added phantom blips indistinguishable from boats that might have changed course and headed toward them. Worse, the wiper at the wheelhouse window by the helm had become too sluggish to cope with the volume of spray. He stationed Terry outside the windows at the bow, and Mo and Ham by the port and starboard rails. Nevertheless, he continued full throttle, since changing pace meant falling behind into the track of other vessels.

Not since his navy days in convoy had he traveled in so much company at sea. Whenever they entered a gap in the fog he quickly checked the horizons. None of the swaying masts and bucking hulls around them had changed relative position. Without landmarks to show passage, they might all have been thrashing stationary in a vast tub.

At first, lookout duty brought lusty yells from Terry, Mo, and Ham, charged to be back on the water. But the wet novelty soon ended. By the time Hank relieved them with Odds, and later with Seth and Kodama, each frowning at duty they considered menial, they stumbled to the galley glum and dripping. For a while, only the *whoosh* of water above the engine throb and the chatter of radio bands provided him company alone in the wheelhouse.

Seth, returning drenched and testy from his watch on the bow, went to the chart table and tapped it. "I'm the one who figured out all these places we might fish, while you partied with your new buddy in Japan. You think I can't steer in a fog? Or keep us safe on radar?"

Hank considered. "You're right. I'll take the next bow watch and give you the con."

Indeed, he welcomed open air for a change, to stand looking into the water with his back against the outside of the wheelhouse. He held tight, and enjoyed even cold sea-slaps in the face when the bow plunged and fans of spray arched over him. The bulk of water hit his chest fist-like, and sluiced off the oilskins that insulated him while making him glisten like the anchor chain. But frigid water trickled inside his hood no matter how tight he drew it, while deck waves kicked against his boots and even crawled under the rubber bands that sealed the oilpants against his legs.

Soon his feet turned icy, and he shivered even when flapping arms against his chest, but he made himself stand a longer watch than the others. Then he took Jody's Fish and Game material on halibut to his cabin. It would be hours before they reached the grounds beyond Kodiak Island that were open to them, giving him time to decide how far west to venture before setting lines. Let Seth keep the wheelhouse if he wanted it so badly. He raised the rail on his bunk and braced in with cushions against the boat's motion, turned on the lamp to read, and spiraled into sleep.

He woke to Mo's thump on the door announcing dinner. Outside it was dark. The boat had run safely without him. Good crew. He rubbed his head. Hadn't left orders. Slipshod. He hurried to the wheelhouse, holding rails against the motion, rehearsing what he'd banter with Seth to ease his desertion. There was cheerful Terry at the helm. The weather had cleared even though wind still rolled seas at them from the southeast. Lights of other boats shot into the air, swooped to blink out for moments close to the water, then swept high again. Overhead, stars raced across the sky as their own boat pitched.

"This is some like it," Terry declared. "On the water and all. The guys on the *Hinda Bee*? They've been calling on radio. That's them to starboard. And *Lady West*'s to stern of us. And *Lucky Sue* ahead. All the guys me and Ham had that great fight with in Solly's and the jail, and now we're buddies. It's like we've got a Kodiak bar out here, but without the booze."

By now the mass of Kodiak Island showed on radar only in the distance astern. Hank turned on the night-light and studied the chart. Time to commit on where to fish.

"Poor ol' Kodo. He's puked until there's nothing to come up. Not that he didn't stand his watches until things cleared and Seth called it off, but I think now he's dead in the sack. I thought he was supposed to be a fisherman."

"He's used to ships, but he's been ashore for years." Hank said. "He'll find his legs."

In the galley everything rattled in its racks. Mo's steaks and spaghetti slid on plates anchored by a wetted tablecloth. The men had settled into sleepy good humor. "Fishing with hooks and bait," said Mo. "Haven't done that since I done it with bent nails and worms back in Iowa at the old farm pond, Sundays after chores and church."

"You miss that too?" asked Ham, his mouth full.

"Didn't say I missed it. Maybe miss the folks and my sisters. But all that pushing cow shit every day? From asshole to milk floor to field, over and over and over? And both Sunday school then church, and prayer meeting every Wednesday?" Mo shook his head. "Couldn't wait to enlist for Vietnam. Then I did, seventeenth birthday. Papa couldn't say no to serving my country, only way he'd give up his free man. But war ended before I got there, and I was marchin' up and down in Texas where nothin' grows. I guess then I did miss . . . Sure, okay, the folks. I'd sure miss it if I didn't go back every Christmas. Haven't skipped a year yet." He thought about it. "Never will, I guess."

"And you go home," snapped Seth, "and first thing anybody says is . . ." he altered his voice to a high wheedle, "When you going to marry some nice girl and settle down like your brothers and cousins?"

"You too!" Ham turned to him. "You're older than Mo and me, so I guess Vietnam didn't shut down before you got there. We missed it all."

Seth, after a silence, muttered, "Burst eardrums."

Terry, having been relieved on watch by Odds, filled his plate at the stove, crowded in around the table, and reached for the steak sauce. "Me, I was on the pier in Tillimook, bumpin' fish guts on a hook against the pilings, before I was big enough for my daddy to take me on his boat." Balancing his plate, he shook the bottle. Suddenly the sauce gushed out in a puddle. "Whoa, shoot!" He held the plate to his lips and slurped the excess. "Fishing hook and line, all by yourself—I've done worse."

"And beer!" said Ham. "Back then on the farm."

"Not in my house, man," said Mo. "We were Methodists."

"I was like, fourteen, maybe fifteen. Threshing all day. And hot? Then, before dinner, everybody in the icehouse taking turns at the pump? My pop hands me a beer along with everybody else, says, 'you done a man's work today so why not, but don't tell your ma.' Man, I took a sip and a second later it was slurp, never since drank anything so good. As if Ma didn't know the second I walked into the kitchen."

They ate for a while in silence, each with his thoughts.

Kodama did not appear. "I had some of that popcorn ready to go for him," said Mo.

"I guess in Japan the water's not so rough," observed Seth.

"Make the popcorn anyhow," said Ham.

"Uh-uh. That's special for him. To make him feel at home."

"You call popcorn Jap food?"

"Not the way I mean it."

Hank finished, rinsed his plate, then climbed down to the bunk hold. Kodama lay curled with a T-shirt over his head.

"Hey. Doing all right?"

"Of course."

"Come up to dinner."

"No. If time to catch fish, I will come."

Hank wanted to pat his head, refrained. "Take it easy. You'll be fine."

"Of course."

Hank pondered charts for the grounds he should try. The Fish and Game papers said that halibut schooled on shelves at 30 to 225 fathoms. In another hour they'd reach a ridge of continental shelf that dropped from 150 fathoms to the depths. They could set lines along it. By now fewer boats moved in company. Some had already chosen their grounds and halted.

How simple it had been through the seventies, he mused. Then only the grand old wooden schooners went for scarce halibut, going out for three weeks at a time on such traditional grounds as Portlock or Albatross Banks, while other boats prospered elsewhere on crab and shrimp and left them alone. He traced the contours of Albatross with his finger. He'd helped fish there as a greenhorn and thus knew it at least slightly, although Norwegians with lifetime experience had done the thinking on where to set. Now that halibut stocks had risen and even salmon seiners like the one he rode trooped out to catch the big fish, so many boats were pressuring halibut that the openings had been cut from weeks to days. And this restrictive opening didn't even include Portlock or Albatross but only waters to the west of them. New grounds, some of it, but with no time provided for novice trial and error.

In his own brief time nature had changed it all, turning the cycle of abundance from crustaceans to finfish, with crabs and shrimp vanished but flounder everywhere. The biologists talked about weak year classes and hedged on altered water temperatures that may have changed feed migrations, but they hadn't proved a thing. The greenies naturally harped on overfishing, which would make sense if shrimp hadn't also disappeared in bays not fished. As for crabs . . . Like a dream, he remembered, those great years when pots came up choked with crabs. And how many thousands of rejected female and undersized crabs had they carelessly thrown back busted? Probably they had grabbed too much of the stock. Swede had it right. Since crabs were predators of baby fish, when their numbers diminished, the fish flourished enough to turn the tables. Now fish appeared to be gobbling a critical share of baby crabs.

Halibut, though, had to be a different story. They matured slowly and, according to the Fish and Game material, could live to forty years, so the big fish now reported in the water must have grown up somewhere away from predatory crabs and human hooks. They hadn't just turned big in the year since crabs disappeared. No single answer covered it all.

By early morning the men were lined aft baiting hooks. Hank reached the fathom curve he wanted, and shifted the engine to neutral. Seth appeared at once. "Couple of hours yet is where I have us to set lines." He pointed on the chart. "We want to hug that two hundred-fathom drop where I'm pointing."

Hank watched the lights of other boats moving beyond him, and fingered the edge of the chart. His own logic was as good as Seth's, and Seth was beginning to override his authority. "We'll fish here." He braced for a showdown.

After a pause Seth's outraged glare weakened and he looked away. "You're boss." Hank watched with equal portions of relief and regret. His old friend needed to be stronger for his own good. Nevertheless, Hank took the opportunity to add, "Kodama's not going to take your place, but he's under my wing. Lay off him, Seth."

"Shit, Hank. Tell him to lay off *me.*"

"I'll see to that."

"No, you won't. You can't." The voice was almost tearful. "It's all changed."

"Look. We'll fish first sets on my grounds here. If we don't like it, we'll steam to yours."

"If somebody hasn't grabbed the place I marked out."

By two hours before the noon opening Seth no longer grumbled. He held the work deck in control, gravely setting a pace. Under his direction they pulled tarps off the tubs of baited line and set them in rows by the chute astern. Then he slipped back up to the wheelhouse. "Who's going to see it," he said quietly, "if we put a few lines in the water early? We can use the practice. And don't think plenty boats don't do it."

Hank found it tempting but shook his head. Bend the rules once, he reminded himself, and it doesn't stop. An hour later a Coast Guard patrol plane swept overhead, dipping low at each boat to check for gear placed illegally in the water ahead of time. Seth acknowledged his near mistake with a hand passed across his brow.

As noon approached, Hank increased gain on the official sideband channel to make sure he heard the signal. On deck the men assembled in boots and oilskins. Mo, Ham, and Terry danced foot to foot, keyed for action. Seth himself attached the first of the tubs' lines to the flag buoy and then paced, waiting for Hank's signal. Odds stood calmly among them. Kodama kept his distance, frowning but as tensed as the rest.

Under a clear sky the sun had begun to burn off low patches of fog that alternately hid and revealed other boats on the horizon. A chilly southeasterly kicked water an inch or two across deck when the boat rolled. It was easy weather for September in the rough North Pacific, thought Hank. He cruised with the current, hugging the contour of the fathom curve as best he could while watching the chart and Fathometer readings.

"This is Alaska Department of Fish and Game. The seven-day opening for halibut has now commenced in Area Four-B exclusively, from due west of Kodiak Island to Unimak Pass. This opening will close at noon next Friday."

Hank's whistle echoed against others across the water. Seth threw over the marker. The line snaked over the chute astern, coil by coil from the tub, drawn into the water by the boat's forward motion. As Hank kicked the boat ahead, the line slipped out faster with hooks clacking merrily against the chute.

Seth had already directed Mo to place another tub by the first, and he himself attached the end line of the first tub to the start line of the second. "That's how you do it," he announced. "Each tubful of line they call a skate. It's one hundred twenty fathoms, which is seven hundred feet, no, seven hundred twenty feet, six feet to a fathom. We'll set ten skates this first crack. That's a longline of say seven thousandsome feet, which is more than a mile. All of you follow?"

"I've set longline before," said Odds. "If the skipper knows how long, it don't matter who else does."

"Maybe *you* think so." Seth looked at the others, and settled on Kodama. "I guess you know this too, don't you?"

"Of course."

"Come on, man," said Terry gently to Seth. "We seen you studying this stuff all week, and buying drinks for guys so they'd tell you stuff. And this ain't your first lecture, but we're still listening. We respect what you've learned."

"Yeah. Well." Seth tried not to show his pleasure. "When we start bringing this line back aboard, and there's fish on the hooks, we won't stand around long. Man at the roller to gaff the fish over the rail, that'll be me, maybe an assistant if they're big. Then somebody to coil the line back into the tubs. Each man fills one tub, that's one skate. Then he carries it back, chops new bait, knocks off any old bait, and puts new bait on each hook. Each bait, put it on carefully so it don't fall off. But there's about one hundred fifty hooks on a skate, so you can't drag your ass. And you've got to coil line and hooks back into the tub so there's no snags when it pays overboard next time." Seth looked at each of his men in turn but ignored Kodama. "Now. These new circle hooks, like the kind just going out, they take the bait in a different way than the old style; you have to slide it around further. We've got half of each, and after three skates of the new circles we're putting out three skates of the old-style J hooks. That's what we call a scientific method."

"Fuckin' science," said Mo. "That's good."

"We've all of us coiled tons of line from crab pots," said Ham. "That's the one thing's no problem."

"Not with hooks you haven't. Or with line that has little lead weights every few feet to help it sink. This is new." Seth chewed his lip, then turned to Kodama who watched with legs spread and hands behind his back. "Since you're the expert, I guess you know all about how to coil with the hooks laid just right. And about how to bait the different kinds of hooks. Yes? *Hai,* is that how you say it over there?"

Kodama glared at the tone. Finally, without moving: "Of course."

"Then, Kodo, why don't you stand beside each man while he coils, and make sure he's right." Seth's lips stretched. "So any mistakes, I guess we just blame you."

Odds raised his hand like a kid in school. "Come on, Seth, I spent a whole week last year doing longline with my cousins. Nobody needs to stand over me."

"We don't need but one expert. And that'll be Mr. Kodo, since he's the best."

Hank, watching from the wheelhouse above, caught the thin, threatening smile that was becoming a disagreeable part of Seth. The man was now so involved in his lecture that the second tub had half emptied its line. Hank was about to call down (and make his voice sharp to put Seth on notice that the captain watched and stayed in charge) when Odds, at Seth's gesture, slid in another tub and connected the lines.

Hank had been tuning his speed to that of the line as it payed through the chute and into the water. He soon found that if he went too fast, hooks danced wildly and some of the bait flew off. The birds knew it at once. From one or two in the sky, suddenly screeching clouds of them converged to fight for dislodged bait. One bird swooped in and grabbed a hooked chunk of herring. The hook caught its mouth, and the weighted line dragged it beneath the water, squawking. One bird's misfortune did not deter others from buzzing the hooks. When Hank slowed, fewer hooks lost their bait but more birds chanced a grab.

Seth calmly continued his lecture. "And while I'm gaffing in fish and everybody else is taking turns to coil and bait, another man needs to gut the fish. Scrape it clean, mind, or the meat turns sour. Not making that up. Swede Scorden himself told me that, back at the plant. Then somebody to shove the fish down into the hold, maybe the guy gutting. And somebody down in the hold with the ice, maybe two—one to shovel and one to stack the fish in layers of ice. I've lost count how many that is."

"On my cousin's boat we all took turns doing everything."

"That makes sense. Except for roller man, which is the main responsibility."

"I've done roller," continued Odds. "I'll bet Mr. Kodama has too."

Seth folded his arms. "Anyway."

The line had payed smoothly from one tub to the next. Suddenly a snag of coils big as a basketball jerked up from the tub and clogged the chute. Hank had settled on two knots for his best speed. He slowed too late. Some of the hooks locked to a side of the chute and the snag held fast. The line pulled taut from the water, stretched, and snapped.

Seth was in the wheelhouse at once. "Whadda you mean goin' too fast?" he stormed.

The tone fueled Hank's tension. "No damn problem if you hadn't fucked up the coils!" Then he controlled himself. It had been his own fault, of course.

Seth waited, arms folded.

You might be wrong but keep charge, Hank told himself. "Trial and error," he said evenly. "I'll adjust speed. We'll start a new set with another marker buoy. Later we'll go back to the first buoy and pick up the broken line." Seth still scowled. Throw him an ego project, Hank decided. "Here's something. Why don't you figure out a kind of scarecrow buoy to bounce astern and keep birds off the hooks?"

"Serves the fuckers right if they drown."

"Every bird on a hook is one less fish. You're smarter than the birds."

"You can say that," Seth declared, mollified.

"Let's keep fishing."

"Suits me. Any time." Seth resumed his post on deck and they started to lay a new set. Carefully.

Soon Seth had slashed ribbons in an old pink buoy, tied it to a few feet of rope, and dropped it astern. For a while the thing bounced on the water and intimidated a few birds, but then propeller wake made it drift to the baited hooks and the buoy line wrapped around the fishing line. "Yo!" called Seth to the wheelhouse, but Hank had already shifted to neutral. They pulled back the scarecrow hand over hand to Seth's steady profanity, kicked the slashed buoy across deck, and resumed setting the longline.

"What we need to do," quipped Terry, "is tie Seth by the leg and bounce him overboard. He flaps his arms, cusses like that, it's enough to scare any bird."

Seth enjoyed it with the rest. "Don't worry. You think I'm through figuring how to beat fuckin' seagulls?"

Kodama's voice cut in. "Tie rope high from wheelhouse, not from stern.
Then buoy will bounce on water beyond where longline sinks."

Seth stopped laughing.

Without a further glitch they laid two full strings of longline, then
returned to the buoy marking the snapped line of three or four skates,
which had soaked longer than the rest. It was time at last to see what was
down there. "Flag aboard," cried Hank, and blew his whistle.

Mo, at the starboard rail, threw out a grapple, and more hands than
needed pulled aboard the marker buoy. Seth came alive. He grabbed the
line before anyone else, leapt with it over the boards of the checkers, and
spun it around the vertical wheel of the gurdy.

The gurdy turned with an oiled whirr, and the line it gripped began to
come aboard. Nothing could be expected for the first several hundred feet
of line, which, empty of hooks, had merely carried the baited line to the
seafloor. Except for Odds who began to coil, however, they all watched by
the inch. Seth stood tense at the rail, leaning over, the gaff in his hand
raised like a pistol at the ready. When the boat rolled away from a wave
the line drew taut and twanged off drops of water.

Kodama remained apart, standing as stiff as the new yellow oilskins that
encased him. Come on, guy, thought Hank, look alive. Don't make me
sorry I brought you from Japan.

Odds filled his tub with the plain line, and disconnected it from the line
with hooks that was starting to surface. "Me next," said Terry. He slid up
an empty tub, overturned another to sit on, and prepared.

"I've had the experience," said Odds. "If you take back this tub I've just
filled, I'll—"

"Go 'way. In ten minutes I'll be experienced too."

"Fish! First fish!" announced Seth. He leaned so far over the rail that only
his buttocks showed.

"Don't fall over!" cried Hank from above.

"Ahh, we'd fish him back out," said Terry. "Good practice."

"Ha!" Seth's gaff struck down out of sight. He brought up a little
pound-weight cod, its spotted coppery back arching sluggishly. They all
booed. In disgust Seth flicked it back into the water.

"Big fish killer there," called Terry. "Start shoveling. Ice! Ice!" Mo and
Ham took up the call.

"You wait," growled Seth. He banged each hook after it passed through the wheel. It made them bounce out on their gangions, and bait that still clung flew off. The action helped absorb his energy. Seabirds converged in the water wherever the bait fell.

The line continued to come aboard. Soon Terry fell silent as he concentrated on nesting the hooks. Suddenly Kodama squatted beside him, snatched the line, and began to coil with a precision that placed each hook in exact alignment with the others inside the coil. "Thus!"

Terry started to take offense, then saw the perfection and murmured, "Okay, thus." He took back the line and bent to it with increased attention.

"Now. Now!" exclaimed Seth. His arms disappeared over the rail again. *"Hah!"* Up flapping on his gaff came a halibut. Mo and Ham cheered. Seth, his legs and back swaying to the motion, passed the line over the gurdy wheel while holding free the hook and fish. "Eeee-asy does it!" he crooned. "Into the boat, baby!"

"Thirty pounds at least!"

"Forty!"

The fish slapped down inside the checkers and continued to thrash. Mo and Ham bumped shoulders converging on it. The creature slipped from their hands and thumped against their legs. Laughing, they managed to lift it to the hatch top.

"Hold him down," cried Mo. "Just give me time to . . ." He quickly honed a knife against the steel hanging from his belt. "Got to cut him here where they call it the poke."

"Seems almost a shame," murmured Ham as he held the halibut. "Fighter like that and all."

"It's a *fish.*"

"That's true." Odds moved in. "The Lord made all fishes for the food of mankind, so don't feel bad about it. I know how to do this. I'll show you."

Kodama brushed them aside. With a knife already in hand he made deft incisions near the fish's head, sawed out gills and entrails in a piece that he tossed over the side, and began to clean the hole. "Must scraping scraping," he declared.

"Next one!" called Seth. "Coming in smoooooth as hotcakes." He leaned over the rail. "Bigger. He's big! I got him." The fish that rose was nearly double the size of the first. It stayed passive. Seth hit the controls with his knee to stop the gurdy, and grunted to lift the fish over the rail. Suddenly it twisted from white belly side to brown green upper, thrashed free of the hook, and splashed back into the water with Seth's gaff still in its head.

"Pole, pole! Grab him!" Seth leapt madly back over the checkers while Mo and Ham struggled to dislodge a dip net. By the time the net reached overboard the halibut had shaken off the gaff, and its brown shape had flickered and merged into the dark water. "Shit. Shit!" cried Seth.

"Never mind," called Hank from the wheelhouse. With anyone but Seth he'd have made it a joke.

They retrieved the gaff. Seth returned to the roller and started the gurdy again.

"I will show," said Kodama, advancing.

"You stay the fuck away," Seth snarled.

Halibut began to come aboard one by one, and the men slowly developed a rhythm. From above, Hank watched over Seth at the roller, his gaze fixed on the spot where hooks emerged from the water. Sunlight glossed the surface, but fingers of shadow from the boat's side allowed glimpses into the depth. A green-white shape would appear far down. Slowly it would undulate upward, twisting on a hook. Difficult to tell the size until it broke the surface.

Sometimes the hooked creature was a mere fat bullet of cod or sculpin, limp at once in the air. (Hank remembered Swede's admonition, stopped Seth from tossing cod back, and designated a small checker to hold them.) But the halibut, flat as shovels, would hit the air and seem to consider, then explode with energy. Seth needed to lodge his gaff in their heads before the thrash began, or lose them. Two of them tore from the hook and escaped before he realized how soon he needed to act. With gaff lodged, Seth's arm might have been slammed by an actual shovel for the beating it took as he shared weight with the gurdy to bring the fish aboard.

"Let Odds or Kodama take roller for a while," Hank called.

In answer Seth stopped long enough to peel off his oilskin jacket and wipe a ragged sleeve over his face.

Hank's arms ached to hold the gaff and feel the struggle. As captain he'd turned superfluous since the drag of the longline itself kept the boat in position, while at any time he could shift the boat's engine controls to the panel alongside the roller where Seth reigned.

By the time the first set had come aboard—and the broken line was no more than a third of a full set—the deck beneath the checkers had disappeared under a dozen big flat halibut. Terry, Mo, and Ham had each coiled and rebaited a skate—Terry twice—and the latter two had climbed into the hold to stack dressed halibut in layers of ice. Seth's pace had become measured, and only two more fish escaped him. Hank closely watched Odds and Kodama, who held post shoulder to shoulder by the gutting table. Intestines flew from under their knives and blood streaked their yellow oilskins. Odds's incisions into the leathery halibut skin were businesslike and detached. Kodama's became sweeps from the judo floor: ferocious though precise, the work of his entire body. Both men appeared too absorbed to discuss the world's wrongs.

While Hank cruised to the next marker buoy, the men hosed away blood and entrails and took turns washing off one another. Seth paced, massaging his right arm. Terry, his coiling done for the moment, stretched elaborately.

Mo beckoned Kodama closer. "Come on, your turn; I'll spray you down."

"I shall waiting to clean myself."

"No, you don't, buddy. We're all a team. Turn around, let me hose your back. Then you do mine."

Kodama frowned his frown but complied, suppressing a smile.

"*Adele H,* tune in if you hear me," came a gravelly, even voice over the CB radio. "*Hinda Bee* calling."

Hank dislodged the mike from its overhead bracket. "Sounds like Gus Rosvic."

"Right here, Hank. Watching you through binoculars about three miles off your port beam. That's us you see. Now that I've taken to making dockside bets with widows who can't stop talking, I've got to keep my eye on you. Looks like you've stopped hauling. Given up already?"

Hank chose not to admit to a snapped line. "Deck's so full we took a breather."

"That's nice. Shouldn't work too hard and tire out if you're not in shape. Now, I'd say we have five thousand pounds of dressed halibut iced away, and the buggers keep coming. How does that reach you?"

Hank calculated quickly. They were only some four hours into the opening, and that could be eighty to a hundredsome fish depending on size. Maybe bluff. Their own good catch wasn't close to this. Lost time, of course, with the broken line. "Makes me feel sleepy, Gus, sleepy. If that's all you've got I guess we can grab some bunk time while you catch up. Maybe even go ashore and hunt a little."

"You do that, you do that. Now, my boys are working too hard to come to the phone, but Zack down at the roller asked me to tell your Terry he's willing to double their little bet. Naturally I don't approve of gambling. But to buy into a sure thing don't count as gambling."

"I'll tell him, Gus. He's so up to his elbows in fish right now I couldn't pry him loose."

"So I see."

Hank had forgotten the binoculars. Before he could think of an answer, Gus said, "'Course, it ain't nice to take money from widows and orphans, but sometimes you can't help it."

Hank laughed. "Hang in there, Gus. Maybe you'll have better luck later on."

At least one thing was certain. This ridge of seafloor had enough action to keep them both busy.

15

SOAKERS

GULF OF ALASKA, MID-SEPTEMBER 1982

The sky darkened around eight, but on this first day they still had a mile of longline hooks to work from the final set. By now the sight of halibut thrashing in the checkers raised no more grins.

Hank had long since entered the system. He did it responsibly, accepting himself as an inbreaker again after a dozen years at other fishing jobs. He cut chunks of frozen herring, then coiled a skate, then baited it. He submitted in good humor to Kodama's tutelage at the gutting table, although after the first slice through a halibut's springy hide his hands remembered the steps to slice out gills and entrails as the Norwegians had once taught him so exactly.

But, "Ha, no no," corrected Kodama.

It appeared that the Japanese observed a different order of incisions, even though the result remained the same. And, had the old Norwegians scraped the poke—the cavity left after evisceration—so repeatedly? All he remembered was a vigorous pass with a curved tool. "Then scraping scraping it is, Kodama-san." His greater concern was lack of an essential piece of clothing made for steady gutting. How could he have forgotten wristers, the waterproof sleeves with elastic at both ends that locked against elbows and down around rubber gloves? Only Odds had brought a pair. Blood and gurry soon splatted far above the gloves to soak the sleeves of his plaid shirt. A day or two of this would rot the cloth.

Seth continued to grunt aside anyone who tried to relieve him at the roller. Clearly he thought he possessed the job, and just as clearly everyone else wanted his turn. Hank tried to cajole him away but made it no issue. Seth had indeed become adept. His performance turned dancelike in its rhythm. Now and then, when a halibut beyond fifty or sixty pounds nosed the surface, he'd mutter, "Some help here." In the rush to grab gaffs and reach the rail, the others (except Kodama) crowded so tightly that Hank stepped aside. He would watch a flapping creature rise lightly under the multiple prongs in its head while his own arm itched to share the kick of the big fish.

At last a halibut worthy of all the gaffs broke the surface and Seth cried "Everybody! Everybody!" Its weight stretched Hank's muscles across his back. The creature filled one of the checker bins. Two hundred pounds at least. It lay quiet and they clustered to admire it. Ham ran for his camera, "To show my mom."

"What we call a soaker, those big ones," said Odds.

Hank remembered the soaker that had once exploded into motion and broken his arm. "Stand clear. Treat him with respect."

Terry moved to Seth at the roller. "Nice going, man. I'll take over now."

"No, me, I can," said Mo.

"It needs a certain touch," said Seth smoothly, and eased them aside.

Suddenly the soaker arched its back with such energy that the whole flat body rose from deck, then thudded down. The tail thumped the boards in drumbeats, and smacked one board from its grooves. Kodama, without ceremony, picked up a club that had been provided as part of the gear, and pounded the fish's head. At last the creature subsided.

"That's what you've got to do," said Odds. "But it's a shame. Like the white man beating back the Indian people. All these years."

"Eh?" Kodama looked from Odds to the club, and lowered it.

"Let's keep that line coming in," said Hank quickly.

Some time in the early afternoon Mo left work long enough to slap together bologna-onion sandwiches dripping with mayonnaise and mustard. He passed them around on paper napkins, with a wet towel for hands. Kodama stepped back from the one offered him, and the side of his upper lip rose. "Go on, try it," said Mo. "It's good." Kodama slowly wiped his hands, and bit a piece near the crust as he might a cockroach. The frown remained as he started to put the rest aside, then tried another small bite, and continued.

Seth insisted on eating his sandwich with one hand while he continued to gaff at the roller. Suddenly he shouted, "Fuck!" A hook had sprung up on its gangion and lodged in his arm. The others clustered around him.

Hank brought his medical kit and examined it. The barb was embedded deep enough, and merely in flesh, that he decided to push it through by the shank rather than pull it out. "Somebody get me the wire cutter."

"Eahhhh!" Seth yelled and yanked. The barb pulled free with a small patch of skin, and blood dripped to deck. Hank shrugged, and swabbed the wound with peroxide.

"Just wrap your bandage around it quick," Seth snapped. "There's a big one almost at the surface, I need to get back."

"You're relieved," said Hank firmly. "Good job."

Odds moved in to the roller before Terry or Mo could race from Seth's side. Birds by now had become a presence. They rode the water, rising and dipping on the swells, and surrounded each toss of offal to peck until it sank. After Odds had served two hours at the roller he declared, "My arm don't mind a rest." He relinquished his spot to Mo, and took it upon himself to name the birds for Kodama. "The white ones, they're gulls. And those gray ones? Fulmars. Those little ones that skit but don't settle? Kittiwakes, you see 'em all over the cliffs in places back home." Several placid brown birds larger than the rest rode the water among the others, seldom competing for food. "You call them gooneybirds."

Seth listened with growing impatience. "They're albatross. If you'd asked me I could have told you all the rest too, and even given you their fancy names. From a book I have on the birds." He turned directly to Kodama. "Glad to lend it to you. If you'd want to look." It was the first time he had addressed Kodama in more than monosyllables.

Both men paused, surprised. "Yes? Thank you," said Kodama.

Rubber bands now secured a wrap of waterproof plastic around Seth's bandage. He had accepted the need to share in the less glamorous baiting and gutting, swayed by Terry's soothing praise for his performance at the roller, although he dismissed with a glare any attempt at instruction from Kodama. In truth, the muscles in his gaffing arm had begun to pop and complain long before the lodged barb gave him an excuse to quit.

"Like I said," Seth continued, "the big ones are albatrosses. And they're the black-footed albatrosses, one of three kinds around here but the kind most common. Still deep shit if you kill one. I don't just mean bad luck."

A white mass splatted on his shoulder from above. He flicked it off his oil-skin jacket and in good humor called to the birds overhead. "I don't begrudge you fuckers our garbage, but lay off my head! You hear?"

They heard a watery snort. "Hey!" yelled Mo, now at the roller. "You bugger! You bugger!" He leaned far over, banging his gaff. "You see that? Some seal or sea lion here by the line. Bugger's got one of our halibut in his mouth. Just up and chewed it off the hook."

Hank had been watching the sleek sea lion head for minutes, debating what to do. Only a few years before he'd have shot it without compunction. Now the greenies were raising a fuss and Congress might already have passed a law that he'd heard they were debating. But he said nothing as Seth, with an oath, returned from below with a rifle and fired directly at the creature's head. Blood left a pool as the head disappeared.

"And tell your buddies," called Seth.

"Nice shot," said Mo. "Guess he learned."

Odds shook his head. "Hadn't ought to've done that. He'd come to the Lord's table. He's one of God's creatures."

Seth turned, exasperated. "So's a fuckin' halibut a God's whatever. But I see you zapping them after they come to eat your bait."

"That's only a fish."

"Not one of God's creatures?"

"It's different." But Odds looked away from Seth's challenging grin. "Also maybe there's a law same as for gooneybirds not to shoot other things like a sea lion."

Terry wagged his head. "Give the greenies all of their way and we'll get a law not to kill any fish besides. Free to hook 'em and eat 'em so long as they don't die."

"You ever heard," continued Seth, "of sea lions bringing anything but trouble? Albatross are good luck so that law's good. But one to protect fuckin' marauding sea lions? Only some bureaucrat who's never fished would be that stupid."

"It is different," said Terry quietly to Odds. "Birds are nice even if they sometimes steal our bait. They don't steal halibut that people need to eat. I mean, the halibut's why we're here. So let the sea lions go catch their own fish, not steal ours."

Odds, normally sure of himself, glanced uncertainly from the dispersing blood on the water to the blood that streamed from the gutting table.

They returned to work. A steady run of halibut, interspersed with less-welcome cod and the roundly cursed spiny redfish, wiped moralities from the conversation, although both Odds and Terry continued to think of it.

Odds, taking his turn in the hold, snapped the oilskin hood tight under his chin, climbed down the slick ladder, and jumped into the mass of gutted halibut. He slipped through them up to his knees before grounding on solid ice chips. His head touched the low overhead and his breath frosted at once. The chill of the fish bodies reached his skin before he sucked each leg free. Sliding himself over to a bin already stacked halfway up with carcasses layered in ice, he began to pull over the new ones. It was necessary to stow the halibuts with their dark side down and the white side up, so the blood left inside would seep down into the dark skin and not stay in the meat. He did it carefully, and shoveled ice from another bin between each fish.

It *was* confusing, he pondered. All God's creatures had a right to the fruits of the earth. But everybody knew He'd put man at the top. And He'd given man the need to eat things in order to live. Father Petroff would have the answer, so no use thinking about it any more before he could get to church and ask.

Kodama's head appeared in the hatch opening against the sky. "White side top. White side top."

"I know that."

"Ah."

"So does everybody else."

"Ah." The head disappeared.

The Japanese man was getting to be a pain, Odds decided. And a disappointment. Not the companion he'd expected for talking about the white man's injustice. He'd maneuvered to be side by side with him at the gutting table, but the man now only grunted at a conversation attempt, or pointed out something wrong with the way he'd cut into the poke. Had it been only booze that afternoon at the airport that had made them seem like brothers? The deception again of booze. Well. With all this fish he was making good money and some of it could go to God's work along with the rest for family. And it was nice to be with old shipmates working hour by hour, not having to make decisions. No worry about how to spend corporation money, maybe feeling important but also scared he'd make wrong decisions and see everybody's eyes turn accusing. This way he'd sleep when he had the chance, because nothing on Hank's boat would make him need to answer to his people. He thrust the shovel hard into the bin's high mound of ice to loosen chips frozen together. Answer to nothing except working for a white man. The thought made him shovel harder.

On deck, Terry grabbed squares of herring and punched them securely over the barb to the hook, then tucked the hook to hang inside the coiled line. If you didn't have to kill things to get along, he mused, that would be great. But nobody except maybe hippies were going to settle for eating only vegetables. And what would you do without a reason to go to sea? His legs liked that shift of weight to weight as the boat rolled. Land was okay, missed after a while, and the women, of course, but not for all the time. His hands continued baiting but he looked over the water, glad for its busy chops and whitecaps always in motion. Suddenly he cried, "Lookit!" pointing beyond the boat.

"Oh man, gotta get my camera!" Ham doused hosewater against the blood on his oilskins and hurried inside.

A plume shot from the water, followed by a blocky black shape that rose and fell. Farther off, another plume spouted.

Kodama became excited. *"Iro! Iro!"*

All work halted while they watched two sperm whales. When the box-like heads dipped to a distant *huff* sound, the bodies, sleek as submarines, skimmed up along the surface. Moments later the heads disappeared. Then, in perfect symmetry, two fluked tails rose dripping and glided down into the water, and the ocean rolled empty again except for birds riding the chops.

Kodama had begun to breathe heavily. "Special fortune," he declared. "Whale special good fortune."

Ham arrived back on deck with his camera. "Where? Where?"

"Better not be that late for your wedding!" Terry laughed.

"Whose wedding?"

"You're right, you turkey. Who'd ever marry you?"

"Shut up and wait," muttered Seth. "Maybe they'll come back." But the ocean remained empty, and finally Hank returned them to work.

Odds had brought two pairs of the waterproof wrist protectors. When he saw his shipmates at dinner soaking their shirtsleeves in disinfectant he observed gravely, "I guess nobody bothered to think ahead." He pulled

the second set of wristers from his seabag and laid them on the galley table
for the rest to share. "I always think it's good to think ahead."

"Mighty nice of you," said Hank for them all.

By the end of the first day's final set, everyone had served at least one
brief turn at the roller and each other job, and all except Kodama had
snagged a line or lost a fish at least once. They hosed off, and had turned
in by midnight. Not until six would Hank rouse them to work again. Go
easy, he decided, since they were pushing muscles unused for a while.
Tendons in his right arm spasmed now and then from a single gaffing
shift. Around 3 AM he woke to glance from his cabin door and saw Seth
pacing the galley, massaging his arm also.

During the days that followed, although they fished only some sixty
miles offshore in the northernmost Pacific, land became more a memory than real dirt and stone. Often it showed only as a volcano's smoke
plume meandering above clouds on the horizon. Occasionally, it appeared through parted clouds in glimmers of snow sheet on a volcanic cone.
That is, if any of them bothered to raise their eyes from deck to look,
aside from Hank who checked his bearings when visibility allowed.
They all watched the other boats around them, however. The *Hinda Bee*
remained a few miles off port, too far away for shouts but within prime
range for CB banter.

The weather varied from storming to glassy. Hank recorded it in his log
along with the position and yield of each set, all of it information that
blended into a continuum of bait, hooks, fish, guts, and ice. Each man
had his own catalog of sores and aches. None of them could have said
with certainty anymore whether the hooking of Seth's arm occurred in the
afternoon of day one or two, or whether the maddening run of useless little spiny redfish happened in the morning or in the afternoon of this day
or that, or when a snag and parted line had cost wasted hours while Gus
Rosvic offered his crew's cheerful sympathies over the CB. On that latter
night, whichever one it was, they'd decided to make up for the loss by laying an extra set which in practice left them only a wink of sleep. On any
given day, except by checking his log, Hank could barely remember when
exactly, only some few hours before, say, a steady run of hundred-pound
halibut had boosted their luck, except maybe hadn't it coincided with,
say, a shift from calm to seas bubbling foot-high across deck?

Under Kodama's direction they had adjusted the scarecrow buoy. It bounced far enough beyond the point where the line sank astern that it shooed off most birds. Only an occasional mess of soaked feathers came up later on a hook. They could find nothing similar to discourage sea lions. Seth kept his rifle handy. Even Odds accepted the killing, although he'd rush first to throw some object at the obliviously gobbling creature and yell, "Get away before it's too late!"

One stormy afternoon, as they worked their routines while waves pushed across deck around their feet and smacked Hank's face at the roller, Terry exclaimed "Oh, phew!" The others yelled agreement.

"Ai!" from Kodama.

Hank stopped the gurdy with his knee and stepped back. A dark house of a whale reared from the water mere feet off the starboard rail. A big eye on the side of the head facing them, calm and distant, looked them over. Water sluiced from barnacles that clung to the whale's wrinkled skin. Spray spouted from the small round blowhole atop the head and blew across deck. It smelled like rotten fish cooked and rotted further.

"Phew, phew," cried Mo and Ham in unison.

"Hey, stinky," called Terry, and ran to the rail looking up. "Come closer and let me pet you."

"No, no," cried Kodama. "Do not touch."

"Yes. Better not," said Hank. He kept his voice calm. "Mo and Ham, don't jerk or run, but fast as you can get all survival suits from the wheelhouse." He reached for Seth's rifle stacked in the lee of the housing, not sure what he'd do. Moby Dick, he thought. Capsized boat.

Odds dropped to his knees. None of the others noticed.

Seth stood with legs apart. "Nobody shoot, nobody yell." His voice was firm but his grin, usually sardonic, had spread in wonder and pleasure. "He's just lookin' us over to say hi, stink and all. Hey, fellah, how's it going?"

As quickly as he had come, the whale slipped again beneath the surface. The water around him splattered high and slurped into a hole, then settled back into orderly waves.

Kodama continued to stare, his whole body leaning toward the spot. "Special lucky," he repeated.

Ham appeared with an armful of big orange rubber bags. "Take 'em quick so's I can get my camera."

"You doodle," said Terry. "You'll *never* make your wedding on time." His gaze returned to the empty water. "Oh, man. Did you catch his eye checking us out? Like a person. That was something, to be here, and see that."

Odds had regained his feet. "I think, maybe . . ." His voice slowed further with each word. "Maybe that's what . . . facing God is like. Maybe we . . .just now . . ."

"Bull. Bull!" Seth snapped. "Smell like that? All we just saw was Nature. Down our throats."

"God's Nature. His very eye."

"Knock it off." Pause. "Give us a break."

Suddenly none of them felt like saying more. They returned to the work of catching halibut.

Hank resumed his position at the roller. No reason to think it, but the whale had seemed to look through him. He felt shaken loose even though his hand was steady. He'd been closest and the whale had exploded at him, that explained it. And he'd already pulled in big fish for nearly two hours. He was tired.

As the days passed, the muscles of Hank's gaffing arm strengthened, although the ache increased after each turn at the roller. Everything about him hurt. And, since he held off using Odds's precious donated wristers (which any responsible halibut skipper should have remembered to stock), cold seawater trickled in to soak the insulation of his rubber gloves and hold his fingers in chill. Fingers became frozen claws halfway through a roller hitch. There was something to be said for skippers staying in the wheelhouse. Old Gus on the *Hinda Bee* did, to judge from binocular scans. But Gus was decades older, older even than Jones Henry would have been. He himself was still young at thirty-six. Well, dammit, thirty-eight.

Hank at the rail found himself daydreaming of sleep while he stared down at the incoming line. At least the line sometimes vibrated to cause little eddies at the surface before a fish of any size appeared. But nothing could be counted on. He began to tense in spite of himself at any white shape that flapped as it rose from the dark, then to feel ashamed at his relief for each hook that came up bare. (It appeared that the new circle hooks held the fish more securely and less deep in the throat than the traditional J hooks, but he'd allowed the guys to be casual in alternating them on the line so he couldn't be sure.) Hoisting big fish pulled at his mostly healed shoulder, that was the problem. And there was no way to relax between pulls. Sometimes a mere cod showing its belly flashed as bright as a halibut soaker. And sometimes a fifty pounder came up with its brown-green side so blended with the water that it appeared to be nothing until the instant when a gaff in the head meant the difference between catch and escape.

Thus, no sign or signal promised relief from staying as alert as a coiled spring. A good skipper made his own rules and kept them. So it was even more important that he, after jumping into the work cycle like a green kid, let nobody catch him slacking.

A sudden wave would slap him and jerk the line loose at the roller. A flying hook would catch his gaff and pull him back before he could free it. He absorbed all into his pace while cold water trickled inside his hood. At least he'd soon struck a rhythm at the roller, swinging up fish, then with gaff banging old bait from hooks, while his eyes stayed fixed on the water.

Flying hooks had ripped into his oilskin sleeves. All the crew's sleeves (except for Odds's and Kodama's) soon bore telltale patch tapes, although the hooking of Seth's arm had cautioned them against the worst. Hank's only game there was to keep his own rips fewer than the others'. He even once squeezed two into the same patch so that it appeared as only one. He might be fooling only himself, but still . . .

One day he braced his left hand on the rail, leaned down so close to the water that spray salted his lips, and drove the gaff smartly into a halibut just emerging. Let it be a nice small one, he thought. Instead, it thrashed heavily enough to strain his muscles from arm to back as, with a false show of ease, he neatly swung it over the rail and thudded it into the checkers. The angry creature gave a final flap just at the chute that twisted his wrist. Almost at once, since the gurdy kept pulling line, there came the next halibut, and it was already partly out of the water, dangling in air and big enough to thrash free. He needed to set an example of steady pacing, so he leaned down quickly and drove in his gaff, despite the pain.

But, suddenly: in truth this was where he was meant to be! He controlled a gleeful shout.

"Need more to be training training." Kodama stood beside him with the strong judo frown unlike the frowns of recent days. His face bore the same gleam as back on the Tokyo judo mat when his manner changed from office flunky to warrior. "Go, Captain. My work here now. You go be captain."

"Not time yet. Two and a half hours each of us. I'm okay, thanks."

"Ha. But radio calling captain, and only number two man is now talking." He firmly took the gaff. "Go. Go."

Seth, in the wheelhouse, was bantering with Gus Rosvic on the *Hinda Bee* like skipper to skipper. "Right, right, I hear you. Things are tough. Women and foreigners, like you say, good old days forgotten, I don't know." He saw Hank and his voice lightened. "Up the bets, eh? Well, sure, if you're so anxious to lose your money. I'll ask the others. Hey, here's Mr. Hank himself."

"Then put the man on!"

Hank took the mike but kept his gaze on Seth who handed it casually. "Yo, Gus."

"Now, Hank. I don't want this to go overboard. Your boy there sounds pretty confident. I've watched you bring up fish right steady, but I'd say it's no sure thing you've got the bigger catch, since you broke-down crab-pot men don't know a snag from a snarl about longline while my boys are pretty good."

Seth gestured to Hank. "I'm going down to check the guys. *Hinda Bee* says okay to double each bet."

Suddenly Hank felt defensive, and uneasy. "We've already got enough bets. You haven't made more, have you?"

"Yesterday. Everybody here except Odds and the Jap. We each raised bets individual with our beer buddies. Guess you've been too busy dealing with Japs to notice. Now we're just crankin' it up another notch."

Hank kept his voice even. "Guess I should be told when anybody but the captain uses the boat radios."

"Guess then you'd better state your rules."

Hank considered quickly. Kodama had seen what was happening. On the CB, heartily: "Gus, you turkey! We hear you, and will get back. Our main worry is not to see your boys starve this winter while we spend their money."

"You worry all you want, Hank. Oh my! I need to close off now. Need to trim the boat so she don't sink under all this weight of fish."

Hank turned back to Seth, who hadn't moved, and kept himself firm without anger. "I'll state my rules now. You're number two man here. Respected as such. You did the research on longline, and on deck what you say goes."

"Goes if I say it in fuckin' Jap."

"Up here, you're free to answer radio calls when you're on hand and I'm not, so long as I'm informed. That means call me to the mike or tell me soon, not tomorrow. But outgoing calls go through me. Except Mayday emergency if I'm . . . not there. Got it, Seth?"

"Got it clear how you're still playing navy officer prick. But this ain't the navy."

"I can live with prick." He tried to make it light, but Seth's jawed scowl stayed unyielding while his fists remained clenched. Go it all the way. "All right, then, while we're at it. No more calling Kodama a Jap."

"What else is he?"

"He's a crewmate with a name. You're not Jones Henry with a burn. Maybe Jones had an earned wartime burn against the Japanese, but not you."

"You've gone sappy, pulling in some foreigner over us."

"*With* us. We're entering a tight Japanese market and he's the expert. You see how he pulls his weight on deck?"

"Yeah. And it changes everything. Leaves some of us no place to go but out."

Hank felt suddenly set on a course he'd often put out of mind. He'd gone shares with Jones Henry for his first boat. Had it hurt Jones to give up a piece of a boat he'd owned and possessed? Jones had done it to keep the generations going. "Okay, Seth. Soon we go back to Kodiak and kiss this boat back to Adele. Then you've got a choice. We've talked around this before, but maybe it's time to decide. I've saved my *Jody Dawn* but I'm going to the bigger boat for black cod, and I've offered you the choice to skipper *Jody Dawn* if you want. You've done it for weeks at a time. I trust you for the whole show. Then you can play by your rules out there so long as you keep my boat safe and fishing." Hank forced a grin. "And you can hire who you like."

He'd seen it before. Offer Seth real responsibility and his eyes glanced off target while the face lost resolve. "Not the same," Seth muttered. His breathing turned heavy. "We grew up in this together. People called us a team, once, you and me. Not separate on different boats."

"We still are. But teams change direction."

They stared at each other, neither willing to break away.

"Hey, up there in skipper heaven," shouted Terry from deck. "Stop ol' Kodama-san from gaffing in halibut or get down here. He's filled the checkers faster than we can . . . Come down with the peasants and get blood on your shoes."

Thus began their biggest run. A fish came up on nearly every hook. Flat thrashing halibut became their single sight. Even the stink of a looming curious whale now barely stopped them for an instant. A fistful of guts thrown its way was (except on Kodama's or Odds's part) more an objection to the stink than an offering.

Meals became candy bars on the go. "Get your fuckin' deck steaks," Mo would call, tossing them around. When the bars gave out—who'd have thought three gross would go that fast?—they dipped crackers and even fingers into the peanut butter.

Seth shunted between spooky silences and explosions of convivial energy, although he continued work at full capacity when fatigue made even Kodama lag. He found ways to join Mo at the gutting or baiting jobs. Their muttered talk was unremarkable since the two had crewed together the longest; Mo had in earlier days been regarded as Seth's shadow. Still, it seemed to Hank, they talked with unusual earnestness for mere work-chat.

Oilskin sleeves turned into conduits for salt water and sores; hands stayed cold and wet inside rubber gloves, while abraded circles around wrists rubbed increasingly raw. There began a tussle for Odds's spare waterproof wristers, followed by hints, sometimes sour, that he share also his first pair, until finally both pairs became common property, and strip by strip they tore apart. Angry shouts increased although no one found the energy to pursue a difference further. Fingers opened only with pain. Arms throbbed clear to the neck. And, during only four hours' sleep Hank now allotted them each night (without polling whether they agreed to it or not), big fish flapped over them, white then dark, throughout unremitting dreams.

Occasionally while they worked, Seth or Terry would remember the bets with the *Hinda Bee,* wipe hands, hose down, and stomp to the wheelhouse to grab binoculars and study the distant rival boat. How low was she riding and thus how full? "Ol' Gus there's got his rails almost to the water," Terry reported on the next-to-final morning. "He's low like us. It's going to be close."

Meanwhile, they had filled the side bins in their own hold, and they began to pile halibut in the hold's walk spaces.

By sunrise on the day of the noontime closure Seth reported to Hank, "Hold's plugged. Not even man-space down there. Time to stack on deck I'd say." He peered through binoculars. "Shit. *Hinda Bee*'s doing just that!"

The morning weather forecast had contained no warnings. Hank studied the water. It was only choppy and the crests barely licked into the
scuppers. "Stack on deck it is!"

They packed the checkers with halibut, then boarded off the rest of the
deck and continued to stack. When at last the one-week season ended,
they were wading through fish and gurry to their knees.

Hank turned the boat immediately toward Kodiak for the long trip
home while the others finished gutting the last of the catch, hosed blood
from every corner, secured canvas over the deckload, and with groans of
relief peeled off oilskins grown clammy inside. Most of them headed for
the bunks stuffing down only what food they could grab on the way. For
a few minutes Terry studied the *Hinda Bee* riding low, but he nodded and
the binoculars soon wavered in his hands.

Broad daylight though it was, Hank dosed himself on coffee and wake-
up pills. He was as tired as the rest, but he was captain.

Only Seth lingered in the wheelhouse. He fingered charts and touched
electronics boxes in a constant pace. Hank at last said, "Come on, buddy,
go get some sleep."

"I could take first watch."

"Go."

"Guess call me in an hour, then."

"We'll see. Go."

"I . . . I don't know. I mean, about taking over the *Jody Dawn* full-time."

"Understood. Sleep on it. We're friends either way. Scram now."

Seth sighed, and slowly went below.

Alone, Hank placed the boat on autopilot, but kept himself from sitting
down. Sleep beckoned in tunes and voices. Shapes of other boats around
him swayed with more than sea motion. Their images blurred, then focused
back with razor clarity. He did push-ups to keep his blood pounding, held
his breath until he needed to gasp, sang, and paced. Finally, assured that all
the boats around him were keeping distance and course, he allowed himself
to close his eyes while his hands gripped the rail by the windows. It gave
him a grateful swoop into sleep, halted by his face bumping against hard
glass. Radar and horizon check, grip retightened, another grateful swoop.
Thus three hours passed.

At the sound of steps on the ladder he straightened. "You didn't call
me," said Seth.

"Was doing fine."

"If I skippered the *Jody Dawn,* could Mo go with me?"

Hank considered, taken by surprise. So that was why Seth had begun working beside Mo so often. He hadn't meant to lose two men but he understood Seth's need for a constant. "One good cook lost, but sure, if he wants."

"Then . . . maybe."

"Congratulations!"

"I didn't say yes all the way, yet."

"Take your time and be sure. You've slept?"

"Enough."

Hank slapped his shoulder. "Then she's yours. You know the way. But call me, no bullshit, if seas pick up even a little." He drifted toward sleep even before he reached his bunk and tumbled in.

Next day at the fish plant it remained for them to unload. After sending up the fish on deck, Terry, Mo, Ham, and Odds crawled down into the icy hold to dislodge each slick carcass and heave it into a cargo net. Filled, the wide-meshed net rose, dripping slimy brown ice. Seth on deck checked the scale attached to the net as it rose, and Hank on the pier checked weight again just before the net disgorged into a hopper. Since every pound might count toward the bet, even the loss from drippage might be at issue.

The *Hinda Bee* had arrived just enough ahead of them to be unloaded first, so that her final count was established. Gus Rosvic sauntered over to stand beside Hank. He peered at the scale and scribbled the weight of each netful. His crew gathered on the side of the dock to gaily heckle Seth while they too watched the scale. A heavy rain bothered no one. Farther off under an umbrella stood Adele Henry, wearing her now-routine boatside bandanna and slacks, with high rubber boots on her feet for the occasion. She was discreet enough for once to leave alone the men who had fished her boat.

Kodama stood apart again, his services unneeded. It puzzled him, such different aggression in these Americans! The aggression that he understood and felt came from the samurai's need to defeat the enemy and destroy him. These people gave the same energy to mere competition, and the loser merely shrugged without disgrace. He stroked his chin and made himself appear unconcerned, although, he conceded wistfully, it might have been agreeable to have placed money of his own with the others

and be included in their comradely levity. When he saw Captain Carford's wife, whom he was expected to call Jody but of course could
never do, hurry over, kiss her husband lightly, peer at the scale and joke
with Captain Rosvic, then hurry off with a wave announcing she needed to pick up the children, Kodama's ache for his own family made him
turn away.

Both boats contained an approximate 50,000-pound hold capacity. The
Hinda Bee had managed with its deckload to deliver 54,831 pounds.
Slowly the cargo netfuls that rose from the *Adele H*'s hold passed the
50,000 mark and approached 54,000, but the fish grew fewer. Seth knelt
and called into the hold. "More, more, keep it coming!"

"Hardly more left," called back Terry. With their final netful the *Adele
H*'s total came to 54,297 pounds.

"Now that's too bad you ain't got a fish or two more," soothed Gus.
"But you crab-pot boys done better than anybody expected. We almost
hate to take your money."

"We do appreciate your concern," said Hank, keeping an easy humor.
"Just give my guys time to hose down and we'll settle."

"And then drinks and dinner's on the boys of the *Hinda Bee*."

"Thanks for the others," said Hank, "but I'll cut out to find Jody and
my kids."

"No no, Hank, them too." Gus saw him hesitate. "Don't worry. It
won't hurt a soul of us to watch our tongues for one night among your
fine children." He glanced at the staunch figure of Adele. "Guess we'll
invite the old battle-ax besides. She's got to cough up five hundred dollars
in bets to me, as I recall. That might quiet her for a change, poor woman."

"Ohh, I'm so thirsty," crowed Zack of the *Hinda Bee* from the pier as he
stretched and capered. "Wonder if I can afford to throw a toot tonight
and still buy me a Cadillac?"

Seth aboard the *Adele H* shrugged and gave him a wan smile.

The men in the hold began to scrub down with pressure hoses and disinfectant. Suddenly a *Yahoo!* echoed from the hollow space, followed by
repeats. Terry called up, "Just lower that fuckin' cargo net again!" Odds
had hosed into a mound that they'd mistaken for unused ice, and there
embedded throughout were halibut!

The extra fish brought their total delivery weight to 54,940 pounds.
Hank announced the count, Gus nodded confirmation, and the deck of

the *Adele H* erupted in dancing and shouting. Adele suddenly came to life, left her umbrella on the pier, and with a commanded "Help me down, boys!" climbed to her boat. Despite the gurry on their oilskins she only stopped hugging each of the crew—even the startled Kodama—when they backed away.

Jody appeared again with children in tow. She enjoyed the sight but hugged only Hank.

The men of the *Hinda Bee* took their loss in glum good humor and the dinner of the two crews was held as planned. Only the hosts who paid for it had changed.

Odds returned to his duties with the native corporation, glad for the extra money—it would be around five thousand dollars after all boat-share expenses were settled—relieved that his arms might soon stop aching all night. No wonder he'd left fishing! But he blessed the opportunity for communication with godlike whales, although by their third or fourth appearance he'd decided that they were indeed only whales, because God Himself could never smell that bad. The fact that Terry, Seth, Mo, and Ham, independently as soon as they had finished celebrating their victory, had bought him one to three pairs of new wristers each, earned only a wan thanks. He'd glimpsed the dark side of their souls and confirmed what he'd expected of whites. Only Captain Hank and Kodama had not worn the cursed things or at any time demanded them.

Seth, with sinking heart, declared himself committed to taking over the *Jody Dawn*. Mo, torn between allegiances to both Hank and Seth, and anguished by Seth's urgent persuasions, finally asked Hank to break the news that he wanted to stay with Hank and the new venture. But, almost immediately, Mo began to reconsider, remembering all he owed Seth for teaching him to fish. Just as Hank at the Ship's Bar was leading Seth up to the bad news, Mo burst in, his heavy face red and troubled, to declare gruffly, "Okay Seth, I'm with you."

Kodama watched, understanding less than he imagined but judging it all. His aches and sores were like battle wounds to be endured and cherished. Happy he was to be there! These men didn't shirk any more than did the dutiful Japanese, but neither would they have merely bowed and accepted hardship with heads lowered as would his endlessly enduring countrymen. He had begun to respect them all, even Seth. But he gladly heard the news that Mr. Sour Number Two was leaving.

PART III

The Wide World

OCTOBER–DECEMBER 1983
ALASKA, MARYLAND, ALASKA

16

UNFREE

KODIAK, GULF OF ALASKA, LATE OCTOBER 1983

The rain webbed first in the canopy of spruce, then plunked onto the rooftop, then collected below into puddles that overflowed outside the house. Jody turned up the heater and started coffee. As on most mornings she yawned by the big living room window, and studied the weather across the field of water that stretched from shore to the glazed lights of Kodiak miles away. The norther that had blown for days pushed rows of little whitecaps and bent the branches ashore that framed the sight. Out at sea the blow across the Gulf of Alaska, unhindered by land for hundreds of miles, would have built a steady roll against Hank and the guys. She kneaded bare toes in the carpet, and savored the quiet.

Hank had now been more than ten months away on his big new long-liner for the Japanese. Even radio contact was spotty. He'd been able to grab only a few days ashore on two occasions when he'd found excuses to return to Kodiak for business, leaving the *Puale Bay* under Terry's apparently uneasy command overshadowed by Kodama.

Jody looked out at distant rain-blurred lights. A second dark winter without her husband was approaching. Six thirty on a morning still so dark that her coffee cup remained a shadow in her hand. It was half a life without him. Now that her own adventure skippering the *Adele H* for salmon had ended for a second year, and Hank wasn't there again when she had the time for him, she could wonder whether they weren't losing

something more precious than work satisfactions. Their lives were slipping on. The stimulus of running her own boat, in the faces of all those
macho male types, had made her careless with his feelings. Hadn't he
trained her as best he could, reluctant or not, and ensured her success by
giving her Terry and Ham off his *Puale Bay* for not one, but two seasons?
It was time she accepted the fact that he'd put their home on the table as
part of the bargain, even though the mere thought of it still turned her
angry. But it was a fisherman's nature to do anything to save his boat, and
she'd married a fisherman.

"Mommy!" announced Dawn from her bedroom. "Are you there? Do you
know what kind of dream I had? It was all about horses. Are you listening?"

Jody pulled herself together to face the day. "Listening, sweetie."

As Dawn launched into her recital, Henny shuffled from his own bedroom wrapped in a blanket Indian fashion. "Who cares about your old
dream," he muttered. The hood pushed his hair down to his eyes. "Morning, Mom." They hugged.

"Mommy cares, that's who. Because it was a very interesting dream, and
I can't wait to tell my very best friend Melissa."

"Last week you said ol' Linda was your best—"

"A person can have two very best friends so that's how much you know.
Isn't that right, Mommy?"

Jody chose not to answer.

"Mommy? Isn't that right?"

"Possibly."

"See, Henny. See?"

Jody patted her son lightly on the buttocks to point him toward the
kitchen. "Blue shirt on the ironing board, that's what you wear today."

"Okay."

"What should I wear, Mommy?"

"That green corduroy jumper's nice, honey. I washed it two days ago
and it's hanging in your closet."

"Well, I think my denim jumper's better, because we're making a sand
table of Africa today and the boys in my class are very messy."

"That'll be fine. And your yellow top."

"Why?"

"Because it goes well."

"But I like my red top, why not my red top since I like it better?"

Jody kept her voice even. "Then make sure it's clean." (And I was an even worse pain, she thought. No wonder my mother chain-smoked, and escaped to those damned bridge games whenever she could.) She walked to Pete's room. The child's nose peeked from covers wrapped around his head. She snuggled him lightly. He woke, wrapped arms around her neck, and they exchanged a smacking kiss. "Now up you go, teddy bear. Move it along."

He wriggled away with a grin. "No."

"Oh yes, buster." She laid out his clothes.

"Okay." He jumped from the covers and began to dress.

Dawn was already dressed and breaking eggs into a bowl as she told Henny, whose morning chores included feeding the dog and cat, that he'd better hurry.

Nothing was wrong, thought Jody. Warm house, good kids. Except the main thing.

The bumpy hour to town was routine. She had herded the kids quickly into the van so that their raincoats shed little water to increase the musty smell that had settled over everything during the prolonged rain. The sky remained gray, without a shaft of sun. Water bubbled over the sturdy planks bridging the stream. Scrub stretched to the foot of green mountainsides whose snow peaks rose only dimly through haze.

Three horses grazed in a paddock that had been cleared and fenced. "See the horses, Petey?" announced Dawn. "Their names are Jackie, Major, and Sweetpea." Pete continued to turn the pages of a picture book and mouth the words printed in big block letters.

"You talk-talk about those horses every day," grumbled Henny.

"But those are my very favorites of all the horses in the world, and Petey ought to know."

"If he doesn't know he's deaf."

Jody had already talked to the owners about riding lessons for Dawn. They'd said it would be better to wait till the child turned at least eight, but they'd go with seven and a half if her legs reached the pony's stirrups. It would be a surprise next spring—at least by March the days would be growing longer—although it would add one more commute and clutter up the precious town-free weekends.

From an empty road the traffic increased by a vehicle or two after they passed a settlement, then swelled to a dozen cars and pickups near the

Coast Guard Base. When they reached the bend overlooking cannery row and the harbor, with frame houses scattered in the mist down the slopes on the other side of the road, a string of braked tail lights slowed passage for the final quarter mile into town.

Jody dropped Henny and Dawn outside the elementary school and waited until they disappeared inside, then drove to another building and walked Pete to the kindergarten classroom, then parked for the day. (Other moms at the office let their kids walk the blocks to school. If Hank were home and available, she'd also feel that relaxed.)

At her desk in the social services office a drug-abuse client already waited, restless and impatient to be done with his mandatory check-in. Cleo, the secretary, had already spiked four phone messages to be returned. One, from the hospital, reported a client gone from methadone back to mainline overdose and they needed papers at once. The next was from a fellow fishing-wife, to set up lunch to plan strategy before the town council in three days in their fight to deny pleasure boats a slip at city docks. (At least this part of the day's for my own stuff, she thought, and scribbled under Council Talk on a clipboard: "Not enough berths as it is to tie boats that *work* for a living.") Another note, from Adele Henry, wondered where she and the children were. (Catching a breather from you, Adele, much as we love you.) The final note, from a name she didn't recognize, asked her to call.

Jody's day, started nearly three hours before, began.

And Hank's day: in the Gulf of Alaska two hundredsome miles east of Kodiak, routine fifteen-foot seas smacked the metal hull of the longline vessel, *Puale Bay*. The ship rose, pitched, rolled to clanks of tubs securely chained, and steadied for seconds before the next sea-thud initiated another round. In the wheelhouse Hank's legs bent automatically to absorb the motion. They had started the day's haul three hours before, pulling line that had been laid to soak near midnight. Now daylight had begun to dim the deck lights and to soften the sky from black to gray. It replaced the phosphorescent underglow of foam caps with a soapy white.

Hank checked his screens. The radar displayed boat blips beyond visual range. The depth sounder showed seafloor at four hundred fifty fathoms, half a mile down, where his line lay among black cod hooked or milling in wait to be hooked. He quartered the ship between troughs and kept its open fishing bay in the lee, flush with the incoming line. Lights from the work area slicked a path on the water. Only by pressing his forehead against a starboard window could he see the actual line with hooked fish coming aboard. It was sure as hell a glitch in the ship's otherwise Japanese-efficient design.

A spinning circle of glass centrifuged water within the pilot window and kept it clear no matter how heavy the bow spray. His ship had port and starboard screws for maneuvering, and the latest in SatNav, loran-C plotter, radar, color sounder—all electronics were state of the art. For the first month trying each new device to its capacity had kept him involved. Now after nearly a year they were all mastered and second nature, their challenge understood. How had he ever chased fish and crabs without them?

The life of the ship murmured and called beneath him, from directed crew to thoughtless prey. He controlled it all aboard the 130-foot ship registered in his name, owned at least on paper. The thought made him stretch and smile. A lone seabird, perhaps stranded too far from land to return, rode a swell that rolled toward the boat. It flew free before the swell tumbled across deck, its white wings suddenly yellowed from a ship's light. Then down it went comfortably onto the next swell, and plucked a stray bait that an unseen crewman tossed. "Take it easy, bird," Hank muttered. "You're lord of the waves just like me."

He poured himself coffee from an electric pot clamped against the bulkhead. Old and bitter. Through the mike to the deck speaker, he said, "Somebody bring fresh coffee to the bridge." His own amplified voice echoed from below.

A few minutes later Ham appeared. "Morning, Boss. Nice and fresh." A once-blue cap was slouched over his face, its bill whitened by flecks of scales and bait. Some of the flecks clung to his wide cheeks.

"Hey, you could have sent one of the junior apes up with that."

"Naaah, good excuse. This wheelhouse is something else." Ham glanced around and headed for the color sounder. Its bright electronic yellows, greens, and reds reflected on his face. "Man, the stuff up here! Makes our old boat look like yesterday." His eyes remained fixed on the screen.

"Go on," said Hank. "Play with that knob the way I've showed you. Scale it fifty fathoms, a hundred, three. You won't hurt anything."

"Thanks anyway, Boss. I'd be sure to break something." He backed away. "But just look at all those colors."

"Remember what I told you they meant?"

"Red means the big stuff's down there, right? And yellow means there's zilch."

"Good for you. How's it going below, this morning?"

"Oh . . . those big black fish, Boss, they keep comin'. Even in your dreams."

"Nothing beats steady fishing under shelter, out of the rain. And money you can count on. Does it?"

"You said it." Ham started to leave although his eyes remained on the color screen. "But it was sure nice, last summer when you sent Terry and me back to help Jody fish salmon for a while. Even if we didn't make as much money. And remember how, Boss, when we was half this crew size with just Seth, Terry, Mo, and me, our good ol' boat half this big and none of this fancy stuff? How we'd park in the wheelhouse between sets and talk or just watch the water?"

"It *was* nice. Different."

After a silence, Ham said, "Well, lots of lines to bait. Don't want to fall behind. Just call if you need more coffee."

Hank wanted to prolong it. "Say, uh . . . does your buddy Mo ever write? How's he doing out there with Seth? I talk to Seth all the time, of course."

"Oh. Doing good. Good. I guess. He did send a postcard from Dutch Harbor. Picture of a mermaid with big . . . tits, you know. Wrote that's what comes up in their nets now they don't have, like, my ugly face to look at. Funny stuff like that. I sure wish . . . Well, you know, Mo wasn't such a bad cook."

Hank felt like lingering over it. "No, he wasn't." He started to tell Ham to sit a while.

"Hello! Hello! Ham sleeping?" Kodama's voice came so sharp and loud that it must have been positioned by the stairs to the wheelhouse. "Where is Ham? Time Ham working. Somebody better wake Ham."

"Shit, Boss, he saw me bring you coffee."

Hank glanced away. "Talk to you later. Thanks for the fresh."

"Sure, Boss, any time." And Ham was gone.

"Last hooks aboard from today's line one," came Terry's voice over the speaker from the fishing deck below.

Hank set course for the next line several miles away, checked radar and visual to ascertain clear passage, shifted the steering onto gyro, and paced his wheelhouse. Kodama might ride the guys a bit but he did keep the fish coming aboard. The operation clicked like the factory it was, converting fish into money. But *Jody Dawn,* dear *Jody Dawn* indeed, his *Jody Dawn* with her good ol' team. He did a few push-ups, adjusting them to the ship's motion. Mo's straight-out cooking had been nice, although the chow that Arty served was okay—even though it swam in grease. And Seth was missed, sour face and all—Seth and Mo now making money out in the Bering on *Jody Dawn,* part of a Japanese joint venture of the kind they'd all hated. Seth might complain, but at least he worked from a wheelhouse just a hop to deck, in touch with his crew.

He rose panting, checked position and controls, then dropped to force a few more push-ups. The strain felt healthy, *genki,* first-rate Japanese word that encompassed well-being. Well, Kodama kept deck in genki shape. And tomorrow when the Japanese freezer ship came to take their month's catch, there would be that Japanese wardroom hospitality with volleys of interesting food.

Without warning the earth-soap odor of Jody's hair filled his nostrils from nowhere. Oh Jody. The smell and taste of her neck and breasts followed: something between daisies and melons. He could feel his arms drawing her bare shoulders against his bare chest. Wet skin and warm. The rub of it smoothed and caressed all the way down his legs. Thinking of it turned his penis stiff against his pants like a schoolboy's. And then her whisper while her hand explored his back. He checked the ship's bearings, then did more push-ups.

The memory of her light voice touched him more than physically. Her presence: he felt wrong without it. He glanced dispassionately at the metal and the black plastics of his wheelhouse, bare despite all the electronic wonders he'd assembled. Bare also the home he'd designed, with its thick carpeting and picture window, if Jody wasn't there. Any place without her lost its savor.

Oh Jody. What if he ever lost her? He'd put her out in that remote, beautiful place when he knew she'd rather be close to town, and now he went off to sea for months. What did she do every night without him? What if she ever tired of the distances that fishing put between them? Met some fellow tied to land who came home every night? Who liked the kids and they liked him? His children! Growing up without him. The thought of their soft, warm little bodies tumbling over him brought a new ache of loss.

She'd forgiven his Helene affair in Tokyo, but never, really, his allowing Tsurifune to connect the security of their house with his boat. Why hadn't he read more closely the small provisions in that contract? Even though his earnings for the year had accumulated, Tsurifune father and son still—with Shoji's trademark pleasantest assurances delivered third-hand through the agent on the freezer ship—had applied the money against the big longliner without letting it pay off debt on the house or the *Jody Dawn.* He needed to talk with them again face-to-face.

Melons. Like melons fresh and ripe, Jody's precious scent . . .

"*Puale Bay,* you read me? Over."

Hank hurriedly grabbed the radio mike. "Tolly, you horse. Where've you been?"

"Scouting, my man. Finding new places I'll never tell you about. And gone into town. Some of us don't run a factory ship that freezes cargo, we need to ice down and deliver ashore. But we have a load now for your Jap freezer ship since it's here. She's due alongside you tomorrow, right?"

Hank wished that Tolly would not have broadcast the information. "Noon, expected," he answered curtly, and changed the subject. "You catching fish?"

"When there's fish I catch 'em, buddy."

A deep, new voice interrupted. "Yah, catch for de Japs. You makin' it hard for de rest of us, you fellahs on de Jap payroll."

Hank felt himself flush. "Hold on," he began.

"I'll second that," said another voice. "We're out here trying to prove Americans can take the whole quota, and you guys—"

"Yah, us good Americans, and you fellahs—"

"Sounds like Olaf Trygvisen there," said Tolly heartily. "Your wife and kids still back in Norway, Oley? Last I heard Stavanger's still where you call home."

"Dot's different. Plenty of brothers and cousins in Ballard, *dey* pay American taxes."

"Guess I'll add my two cents, Hank." It was Gus Rosvic. "We hear, and it ain't just rumor anymore, that Jap buyers down in Washington and Oregon, and in Prince Rupert, Canada, pay six cents more than in Alaska for black cod. Same fish, caught no farther off the coast than our grounds is. Now, we can't afford to go all that distance extra, so we're stuck with what they pay us. But I expect that you boys working for the Japs get that Seattle price. Am I right?"

Hank felt his mouth go dry. "Sorry to disappoint you, Gus," he said abruptly, and switched channels. Now he needed push-ups! Goddamn. Goddamn!

"Oh the policeman's feet are big, high-o the fuckey-o policeman's feet are big," sounded Terry's voice coming up the stairs to relieve him. Deep voice for a man not tall. Terry bounced in wiping his hands on a cloth. "Hey, Boss, ready for relief? Battery water, oil and water temp, all just checked."

"She's yours." Hank kept his face averted in case it betrayed malaise.

Terry stretched, and danced a few punches. "Got to wake myself up. Even though I just did two hours at the roller and then hit the engine room. Funny how, out here with everything like clockwork and a full six–seven hours of sleep every night, all you want to do is sleep."

"I know."

"Yet here we've got more sack time that you can count on, than ever we had on the *Jody Dawn*. It's interesting, how that is. Sleepy, I mean. Maybe because there's no surprises." He handed Hank a fold of papers wrapped in plastic and sealed with tape. "Catch record for the freezer ship tomorrow. Mr. Production Master sends."

"How'd we do?"

"You know ol' Kodama. He don't make public announcements to the peons."

Hank pulled off the tape and without looking handed Terry the papers. Terry wiped his hands again, read, shrugged, and returned them. "I thought we'd done better than this, to tell the truth. A fish about every three hooks whenever I was at the rail. The Japs and Koreans sure had it gangbusters here before we wised up and moved in."

Hank busied himself logging the new catch figures. It had certainly seemed that, earlier with the same effort, they'd caught more during the first monthly deliveries to the Tsurifune freezer ship. Yet he trusted Kodama's figures. "Terry? How's Kodama behaving?"

"*Mr.* Kodama? No different. He knows his stuff. Ham still gets bugged. The others had his pickety-pick from the start so they don't know different."

"And you?"

"I look him in the eye. We get along."

They still had a ninety-minute run to reach the marker buoy of the next set. Hank checked Terry out on their course, then went below to make an appearance. Over the months he'd concentrated on fish location and ship handling, and paid less and less attention to the routine operations down on deck since Kodama obviously knew his job. Had things slowed even under Kodama's steady drive?

The deck might have been roofed, but cold wind blew across it from the open sides. After the close heated wheelhouse, Hank shivered. The scene had the usual repetitive factory bustle. Two men were lined up at the long baiting table spearing chunks of herring onto hooks under a speaker that blared a rock beat. At another table Ham and Arty stood amid a welter of red intestines and hose water as they sliced and gutted the fish just caught. Busy hands and blank faces all around. It could have been a shoreside cannery line except for frosty breaths and the occasional slosh of sea that hit the side of the ship with a thud and then gurgled around their boots and through scuppers.

Kodama paced the length of the gear alley with hands behind his back like Captain Bligh himself. His eyebrows had acquired an upward twist that, along with a ramrod posture, made him seem taller than the largest of the others. His energy filled any space he occupied.

"So. Captain!" Kodama exclaimed with gold teeth exposed. "Seeing all is good. Strong product, hold filling, workers happy because productive." The hands remained clasped behind his back.

Hank smiled. "All genki, right?"

"Genki, hai!" Kodama's face, smoother now than in office days, had developed a ruddy confidence in place of the old scratchy edge. His gaze retained its directed burn, but it now fitted the man's package differently to include heavy-humored animation. "Freezers filling filling. Soon vessel so low in water that fishes swim aboard without hooks, thusly saving bait. Ha-ha. Therefore, fortunate that freezer cargo vessel comes tomorrow for collection of product."

Hank walked around. He paused by the baiting table. Kodama moved in at once to declare, "Tom. Must push bait further into circle." The man nodded without looking up. They next went to the gutting station, and Kodama continued with, "Ham. Must scrape out intestines harder, harder. See how Arty scrapes."

Ham, whose face had been blank, glared as he held up a carcass and shook it. "You see any gut left in there?"

Kodama studied it. "Good. That one good perhaps. Satisfactory."

"*All* of them fuckin' good." Ham's glare settled on Hank. His wide face had reddened and his usual earnest, unquestioning expression had tightened at the mouth.

"Looks fine to me," said Hank, making his voice firm. "Looks very fine."

"Perhaps." Kodama brushed it off with a hand. "Back to work, Ham, steady, steady."

"You guys are doing fine," Hank declared, but felt lame as he said it. He continued down metal stairs to the lower deck and Kodama followed. The Japanese held open the hatch door to the packing room and beckoned Hank through first. Inside, two crewmen glanced up from the fish they were hosing at a long sink, greeted him with a casual "Yo Boss," and continued to work at an easy pace. Then Kodama entered. Was it imagination, Hank wondered, or did those two sets of hands suddenly start to work their brushes harder?

Hank enjoyed the sight of the sturdy black sablefish carcasses with their exposed thick white meat where the head had been lopped. It was indeed a handsome product he was delivering. The fins flicked on hides not yet stiffened, creatures still alive not an hour ago. He spot-checked tray weights. It all seemed right.

Kodama's hands returned behind his back. He watched the two men in silence. Without looking up they vigorously brushed inside the gutted fish, hosed and brushed further, then arranged the carcasses eight to a tray. They now worked with such animation that hose water splattered from their aprons and dripped from straggles of adolescent whisker on their chins. Both kids' shaggy hair was tucked into white sanitary caps. It made their young faces look skinned.

Kodama slowly drew a pair of white gloves from his pocket and slid in his fingers. He picked up one carcass after another, examined it, then returned it either atop the steel rollers where it waited for storage or to a tray if it had already been packed. At last, "Ha!" he said as he waved a fish. "Grade two in grade-one tray!"

Both kids looked up warily.

Kodama pointed to a nick in the tail. "Who has done this? Inferior product. Kenny? Slim? Which has failed to see? Very bad."

Hank drew a breath and faced it. "People don't eat the tail. Doesn't affect the meat and hardly noticed. Look. A cut the size of my little finger. Just something a hook snagged."

"Ha! In Tsukiji noticed of course, perhaps."

The two kids watched. Hank realized that he needed to take a stand. "This is still a grade-A fish. For somebody's table, not to hang on a wall."

"Captain! In Tsukiji very high standard!"

Hank firmed his voice. "I truly respect your careful eye, Kodama-san. But this is a keeper." He tapped the tray from which Kodama had lifted the fish. Kodama paused, then with a frown returned it. Hank noted that the crewmen exchanged glances. Their mouths twitched in quick grins as they bent back to scrubbing fish.

Kodama started to lead him back to the main deck. "While I'm here," Hank said, "might as well check the freezers." It was a chore he seldom performed.

The muscles around Kodama's eyes flickered. "Very cold in freezer." He waved toward the trays. "Only trays like thus, frozen cold cold."

A fleece-lined jacket hung by a hook alongside the freezer entrance. Hank slipped it on. "Let's go."

Kodama seemed to hesitate, then declared with his usual vigor, "Of course."

When Kodama pulled open the heavy insulated door the frigid air blasted over them. Inside, seen through their breaths, the white-glazed metal racks held trays and trays. Hank dutifully raised the lid of one to touch black shapes inside for hardness. "Good show, Kodama-san. Nice product."

"Of course."

Hank began to count the full trays in one of the high racks. He lost count, then started again.

"Cold, cold," said Kodama. He sounded anxious, even uneasy. "Bad dangerous to stay here long. Let us go."

Hank saw that he had no coat. "Go. I'll join you in a minute." Kodama remained. Hank totaled the trays in one rack, then counted the racks and multiplied in his head. "Funny. This comes to more than on the manifest you gave me, Kodama-san. By a couple of thousand pounds at least."

"Of course!" Kodama asserted. He hesitated, rare for him, before adding, "Many spaces missing trays."

"Not the ones I see here."

"Trays behind trays, many missing."

Hank accepted. The cold had begun to penetrate his jacket and his fingers were stiffening painfully. He was glad to leave.

Next morning Kodama, in his cabin, slowly changed from coveralls to a clean shirt, filling the time before he would join Captain Carford to board the freezer vessel *Torafune Maru*. More important, he prepared his mind. Nothing in him had changed outwardly. He remained fierce in his devotion to a quality product because this alone now defined him. Only when the *Torafune* came monthly to collect their frozen sablefish and transport them to Japan did the immensity of what he'd done shorten his breath and sicken him. For criminals, it was said, the fifth or sixth crime didn't shatter one like the first. If such were only so.

He stared at the gray metal walls of his cabin. They had become his prison. The air was stuffy despite the ship's ventilating system, since he chose never to hook the door ajar as did most of the others aboard, but this gave him precious privacy. With every object folded or secured, it was a room of bare simplicity. The only object of disorder he allowed was the little paper ship that his older son had given him on departure nearly a year ago. All the red and blue had faded, and a careless tea spill during rough weather had removed the stiffness from one side of the hull so that he needed to prop up the model with a matchbox. Faded also was the Japanese script on the side of the collapsed hull that enjoined him to be brave and honorable.

The contents of the terrible sealed envelope from Shoji Tsurifune had remained unread and virtually forgotten until five months ago during the May delivery to the freezer ship, when agent Muneo Watanabe riding aboard handed him a second envelope. Said the agent in private, with stiff formality, "Combine this with the other instructions, and now please perform them."

Kodama had turned wary at once, but spoke strongly. "I've been delivering a grade-one sablefish product. For the other, I'm a fisherman, not a spy."

"This has nothing to do with your reports on vessel and personnel. Yes, Subdirector Shoji Tsurifune is still disappointed with those. You'd better remember that some day soon he'll become director. But that's for another time. You're instructed now to stop catching so much sablefish."

"Why are we here then? Captain Carford's a good fisherman. I can do nothing about success." Kodama suppressed saying that it was often he himself who drove the crew hardest.

"You control the catch log before he sees it. What you deliver to us must at least show as less on the papers."

Kodama had tried to remain calm despite his feeling of outrage. "That would cheat the fishermen who work for shares, not salary."

"Don't worry. The subdirector can make it up to the captain in other ways."

"And the crew?"

"Common crew's not your concern. American fishermen have become greedy greedy. If they succeed there's nothing left for Japanese vessels. Remember that."

"I'm not a cheater."

"You're a worker for Tsurifune Suisan. You were approved for this position with the understanding that you'd convey information, and that you'd do what you were told."

It turned out that his own reports had helped bring about the subdirector's instructions. To avoid spying on the habits of the captain and the others, Kodama had filled the reports with tabulations of other vessels, even those distant ones counted on radar during wheelhouse visits. The number of vessels kept increasing. It proved that Americans were now banding together to capture more and more sablefish. Said agent Watanabe, "Your own vessel's deliveries using the American quota thus add to the total they'll use against us, to prove that they can catch all sablefish in Alaska and throw us out. Your old envelope contains basic procedures for underlogging and concealing it. Add to that these codes for reporting to us the actual catch. You'll now give us two manifests at each delivery: the one in English where you'll reduce the numbers of what you've caught, and the hidden one in Japanese with coded true figures."

Kodama had accepted the second envelope, read the contents of both with growing disgust, and two nights later had torn them into small pieces that he scattered into the water. During the next month he'd worked his men even harder to achieve quality. This is what will speak for me, he reasoned. At the June delivery agent Watanabe had examined the manifest, then looked up through thin-rimmed glasses. "You've changed nothing."

"First-quality product!"

"No one questions that. Yet you've reported too much as before."

"I'm just a fisherman. The instructions are too complicated to understand."

"Don't talk like an animal! You worked for years in the fishery office. We'll have your replacement on the cargo run next month, ready to take over unless there's full compliance. Then don't expect to stay with the Tsurifune company, or to creep back like a poor dog to the fishery office after the subdirector talks to them." Agent Watanabe returned his glare, and handed him an envelope with new codes for the month.

And thus had Yukihiro Kodama, offspring of samurai, decided that his family needed him to survive, and had taken to dishonor even though he had kept it to the barest minimum.

Now the summer had passed, the Americans had failed to harvest the entire sablefish quota despite their efforts, and just in this month, October, the Japanese fleet had been allowed to reenter Alaskan waters to share the quota's remaining sablefish.

Now, as in the fourth week of each month since they had started fishing, Kodama waited beside Captain Henry Carford for the arrival of the cargo ship. It slid into view, this image of his homeland, so large it barely rocked in the water that made the *Puale Bay* heave and pitch. Its scupper holes, looking like whale eyes, gushed water, and its heavy engine drummed within the steel depths. He watched as the captain skillfully eased their own vessel alongside while both crews adjusted fenders. The rail of the smaller vessel he rode swooped up and down at least four meters against the high black hull with familiar Japanese characters.

A ladder rattled down from above. Captain Carford, impulsive always, went first. He waited for the highest rise of the deck where he stood, leapt clutching the ladder's rope sides, then quickly scrambled up several rungs to avoid the *Puale Bay*'s rail that could possibly surge higher on the next wave and crush his legs. Kodama followed with the waterproof bag of papers bouncing on his back.

On the wide deck of the *Torafune Maru* Kodama exchanged curt bows with the crewmen, a nod and deeper bow with Hoshi Tamukai, who was now only a crewman but had once been a fishing master, and then, in the wheelhouse where he followed Captain Carford, traded deep bows with the freezer ship captain and with company agent Watanabe.

The two Japanese officers spoke enough English for pleasantries and shook hands western style. Then in the wardroom Kodama translated business exchanges as they examined the manifest and signed papers. A white-coated steward placed Japanese tidbits on the table. Captain Carford began eating them at once with his near-impolite American energy. Kodama sampled a few, but without the pleasure they had once given him during the earliest visits.

The agent addressed Captain Carford in English. "The product of fishing vessel *Puale Bay* is always good quality. We find it is not necessary to check it."

Carford-san nodded toward Kodama. "That's because I have such a quality fishing master."

Kodama acknowledged with a slight bow while the generosity stabbed his heart.

Carford-san continued to drink green tea from a cup the steward refilled at once, and to attack vigorously the sashimi laid before him. He gobbled even the sliced radish arranged like blossoms that was meant only for decoration. For a man of such authority, Kodama thought, embarrassed for him, Captain lost dignity in the presence of food. Eventually the captain's friend Tolly Smith joined him after making a delivery from his small vessel. His enthusiasm for the food was even more childish.

Agent Watanabe turned to Kodama without changing his bland expression, and spoke in Japanese. "You still under-report just enough to keep us from replacing you, even though the subdirector's going to be disappointed again. Don't you understand that it's now more important than ever to keep the American catch looking small, with your countrymen back on these grounds trying to prove Americans can't catch it all?"

Kodama's stare remained on the agent's face. There was nothing he could say, but to look away would be worse.

"Boy, but I like this raw sea urchin, this *umi*," declared Carford-san heartily. "You don't get it over here, so I look forward to your coming."

The agent told the steward in Japanese to bring more umi for the guests, then said in English, "Enjoy all on the platter, please. More will come."

Another steward brought in carafes of warm sake and cups. The captain of the ship immediately poured some of the liquid into the Americans' cups. Carford-san knew enough to reciprocate. They all drank toasts to Japanese-American friendship.

Agent Watanabe continued casually in Japanese to Kodama, "You don't seem yet to understand duty to your countrymen. It would be easier than you might think to replace you."

"I can't do more than this. The captain's beginning to suspect. He's not stupid."

"Then it's you who haven't done it properly."

Kodama closed his eyes and turned away. If only life were like the fight of equal adversaries on the judo mat.

When the meeting ended Kodama picked up a letter from his wife in the ship's office, then climbed down into the freezer hold to watch the proper storage of the product over which he had expended his energies and reputation. The workers moved as gray shapes in the frosty air. There in rubber clothing and a thick jacket was former fishing master Tamukai, lifting heavy boxes from the pallet and carrying them with bent knees to the storage lockers. If Tamukai had not been working they'd have talked, but this sometimes embarrassed them both so that Kodama was glad enough merely to nod. With so few Japanese vessels able to fish anymore in Alaskan waters where they once were the kings, even a fishing master was lucky to have work back on the sea.

Tamukai came from the locker. He studied Kodama with teeth clenched in a smile that was not friendly. Suddenly Kodama realized: This man is the replacement they have waiting if I fail them!

Jody's day ran its course. The unidentified-caller message from the morning came from a woman who wanted to turn her husband in as a drug addict. Jody explained that the man himself needed to request treatment or it wouldn't work. Later a drunk staggered into the office claiming that big worms were waiting outside to eat him, followed just at lunchtime by a native whom she knew to be a hard worker when sober, whose knees simply buckled by her desk. Both needed attention and all the consequent paperwork. By the time she was able to join her fisher-wife friends to plan out their newest civic challenge on behalf of the boats, they had all finished eating and needed to return to their jobs. "But we've picked you to speak last at city council and sum it up," said Madge Farley. "Don't worry, you'll be fine." Waiting when Jody returned to the office were two earnest young men in black, performing their year of Mormon missionary work, who tried to convert her while phones rang and she tried to be polite, until she lost patience and ordered them out despite their hurt expressions.

At two the kindergarten called to say that Pete was sneezing and had a runny nose, so would Mommy please come get him right away before he infected the others. By the time she collected him the sky was so dark that lights reflected in squiggles on the rain-slick roads. She might have returned with Pete to the office, but drunks and addicts weren't child's fare. She could have knocked on Adele's door, but that would probably have led to a prolonged dinner with yet another rerun of Adele's latest trip to Paris France, and inadequate time left for the kids' homework. Instead she and Pete nursed soft drinks in the car with the wipers flicking and the engine turned on occasionally for heat, until she could pick up Dawn and Henny for the ride home.

The hour-long trip through darkness started with children's chatter and bickering. Rain drove against the windshield and the glass steamed as the temperature dropped. Jody leaned over the wheel to concentrate. They might have been traversing a walled corridor for all that was visible beyond the headlight beams on the road.

Blessed summer was such an endless time away, when she'd again captain Adele's boat for the salmon run and Auntie Adele would take over the children. Henny and Pete would fly to Hank's parents in Baltimore for visits, then independent Dawn by herself since all of them together had been declared too big a package. (And come home restlessly spoiled but so what; Jane and Harry Crawford were warm and had good standards.) Her own mother, fortunately, never tried to take them although she sometimes whined about lack of visits. Need to invite her to Kodiak again, sometime. Give Hank a break and make it before he came home at last for Christmas. Or after he'd left again on that damned *Puale Bay* that was draining their lives.

"Mommy," said Dawn. "Why don't we sing?"

"Good idea, sweetie. Do you want to start?"

"Old MacDonald, because there's a horse in it and that's my special part, so everybody else keep quiet when we get to that part." They all sang and took turns imitating animals. Jody did the hee-haw, Henny oinked the pigs, and Pete eek-eeked the mice between giggles.

At the chilly dark house surrounded by dripping trees, the real animals greeted them with meows and wagging tails. The kids hopped at once to their tasks. Soon there was light, heat, and cheer. After all, it was a good place to be.

Hours after the freezer ship had departed, the dark engulfed the *Puale Bay* like soup. Hank again strode his wheelhouse. A red light on the chart table dimly outlined his skipper's chair and the boxes that held electronics, while colors danced on the hooded and dimmed-down screen of the fish finder. Voices droned away on the radio bands.

The norther had begun to shift east. A heading sea hit the bow and the ship shuddered. Grape-sized globs of water banged at the windows and snaked a trail down the thick glass. The ship was watertight and secure. Its engine missed not a beat, and with Terry as engineer its machinery would chug faithfully through any weather. And it had a sensible enclosed work deck to keep the crew dry. (It. It. Whenever he tried to think of the *Puale Bay* as "she," the word stuck in his throat. She-vessels were the ones that you'd made a part of you.)

On a smaller boat he'd hear yells from a drenched crew on open deck, would yell himself from sheer spirits, and enjoy the cascade of water down his oilskins. But who was he kidding? He was dreaming from a heated wheelhouse where his body craved exercise. On a smaller open boat those high spirits would come only in the first hour, before chill and wet entered the bones. Better to stay dry and relatively warm.

What was Jody doing now? Home with Henny, Dawn, and Pete in their warm house, that's what. Getting ready to turn out lights and snuggle under covers. Jody under covers alone. And the night quiet outside, secure and sleepy. Kidding himself indeed, to think a good life meant tossing in darkness with hours to go before the final line was worked, then having to set fresh lines to soak overnight, all before the next gleam of daylight and his call to start fishing again. When had this ever seemed the good life? The thought would have startled him except that it had crept over him more and more since he'd taken over the *Puale Bay*.

"*Puale Bay*. Switch to channel," came the voice of John Gains over the sideband speaker. Hank complied. "Yes, Hank. Call from Tokyo. You're directed to finish whatever lines you're working, then steam at once to a new position that I'll give encoded."

"We're doing fine here. It's my own spot. And moving takes hours, so we won't be able to soak the lines overnight."

"All very well, Hank, but the director's apparently dissatisfied with your last delivery. He's anxious that you relocate as soon as possible."

Hank felt his face burn. But he himself had been unhappy at the delivery totals. "Let's hear the location," he said grimly. Static interrupted and he asked for a repeat.

"Didn't you copy? It shouldn't be broadcast more than necessary even in code. We're not playing for marbles here, you know."

"I said, repeat."

"Listen carefully this time." The transmission stayed clear. "And I think it's best you report in as soon as you arrive."

Hank decoded the new location and checked it on his chart. Reaching it would take all of a day, and it placed him over a ridge of seafloor shallower than conventional sablefish grounds by more than two hundred fathoms. "Some mistake here. Black cod school far deeper. You say the director gave this order? The old man?"

"As you surely know, Shoji speaks for him and handles the day-to-day. It's the same thing. Shoji's anxious that you get there soon as possible."

"What the hell's he trying to do? Down my catch to zero? That's bullshit, John. Not going."

"Hank, don't make me remind you of contracts."

"Better you remind your Shoji that I'm captain out here, and I know where the fish are." When John started again to speak of contracts, Hank interrupted with, "What's this I heard that the Japanese—including, I assume, Tsurifune—pay longliners fishing off Washington and Canada six cents a pound more for their damned sablefish?"

Pause. "I wouldn't know. Unsubstantiated rumor, I'm sure. Your job is to fish and deliver. Those people are taking good care of you, don't worry. In your case, there would surely be some adjustment if what you said . . . Unsubstantiated, Hank. Don't speak of that again. And go now where you're told. Don't make trouble for yourself."

"Not going, John. Tell Shoji he's made a mistake. Now I'm signing off. Out."

Hank, alone again, performed push-ups.

17

MOONJOG

GULF OF ALASKA, EARLY DECEMBER 1983

During the next few weeks the weather progressively roughened, then eased into a patch of deceptive calm, then entered early winter with full-blown venom. The Tsurifunes sent no further instructions through John Gains. Shoji must have realized how mindless his orders had been, Hank decided. The incident made him reconsider his position with them. They might be heading him toward eventual prosperity, but he'd no longer let them jerk him around.

He also decided that it was time to stop feeling sorry for himself locked in the wheelhouse. He'd fallen into a trap of advancement from skipper to captain—from senior net-puller at one with his men to remote presence—that he'd seen happen to others as they climbed the ladder. Solitary at the top and out of touch. He realized that he barely knew this *Puale Bay* crop of crewmen, at least in the manner of the old days. They answered to him as did Kodama, of course. But they jumped only to Kodama's bark.

Despite Kodama's disapproving frowns he started working periods on deck, giving Terry longer stretches in the wheelhouse. It quickly changed the balance with his crew. Kodama nagged them less in his presence. Despite bad weather, everyone seemed more relaxed and cheerful. Another thing was surely just a coincidence: the daily catch figures increased.

Terry enjoyed the change too. When it came time to switch places he would slide from the padded captain's chair and stretch. "Ahh, that was a good loaf, warm and dry. Skippers sure have it easy."

One morning before daybreak, Hank in thermals and oilskins took position at the rail. Scudding hills of dark water rose and fell ahead. The worst of weather that had turned his stomach coffee-sour in the stuffy, rolling wheelhouse invigorated him now as in the old days. He braced with one hand while he gaffed with the other. Geysers of cold spray hit his face. Hooked black cod rose dripping on the line. He brought them in like so many potatoes, one every minute or so, enjoying the struggle to keep his balance.

Ham faced him on the other side of the line, and knocked off any fish that Hank's gaff failed to shake free at the pace they maintained. To judge from the drip down Ham's face and sleeves, the pitch of the wind wetted him even more. Hank hoped that the sweat pushing from under his own wool cap would pass for spray. He'd been too long in the wheelhouse without real exercise.

Behind them, under Kodama's hearty push, the coiling, baiting, and gutting continued in the low, chilly gear alley. "Captain! Must gaffing faster, faster, ha-ha," called Kodama.

Hank joked back.

"Hey, Boss," yelled Terry suddenly from above. "Come quick. Jody on radio says it's urgent."

Jody's voice was brisk even through static. "Hank. Bad news. Your mother just called. Your dad's had a heart attack. Serious. She thinks you should come." A pause. "I do too."

Hank's voice caught in his throat. He controlled himself. "Get me flight schedules. Still that Anchorage overnight direct to Chicago, or do I lose time through Seattle?"

"Seattle. I've checked."

"Reserve me tonight."

"Can you make it in time?"

"Reserve me. I'll try."

He called below for Kodama and Terry, pulled the chart for Seward, the nearest port, and started to plot course, keeping his anguish in check with action. Make lost fishing time up to his crew somehow, later. "Cut the line we're working and buoy it. I have to get ashore." He quickly explained why. "Terry! Going to run the engine full."

"You got it, Boss. Sorry for your dad."

"Captain! Must not abandon fishery without permission." Kodama said it sternly.

"Doing it this time, Kodama-san. Go. Go."

"Irregular, Captain! What will Director Tsurifune say?"

"Ten minutes, Mr. Kodama, or I'll come down and chop the damn line myself."

Gus Rosvic's voice came on the radio. "Hank, we heard. Listen. We're pulling our last string, and we're loaded to deliver. Take you to Seward if you need a ride."

"Really appreciate it, Gus. But I'm trying to make a flight tonight. Aboard here I can do it."

"Well now, don't underestimate a boat built for weather or a skipper who might have once rum-run a little before you was born. If somebody meets you at the Seward dock with a car, we'll get you to that overnight Seattle plane with time to spare. All we got to do is figure how to get you from your big rust bucket to a boat the right size for catching fish."

Hank turned to Terry. "Do you feel right to handle the ship without me? I know you're ready."

"I can."

"Irregular, Captain!"

Under a sky dimly gray just before daybreak, in water too rough for Gus's boat to come alongside without risking damage, Hank balanced on his own deck and zipped up his survival suit. Across the water, the *Hinda Bee*'s lights swooped crazily. She took seas harder than his large *Puale Bay*, but she righted at once when a sea struck her. He tugged once more at the clamps and body strap that secured him to the heavy line passed between the vessels.

Do it! With arms around chest he took a breath and jumped. Water sucked over his head. Frigid shock hit to his teeth even though the water-tight coverall sealed all but his face from feet to forehead. At last the suit's buoyancy shot him back to the air spitting bitter salt.

The sea kicked him about like a doll. A cold trickle entered beneath the chin strap and penciled a chill down his chest. Water pressed against his stomach and legs through the insulating rubber. He tried to swim and speed the passage, but the heavy material encased him as if he were in a bag. He was helpless, in the hands of others. From surface level, waves rose to hide the drunkenly bouncing *Hinda Bee* toward which he was being pulled, then revealed glimpses of yellow oilskinned arms at her rail. The *Hinda* seemed more frail than when seen from a deck. He twisted to see through salt-slapped vision his friends on the receding *Puale Bay*. Friends! All of them. Suddenly he'd have hugged them each. There they stood, securely braced on a ship that rose and fell sturdily, while water batted his head toward the sky, then nosed him under.

It had happened before, he told himself, subduing panic. He'd made it back from overboard once in the raw cold without support and with death staring truly. But facing the great force alone hit fresh each time. Jody, he thought, I love you, want to be . . . He controlled himself. Needed to stay passive, breathe between blows of water in his face, and trust the pull of those yellow-clothed arms.

The hull of the *Hinda Bee* seemed to thrash even more as he was pulled close. He looked up. The bow towered like a fortress, then plummeted, pushing spray.

It ended quickly. The *Hinda*'s rail descended into a trough, and with a yell and heave those on board drew him in. Hank clapped his hands clumsily encased in rubber against the rail. Their hands clutched his arms. As the boat swooped upward his body followed in the grip of others, over the rail like a sack, onto the deck.

"Thanks, guys," he muttered as they helped him to stand.

A whistle tooted. It was answered across the water by the *Puale Bay*, where his men waved. He watched them toss over his seabag wrapped in plastic. It bounced toward the *Hinda Bee* on the end of the line that had steadied him. He waved back, then duck-walked across the slippery deck into the cabin.

The welcome heat changed the numbness on his face to sweat even before he could unzip the survival suit. Water dripped from the suit to puddle around its floppy orange feet. "Never mind that, Cap," said a voice. "Coffee black or cream?" Braced against livelier sea motion than on the vessel he'd left, he peeled out of the suit arm by arm and then leg by leg, and slumped gladly onto the bench around the galley table. A steaming mug came down in front of him on the table's matting. Someone dropped his seabag beside him. He acknowledged each, but kept eyes fixed on the coffee's sway with the boat. The drag through water had left him shaky in spite of himself.

Hank steadied his hands around the cup and looked up. It was the same crew that last year had landed in jail with his men, the same ones with their endless bets. "Nice pull, guys. After you washed my face a few times."

"Sorry about that, Cap," said broad-shouldered Alec heartily.

"My man Ham," said Bud with the broken nose in a voice deep as his saunter. "He behavin' himself?"

"Finest. Said to tell you he's ready to beat your ass at hoops whenever you're in town together."

"That'll be the day, tell him."

Alec laughed. "How do you tell who's won, by the blood? You two bang on each other like it's football." He turned to Hank. "Sorry about your dad, Captain. Skipper says take the upper bunk in his cabin any time, but if you go up to the wheelhouse he'll tell you some fish stories. Or he'll be down after we finish on deck and somebody relieves him."

"Thanks. I'm on my way."

Gus Rosvic slouched comfortably in his captain's chair. The signature black cap pulled close to his eyes accentuated his shaggy white sideburns. "Settle in, Hank. Long trip ahead. Incidentally, we got a radio call from that Jody of yours. Somebody's meeting you in Seward. There's a lady gets things done. My boys show you a bunk?"

"Took care finest, Gus. Thanks." Hank's eye quickly scanned the wheelhouse. Gus's radar model was at least five years from the newest; depth sounder in black and white, no color; loran-C but no latest SatNav. Duct tape patched his skipper's padded chair. But bits of polished brass shone in the dull light along with woodwork rubbed and mellow, everything in place. All of it right, even to smells of old coffee and damp wool. The kind of boat he liked best. Ahead the bow rose and plunged. The deck rolled degrees more than that of the larger vessel he'd left, and with a snap rather than a lurch. Don't get seasick, never live it down.

The wheelhouse radio sputtered. It was Terry from the *Puale Bay*. His voice, confident and easy, dispelled any doubt in Hank that he could handle the boat. With questions answered Terry became his usual light self. "Boss! You dried out yet? Ham and me want you to know, you got a new name with us here. After the way you hit the water when you jumped? We call you 'Splash' now. 'Splash Gordon' like that guy in the funnies."

Hank enjoyed the name. " 'Splash' it is then." But back with Gus he paced and his stomach tightened for the days ahead.

"How old's your dad, Hank?"

"Sixty-three, I think."

"Oh, then he'll pull through fine." Gus's deliberate voice had the hon-eyed ease of age comfortable with itself. "Look at me, near ten years older and still pissing. He a vet?"

"World War II Navy. Off on South Pacific duty when I was born in forty-four."

"Well, that's interesting. So was I. And now his kid's in my hair with his crew and their bets trying to send us broke. And his kid's lady rocking the fleet because she runs a seiner and don't mess up. That's what's hard to take. She don't mess up."

Hank smiled. "Wish I could help you there, Gus."

"Well, boy, you could stop kissing Jap ass." The easy voice didn't change. "But never mind that now. Don't worry. Your dad'll make it fine and we'll get you there."

Hank started, then pretended he hadn't heard. I'm only making my way like everybody else, he told himself. Saving my boat. Family's daily bread.

The sun had risen. It shone briefly at the horizon, then disappeared into the sky's low cover. Hank studied the water. Wind blew laps of scud atop green crests and rippled the glassy surface beneath. In troughs the hue turned black and beckoned downward. Watch me, it said. Come along. Let me take you in.

Someday, he thought, my kids will wait at my hospital door. Or throw a wreath on that water I'm watching. What will be their summation? What's mine now for my dad? He suddenly felt too weary to brace against the boat's motion. "Maybe I'll shut my eyes for a minute, below."

"You do that, Hank. Be my guest. We'll wake you for chow."

The day had cleared by the time they entered Resurrection Bay, passing among the high guardian rocks. Wings of small birds from nearby bluffs filled the air. A late sun pinked snow on the surrounding peaks, and flashed golden on surfaces of ice within the mountain snow. The boat's motion turned steady enough that her wake cut a clean-frothed triangle astern. Hank had slept all he could and eaten more than he'd wanted under their hospitality. When he bantered they bantered back, but they respected his silences. Gus had also napped, but now steered again to dodge floats of crusty bay ice. He'd said no more about the Japanese.

By Jody's arrangement, Swede Scorden waited with a car at the municipal pier. After hurried thanks to Gus, Hank found himself in a vehicle that was stable on the road while his inner system continued to swoop with the waves. In the long twilight, lamps and neon lights were already bright along Seward's main street. By the time they reached the highway to Anchorage the mountain snows around them had turned darkest blue against black sky.

"Nice of you to come yourself," Hank began.

"Jody caught me headed for Anchorage. Thank the usual politics before the next Fishery Council. Hot enough issues that young Tsurifune plans to be there, incidentally. If the Japanese can persuade the Council to hike up the black cod quotas it would leave enough for them, even if Americans gear up to take more than in other years. For the same reason, Americans want to keep down the quota so it'll be easier for them to take it all. Part of the Game, as I've said before."

The car passed through hilly forest where dim fir trees bowed under the snow. Hank would have been glad for silence while he collected uncertain thoughts, but Swede's dry voice continued. "Feel you're pulling your share out there?"

"Can't complain. Sometimes our catch figures seem spotty even though the fish never stop coming."

"I've noticed. The numbers eventually filter to my office." After a pause. "You're the captain. Keep an eye."

"What do you mean? I do keep an eye."

Swede changed the subject abruptly. "You like eating black cod?"

"Maybe as delicatessen sablefish back East. But Arty our cook tried to bread and fry some fresh. The smell sent us puking. Stuff went overboard fast but the galley stank for a week, even the pans. We got a lecture from Kodama on marinating first and so on, but the crew said they'd throw the kid overboard if he ever tried to serve it again."

"You're all peasants. A chef friend's place is on the way to the airport. I phoned him to fix some for us. About time you knew what you were catching."

"Well . . . good. If we have time."

"If? Everything in the fish business is 'if.' Likely we'll have time."

As they progressed, a moon rose to turn the scene around them white. Eventually they left the forests for open stretches along the wide Turnagain Arm. Hank shifted restlessly under the seat belt. His balance still swayed from the sea. Under moonlight, hummocks of ice cast shadows along the arm's frozen water, and snow peaks above the ice glowed brighter than in daylight. Terry, back in the wheelhouse, would be watching the same light rise and fall on rolling water. And Jody . . .

He glanced over at Swede's face in profile. Chin still defiant, and with his wrinkles erased against the brightness outside, no older than when he'd first met the man nearly two decades ago. Face it. "Swede . . . How do you feel about this, working for the Japanese? I'm taking flak out there from other fishermen. Is it just prejudice? Jones Henry went too far, but now it sounds like everybody's gone anti-Jap. I know I'm under a Japanese wing. But I'm just sharing a resource while I help develop the fishery and pay my bills."

"That sounds like whining, Crawford. Deals are being made all over. You've watched American fish investment go to zero since the crabs collapsed. In this time and place, if you want to do anything bigger than fish the same little boat all your life, you're stuck signing with foreigners who know the value of fish. You made a practical decision."

Hank decided to admit what bothered him most. "They act like they own me."

Swede's laugh wasn't pleasant. "Get used to it."

"There've got to be alternatives."

"You know yourself American banks are scared since king crab collapsed. You accept foreign help or go scratch. Now, being in a Norwegian pocket might be the easiest, since they're closer to our own culture. Sign your soul and house again to, say, Christiana Bank. They're funding new trawlers for Bering Sea groundfish, with American ownership on paper. That's of course what you're already doing in a different fishery with Tsurifune. The Scandinavians are cool, reasonable people. But when it comes down to the money, sharks like the rest. Like you'd better be whatever you do to make your way."

Swede braked, swore, circled a boulder in the road, then gunned back to an even eighty miles an hour. He resumed calmly. "You might as well stay with the Japanese. They won't shake you around any more than the others, and for all their scheming they have a sense of honor."

"But with Tsurifune, sometimes I get almost paranoid and think they're screwing me. Listen. You're in their Kodiak office whether you run it or not. Tell me this straight. Is it true your plant in Seattle's paying six cents more than Alaska for the same black cod?"

"You want it straight? The answer's yes. And you'll find it so in Canada too. In case you didn't know, the lower forty-eight and Canada have both banned their black cod grounds to foreigners, which means to Japanese mainly. So the Japs are desperate to keep their Alaska quota. Their strategy is to make black cod unattractive to fishermen up here by paying a low price, while keeping Tokyo supplied by paying what they need to in other places where they've lost the fight. Maybe, they hope, your fishing friends who give you a hard time and are so hot to take over all the black cod will get discouraged and fish for something else, and they'll get to keep their quota."

"Son of a bitch!"

"Don't judge too fast. Tsurifune and others at his level need to work every angle to stay in business. That means continuing to get what fish of ours they can with minimum sacrifice, and only giving in when they might anger us enough to cut them off. Collectively they've had to idle hundreds of their fishing ships and thousands of fishermen since we took back our two hundred miles and other countries followed."

Hank shrugged. He remembered his encounters at sea with foreign fishing ships before the Magnuson Act of 1976. It had been a toss-up whether the prize went to the Soviets or the Japanese for greedy overfishing and their indifferent overrun of gear laid by smaller-boat American fishermen.

Swede began a long account of a meeting in Anchorage he had just witnessed. A coalition of American fishermen, fish processors, and marketers had presented a united front to their Japanese counterparts to demand that they lower tariffs and open their closed markets to processed American fish. "You could hear the collective suck of Japanese breath at the proposals," said Swede with a relish rare for him. "Top people from Japanese fishing. They didn't want to come, but they were afraid of Reagan's new State Department if they didn't. Your Tsurifunes were there. The last thing those people want is to allow fish into Japan that's already cut their workers from the loop and that'll then compete with their own product."

Hank listened only sporadically. He had begun to wonder: If Tsurifune and his friends played sly with the price they paid for black cod, what other tricks were they playing?

Swede continued to enjoy his story of the conference. The Americans held an ace, with a bill by Alaska Senator Ted Stevens that set a near-immediate date for the phaseout of foreign fishing within U.S. waters. "The Japanese tried to offer concessions that would have benefited one of the three American interests over the others. But the Americans didn't break ranks. Both sides just stared. Sometimes nobody spoke for half an hour." On the final day the Japanese gave in, partially, by agreeing to buy fifty thousand tons of U.S.-processed fish and to approach their government to lower tariffs. "That might not sound like much, but it was a hell of a breach in the Jap wall. They'd never had to deal with the whole American industry united, and with the threat of our government behind it. To my knowledge, Stevens has now shelved his bill. It served its purpose. But you can see how the pressures on Tsurifune are closing in."

Swede appeared to wait for his comment. "Well," said Hank at last, "I can see their problems. And I like them, especially the old man. Their hospitality's great. We probably shouldn't begrudge foreigners the fish that we can't take. In a hungry world we shouldn't hoard food we'd waste. But—"

"I'm glad to see you're not as provincial as some of your buddies, Crawford."

"But that fucking six-cents-a-pound difference mounts to thousands of bucks I need. *Other* Kodiak guys need. So Japanese still hold the cards. They've got the money and the market." He lowered the window for a blast of fresh air. The moon's reflection sped along the iced water of Turnagain Arm. "I'm still stuck with them."

"And they're stuck with you. You've got the things they want at the moment: your American quotas and your good reputation. That happens to give you more power than you might think." After a while Swede added quietly, "Just stay on guard."

"You've told me that twice now. What do you mean?

"Well . . . Here's an example. Something little known yet, just a rumor. Last year the Coast Guard might have inspected a Japanese longliner and found what they think are double logbooks: one for the inspectors showing a modest catch, and the other recording what they really caught, which might be twice as much. An old trick. It was the ship of a Tsurifune colleague, incidentally, not the old man's. I won't ask if you've been approached on anything similar, but I'd caution you to—"

"Never. And I wouldn't!"

"I believe you."

Suddenly Hank pictured Kodama's reluctance to see him count trays in the freeze locker.

Swede pulled to the side of the road. "Piss call, Hank. Age calling. You suit yourself."

They separated to do their business. The highway was wide and smooth, built for traffic, but they occupied it alone. With the engine off, the creak of ice sounded clearly from the bay a few hundred feet from the roadside. Moonlight glowed on it all. A chilly breeze blew ice odors that combined with those of spruce trees rising dark above him. They could have been at sea for the isolation.

Out there on the longliner, Hank wondered, could trusted Kodama be pulling tricks?

Twin car lights meandered in a distance, disappeared behind rocks around a bend, approached, and flooded them. The car stopped. "Need help?"

"No problem, thanks," said Swede, and the car continued.

If, Hank said to himself, someone had stopped like that in Baltimore, I might have thought robbery. One reason Alaska holds me here. Am I letting it turn to shit on me?

Back on the highway Hank continued. "I'll ask again. Why tell me to stay on guard?"

Swede drove a long time before he answered. "I didn't want to put ideas in your head. But their game with your boat might now be this: to hold back the perceived American catch wherever they can. Your deliveries go toward the total that Americans accumulate toward proving they can land all the black cod with nothing left for foreigners. For Japanese. The less you catch, the more's left for them."

"And Tsurifune tried to send me off to fish on grounds too shallow for a good catch! The bastard was screwing me! How should I do it, Swede? To save myself and get back at them?"

"You could give up your fine crabber and your house, go back to a little seiner, and build your family a log cabin."

"Wish I could."

"No, you don't. You're ambitious. There's too much out there. You just need support to help get it. So if I were you, Crawford . . . Keep to your contract, don't blow your chances. Stay cool and fish your ass out of this hole. Just take nothing for granted. Check everything."

"You're fuckin'-A I'll check. They can watch out for me now!"

"And save your firepower. Japanese hate confrontation; they'll do better by you without it. You're valuable to them. Produce well for 'em so that everybody's happy, and by contract you will get back your securities and the controlling shares you now own just on paper. Then get out and do again as you please. Go cautious if you like. Or get savvy, learn the politics, name your terms, and jump into the game with your new chips. Play it calm with Tsurifune and you might end up owning most of a fishing fleet."

Hank lowered his window again and let the moon-drenched night blow around him. It calmed him and brought his thoughts back to earth. "All I think I ever needed was a limit seiner and three or four crew. That's the fishing I love. Then, okay, expanded to my fine, big *Jody Dawn* but still with the same-sized crew and the wheelhouse still practically part of the deck. With crab I owned the damn world out there for a while. Now I watch everything changing under my feet."

"You owned nothin' unless the system protected you. But you're American in the right time and place so you've got more of the world than most. Don't feel sorry for yourself. Remember that the fish is here with us, not with foreigners for all their interest and schemes. If we can take the fish, it's ours, not theirs."

"Ours? I thought you were working for the Japanese."

"For salary."

Hank's thoughts were too heady for anything but a joke. "When I get that empire, Swede, I'll put you in charge, go back to seining salmon all summer, and take my family to Hawaii for the rest of the year."

Instead of a dry laugh, Swede's voice deadened. "Find somebody else. I'm done fighting. The Japanese have given me safe harbor. It suits me now to play safe and watch it all become history. The best I could do was caution you. Now you're on your own."

Swede's steady foot on the pedal brought them to the restaurant on schedule. His chef friend had a charcoal grill fired and waiting. Fat dripped from the marinated black cod filets and sizzled from within the meat.

Hank forced himself to be polite and accept a serving. He was unprepared for the fish's depth of flavor, and a heavy richness equal to sirloin. Before long they were driving again toward the airport. The taste lingered in his mouth. "Pretty good, I've got to admit."

"You'd better."

They reached Anchorage with time to spare. Hank checked in for the flights through the night that would take him via Seattle to Baltimore by the next afternoon. Then he turned to Swede for a final question. But Swede had disappeared.

18

CITY LIGHTS

BALTIMORE, EARLY DECEMBER 1983

Shoji Tsurifune's near trick occupied Hank's thoughts between sporadic naps during the long connecting flights from Anchorage. Fantasies of payback alternated with concern for his father. At the Baltimore airport, however, when he saw his cousin Bobby and Bobby's wife, Alice, waving, their familiar friendly faces helped dispel dark thoughts. Need to put all that from mind for a while, he told himself. "How's Dad? How's Mother holding up?"

Alice hugged him. "They'll be so glad you're here. Aunt Jane says he's doing better. We'll take you straight to the hospital."

They drove into the city, past the new baseball stadium and new convention center, into the harbor area now bordered by walks and restaurants. Hank forced himself to relax. Sea spray and endless longlines of thrashing fish began to seem far away. Even at midday early holiday lights festooned lampposts as well as the rigging of the historic sailing ship moored at the quay. People bundled up against the early December chill strolled the open space with no apparent purpose other than leisure.

"Look at all this, Hank-o," said Bobby. "You left just before the city came alive. I can't even remember the old stuff that was here. Factories, something like that. Torn down and now we've got condos right on the water, and see that marina over there? Great places to eat and watch the scene."

"And shops," added Alice. "Just a zillion nice stores."

251

"I remember crabbers and oystermen who tied up here and sold their catches. What happened to them?"

"Oh, those stinky old boats, I do recall. That was sooo long ago. Thank goodness we got rid of them." Alice turned to him with wide sympathetic eyes. "It's an emergency I know, but such a shame Jody couldn't come too. Up there God-knows-where in Alaska with the polar bears."

"Come on," Hank chided in good humor. "What have you been reading?"

"Those long dark nights they talk about? Without first-division teams or even a bitty stadium or cultural stuff like musicals, or . . . or formal dances? I know you've got your big company or something, but don't you and poor Jody go crazy? I'd just die up there and so would Poodles. Wouldn't you sweet?" Bobby grunted. Hank noticed that both cousins had put on weight in the year or so since he'd last seen them.

He tried to picture Jody at one of the stuffy formal fund-raisers. That would be the day. (But how long since they'd danced except to a bar juke-box? Did Jody even own an evening gown? Had she ever wanted one?) He concentrated on city sights that had been part of his growing up.

They turned up Charles Street. "To the right," said Bobby. "That big entrance? My office is on the twenty-seventh floor, view of everything. I just walk to work from Federal Hill across Harbor Place. Like I said, Hank, this town's got it all."

"How's business? Sporting goods, isn't it?"

"Athletic shoes. Hank, you wouldn't believe how I'm doing. Old canvas sneakers are history. So many kinds now that the yuppies need to buy different shoes to run, walk, sit, shoot hoops, run bases, you name it. Then, ho ho, every year or so we change styles so they have to buy new. Bonanza."

Hank wondered aloud about the Merchants' Club down one of the streets. It had been a mainstay of his father's life, where businessmen of substance met at lunch in paneled rooms, served by discreet waiters all called by name. "I always felt like hot stuff meeting Dad there."

"Uncle Harry's invited me now and then," said Bobby. "Actually, well, my crowd belongs to places with more pizzazz."

Their course up Charles Street took them through lines of genteel shops and townhouses to Mount Vernon Place with its monuments, stairways, and trees, crowned by the pillar of the Washington Monument. "Nothing's changed here, at least," said Hank. "Do they still have that flower festival in the spring?"

"I should hope!" exclaimed Alice. "I help at the Federal Hill booth. Before that at the Roland Park booth, before we moved downtown. Remember Peabody over there, Hank? You surely went there Saturdays like the rest of us."

"I did. I did. Two years of fiddle lessons from hell before I persuaded Mom to give up on me. I might have stayed if they'd given me drums."

Pleasant laughs all around. But no amount of talk could quiet Hank's trepidation.

Farther uptown they passed the front of Johns Hopkins University. The slopes lay brown and empty now in winter, turf where he'd lolled in May green and sunshine with his head comfortably in the lap of who? Nancy? Sally? Names even vague but their faces . . . Married now? Kids? Gone fat? Was he remembered? Would they gasp at the news that Henry Crawford now owned a 108-foot million-buck Bering Sea crabber, skippered a bigger-yet longliner in the Gulf of Alaska, and commuted to Japan? (Never imagining the underside of all that.) Hell, they wouldn't understand any more than Alice. He watched two kids with trailing bright scarves who wandered hand in hand past the library doors. Others now owned the place, himself forgotten. Nearly twenty years ago, was it possible?

"Hopkins lacrosse. They winning these days?" he asked to keep the conversation going.

"You don't follow?" exclaimed Alice. "Alaska must simply be a wilderness!"

"We generally keep the polar bears off our front porch," Hank said mildly. He stretched. What had he given up by leaving? Without that first Alaska jaunt he might now be king of something like the sneaker trade in Baltimore. Ship-related at least. White shirt and office, but doing business with Brits, Germans, Russians, even Japanese—eye to eye without being screwed behind your back. He watched the big homes they now passed, with their spacious lawns, handsome trees, and tended shrubbery. All that lost to his children, the East Coast's whole surrounding style of history and comfort. But not going north would have meant never meeting Jody. He'd be married now to a cheerful ditz like Alice. Get yourself home soon, he told himself.

Inevitably, the road snaked down through trees toward the hospital. "I don't have the details of Dad's . . . " His tongue stalled at the word.

"Just must have happened, Hank," said Bobby. "That's the best we know. Immediate family only at the hospital. We haven't seen him since we had hard crabs on the patio last July, when he was in fine shape."

"You've got to promise to call us with a full report," added Alice. Her voice turned husky. "Uncle Harry was so straight and handsome, it's just inconceivable he won't be all right. Oh, Hank." Her hand touched his shoulder again.

When he entered the hospital lobby a faint smell of antiseptics oppressed him at once. He took the elevator as directed. On the patients' floor the medicinal odors turned heavy. A sinister machine with tank and dangling mask stood in the gleaming scrubbed corridor. The sight brought him close to panic. He ran to reach the door, tapped, entered, and stifled a cry at the haggard old man connected to tubes. "Dad?"

"Who are you?" A startled woman peered from behind a screen.

It was the wrong room. In the one adjacent, the recognizable head lay on a pillow, eyes closed. Before he could advance, his mother rose from a chair beside the bed, hurried over, and hugged him with her head on his shoulder. Her hands clutched his arms. They both began to cry.

"How is he? When did it happen?" She only gripped him closer. "It's okay, Mom. It's okay."

"That you, Hank?" Dad's voice was remarkably clear.

His mother released him and Hank hurried over. His dad's hand was weak but still had a grip. On impulse Hank bent over and kissed him, something he'd not done since he was a kid of about five.

"Hey, fellah. Good to see you. How's fishing?"

"Good, Dad, good. What's this you're pulling here?"

"I wasn't getting enough attention." The mouth stretched slightly in a smile, but the voice turned thin. "Look now. Lots of . . . atten . . . shun." The eyes closed.

"Dad? Dad?"

His mother's hand took his arm. "He drifts in and out. Dr. John Murphy says it's normal with this particular . . . He'll recover and be fine. John assured me." Her voice caught. "But he's so weak."

Hank touched his father's face. Stubble on the chin, unlike always-shaven Dad. Lips pale and dry. The dim yellow of his forehead and cheeks was the most unnatural part. At least the gradual graying of Dad's hair and mustache, both once so dark, had occurred gradually enough that he'd seen it before. Yet Dad's face—suddenly the beloved face—retained its grace even though it now showed vulnerability.

Hank sat on the edge of a hard metal chair, hands clasped at his knees. He watched his mother's face. It had aged smoothly, but was puffy and tired. Dark blotches had begun to appear on her hands. "How did it happen?"

"We'd finished supper, I remember that. We'd headed upstairs to the study for a TV show. Without a word Dad sat on the steps. Not like him at all. And he didn't answer when . . . It took me a minute to understand. He's always so healthy. I'm the one who gets sick at times. I never thought . . . " Her voice wavered and she stopped, looked away, then collected herself firmly. "Well, thank goodness I phoned nine-one-one. It all happened so quickly. The men with the stretcher—and one woman, that was interesting—they were all efficient but were still kind, I thought. One was even black, but very kind." She sat back, now in control. "In ten minutes the whole world changed. I'm glad you're here. Now tell me about the children."

He gladly shifted to talk of Dawn, Henny, and Pete, but glanced often at the still figure in the bed. "Henny's gotten taller since you last saw him. Very serious. Likes to stick around the boats." He felt pride in adding, "So does Dawn. You know how she talks a blue streak. But underneath there's real work savvy, and she pitches in everywhere. I'll make both into fishermen yet."

"I suppose you will with Henry Junior, dear, whatever anybody says. He is a sturdy young fellow. But Danielle? Please don't expect me to call the child Dawn after we persuaded you and Jody to give her such a fine old family name. You and Jody should be grooming her to become a young lady." His mother waved her hand to imply enough of that now, then thanked him for a coffee-table book of Alaskan scenes and asked about gifts she had sent. "How does Jody look in that green-checked jacket I mailed last September? It seemed so perfect for her in the store that I couldn't resist. She wrote and thanked me, of course. And apparently Danielle loved the party dress I'd shipped earlier. The child is a girl, you know. And Pete's alphabet blocks? It's never too early to start."

"Pete. Really likes the blocks," he improvised. "And Jody. Looks great in the jacket. Great." But he knew nothing of any gifts, nor the book apparently sent by Jody. He'd barely seen his family for months. So they exchanged stuff not only at Christmas? How much else didn't he know, had missed by life at sea and the rounds of fish?

"Let's talk about details, Mom. Bills for the hospital. What about expenses at home?"

A pause. "Well, I'm sure your father can see to any of that as soon as he gets well."

"Hey . . . Hank."

Hank rushed to the bed. "Dad! How're you doing?"

His father's eyes showed a moment's spark. He held up his right hand with thumb and forefinger joined in a circle of okay. Then he drifted back to sleep.

Hank watched, still frightened, but relieved.

"I'm sure he's pulling through," he told Jody that night when he called before she left her office in Kodiak. "Might take a while, but . . . Kids all right?"

She reassured him, then added: "I wasn't that close to my father. But I'm glad whenever I think of it that I got myself to Colorado before he died."

"Dad's not going to die!"

"No. Of course not."

"Now, Terry," Hank continued. "I told him to call you every day. I have a message for him."

"When I talked to him last night, after I got home to the marine radio, it was all going fine. I've already told you that, when you phoned before your flight from Anchorage. I'll have an update tonight when we get home."

"I need you to tell him this: Keep fishing deep water, that's where the black cod school. Don't obey orders from Gains or Japan to go shallow. I trust Kodama, but maybe Tsurifune's playing tricks. How you pass that to Terry without the whole fleet hearing I'm not sure. Try." He told her the suspicion that Swede had raised. "I'm not sure yet how I'm going to handle it." As he told it his anger returned. "Damn them. Treating me like a chess piece! I need to get out from under."

"If we'd talked this over back then, before you signed—signed even our house away!" Hank tensed, and was relieved when she continued reasonably: "Let's not go over this now on long distance, Hank. Fix yourself a drink and go to bed."

His voice softened. "I miss you."

"And I miss you. We all do." But her voice remained steady. "Kiss your dad for me. And . . . I'll try to warn Terry. And—don't get upset—I'm being practical. God knows how your mom would fit into Kodiak without her garden clubs, but she's a good egg and she'd be welcome."

"Dad'll be fine," Hank said hastily. "But thanks."

In his old room on the third floor, preparing for bed after wishing his mother a good night, he looked around and grew nostalgic. During the few times over the years that he'd visited with his brood he and Jody had stayed up here, but he'd been too occupied to re-wander its corners. He now noticed that the room remained intact as he'd left it two decades before, and dusted at that. A lacrosse stick hung on the wall over books whose spines read Dumas, Twain, Kipling, and *Julius Caesar* (the only one of those famous plays everybody claimed were so great that had ever grabbed him). A high school trophy for track with its gilt worn to brown at the edges. Even a faded paper lei from some dance, draped over the Winslow Homer print of men in a dory. He'd forgotten the stir that picture once had given him, long before Alaska.

He patted the carefully stitched flowered quilt on the bed, the work of Mom's grandmother, stroked the polished old headboard with scrolled posts from some Crawford generation, and slid open a drawer from the chest whose carved handles resembled lion's heads. Each piece bore family history from households and people vanished before his time. When he settled into bed, familiar odors surrounded him. It all brought memories.

Three hours later the phone rang and his mother called up, "It's Jody for you, dear. Don't scold her. She probably hasn't counted, to know the time back here."

Jody got to the point at once. "You're not going to like this. Those Tsurifune people in Tokyo must have set it in motion even before you left Anchorage. They ordered *Puale Bay* to Seward, and Terry thought it was to unload even though their hold wasn't full. At the same time they were flying over a Japanese captain. This afternoon they sent him on a charter boat to meet the ship halfway down Resurrection Bay so that *Puale* didn't even dock in Seward. It's already happened."

"I'm calling Tokyo, then flying home first thing tomorrow to settle this!" Hank exploded.

"No, you're not." Jody's voice was firm. "Stay with your folks or you may regret it. Call Tokyo if you want, I suppose. But frankly, I think you ought to simmer down before doing anything. Terry didn't sound that upset. He may even be relieved. We'll still get paid for your share of the catch."

"Treacherous bastards!"

Jody called something to Dawn on how to work the chopped onions into the hamburger. Her voice was lighter when she returned. "Sorry, I didn't hear, but I assume you were just cussing. Remember, you don't want to shock your mom if she's in earshot. Go back to bed and sleep on it."

After he hung up Hank struggled with his anger, and finally dressed and slipped out of the house to sprint along deserted tree-lined streets while he tried to think. They even controlled his *Jody Dawn!* Fly to Tokyo and have it out? Need money, money for that. He remembered Swede mentioning that the Tsurifunes were coming to Anchorage for the next Council meeting. Take them on there, then, in eight or ten days, check the date.

What if he could find enough to buy back the *Jody Dawn?* Loan from Dad? No, terrible timing even if he had it.

What about Seth? A bachelor, not a heavy enough drinker to blow his savings, surely he'd saved money from the good crab years. It was time that Seth began to commit. Then what about Terry?

Back at the silent house he kept his voice low as he called Jody back. "Radio Seth on the *Jody Dawn*. I assume he's still off the Aleutians. Tell him to call me from Dutch or whichever next port he reaches. Give him Dad's number at the hospital as well as here. I need to talk!"

Seth reached him at the hospital late the next day. "Better be important, man," came the deep voice. "Like Jody said it was. We were headed to Dutch but we pulled out of our way into Adak. What's up?"

Hank glanced at his dad asleep. His mother had gone to the gift shop. He decided not to break the call to find a pay phone for privacy, but he kept his voice low. "Think about this. I know you've saved. What would you say to buying a piece of the *Jody Dawn?* Say ten to fifteen percent."

"No way, man! I decided long ago I don't want that strain of owning things. Paperwork shit, and . . . No offense, but look what it's done to you. Japs have you jumpin' on a string."

Hank felt himself flush. Was that how it appeared? "Hey, just half joking. Forget I brought it up. Thanks for calling. Safe trip." He vowed to ask no one else.

Three days later the doctors reported the worst crises had passed. Multiple tests had defined the limits of the attack. Medications and future procedures were being mapped. The senior Crawford now sat up in bed much of the time, and conversed or read for at least an hour before his eyelids shuttered down.

"You dodged the bullet, Harry," said Dr. Murphy heartily. The two knew each other from the golf course. "We'll make some clicks in your lifestyle, send you home to rest, and by spring, maybe, we'll see you back on the green."

"And when can I return to the office?"

"Ohh . . . that might be a different story, buddy. Depends on the pressures there, doesn't it?"

"Come on, John. I'm only sixty-three."

"A mighty healthy sixty-three except for this little thing. Let's see how it plays."

The elder Crawford frowned. He doesn't like doctor condescension any more than I do, thought Hank, and was about to press for specifics when his dad demanded, "What about my evening highball? Are you going to say that'll hurt me?"

"This is a hospital, buddy."

"But not a damn monastery."

The doctor studied his chart without looking up. "This son you brag about. Alaska fisherman, probably half pirate, so I don't know how we could stop a skilled smuggler, eh? But in that case I'll cut down any sedative for sleep. And I'll tell the smuggler that one stiff shot's the max, got it?"

Hank laughed for the first time in days. "You've got it, Doc."

19

SHAFTSMANSHIP

BALTIMORE, EARLY DECEMBER 1983

Another three days and Dad was home, walking about at least from chair to chair. Mother wore an apron more often than her painting smock or going-out clothes while she fussed over pots and baking dishes to fix what father and son liked best. Sarah, the household's part-time cleaning and laundry help for decades, moved about them discreetly, although her admonition, "You oughtta be spanked for livin' so far from your folks," came from distant times when he'd been a toddler.

Hank took his mother to lunches—saving dinners for home with Dad—and trailed her at the supermarket to take in bulk sizes she would not otherwise have bought. He forced himself to watch her objectively. She'd always cared for herself, and her hair and clothing remained impeccable even when directing the grocery cart he pushed. She walked deliberately but favored one knee. Could she still dance? (He remembered his childhood savor of perfume and swish of silk when she'd wave gaily from Dad's tuxedoed arm as they left for a big party.) He knew she was anxious for the future, probably frightened, but her cheer never waned. She'd have called it good breeding.

Bobby and Alice insisted on entertaining him one night at their country club among some of their friends. Clearly he was on display, complacently accepting their jokes about his life in the wilderness, while still enjoying the well-being of the place. Walking back from the washroom, Bobby suddenly said, "I sure envy you, guy. You've made your life an adventure. This here is all mighty nice, but . . . " Hank started to invite him expansively to come ride on his boat and pull a line or two (joke and bully his ass into a sweat he wouldn't forget), then glanced at his cousin's tubby middle and thought better of it. "You've got a good world here, man. Enjoy it."

He looked forward to the five o'clock highball ceremony he'd started at the hospital. He and his father sat in the living room as the day's last light filtered through the curtains, their outlines darkened.

"You're still successful in Alaska?"

"Doing real good, Dad."

"Finances steady?"

Hank hesitated, then said, "Steady."

"Your mother keeps daydreaming that you'll bring Jody and our grandchildren back East to live. By now I suspect that's a dream."

"I think you have it right, Dad." He started to say that Jody was bonded to Alaska, but knew it wasn't honest to let her carry the blame. "I'm doing the only work I ever wanted to do, and in the place where fishing's in the bone."

"I'll be devil's advocate. New England's famous for fish and fishermen. So is Chesapeake Bay. Both closer to your roots."

Hank took enough time so that he appeared to consider, although his impulse was to declare 'no way!' He'd seen Gloucester fishing boats only as a summer tourist long ago, but even so. The bright wooden boats had attracted him at once but they were quaint, quaint. And their cargoes were limp fish without the dash and fight of salmon or even black cod. As for Chesapeake Bay—an elegant book of Bay photos lay on the coffee table in front of him. The cover showed a man standing on the rail of a scuffed boat with a cabin the size of an outhouse, holding a pair of long poles that disappeared into the water. "Sure. I could tong like this for oysters. Be like harvesting rocks. Pretty exciting." His dad waved a deprecating hand. He understood.

How to say the rest in Mom's ordered living room, Hank wondered. Kodiak might lack old class, but in Alaska a fisherman had a place in any society he might choose. "I'm sorry, Dad."

"Don't be. Don't let being sorry trap you."

On the day before Hank's return to Kodiak his dad felt well enough to declare that they'd go to the Merchant's Club for lunch as in old times. On the way to the car the elder Crawford stumbled on the doorstep and tore a ligament. He took the accident in good spirits, but Hank, seeing his mother clearly upset, canceled his flight and rebooked three days later. He could still reach Anchorage in time for the Council meeting and whatever face-off awaited with Tsurifune.

During the next day, while his father napped with his cast-covered leg resting on an ottoman, Hank wandered old haunts and found a few friends who had not drifted to other places. Each encounter confirmed that his life and future lay north, with no regrets. He became restless and it showed.

"Take the car tomorrow," urged his father. "Find some fishermen. Kent Island, say, a couple of hours from here across the bay. We see fishing boats there when we drive to Rehobeth."

"We'll be fine," his mother added. "And I'll have a big dinner waiting when you get back."

Next morning Hank took the time to help his father downstairs and settle him before leaving, so that it was past noon by the time he crossed the Chesapeake Bay bridge to the Maryland Eastern Shore. He followed a dirt road branching from the highway and found a pier. Sounds of activity came from an adjacent low cinder-block building. A pale sun shone, but frost remained on the gravel still shaded by the doorway.

Inside a long chilly room stood a few women shucking oysters. Most were black. They wore bandannas, and had plastic aprons tied around their bulky middles. Muddy heaps of the mollusks lay on the table before them. Their gloved hands speared open the shells with thin knives, then sliced the limp creatures inside into shiny metal cans of gallon size. Their work had the concentrated speed of a factory line, and none looked up, but they appeared relaxed and in good humor.

An overweight man in a checkered shirt strode through with a shovel. He frowned. "He'p you?"

"Mind if I look around? I'm a fisherman myself."

The man's glance traveled doubtfully over his city clothes. "You don't want to get in the way," he said, and continued outside.

Hank followed him to the pier, where a low boat was unloading. Its stern bore the name *Clara*. A black man in coveralls on the deck below shoveled oysters into a bucket. After he had filled each bucket he made a circle with his hand, the worker above him on the pier who had spoken to Hank called "Yo!", and a crane raised the load. The worker tipped the oysters into a bin mounted on a forklift, then shoveled up the spillage. The leg of another man, who operated the crane and apparently tabulated the delivery, protruded from the open door of a small shack with smudged windows.

Another boat eased in from around a point of low pines. Like the one delivering, it was about thirty feet long and painted white, with high sides and a small cabin forward. An engine housing, capped by a rusty exhaust pipe puffing gray smoke, crowded much of the deck space. When the boat came closer, Hank saw its name, *Aggie*. He grabbed the mooring line thrown by the younger of two men aboard. They acknowledged with a nod but called over the engine noise only to those they obviously knew on the pier and the other boat.

"*Aggie* down there. Howdy," ventured Hank when the engine stopped. "Good haul today?"

The older man looked up. A toby-jug nose dominated his wind-reddened face beneath a black wool cap. "Come back, sir?"

Hank waited, then realized he'd been asked to repeat the question. "Just wondered how fishing was out there today."

"Eighteen–nineteen bushel apiece, sir. Quota's twenty-five bushel, so you go figure."

"Too bad." Hank felt self-conscious but still he added, "I'm a fisherman myself, so I understand low catch some days. I fish in Alaska. For a living."

"That so? Alaska. Be a piece from here." He said it with no particular interest but the younger man looked at Hank sharply.

Hank's hands sought his pockets as he watched them shovel their oysters into a bucket. He hadn't dressed for the raw chill that breezed from the water. When they finished, the younger man climbed to the pier and limped toward the shack.

"Tom," called the older in a voice mild but full of gravel. "You ask has he got coal oil. Half can'll do. F'ar's gone out to the stove, I forgot to check 'im."

"Right, Dad."

"Just pass up that can while your boy checks the weights, Cap'n Bart," said the man on the pier. "I'll go fill it." They spoke in an easy cadence.

After the man named Captain Bart handed up the can he drew a bucketful of water and splashed the deck. He seemed friendly. Hank asked if he could come aboard.

"It won't but mess your feet, sir. But come down if it suits you."

Hank jumped aboard. Since the captain had now begun to sweep mud and shell, Hank drew up more bucketfuls of water and sloshed the debris through a scupper.

A voice came from the pier, "Yo, Cap'n Bart. Got you helper there."

"Ain't it though!"

At least he was now acknowledged, and surrounded by their voices even though nobody addressed him directly.

"Tell him come yere when he's done with you," called the man aboard the *Clara*.

"I'll do that, Bernard."

When the deck had been cleared Hank asked if he might look around. "He'p yourself, sir. She's a deadrise maybe forty year old but I keep her good. Don't leak neither drop."

Thick paint on the boat's housing appeared to be only a few months old, but it covered tenacious flakes of former paint that had layered high enough to cast shadows. The rails, scuffed to the wood, were built wide enough for a man to stand on. Hank raised the engine cover, avoiding the exhaust pipe that remained hot. The engine looked like it had come from a car. A jerry-rigged wire replaced a bolt on the assemblage that connected the choke cable to a lever at the rail. Hank smiled to himself. Funky by Alaska standards, but done with the ingenuity of real fishermen.

He needed to step around pairs of wooden poles that lay the length of the deck. He lifted one. Heavy! He balanced it with respect. Places on the grain had worn smooth where hands must have gripped thousands of times. These were tools of fishermen who worked hard. Chunks of black mud clung to metal teeth on the end of each pole. An oyster shell poked through one chunk. Hank pulled it free. Its surface was gnarled and mostly gray, with sharp edges that held grit beneath like dirty fingernails. Hank bounced it in his hand. More weighty than it appeared. Creature inside. Something more than the "rock" he had termed it.

Tom the son returned with a slip of paper and some dollar bills. He handed the money to his father who put it in a plastic bag, then turned to Hank. "You say you fished in Alaska?

Before Hank could reply, Captain Bart declared, "Guess we'll go now, mister."

Hank started to climb to the pier, considered, and turned. "Any chance you'd let me ride out with you tomorrow?"

Father and son exchanged glances. The son nodded.

"It's early time, sir," said Captain Bart. "We gen'lly leave shore 'bout five. Around to another creek from here."

"Tell me where."

"We bring our own sandwiches and thermos. Ain't no cooking stove yere."

"I'll do the same."

"I'd dress warm if I was you."

They mapped out the roadside place that opened early for watermen. Hank felt more lighthearted than he had in weeks. On his way back through the city he found a surplus store and outfitted himself with padded coveralls, boots, and gloves. At home, in time for the evening highball and dinner, his bright mood affected both parents so that it became the most convivial evening of his visit.

His father noted, from a piece in the *Wall Street Journal,* that two days hence the Senate Commerce Subcommittee that Hank had once testified before would hold an open session on fishery updates. "You might be interested."

A few hours later Hank sped back toward the bay on dark empty highways, while blanking out thoughts of the approaching showdown with old Tsurifune as best he could. He reached his destination only three minutes late. It was the only lighted building within sight. Pickup trucks filled the entire space in front of a porch and spilled back beyond the illumination. He parked his dad's Mercedes as unobtrusively as possible between high truck panels.

The wooden steps were icy. Inside it was warm and smoky, with odors of soap and brewed coffee. Hip boots hung from the ceiling among shelves of cans and bottles. A counter lined one wall. Men in baseball caps and heavy jackets occupied nearly all the stools in front of it. Their thick backs formed another wall.

"Now didn't I say he'd come?" declared Captain Bart. "Sit right here, sir. Saved you a chair. The man needs coffee there, Ruby." The mug was already on its way.

"Need anything else?" asked the pleasant fat woman who delivered it. Hank asked what sandwiches she could make. He'd slapped together only two of leftover pork roast and he already had an appetite. "Baloney and cheese, honey." Hank ordered four. He added packages of cakes, asked for his coffee in a carryout cup, and told Captain Bart he was ready to go.

But there seemed no hurry after all. The talk along the counter continued at an easy rhythm among blacks and whites together. Some of the drawls were so thick that Hank lost entire sentences, but the subjects never seemed to stray from boats and gear any more than with fishermen in Alaska. He felt both a stranger and comfortable among his own.

"This man yere's from Alaska," Captain Bart volunteered at last. "Says he fishes there."

"Name's Hank. Hi."

"Alaska, now," declared a man halfway down the counter. His elderly face was lined and jowled, but his shoulders looked still able to carry heavy weight. "They got crabs up there too, do they? Not good as ours, I judge."

Hank smiled. "Both pretty good."

The man persisted. "I'd say ain't neither crabs beats a Maryland jimmie."

"Leave the poor man be, Cap'n Billy," said Captain Bart.

"Now what you use for crab baits up there in Alaska?" asked Bernard, the black man of the *Clara*. "They got chicken necks way up there?"

The questioning lasted only a short while before the talk returned to local matters. Maryland's limit on a boat's daily oyster catch affected them all. Hank gathered that the oyster and crab populations had plummeted in the lifetime of all the older men. The men disagreed on whether the catch limit would do any good, and who was to blame—maybe it was Virginia people farther down the bay. All concurred that the politicians in Washington, D.C., wanted to get rid of watermen so they and their rich buddies could play-fish what was left.

"Bureaucrats might say arsters is scarce," Captain Bart said, pumping a fist on the counter. "And it may be, but not because they say it. Lazy, those boys? They never been to all the places I could show 'em."

"You could show 'em places not yours to show," observed Captain Billy.

"Now what you mean by that?"

"Guess you know what I mean."

After an uncomfortable silence: "Come on, Cap'n Bart," said another. "You catchin' like your daddy did? Crab and arster ain't like they was."

"I know. Maybe not. I know." Captain Bart spread out his thick, puffy hands. "Ain't nothin' you can do about it. Got to live. City people retire down yere with money, they ought to be made to stop building houses one-two-three right along the water, that's one thing. Then they complain that the boats we fish from smell bad next to their fancy boats. But who's going to stop them? Other bureaucrats?" Several of the others grunted agreement. "And then let's say you start to fish good again. Uncle Sam ain't goin' to let you keep it. Make it, you're still goin' have to give it back."

"That's a fact, Bart."

"Nothin' on this earth you can do about it."

One of the younger men, muscular and ruddy faced with his hair in a ponytail, rose and threw a dollar and change on the counter. "Don't give it up like that, Cap'n Bart. Listen to Larry Simns and his Watermen's Association when he calls us to go to legislature like your boy does. We can go worry hell out of the politicians, that's one thing. Then bureaucrats and scientists got to listen or lose their soft jobs."

"Ssshush, Henry," said Captain Bart in a voice easy and reasonable. "You're a good boy. But all that time you and my boy Tom and others spent up there in Annapolis? What good it do? They still regulate. And arster still scarce as pearls."

Tom had risen. "Daddy. Oysters don't come from talk at Miss Ruby's."

"That's true, boy." To Hank: "You ready, sir?"

"I'm ready." He kept it light. "And my name's Hank."

"Well, now. Hank it is then, sir."

An icy slick covered the boards of the pier and the *Aggie*'s wide rail. Tom walked with a limp, but after casting off the forward line he bounded aboard with boots barely touching the sides. He played a flashlight beam along the wood while his father grunted over seat first. "Step careful," he advised the guest. Hank debated his own seaman's image, chanced it with a leap, and landed successfully on deck.

Flashlight beams wandered the structures of other boats around them, and engines started with general coughs and rumbles. An oily smell permeated the *Aggie,* but Hank enjoyed it, along with the feel of his feet on a deck about to put to sea. He took stock in the dark and wondered where to be useful. Everything was cluttered and cold to the touch. Captain Bart entered the cabin. (No lock on the door, as they increasingly needed in Kodiak.) A match glow showed he was firing the kerosene stove. Tom moved a crate holding down a tarp and raised the engine cover. Hank recognized a routine, and backed out of the way.

The engine started with a rattle, knocked a few times, then leveled out. Its chug reverberated throughout the boat. They moved from the pier. A dim orange first light silhouetted trees, houses, and low spurs of land, and slicked the top of ripples in the black water churned by a boat ahead of them.

Their motion generated a chilly breeze. "Warm yourself in yere to the far, sir," invited Captain Bart from the cabin.

Hank thanked him, but moved instead to stand by Tom at the tiller and watch the water. The son stood erect with his hand on the controls, looking straight ahead. Hank raised his voice above the engine noise. "Guess you could steer in and out of here in your sleep."

"Yup."

"Been at it long?"

"On and off, sir."

Hank tried another tack. "Does the water here ice up, later in the winter?"

"Happens."

They both stared ahead. Tom shifted course to skirt a point of land. Hank decided not to press conversation and to enjoy whatever part of the ride he could.

Minutes later Tom volunteered, "Put us ice sheathing to the hull two years ago. Lets us go out except if shore ice goes thick." Suddenly his voice turned hard. "Mister, you come down here from the gov'ment to spy on my old man?"

"No! Hell, no. Listen. I carry my Alaska fishing license in my wallet. I want you to see it if you think such a thing."

There was enough light for them to study each other's faces. Tom's eyes were clear and direct. His tension faded. "Well then, sir, I'll take your word for it." Slight smile. "Guess I never seen a gov'ment spy help wash the deck. Hank, is it? I'll take your word." He added: "Alaska!"

Hank wanted to ask why they so feared the government, decided against it. His own caution against bureaucrats was nothing compared to this. Were they hiding something? It wasn't his business.

His reassurances relaxed Tom enough to talk. He volunteered that his dad, now seventy-seven, could have retired long ago if he'd chosen, what with arthritis and enough other ills, and with savings and Social Security enough to maintain the four-room house he'd bought after the kids grew up and left. "But the ol' man ain't chose to sit home and get on my mother's nerves." Tom's voice softened. "Not him."

The sun began to rise in a glowing ball. It bathed Tom's face and made him squint so that lines appeared on it everywhere. His face had scars along the hairline that Hank hadn't noticed before. The sun's fresh warmth, or the companionship of a stranger close to his age who lived too far away to carry tales where it mattered, made Tom voluble. He had three other brothers, and at twenty-six he was the youngest. "We all followed the water. Once I thought I wasn't. Which is why I own just two-thirds of the ol' man's boat and still buying it by the piece. But keeps him going, the ol' man. Except he ain't used to all the regulations now. In his time he'd go out, shaft-tong oysters all day winters, crab summers, work rockfish or eel times between, take where he found it and as he pleased. Me and my brothers, each in turn, be in boat with him from about age eight, nine, weekends after school and summers. That's how it was. Hard work sometimes. But oyster and crab there for the taking and no bureaucrats. No needing to go stare at politicians in the legislature and what good does it get you?"

They were chugging with other boats across an expanse of water. The shoreline dimmed, but remained close enough to show trees and the occasional white of a housefront. One stretch had several housefronts, and a marina with cabin cruisers. Tom pointed. "Outsiders moving in who don't work the water, just pleasure theirselves on it. Take pictures of us in our boats but only talk to theirselves."

"Would you talk to them?" Hank smiled.

Tom returned the smile. "Huh."

"Sounds like a good life anyhow."

"All scarcer now, everything different. Oysters got diseases we never heard of before, whole beds closed down. That's what the ol' man don't understand. He thinks the gov'ment should stop the outsiders, not regulate him." Tom frowned ahead. "It's not enough left for everybody. That's bottom line. I guess Alaska's different. That's why sometimes I wish . . ." He changed the subject abruptly. "Also got two sisters, one of them's married a waterman. Other one, Sarah, works to an office in Salisbury and ain't married." Careful smile. "Like me, independent, I guess—so far. Started late. Neither girl around here but was hooked when I come back."

"Vietnam service? That interrupted things for a lot of us. I know. Navy, myself, over there. What about you?"

It closed the conversation.

The early sun was casting long yellow-orange rays by the time they reached a place where Tom slowed the engine. At the diminished sound Captain Bart emerged from the cabin. He peered around. "Further in, Tom."

"I see it."

"Just easy, easy."

"Yes, sir." To Hank, in an undertone: "I know it good as him but let him do it."

Captain Bart examined the land on both sides of the bow moving slowly toward shore. He waved to port, then to starboard, then put his arm down and said, "That'll do it now." Tom idled the engine and walked forward to the bow.

Bart looked around him and drew a long deep breath. "Now ain't this good life, sir?" he said quietly. "Be on the water and watch the sun rise? Never tires me, all these years."

"It *is* good, sir." They savored the moment together.

"Found the reef square-on," called Tom. He splashed over an iron bar for anchor. It broke the mood.

"Nice reckoning, Cap'n Bart," said Hank. "What points ashore did you triangulate on?"

"Come back?" After Hank clarified: "Ohhh. Look, sir. Big dead tree yonder, just line 'im with the port scupper."

Hank peered, but saw only a whole woods of low pine.

"Now to starboard . . ." Captain Bart grinned up at Hank and patted his back. "You think maybe a mermaid that side?"

Hank laughed with him. "I didn't want your secret, Captain."

"Neither did you get it, sir." Bart pulled a rubber apron from a hook and tied it around his waist. "Eighteen-foot shafts do it this tide, Tom," he declared over his shoulder.

Tom had already selected a set of the poles. "Shaft tongs," he explained to Hank. "Got different lengths for how deep. Stand clear when I swing 'em." Each pole had metal teeth attached to the ends. The double poles were hinged like scissors so that pulling the tops apart spread the bottoms, and the bottoms with the teeth would then close when the tops were pushed together.

The shafts clattered as Tom balanced them at their fulcrum and stepped up to the wide rail. He swung them teeth down into the water. It looked easy to Hank. The shafts slid through Tom's hands until they bumped the seafloor. He then pulled them open, jiggled and pushed, then closed the shafts, and pulled them up rhythmically hand over hand. His whole body entered the motion while his feet kept balance in a dancelike shift and shuffle.

The teeth that emerged were a steel cage of dripping black mud. Tom swung them across the rail to the table by the cabin, and scissored them open. Out tumbled a few muddy oysters clotted together. Captain Bart's gloved hands began at once to sort them, while Tom splashed the tongs back into the water.

The hinged shells of only three oysters were clamped tight. The others lay open with pearly white insides. "Now see here, sir, all the dead arster? Used to be every one was a keeper, firm and solid. You tell me what's happened." The captain pushed the keepers through a hole in the table, then scratched through the mud with a tool that combined hammer and pick. He found one more whole oyster. It was not large. He considered. "Hank, is it? Hank, come yere then. Show you to cull." He maneuvered the shell against a ruler until he found a thin point that barely reached the three-inch mark. "Don't matter how close she gets, long as you get her there."

"That little spit of shell's like paper. Anything could break it off."

"Then treat it gentle." Bart plopped the oyster through the keeper hole, then swept the open shells overboard.

The shaftloads from Tom continued to yield more shell than whole oyster. Captain Bart's hands flew over the mass, sorting easily before the next load arrived. He allowed Hank to sweep the open shells overboard after he had cleared them.

"Arster gone to hell, sir." Captain Bart pulled apart a hinged shell that looked whole but had an open gap at its point. The creature inside was dark and shriveled. "Do neither good to theirselves nor us. Got that thing called MSX says the bureaucrat scientists. Didn't use to be MSX. Now you tell me what's happened, Hank. You tell me it ain't something their science boats leaked overboard. Or come from all them new houses with strangers, come to run their fun boats and dump shit into the water. Good healthy arsters used to be everywhere, and no twenty-five bushel limit. Now, see, even the grasses gone scarce."

"Grasses?"

"Seaweeds. All along the shores. Used to get in your propeller and we'd cuss it, but there's where all the baby fish and crabs growed, used to. Now you don't hardly see grasses where they used to be. No wonder it ain't much of a living no more to follow the water. Bought my first boat age nine or ten, eighteen-foot skiff. I been captain of a boat ever since I was eleven or twelve. And the way we'd pull in arster! No more."

Hank spoke sympathetically, and thought of king crab gone in Alaska. But Alaskan waters still had other abundance.

The sun shone clearly and warmed them despite a chilly breeze. It was turning into too nice a day for steady gloom. Captain Bart continued to talk when he found that Hank was interested. "Watermen don't have no whole lot of money, that's a fact. But, I don't know, one good reason they don't have none, they get paid every day, they spend it."

Hank laughed. "Sounds like fishermen everywhere."

"That so?" Hank asked whether he felt he was getting fair price for his catch, and the captain exclaimed, with a new burst of energy, "No way! It ain't no money into arster business. It takes so much to operate with. 'Fore you leave the dock you got ten or fifteen gallon of gasoline, that's eight or ten dollar right there. Then you got your drinks, sandwiches, your coal oil . . . Takes at least twenty dollar before you untie your boat. Little better money in crab business, sometimes." He threw up his hands. "But ain't no use to complain. What else does a man want to do?"

After Tom had maneuvered his shafts the length of the boat's rail and worked out the portion of the reef under the boat, he went forward to let out the anchor line and drift to a different stretch of the reef. The cull table emptied. Hank waited to follow Captain Bart into the heat of the cabin. His feet had chilled from standing in one place and so had his fingers despite their motion. Yet the captain merely stretched out his neck like a turtle and peered around.

A half dozen other boats lay scattered along the horizon, but only one other worked close by. The man aboard it stood alone. Shells and mud were piled high on his table, waiting to be culled. Hank didn't recognize him from the breakfast diner until Captain Bart shouted over merrily, "Bible says love thy neighbor, Billy. You reckon that means me and you?"

"Jest keep to your side, Bart."

"If I decide to move your way, tell you what." Captain Bart slapped his leg and winked at Hank. "I'll take my pants down and let you scratch my tay-ul."

Captain Billy bent over his shafts without replying.

Captain Bart nudged Hank. "Now listen to this next." He raised his voice again. "You there, Mr. Billy?"

"Leave him alone, Daddy."

Tom said it with enough authority that his father shrugged, muttered, "Need to get warm," and entered the cabin.

Tom turned to Hank. "Daddy and Captain Bill both think they discovered this bar and own it. Don't get me started on that one. They used to be buddies. Used to enjoy complainin' together all night long. Bill's even my godfather." He motioned for them to go inside. "I've got some questions."

The cabin's heat was welcome despite the close odor of kerosene. Hank crowded with Tom on one of the short benches since the captain had spread himself comfortably on the other. They unpacked lunches and soft drinks.

Captain Bart cut his sandwich into small pieces. "Don't never let no dentist at your teeth, Hank. Lest you want to lose 'em every one."

"Alaska now." Tom's eyes traveled over Hank's shoulders and face. "Hard fishing up there? Anything hard like here?"

"Ohh . . . at times." Hank decided not to embellish beyond a brief description of a Bering Sea winter. When Tom pressed for more, he summarized, "I've seined for salmon, worked pots for crabs, once trawled for bottomfish. Now I'm longlining for halibut and black cod. One thing you have up there's variety."

"Variety here, too," said Captain Bart at once. "Only what you see now is arster. But springtimes we run eel traps, sell some for expenses, keep some for bait. Gill net for rockfish. Summers put up a pound net and use that bait. Then go for the crab. It's busy here all times, whatever you make it."

Tom snorted. "Not the same."

His dad quickly changed the subject. "You ain't said how you catch your arsters, Hank. Same as here?"

Hank shook his head. "No oysters, far as I know. Clams now. I've dug clams at low tide sometimes, for fun."

Captain Bart threw up his hands, then slapped them on the table. "That does it for Alaska!" He nodded significantly to his son. "Be grateful the Good Lord put us yere in Maryland on Chesapeake Bay where there's arster."

"Yes, sir." Tom shut his eyes and drew a breath, then turned back to Hank. His naturally flat voice remained quiet, but his questions increased in detail and persistence. He wanted to know all manner of sizes—boats, crews, fish, crabs, nets—as well as matters like the fight you'd expect from a salmon, what came up inside a bottom trawl, the single girls in Alaska, the new color electronics. As Hank answered, Tom's hands crept over each other while his tongue explored his upper lip. "Make good money up there too, I bet."

Hank sensed the direction of Tom's drive and chose his words carefully. "Fair money, sometimes. Plenty of nice people, sure. But not cheap to live. Everything's expensive. And most good boats have crews that hang on, so—"

"But a fisherman that's experienced? Not afraid of cold water? Bound to be somebody'd hire him."

"It does happen."

"Now *our* boat," said Captain Bart. "She's strong. Lot of these boats around yere ain't nothin' like good as this boat." His look toward his son was anxious. "Don't leak neither drop. And own it every bit, motor and all."

"Owned it for years and years, Daddy. Nothing's changed except that everything gets scarcer."

Captain Bart shook his head. They ate in silence for a while. Hank drew a breath and broached an immediate subject on his mind. Father and son looked at each other, back as a team again, and joined in a chuckle. "You want to do the shafts, Hank?" Tom's uncertain manner changed to confidence. "Well then, maybe you could try."

Captain Bart slapped his leg. "But Hank, listen yere. You fall in, son, do us a favor. Fall close to the boat, make it easier to fish you out." Hank shared their laugh.

Back on deck, Tom turned over the eighteen-foot shafts to Hank and took up the next longest for himself. They stationed him on the port side while Tom continued on the starboard. "So's neither of us bangs the other," said Tom diplomatically.

Hank gripped the shafts with a sense of ceremony. They were heavy, but when he found their fulcrum the weight evened out. He brushed a hand over the gunwale to make sure it wasn't iced, then stepped up to it with knees bent for control as he would on a storm-pitched boat. Suddenly the shafts swept around on their own and nearly twisted from his grasp. When he leaned forward to right them he nearly lost his balance. Only the spring of his knees kept him from falling overboard.

"Steady there, Hank," said Tom with a grin.

His feet explored the few inches of flat surface. Enough to hold him although tight for maneuvering. No stepping forward or back, just sideways. He was glad for calm water. And glad he'd bought boots with heavy treads.

The shafts were both graceful and clumsy. As soon as he dipped the tong end toward the water and his hands left their fulcrum, the weight pulled him outward again, but now he knew to compensate by leaning back. The poles eased through his hands. He liked their solid feel, and the scrape that passed through his arms of open tongs on hard seafloor.

"Push into it, Hank. Got to dig."

Hank pictured claw machines in old amusement parks. Only if the claws raked down while their teeth closed did they grasp anything. He gripped the poles in open position, jiggled them, and pushed down. It unbalanced him again. In rough seas the boat might have slid from under his feet to leave him swaying on the poles. He shifted quickly to weight himself back on the rail, and hoped those watching hadn't noticed.

"Wish I had a camera now," drawled Captain Bart. He was already culling Tom's first load. "Keep at it, son."

"Hi yo!" Hank countered, but suddenly he felt like a child given a toy tool to keep him busy. He mustered his forces, drove down the shafts, and pushed them together. When he pulled up, ha! They had extra weight. He gripped the shafts and started to raise them hand over hand. Weight indeed! And now there was true unbalance. Holding his back stiff didn't help. He tried to copy Tom's dancelike sway with hips in an easy pivot. The weight and the drag both seemed to increase foot by foot as the poles rose above his head.

At last the tongs broke water. His grip was too close down to swing them over to the culling table. With bent knees he shifted hands on the poles to gain back their length. It was clumsy. They swayed, the tongs dipped back into the water, and the weight twisted his wrists.

Panting now, he brought the closed tongs to the table and pulled them open. Out dropped a single open shell, followed by a dribble of mud. Tom deposited his next delivery on the other side of the table. It tumbled into a high heap. Worst of all, neither Tom nor Captain Bart joked or commented. He was now being judged.

The day progressed. Hank shrugged off pride, developed a rhythm, and with perseverance finally produced loads large enough to make a clatter on the table. There was never one to equal a third of those Tom delivered. His back soon ached, then his shoulders and arms, then his wrists, but he continued to enjoy himself. Out of the question to give up.

The afternoon sun began to cast long shadows. Winter daylight would last no more than another two hours. The piles of keeper oysters had risen although Captain Bart grumbled that if it was thirty bushels he'd dance a jig. The law allowed them twenty-five bushels apiece a day, caught sunup to sundown. When it came time to move again, Captain Bart gestured toward the boat of Captain Billy. "Jest ease over longside of him, Tom, and we'll dip some there." He nudged Hank. "Fourth of July might be over by the calendar, but might be you'll see some Christmas fireworks."

"No, Daddy. That's his side."

"What? When I found this whole reef myself?"

Tom's face tightened. "You both found it same day," he snapped. "Let it be."

While Tom went forward to pull his makeshift anchor, Bart muttered, "Boy gets itchy sometimes, Hank. Ever since Marines and Vietnam. He was hurt, you see. Now, except for the limp, he's got over that. But Tom's off by hisself, just a rented room and kitchen. Single like he is, there's room for him at the house and his mother be glad. Hardly ever goes out, sometimes drinks heavy. Now does that seem right to you? I come back from Army against the Krauts, and seen some bad things. But I went right back to the boat and raised my family. Where's the sense of remembering?"

Hank kept his reply neutral. Tom could be like Jones Henry who never forgave the Japanese. He himself had seen bad enough in Vietnam from the deck of a river craft, but knew of horrors on land that might never heal.

They left the grounds for another. Captain Bart steered. Tom, long over his anger, briskly shoveled and kicked overboard the random rejects that had fallen from the cull table. Hank joined him. Tom glanced back at his father, then lowered his voice. "Hank. Tell me for sure. There's boats and good catch up in Alaska?"

"No guarantee. But maybe." Hank didn't want to encourage Tom and open a floodgate, yet he knew that as captain of a multicrew longliner he could find a berth for a hard-working fisherman. He surveyed the scuffed little *Aggie* and the tools of grunt labor that scratched up passive oysters from seashore water, and at the scrub shoreline. Was his problem so bad after all? Free from the worst of demons that Vietnam had left with others, and captain-owner of a ship that harvested vigorous fish from the sea surrounded by the great mountain country that he loved?

Tom's face was young, but lined with a strain beyond youth. The contrast showed especially in his narrowed eyes, alive and searching, but guarded. "It's nice country here, Hank." He seemed to consider. "And on the water like this you feel good. But I don't know."

"Don't know?" Hank slapped his shoulder, and made it as hearty and noncommittal as he could. "Join the crowd, buddy."

By the time to quit for the day and deliver, the sun was orange on the horizon and a chilly breeze blew, but their spirits had turned high. Father and son exchanged banter with other boats heading in, some of it gleefully obscene. Mud caked Hank's coveralls from neck to boots, his hands were blistered even through gloves, and he felt the enormous contentment of a day worked at sea in good company. The only job left at dock was to fill buckets with oysters for the crane to raise. He gaily started to compete with Tom at the shovel, filling a separate bucket and tamping it down.

"Hoosh!" hissed both father and son.

Captain Bart took Hank's arm and pulled him back. "Now you done enough for the day, you jest watch. See how Tom slides in arster easy off the shovel? Don't push 'em down? Leaves lots of air? We get paid by the bucket, Hank, not by weight."

"Oh, boy. I haven't learned much today, have I?"

Father and son together squeezed out forty-two bucketfuls of oysters. Captain Bart had saved aside a few. He handed one to Hank along with a shucking knife, then began to open another himself. Hank slid the blunt tip of the knife along the tight-closed edges of the shell but found no opening. The blade slipped and nicked his hand.

"Good thing you live in Alaska where's nary arster!"

Hank sucked his wound. "Guess that's another thing I didn't learn today." Captain Bart showed him how to ease in the knife at the bivalve's muscle. Hank followed clumsily. He parted the two halves of the shell with such a jolt that the juice spilled over his hands. "At least I can handle what's inside," he joked, and slurped down the oyster. It tasted more briny, and sweeter, than most he'd eaten in restaurants.

When they parted Hank felt a surge of affection. Both Tom and his dad knew heavy work on the water and savored it. Someday such a pairing might be his luck with Henny or Pete, even Dawn. He grasped their big, water-puffed hands in turn and thanked them for their hospitality, resisting the urge to hug them as he might have done in another place and culture.

Captain Bart produced a plastic bag. "Some arster I saved for you to take home. Tell 'em home it's reason there's mud over your suit. If you're sure you ain't going to bleed to death opening them."

"At least I'll keep a bandage handy."

Tom became quiet. "You can say hello for me to those big fish and crabs in Alaska. Not likely I'll do it myself."

"Never a need to, boy." Captain Bart patted his son's shoulder. "Never a need."

Nothing was left but to throw off their lines from the pier. Hank watched the letters *Aggie* on the stern recede above the wake of the darkening brown-green water.

As soon as the boat left, Captain Bart turned away and busied himself. Tom watched Hank until the boat rounded a spit and disappeared.

20

HONOR

BALTIMORE, DECEMBER 1983

Hank considered his next day's soreness laughable for an Alaska fisherman once hardened to thousand-pound king crab pots. He hurt from pelvis to neck. But he allowed no trace of the pain to show in his stance or walk.

During the days of his stay in Baltimore, Christmas decorations had sprung up everywhere. "It's so close, dear," said his mother. "Call Jody and the children to come join us."

"Their plane fare would be our pleasure," said his father.

"We'll decorate a tree again like old times. And the Hutzler's Santa! Maybe Danielle and Henry have outgrown it, but little Pete would love him."

It troubled Hank to say no. The Christmas trip east two years before had been lovely despite the hassle with three squirming kids. But so many reasons. He tried to explain. His boat required him back. And their Christmas Day open house had already been committed. Not mentioned was Jody's decision that the children's school plays and their own social life took precedence for the next few Christmases; the holiday was one of the few periods when fishermen all came home and families could count on being together.

John Gains had called while he was out oystering. Hank returned the call reluctantly—the man had nothing to nag about that couldn't wait until his return—and was glad that John had left for the day. Growing in

Hank was the need to face up to Tsurifune, whichever one, over their meddling with his command.

Meanwhile, he took his father's suggestion and drove to Washington for the congressional hearing. He'd not been there for nearly a decade, since testifying before the same Senate subcommittee during the fight to control the nation's two hundred miles of seafloor. Awesome, he realized, how that eventual law, since it had gone into effect in 1977, had so dictated the turns of his career. Without it he'd still be fighting without recourse for a place on his own waters against Japanese and Russian factory ships—unless they'd fished it out for everyone by now—and the foreigners would still be looking down from high decks to thumb noses and toss rotten fish at little American boats below. Nor would the Japanese now have the need or interest to fund an American to catch Alaskan fish for their markets.

Parking in Washington was the first problem. Even though there were vacant spaces, every street around the complex of Capitol Hill bore signs requiring a permit. He cruised the roads in a widening circle beyond the grandiose official buildings, past brownstone rowhouses at one end and museums at the other. Restrictions everywhere. How did these people manage? No wonder he'd moved his life from this part of the world! At last in exasperation he backed into a gap along a permit street across from one of the long white congressional buildings. Let them goddamn ticket him and he'd appeal it. Citizen's right to see his government in action.

The Senate committee hearing room was as large and ornate as he'd remembered. To reach it he traversed strangely empty marble corridors, and entered through high doors of heavy polished wood. A single senator, whose name Hank recognized from his nameplate (he came from somewhere in the Midwest), sat at the center of the dais flanked on either side by a half dozen empty chairs and corresponding nameplates. Behind him a busy woman handled papers. A man at a witness table faced the dais, and read from a document in a voice that droned with little inflection. Nine people sat scattered throughout the wide audience portion of the room. They all followed the talk from identical sheaves of papers. When the witness turned a page, the others turned one also to a collective rustle.

Hank's brown tweed jacket from the closet of his old room, and his once-favorite red wool tie with ducks in flight, contrasted with the uniform dark blue suits and tight-patterned silk ties of all the other men. The women's dresses were equally dark and businesslike. He shrugged off the difference as he went up to receive a copy of the statement from the staff person, but he chose an isolated seat in a back corner.

When he himself had testified before the same subcommittee in the same room, senators filled the entire dais and listened gravely, an audience had packed the place clear to standing along the walls, the list of witnesses filled two sheets, and stacks of printed statements cluttered several tables.

Heady times! Everyone had felt the fate of the oceans to be at stake. Fishermen like himself had come from ports on both coasts to tell of foreign depredations on their gear within sight of their own towns. Bolstering the case were biologists who confirmed that several Atlantic and Pacific stocks had been overfished to depletion. A National Marine Fisheries inspector testified that by his direct observation the Soviet fleet fished three times the mackerel it reported. Nobody was neutral. But if you were an American fisherman you knew exactly where you stood. In the waiting rooms of influential congressmen, American lawyers hired by Japan and other countries waited their turn alongside stony-faced fishermen. Wise congressmen received constituent fishermen first, whatever else influenced their final vote.

Only a few years before that time, it had seemed a bold step when the nation legislated control over sea resources within twelve miles of the coasts. Now two hundred-mile occupied the table, and only the Ford administration itself had dragged its feet. At hearings, others had stirred with resentment (and uneasy doubt) when State Department spokesmen warned against declaring two hundred-mile control because this would compromise high seas freedom elsewhere for the nation's ships. Well, that warning hadn't come to pass, Hank told himself. We were right.

For fishermen it had been a time of bonding. Among those who came in groups to testify, Hank remembered late-night drinks and tales with men from Maine, New Bedford and Gloucester, from one of the Carolinas, from Eureka and Tillamook on the west coast, and plenty from Seattle. When his own delegation of three from Alaska told of their boats crowded out by Japanese, Soviets, Koreans, Taiwanese, and even Poles, those from other regions grunted support.

That Alaska three. How they'd strutted through the halls in a conscious costume of wool shirts and jeans, to the amusement of their sponsoring senator, Ted Stevens, and Alaska's single representative, Don Young. It was exhilarating the way private office doors opened to them and reporters copied their words. Their indignation had been pure: a fight with a clear goal. He could hear Jones Henry still, seeing him off on the plane east, "Tell it, Hank! How the foreign fuckers rape our fish . . . don't be afraid to say rape because it's a fact!"

"I will, Jones. I will."

And Hank remembered the little delegations of foreigners, especially, in retrospect, the anxious Japanese who stayed close to their lawyers. They were common enemy along with the remote State Department types. No shades of gray back then. The issues had been clear and clean.

And now an audience of nine? With one senator of only junior authority and not even from a coast, listening with hand on chin, maybe asleep. And how was he himself honoring the great work of his time, or the legacy of Jones Henry? By creeping into the pocket of the very people they'd fought to remove from the fishing grounds!

The hearing concerned amendments to the two hundred-mile law and to the 1980 Fisheries Promotion Act that had grown logically from it. Hank scanned through the pages of the statement being read. Nothing in it appeared relevant to him until, twenty pages further on, it recommended continuing foreign fishing quotas based on each nation's cooperation with U.S. tariff laws. He still ached from his day on the water, a comfortable ache warmed by a good feeling for salty Captain Bart and restless Tom, so able with the shafts. They worked the water—not his version of it, but how they worked. He closed his eyes to wait for the reader to advance a few more pages.

The staff woman shook him awake. "I think they want to lock the doors now." The place was empty except for the two of them. He started to cover his embarrassment. "Don't apologize. It's all pretty boring without the full committee. This hearing was just to get some statements on the record before the year closes."

"With only one member listening?"

"You don't come here often, do you? We've been in recess since before Thanksgiving." She gave him copies of some other statements that had been submitted for the record. Soon he was back wandering the empty corridors.

Two hours after he had parked, he returned to his car for the drive home. The vehicle had been ticketed for illegal parking, and a steel boot locked one of the wheels. It took him another hour and a half to find the appropriate authority, take a taxi to the local police station to pay the fine, and wait for the boot to be removed. His outrage, over a citizen's lost right to park close to his government in action, might as well have been voiced to the bare tree branches as to the cops who handled his case.

He left his nation's capital in a dark mood. Suddenly, he thought, how dared Tsurifune replace Terry, put in charge of the *Puale Bay* by the captain himself! And they had tried to shunt him to poor fishing grounds. By the time he reached home his anger was steaming in all directions.

"You broke the rules and got caught," said his father calmly during their evening drink. "Grow up, son. Parking over there would be a free-for-all without restrictions. I should have told you to take the train."

Hank calmed down and felt foolish. This East Coast wasn't his place anymore, and the matters he needed to face waited elsewhere. After another few sips of highball, he felt detached enough to think out loud. "Question, Dad. You fought Japanese in the Pacific. How do you feel about them now?"

"I'm realistic about it after all this time. I've done business with them when I needed to. It doesn't mean I've forgotten. We took in Tokyo on our world cruise year before last. Everybody was polite enough. You couldn't guess behind those friendly faces what they'd pulled on us forty years ago. You've become pretty friendly with them, I judge."

"They make it easy with their hospitality. And I have to be realistic too. They just about own the fish trade, since fish is their food. You can bet they know it, though, how what they pay for fish dictates price clear to Alaska. So you don't mind doing business with them?"

"No. That war of my time's history. Your generation thinks of Vietnam, and there was Korea in between, so still being a prisoner of my Jap-German war would just brand me. I have the choice of being history, or living as it comes."

The light had grown dim but neither moved to turn on the lamps. The senior Crawford cleared his throat. "Son, you know that when your mother phones her grandchildren she and Jody talk. Do the Japanese have you in their pocket?"

Hank was glad for the dark. He swirled the ice in his glass, drank the last, and wished for more. "Maybe a little."

"For how much?"

"Including my own boat, *Jody Dawn,* and my piece of the new longliner . . . " He decided to minimize. "Vicinity of a million."

"My Lord, son. I couldn't help you make more than a dent in that, and still make sure your mother's secure."

"I didn't ask you to, Dad."

"But I think I woke one day in the hospital to hear you on the phone asking somebody in Alaska for money."

"Seth and I've fished together for fifteen years, Dad. It's different. King crab once made that kind of money."

In the silence the ice clinked in his father's glass. "At least you kept your other equities out of whatever you've signed. Your house."

"Afraid not."

"You fool!"

It came like a blow. Hank could have been a boy again. His mouth went dry, but he tried to keep his voice even. "Nobody asked your help. We'll manage. I've never asked for help."

The sudden change in mood was so abrupt it halted them both. At length his father said, "Go freshen our drinks, son."

Hank felt back in charge of himself. "The doctor said one a day, Dad."

"That was at the damn hospital."

"The bottle's in the kitchen with Mom there. She guards the house."

"Get it anyway."

Hank complied. His mother stayed busy at the stove. She spoke only routine pleasantries, in a voice unusually careful, and made no objection when he poured. Had she been listening?

His father reached out in the dark and their hands brushed before he located the glass. "Thanks." Hank wanted to run, but he resumed his seat.

"What about your children's education?"

"Alaska has a good public school system, Dad. It's my time to take chances."

"Not with your family's future."

"My life's different from the one you made."

"I left nothing to chance for my one kid growing up, and you have three. My bride, of course, is now my first responsibility. I've made sure your mother will live in this house or anywhere else without financial worry. We've started a little trust fund for our grandchildren, but I didn't think I'd need to worry about their future all the way."

"You don't! Know that I can take care of myself."

"With a million in debt including your house? Working for yourself? We've just seen with me how close things can come. But, if I die tomorrow, my responsibilities are covered. You've nearly drowned twice that I know of, and what haven't you told us? What kind of insurance do you have?"

"Enough!" But he knew it wasn't so; he had more insurance on the boat than for the family. Jody had taken the initiative on that issue, to save money, declaring that she'd always worked and would never need a damn widow's pension. "Enough."

"I hope you're right. My work's had no physical danger. And it's been with a company, for salary, earned up the ladder and saved step by step. Not always doing what I wanted, incidentally. I've never been in debt except for the mortgage on this house, with even those payments carefully calculated. You're swinging on a limb."

"My boat's worth a million and a half. I have equity."

"Worth that since crab collapsed? With my son in the fish business, you know I keep up with the situation through my newsletters. Sure you're not kidding yourself?"

"I'm not." Hank firmed his voice to mask unease. "That fish out there has a future."

"A hell of a gamble from where I sit."

"My business is a gamble beyond anything you know, Dad." Hank snapped it, surprised at his own asperity. "It's part of the life when your nets can come up full or empty. Jody and I are okay with that life. We chose it. There's money in it when the time's right. But the people who understand that gamble now are foreign, not Americans. The market for the things I catch is Japan. Sometimes it might get to be survival of the fittest, but I'm on top of things."

"Now I'll be blunt again. We've had some notion of your problem with Jones Henry when you signed with the Japanese. Remember that, since our visits to Kodiak, your mother and Adele Henry phone each other now and then. What we don't know is whether we should admire your independence, or worry for what it might do to you. Whatever your gamble, don't forget you're part of a community. Maybe I'm being conservative. But I'd caution you—don't sell out your community. I don't think you want to go it alone."

"Most people up there understand. They all have to adjust or go under. I was in danger of losing my boat. I just had to be realistic." Hank felt the need to continue his point. "We're all right, Jody and me. And the kids." Saying the words dispelled his own doubt. But he realized that now he'd never be able, in pride, to ask his father for help, whatever happened.

The clank of pots in the kitchen gave a normalcy that, at last, helped by the bourbon, calmed them both. Hank's father apologized for his outburst and asked Hank to explain more about his relationship with the Japanese.

Hank felt relieved to sketch out the Tsurifune bargain to a third party with no stake in fish. He decided to be fair about it, not color the facts with his new anger. "I'm with a family company, not one of the big impersonal ones like Taiyo or Mitsubishi. Boats and fish, nothing else. The company goes back a generation, to the present director's father in 1917, they told me. From what I can gather, about two hundred employees, though there were nearly twice that before we declared two hundred-mile. The old man runs it, the son's next in line. We get along. They have a reputation for being honorable." He stopped. Had the Tsurifunes been waiting for the chance to switch to a Japanese captain? he wondered for the hundredth time.

"They sound like solid people. Have your fellow fishermen made deals too?"

"Some. Tolly has."

"That's one. Does that mean you're mostly going it alone?"

"If they've singled me out it's because they know I can deliver." The statement jolted. He'd made it sound too rosy even to himself. "Don't worry. I'm working to get out from under them. They *are* overbearing as hell." He checked himself from blurting that they goddamn owned and had now humiliated him. Too ashamed to admit it. "I'm working to get out in any way I can."

"Are you bending laws that could turn around and bite you?"

"No!"

"Does that mean you've checked?"

"Sure." But Hank shifted uneasily.

"And now a very hard question. I don't like to remind you of this. But you're pushing forty, son. In most men's lives I've seen that's the time to consolidate, or it's their last practical chance to change and still have space to make something of it. I have to ask. Are you certain you're on your own right track?"

"I'm on my track, Dad." Hank gulped from his glass and hoped the conversation would lead elsewhere.

"I sit here kind of helpless," his father continued. "I've accumulated years of business knowledge, and I have a single child to share it with. A son who carries my name. But my knowledge is tied into structure and you're venturing outside of the structures I know. You work harder than most, and in more danger and chance than most, so if that's the life you choose, my hat's off to you. It's an honest and ancient occupation. I'll correct that. You've made it a profession."

"Thanks."

"You say that you think the Japanese are honorable. Good for them if that's so. Then I hope you'll find your way honorably too, whether they're true to it or not. When you look back, far-fetched as it may seem, that'll mean something to you."

It took a while for Hank to find his voice. "Yes, Dad. I'll try . . . I will."

Two days later Hank's father was able to stand in the living room to see him off, and their hug lingered. His mother's hug lasted even longer. His cousins drove him back to the airport. Alice talked gaily of the fortieth birthday party Bobby was going to have in a couple of weeks. "Then he'll be so *old!*" When they parted at the flight ramp Bobby found the chance to mutter, "Man, but you lead the life!" Hank boarded the plane slowly, and looked back to wave. Then as the plane circled he watched the city skyline, and a final spur of Chesapeake Bay. Only when the terrain below became impersonal fields did he relax, buy a beer, and settle in for the long connections to Kodiak through Denver, Seattle, and Anchorage.

Forty indeed, he thought. He himself, in just a few months—old by Alice's definition. With luck, Jody would let it pass without drawing attention to it. Over wine with the airline meal his thoughts began to settle on details of family and boat. His father's challenge of honor kept returning. Pull it all together at forty lest it be lost. Later, as he sipped a scotch, honor seemed tangible, a shared value among all men of goodwill. A plan grew in his mind. He began to outline it. At least one Tsurifune would be at the fishery council in Anchorage. The more that he detailed the proposal he'd make, scratching figures on a pad, the more it seemed right. Not only clear, but practical.

Hours later, when he reached Seattle for the final connection, his plan, come to fruition in his mind, had him feeling expansive. He scanned the people waiting for the flight to Anchorage. Since the December meeting of the Council started the next day, it was no surprise that he knew at least a third of them. There were voting members from Washington and Oregon, fishing organization reps (always good for a free drink), and editors of *National Fisherman, Alaska Fisherman's Journal, Pacific Fishing,* and others, many from each group former fishermen themselves. He kept his rucksack on his shoulder and passed from one to another with hi's and handshakes, heading for Nels Tormulsen's halibut crew where he could talk fishing instead of fish politics.

"Well, Hank! At last!" John Gains appeared behind Hank with the overweight Seattle lawyer for the Japanese (what was his name?). No way to avoid them. Every time Hank saw Gains he looked more sober in his dark suits. His former crewman's strong handshake showed that John remained athletic, even though he'd otherwise become an office creature. "Too bad we didn't connect," Hank said pleasantly to take the initiative.

"Why didn't you return my calls? Shoji's still upset at the way you took off from your ship. I can tell it from his voice. By the way, hope your dad's all right?" Hank nodded. "Well, my purpose was to get you back in time for Council, and here you are. You'll be useful there for the next few days."

"I want to see Tsurifune tonight. But then I'm headed for Kodiak first flight tomorrow, John."

"Not wise. The fights over sablefish harvest levels and allocations are coming to a head. They don't tell me everything, but I know the Tsurifunes took a beating last month on the tariffs conference, so this fight means even more to them than usual. Incidentally, Hank, you should know: Shoji—Mike—is taking over more and more; keep that in your blender. Shoji's got vision."

The lawyer joined them, and offered a limp Asian-style handshake worthy of his employers. "We'll brief you later after I decide how you can be useful." The puffy hand squished sweat.

"Write down our seat assignments," added Gains. "Go change yours to join us. Now, I guess changing your flight to Kodiak from tomorrow to late Friday has to be done in Anchorage. Actually, Hank, it would be better if you skipped Kodiak altogether and went straight to your ship from Seward after Council. Certainly Shoji would take that as good faith."

"Kodiak tomorrow morning, John."

The lawyer watched him with appraising eyes, but said nothing.

"Hank!" continued Gains. "You should realize that Shoji's concerned. A Japanese relief captain in charge for too long might compromise your boat's American status on the grounds."

"Then he should have left my American Terry in charge!"

"I don't know Shoji's thinking. Not yours to say."

"See you at baggage in Anchorage," said Hank firmly, and continued toward the halibut men. Gains called after him but he ignored it.

Dr. Lester Kronman, one of the Council members from the lower forty-eight, stopped him when he passed. "Henry Crawford, isn't it? You're fishing sablefish, correct? I have questions." Kronman was bald, and large at the middle, but tall enough to be imposing.

Hank forced himself to cool down and listen. He'd always known Kronman to be legitimately concerned for the fisheries, and friendly enough, although pompous as befitted a Ph.D. among the lesser educated.

"What's it look like out there, eh, Henry? Useful to know when we vote on yield." Kronman raised bushy eyebrows to look through the middle lens of his glasses, and stretched his mouth in the best he probably could do for a smile. "Plenty for everybody, I'd assume you'll say? Eh?"

"Well, Doctor. Abundant enough in spots." Hank chewed his lip in a show of considering the question. "Plenty" would have been his answer had it not been for Swede's caution that Americans wanted to hold down quota to an amount they might take entirely. Loyalty where? "Who can say in a big ocean? We've done pretty well ourselves."

"So I gather. And size?"

"Oh, big, big."

"Exclusively?"

Hank alerted to the emphasis. What was the experts' wisdom about size? Dr. Kronman's appointment to the Council, if Hank remembered, hinged on his involvement in marine science. But was Kronman independent, or did he answer to some company? And if so, was it to processors or catchers, and to American or foreign? "Not all big, no," he hedged.

"Size matters, you know. Exclusively large could mean no healthy year class coming along to take their place."

"Not exclusive at all. Just a lot of good size."

"Well, I hope you're right. Now, gear. You're fishing longline I believe? People tell me that pots and trawls laid for sablefish interfere with longline sets. Your comment?"

"They do. They do." It was a question Hank could answer as he felt since both sides of his own conflict used longline. "Our hooks snag on pot straps, and pull up all kinds of net torn loose from trawls. I wish the Council could declare separate grounds."

"Interesting. At least you're not trying to eliminate competing gear the way some of you folks are. Now, you have another boat too, don't you? A former crabber now trawler?"

Hank smiled. "You know a lot about me."

"Homework, Henry. I take my appointment seriously."

Hank endured a few more questions, each edging closer to his personal business, and finally managed to excuse himself. He headed straight for the halibut men.

Nels Tormulsen and his crew had a raw, scrubbed, outsider look that promised relief from the suits and businesslike drivers, even though the plaid shirts that stretched over their muscles had become as much a uniform at Council as others' silk ties. Their circle opened to include him. "Here he is," said Nels easily. "To join us or spy on us, I wonder?"

The tone was unchallenging enough that Hank could reply in kind, "Here to spy, count on it. Why else would I go out of my way for company like this?"

"Maybe for fresh air."

"Fresh air?" Hank relaxed and waved a hand in front of his nose. "You guys? Didn't you wash before you left your boat?"

"No room for soap," laughed Kaare, a compact, first-generation Norwegian cousin within Nels's family. "De black cods take up all our deck and into de bunks. Too bad for you udder guys out dere, Hank."

"Funny. I'm catching so many blacks I assumed you'd forgotten how to bait and they were slipping off your hooks."

"Naah. You catch de vuns ve t'row avay."

Nels faced Hank suddenly. "Thursday at Council. We're going for it all. Last year we screwed up and didn't meet the black cod quota we said we could. Not anymore. Your Japs are going to be out."

Hank kept his manner steady. "I wish you luck."

The announced boarding for the flight to Anchorage saved further comment. Hank was grateful that his seat placed him beside a stranger and several rows away from all but two other Council members whom he barely knew. How had he allowed himself to be twisted away from the boats and people he called his own?

Fog and then darkness obscured the rest of the trip. He faced his reflection in the window, leaving no easy escape. He tried to think of things free of guilt or commitment. Back to the shaft tongers on Chesapeake Bay. What would become of them if oysters and crabs continued to fail? His own options were vast compared to theirs. That's what he'd achieved by changing coasts. His reflection continued to face him. Achieved only by splitting his loyalties. He pulled down the blind and reached for an airline magazine. An article on dogsledding occupied him for the rest of the flight.

At the Anchorage baggage pickup he tried to stay distant, but John Gains strode over from a public phone and spoke abruptly. "We've booked you at the Captain Cook along with the rest of us. Shoji's already arrived. Dinner's top floor at seven thirty. You can share our car to town."

Hank started to say that he planned to stay at an airport hotel for the earliest morning flight to Kodiak, and was only heading for town to find Tsurifune for a talk. Instead he nodded. Gains was actually helping make Tsurifune available.

The driver who picked them up was Swede Scorden. Hank started for the passenger seat, but the lawyer stopped him, saying, "Hurts my back to crawl over seats." Indeed, the man struggled and huffed to crowd in his nearly three hundred pounds. Swede, after a cursory question about Hank's dad, said nothing further and stayed hunched over the wheel. The lawyer and Gains began to discuss the lawyer's testimony next day before the Scientific Committee.

"You'll need to hammer home, Justin," said Gains, "the hardship to the Japanese back home. I've written out some examples for you."

"Save 'em. Nobody here cares what happens to people in Japan. I've lined up better hardship."

Justin Rider, thought Hank, that's his name. He remembered now why the man turned him off. Rider had invited him to dinner once, lectured him, then pumped him for information, then left the bill on the table until they split it, cheap asshole.

"The better hardship case is this," continued Rider. "There's a nice little native co-op for herring up north. They deliver to some of the same Japanese fleet that first pays its way by hitting sablefish in the gulf. If our people lose their TALFF sablefish quota, the owners can't justify sending ships from Japan just to pick up that herring. We'll use that, since when you say 'native rights,' everybody jumps to cross himself. I've lined up some Aleuts to testify in full council."

"I learn from you every day, Justin," said Gains admiringly.

The lawyer turned his bulk with a grunt to face Hank. "We're talking as family here, Crawford, you understand."

"I'd assumed that, Rider."

"Frankly, I hadn't realized how useful you could be until I saw you working Dr. Kronman back there. And then working the longline people. You're a valuable resource. I assume you knew enough to tell the good doctor there's more sablefish in the gulf than anyone can catch. He's pivotal on the Scientific Committee, and tomorrow they've got to recommend either raising Domestic Allowable Harvest or sustaining Japan's Total Allowable within the old Optimum Yield to keep us in business. And the fishermen. Did you learn their strategy, Crawford?"

"Only their determination, Rider."

"I hope you told them they'll fall on their faces again this year. You could save them embarrassment. They're being unrealistic as usual. We should be able to manage getting Japan a TALFF every year for years to come, before those locals get their act together, if they ever do."

Hank watched Swede to see if he would react. Nothing, even when the lawyer told him to drive faster since they didn't have all night.

The hotel lobby was crowded with the usual Council-time collection of lawyers and industry reps. It was all becoming predictable.

Hank followed Swede. "Busy time," he observed lamely to start them talking.

"Seems so, Crawford. But I see you're getting the hang of it." And Swede walked off.

"Seven thirty, top floor, Hank," said John Gains. "Don't be late." As an afterthought, he turned to add, "Please."

21

SPLASH

A phone call to Kodiak left Hank restless and yearning. The kids had spoken one by one. Dawn told of a horse she loved especially that they passed every day on the way to town. "And, Daddy, I'm drawing him with sleigh bells just for Christmas to hang on the tree." Henny gravely declared that he was building a model in school. "It looks like your boat, Dad. I'm trying to make it look like your boat." (Jody's voice in the background said "Weren't you saving that for a surprise?" and Henny muttered, "Oh, I forgot.") And Pete the playful, still shy with words, "I have three . . . five . . . *seven* keys, Daddy. Bet that's more than you have. But five's my best number because I'm that old."

"There's a new restaurant out by the Flats," said Jody. "They say it looks over a stream. I thought we'd eat lunch there tomorrow after I pick you up."

"Great. Great. Then let's leave time back home before we pick up the kids. I miss you!"

"I miss you too. More than you think."

Be firm tonight, he told himself. First flight out tomorrow. Maybe fly back in two days for Council if it really matters.

As Hank left his hotel room for the restaurant, Oddmund Nikolai and another man emerged from a door farther down the corridor. They all waited by the elevator together. Odds introduced Joe Ketchinoff, a man with the lean cheekbones of an Aleut.

"Joe here," said Odds, "he fishes from Dillingham summers for the reds and kings, but he and his people are doing good now with herring they deliver to the Japanese. He's here to testify on that, so's Council don't cut off the Japanese longliners that need to come buy the herring."

"I guess you know that lawyer, then," said Hank. "Justin Rider? Fat man?"

"Oh, is he fat all right. Sure. Mr. Rider. Very important man. He gives us good advice."

Swede had mentioned that Odds now helped control native claims money. "They say your corporation's making out with timberland. Congratulations. Anything with fish?"

"Especially, Hank. Especially. There's money we need to invest. We're close to buying a plant in Kodiak for groundfish. But a manager—we need to find an experienced manager. There's a lot of things we're doing."

They entered the elevator. It stopped two floors up to admit Nels Tormulsen and his crew along with the organization rep for the halibut longliners. The rep, a lean, short young man, was talking when they entered. He stopped in midsentence at the sight of Hank and the two natives. The fishermen's bulk crowded the tight space. Nels pushed against Hank playfully. "Get in your own corner, man."

"Saying my prayers. Elevator cable's going to break with all this squarehead weight."

"Hank here's with the Japs on this one, Stanley," said Nels easily. "But I don't care if he hears us. Just as soon he hears us."

"Good enough," said the rep, and continued. "So I'm not sure about the Scientific Committee people tomorrow afternoon. You never know about Dr. Kronman until he votes. Two others told me flat out they didn't think we could take full quota, so I think they're in the Japan corner. So we've got to talk up every voting member we can find. The guys from *Vansee* and *Grant* are supposed to be flying in soon; they'll help."

The elevator took them all to the top floor. The restaurant had large windows along two sides. In daylight they offered a view of the snowy Chugach Mountains that Hank always enjoyed. In the early winter dark the windows merely reflected tables in the wide room and rails of the raised bar in back. A waiter passed with platters of thick steaks still sizzling. The sight and aroma made Hank's mouth water. That's for me, he decided.

"You alone, Hank?" asked Odds. "Come eat with us and maybe you can give us some advice."

Hank thanked him but said he'd committed with others. Then he glanced at a far table. There sat Mike Tsurifune, in from Tokyo indeed, talking coolly to two other men whose faces Hank could not see. John Gains, sitting alongside Rider the lawyer, motioned him over. Hank looked away. He wasn't yet ready to tackle what he had in mind with Tsurifune, and he realized he'd been hoping that it would be the old man he'd have to face. "Well, Odds, I might just join you for a quick beer."

"Oh, Hank. You should know by now. We don't like booze around. It's against the Bible."

Just then Nels Tormulsen slapped him on the back in passing and said, "Buy you a brew, man, before we start our secret plans without you." Hank told Odds he'd connect with him later (Odds now seemed relieved), and followed Nels to the bar, glad for the excuse. But go easy on the drinks, he reminded himself, since the Japanese would probably do toasts.

At the bar Hank began to banter with the guys from Nels's crew when two men wheeled on their high stools and hailed him. Suddenly the greetings turned noisy. There was big Joe Eberhardt, Hank's one-time skipper nearly a dozen years ago, aboard the old *Nestor* that eventually had become Hank's first temporary command as an anxious young relief skipper. And Arne! Arne Larsen, the hard and robust Karmøy Norwegian, some gray now in his hair, who had offered Hank advice during that early skipperhood, then later fished crab near him, boat to boat as a competing equal.

"Haven't seen you since crab went bust!" Hank exclaimed. After slapped backs, he asked, "What are you up to?", hoping that they'd survived the crash.

The two skippers had been fishing for what remained of red king crab off the Aleutians, sometimes in sight of Hank's own *Jody Dawn* under Seth. Their boats were now tied in Kodiak for the holiday weeks. "Doing good, good," said Joe easily. "In town between planes. Council time's good for a look at things, since I'm headed below for Christmas anyhow."

"Oregon, right? Susan. How's Susan?"

"Divorced, Hank. That's history. Still Oregon. But it's Sherrie now."

Arne was also headed south, to Ballard, where his wife's mother and one of his own brothers would be visiting from Norway for the season. "Den maybe I come put on trawl gear for roe pollack in Shelikof. What the hell, everybody says big money. Hank! You know some Jap buyer?"

"Looking myself, maybe. Not sure yet." Hank's glance slipped to Mike Tsurifune's table. Only John Gains looked his way and tried to signal.

Over drinks the talk turned to crab-pot reminiscence. "Ja, you Hank," boomed Arne. "On de crabs vunce in Bering and I come to have a look. Your old lady vas on dot trip, right Hank? They just got married, I think. And they smile and smile while dey pull empty pots they'd just put over, think I don't see how fresh was the baits, har har." The volume of his old-country guffaw had not diminished. "Till I say vot de hell, green young skipper and his Jody, so I go off a few miles. But I got better binoculars than you think, Hank. You think I'm gone you go back to pots with couple hundred crabs each one."

"I'd forgotten how slippery I was," laughed Hank. "Sorry."

"Nei nei, Hank. I do the same, so vas no problem."

Indeed, Hank had felt guilty at the time, since Arne the season before had been a mentor, but this was not the place for an apology. "Hell, I mean sorry I was shithead dumb enough to leave fresh hang-bait in sight. Sure, I was hiding my good pots."

Everybody laughed and laughed. In retrospect it all seemed the best of his good times, the lighthearted days of early marriage to Jody before the kids, when she rode as cook, and Japs were as much the unquestioned usurping enemy on the grounds as Koreans and Russians.

The talk drifted to fishing and boats in general. "Anybody's got a long-liner and dragger both," called Jeff Mathews of the *Sleepthief Two* from another bar stool, looking at Hank significantly, "this year he can grab the big ring. For longline he's got black cod in the gulf. Zoom. And then for the dragger, Fish and Game says the pollack spawners is going to hit the Shelikof smokin' next month. I mean in smoke. If I had the right boat for that, say, a crabber I'd converted to go drag . . ." Another glance at Hank that included Arne and Joe, "I'd start gearing the day I sobered from New Year's, then steam my ass to down off Karluk and wait my chance."

Several of them turned to Hank. He realized suddenly that it was with interest, even respect. "Nobody can do it all," he muttered, and sipped his beer.

"Guess you know that when Terry called you 'Splash Gordon' over the sideband out there earlier this month, and people heard," continued Jeff, "some of us started calling you Splash, Hank-o. That's what it looks like you're headed to make, a big splash. Didn't go bust when king crab went

tits-up. Found a way to save your crabber instead, and now she's ready to
drag anywhere you want. Then got yourself a longliner in the gulf under a
deal with the Japs. Even got your old lady seining salmon, summers, on
what used to be Jones Henry's boat. How'd you do it all, Hank?"

Hank started to set them straight with an outline of his enslavement to
the Tsurifunes and his unease for Jody's safety, then thought better of it.
Instead, he turned to the bartender and ordered a round for the group.

A half hour later, John Gains tightened a hand on Hank's shoulder and
said, "We're eating." Hank followed. On the way to the table John added
drily, "I don't imagine you need any further alcohol, but you knew you'd
be expected to drink some toasts. We've already drunk the preliminaries.
Whether you apologize to Shoji or not for being late is up to you, but I
have to say he was watching the company you kept."

"Nice of you to tell me, John." Hank felt only a mild buzz from the
drinks he had guarded. He glanced at the table. Four others including
Mike, the lawyer, and the two in shadow with backs turned. Ready now
to take them on. He kept his tone indifferent. "Swede's coming later?"

"Why should he? He's good for taking hold in a cannery situation, but
you should understand by now that Scorden doesn't count at this level.
He merely runs the Kodiak plant."

Hank realized that he'd wanted Swede for moral support. He con-
sciously straightened himself. At the table the fat lawyer turned an
expected sour face toward him, but Mike Tsurifune, groomed impeccably, rose smiling and extended a firm hand. "Looking fit, Hank!" His
voice bore no dark overtone, as he complained cheerfully that he'd found
no tennis club Anchorage and thus his game would suffer.

"Ha!" There, springing to his feet from the shadows was Director
Kiyoshi Tsurifune himself.

"Hey!" cried Hank. He forgot his anger for the moment. Such was the
immediate warmth he felt between them that if the old man had been
American he'd have bear-hugged him.

The director gripped Hank's arm and pounded his back. "Good looking, good looking, Mr. Crawford! So. You are well. And father. Is also
father well?"

Hank grinned down at the shiny bald head and wrinkled face all smiles,
and patted the frail-seeming back in return. "Great to see you, sir! My
dad's fine, thanks. I'd heard you were sick. But good looking yourself,

now. I'm really glad to see it!" He started toward a vacant chair that John Gains indicated.

"Ha!" The director took Hank's arm again, and snapped something in Japanese to the man beside him. The man left his chair at once taking only his sake cup. "Here, Mr. Crawford. Here. Sit!" He rattled the chair. "I must tell you of new acquisition." After Hank sat, he gestured, and Mike handed over the sake cup from the vacant place. The director filled it from a heated carafe. "New acquisition! Yesterday! Jasper Johns number four for Tokyo collection! Impressive, you are impressed I can see."

Hank relaxed. "Very impressed, sir." He filled the older man's cup in return and everyone toasted. The warm sake spread a comfortable top over the effect from Hank's other drinks. The director gestured to his son again, received from him a box wrapped in gold paper, and with a bow and smile presented it to Hank for Jody. Then he continued enthusiastically to describe his new painting. The others listened with polite but disinterested attention, except for John Gains, whose interjections showed he had done homework on the artist. The director, however, barely acknowledged. His lively eyes remained on Hank.

Hank bowed appropriately for the gift. Find something at the hotel gift shop in return, he decided, and leaned back to enjoy himself before getting serious.

The waitress placed a sizzling steak in front of each man except Hank and John Gains. "I'd assumed," said Gains, "that you'd want the halibut with me to show your commitment, whatever the others ordered."

Hank regarded the white chunk of fish before him, often delicious but here lost in the sort of cream sauce he never chose, while the meat wafted inviting odors. He ate nevertheless in good humor. When Mike joked about the dearth of tennis courts in Anchorage, he laughed in sympathy. Rider explained how it was only a wildest dream that American fishermen thought they could catch all the sablefish in the Gulf of Alaska, and Hank nodded with suitable gravity.

When the meal ended, Tsurifune spoke something in Japanese to his son, and Mike looked at his watch. "Come, Hank, show me the hot places in Anchorage."

"I know a few, Shoji," began John Gains.

Mike either didn't hear or ignored Gains as he moved around the table and threw out his arm for Hank to follow.

Hank shook his head. "We need to discuss some things tonight. With your dad. In private. Then, first thing tomorrow, I'm off down to Kodiak."

Mike spoke in Japanese to his father while maintaining his bright expression. The director's answer came in syllables drawn from deep in his throat like a Kabuki actor.

"Too bad, Hank," said Mike. "You must stay tomorrow and sit with us at Scientific Committee to show solidarity. Thus to keep the committee convinced that it's impossible for American vessels to capture all the sable-fish quota, a fact they know. American fishermen will recommend that they deprive Japan of our historic quota. We must keep them convinced with our strong presence."

Time to start, Hank decided. "Nope. Sorry. I haven't seen my family in over two months."

Mike's face lost its ease. "Father says it is not good among friends to be stubborn, Hank. And we have nothing important to discuss further tonight."

Hank made his voice firm although he kept it low for privacy. "You've counted on my American presence out there. But you shipped in a Japanese captain when I left my trusted man Terry in charge. I'm ready to hear why."

"Most unbusinesslike discussion tonight."

Hank continued staring into Mike's smooth Asian face, and said nothing, although he began to tense. Finally, Mike spoke to his father in Japanese. The director grunted, and waved his hand in assent.

"In twenty minutes then, Hank. Father will receive you in his room. Let me give you the number."

"Good." Hank nodded to the others at the table and left. The fishermen at the bar called to urge him over. By now they had absorbed more drinks and become boisterous. Hank gave them a grin and a wave but kept going. The native corporation people were just leaving, and he crowded with them into the elevator but passed only pleasantries when Odds started to converse. In his room he quickly brewed coffee and drank it black while he scribbled notes to remember all that he needed to say.

At the director's door Hank raised his hand to rap and Mike opened it. The old man was ensconced like an icon behind a table laden with papers in neat piles. The lawyer sat beside him. Mike gestured to a chair facing them, and took a seat by his father. No one smiled.

Hank remained standing. Keep cool, he reminded himself. "I'll start with this. I'm pissed as hell that you sent over a skipper to replace my man."

"You don't seem to get it," said the lawyer bluntly. "You own that boat in name only. The money's here at this table. The Tsurifunes have to look out for their interests, and you deserted the boat they'd entrusted to you. Maybe you don't realize that at any time they want, they could decide you're a poor producer and be rid of you. I can tell you it's been discussed, after you left ship the way you did. They could—"

"*What?*"

"—could call in their loans, including the one on your other boat and your house."

Hank felt himself explode and did nothing to contain it. "Call me a poor producer? Don't ever try it!" He advanced, planted stiff arms knuckles down on the table, and spoke in their faces. "Ever see my bills of lading? They prove what I deliver." Both Japanese pressed back in their chairs, and even the lawyer looked startled. "Try dumping me for that and the word'll be all over the fucking waterfront, and clear to the fucking State Department, what doing business is like with the Tsurifunes." He stepped back but maintained his glare as he wondered if the threat were possible. His reputation at stake!

Mike recovered first. He adjusted his cuffs and rose. "You heard mistake, Hank. No intention to do this." His voice regained its smoothness. "We understand why you needed to leave. But this fellow Bricks—Terry, is it?—that you left in charge. We are told he is too easygoing. Thus we had reason to decide he would not be productive."

"Who said? You didn't even give him a chance."

"Never mind. Let's forget it. Go to your ship and continue to produce, and we'll recall Captain Fukuhara at once."

Hank retained his tone. "You can pay your Captain Fukuhara yourself, but not from the funds of my boat. When you examine the books, you'll see that the fishing vessel *Puale Bay* has paid captain's share to Terry Bricks for the time I was away."

After a pause, Mike said, "That's up to you, Hank."

The director had been silent. Suddenly he pointed his finger at Hank. His voice had none of the cheerful bounce of an hour before, and his eyes had turned calm and steely. "You are good producer, Mr. Crawford. Go back to ship and produce. Work hard and make money. Now you go, please."

Hank only shifted his feet. "That brings me to the next thing."

"You're pushing it, mister," growled Rider.

Hank ignored him. He held his ground and his expression.

The director pointed to the vacant chair. "Then you sit, please." He added lightly, "You are very big, Mr. Crawford. But very more big when you stand."

The remark broke the tension. They all chuckled and Hank apologized. He sat but leaned forward. "This next is about money. You're paying Seattle and Canada more for their sablefish than you pay me. Same product. And my quality's at least as good as any other, probably better."

Rider cleared his throat. His voice stayed level and dry. "You're paid the going Kodiak rate. If somebody else wants to pay more, sell to 'em and watch 'em go broke. Examine your contract. All my client has is right of first refusal. If we're not willing to meet a competitor's price, you're free to sell to them."

"Except that, since the Japanese constitute the entire sablefish market, you've all agreed on price."

"What a notion, Hank!" exclaimed Mike.

"You're keeping it low in Kodiak to discourage Americans, make it seem a poor-paying fishery so that we won't kick you off the sable grounds like the Canadians did."

The director said something in Japanese. His son shrugged, and began to scribble figures. John Gains had it wrong, Hank realized. The old man still called the shots.

The lines around the director's eyes crinkled agreeably again. "Mr. Crawford. You are our friend. Friends protect each other. Therefore, we shall pay you four cents U.S. more for each pound of quality sablefish."

Hank smiled back, relieved. "I appreciate that, sir." He struggled with the urge to accept partial victory, then steeled himself. "However, sir . . . "

"Therefore it is settled."

"Generous," muttered the lawyer. "Know when you're well off, Crawford."

Hank took a breath and maintained good humor. "But you see, sir, the price you pay in Vancouver is six cents higher."

"Ah, but in Canadian money, worth less."

"No, as translated into U.S. money. Also six cents more in Seattle."

"Ah." The old man's lips thinned and parted to expose gold teeth. "Seattle, however, closer to banks, Mr. Crawford. And to vessels, closer."

Hank saw that it was becoming a game. "But Kodiak is closer to Japan, sir." He felt calm at last, and had begun to enjoy himself. "At least a thousand miles closer," he guessed.

Long silence. Hank retained it without changing expression. His gaze now remained on the director alone.

At last: "Five cents, Mr. Crawford. But not to speak of it to others."

"Thank your greedy stars Mr. Tsurifune tolerates you for some reason," said Rider.

Hank held himself together. He allowed more time to pass before saying, "Six, sir."

Six became the figure. After grave handshakes, Mike said with resumed lightness, "Don't know whether I can afford it anymore, Hank. But time to see the town, eh?"

Hank studied his large clasped hands, with the stub of a lost finger on his left hand from a wild crab pot more than a decade ago. One knuckle had a red, healing scab, and another a scar that had required stitches. He had debated with himself during the long plane trip, before he'd thought of his new propositions, whether to challenge their honesty if he had the chance. He decided to do it. "I have more to say."

The lawyer had already risen. He snorted in exasperation. Only Hank and the director faced each other across the table.

"You will say then, please, Mr. Crawford."

"Somebody's told me the American Coast Guard boarded a Japanese longline vessel last year and found that it was keeping double logbooks. Not proven yet, but it seemed to show that the captain was cheating. Fishing maybe three times the amount of sablefish he reported against his quota. This vessel was not from Tsurifune, they said. But I want to warn you, sir. In two ways. First, my own honor is important to me, and therefore—"

The director held up his hand, and spoke to his son urgently in Japanese. Hank waited to continue.

Mike took over with cool precision. "My father wishes to thank you for the warning, Hank. Such rumor we've heard. Please understand that some Japanese companies are in . . . desperation, at loss of American fishing grounds and nowhere else to go. We take your warning as proof of friendship, but do not wish to discuss this further. I'll persuade Father, all right, forget about Scientific Committee tomorrow. Please go happily to see your family, then quickly join your vessel and continue to produce. Father is now tired and says good night." Slight smile. "I too am suddenly tired. So, therefore, good night."

Now they're giving me the bum's rush, thought Hank, and wondered if they indeed had something to hide. He tightened the clasp of his hands. "More."

The director hadn't moved, as if he expected further discussion. He nodded, hardly tired. Interested, even.

Hank spoke quickly before it stuck in his throat. "I want you to apply all my earned credit to my crabber-trawler, *Jody Dawn,* not part to the big longliner *Puale Bay,* and immediately give me back full ownership of *Jody Dawn.*"

"Ah, Hank," said Mike easily. "Not possible. You understand, we still have great investment there."

"Read your contract, sir," growled the lawyer.

Hank kept his eyes on the Director, who seemed to be studying him. He made himself speak slowly to avoid needing a translation through Mike. "Sir, also the lien . . ." He needed to pause to lick his lips, which had gone dry.

"Hank, Hank," began Mike smoothly.

"And also cancel the liens you've put on my house to cover both *Jody Dawn* and *Puale Bay.* Within three years, probably much sooner, I'll pay back the rest owed on *Jody Dawn* with . . ." He had prepared to say seven and go higher, but suddenly decided to take a chance. ". . . four percent interest, honor agreement. I know that's less than the going rate, but for this . . . goodwill, I'll continue with goodwill to provide an American presence aboard the longliner, *Puale Bay.*"

The lawyer almost laughed. "Contract, contract, sir."

Hank continued to watch Mr. Tsurifune as he said to the lawyer, "Not talking to you. Stay out of it."

"Interesting idea, Hank," said Mike. "But not practical. And besides, you're already providing American presence, under contract as Mr. Rider reminds."

"I'm talking about *how* I do it."

The gaze between Hank and Director Tsurifune remained steady, and the room became silent. Hank remembered watching the old man on a Tokyo–New York call when he'd bought one of his paintings. The same sense of energy now emanated from all Tsurifune's person, although the wrinkled face stayed composed. One scornful laugh from this man and his own cards would tumble, Hank realized. At least a minute passed.

"Seven. Interest seven percent, Mr. Crawford."

Hank felt relief wildly, but tightened his hands against each other and in spite of himself said without thinking: "Five and a half, sir." After he'd said it—*Why?* He was getting caught up himself in games. He prepared to accept seven, and hoped he hadn't blown it, but kept his expression firm. More seconds passed.

Suddenly, "Hai. Five and half. Honor! Okay."

Director Tsurifune held out his hand. Hank grasped it. The older man's handshake was sturdy, not the weak-fish Japanese kind. They ended pumping as both exploded in spontaneous grins.

At once the lawyer advised against the agreement. The director waved him aside. Mike made no further objection. "Since Father wishes, Mr. Rider will draw up new contract." He added, "When time permits."

Hank controlled a growing excitement as he drew back his chair, sat again, and forced his hands to reclasp. The others, all standing, frowned. He coughed to regain moisture in his throat gone dry and said, "Sorry. More business."

"What now?" exclaimed the lawyer. "Penthouse in Seattle?"

Hank felt able at last to ignore him. And it wasn't difficult, now, to look at the old man with warmth and ease and to address him informally. "I have a new idea, Mr. T. Good idea, maybe."

"Ah?" The warmth was returned. The director resumed his seat.

"I'm told that the Japanese once, until the nineteen-sixties, fished roe pollack in Shelikof Strait. I hear it was a pretty rich time."

"Rich. Hai." Mr. T nodded, then exclaimed, "Rich rich!"

"Rich while it lasted." Hank didn't mention the eventual rapine greed of the Japanese, nor the anger of fishermen like Jones Henry who watched from small boats crowded aside until the Alaska governor forced the issue.

"Much lost," agreed Mr. T. "Very sad time."

"You pretend to know your history, Crawford," said Rider, who had now reluctantly resumed his seat. "Do you know that Governor Eagen of this state acted in contempt of the law? Typical of the cowboy assumptions up here. No responsible court, under laws at the time, would have upheld Alaskan jurisdiction over that whole thirty-mile strait. Except for the three miles from each shore, it was international waters that Alaska usurped. Eagen got away with it because the Japanese are peaceful people, and they accepted the outrageous act."

Hank checked himself from saying: accepted because they were smart enough to see that it was an outrage they'd better soft-pedal to retain the rest of the fishing loot off Alaska. "I only brought up the past," he said aloud, "to talk of the present, now that I'll have back my *Jody Dawn*. Roe pollack in Shelikof Strait has become a rich fishery again. But now, as you know, only for American trawlers like mine. I could catch the fish and deliver them to a Japanese processing ship in a joint venture."

Hank noted that Mike now also paid attention. He didn't bother to look at the lawyer. "In Kushiro," he continued, "I saw at least one Tsurifune vessel, idle because of your lost Alaska fish, that I think you could quickly make ready to process roe. Didn't I, Mike? If you want to bring this vessel over, my *Jody Dawn* will fish roe pollack and deliver to you. And . . . I'll need tonight to go back upstairs to the bar and confirm this . . . two other boats, good friends, will deliver to you if they have my trust and I have yours. On your part, you must promise me the honest, highest price, plus a bonus settlement at the end of the season if your profit in Japan is good. I will guarantee a joint-venture partnership for two seasons. Then we'll renegotiate." He still held the attention of father and son. Go all the way. "And manager of the joint venture ashore will be Mr. Swede Scorden."

"I hadn't gauged you after all," said the lawyer quietly.

Mike Tsurifune spoke to his father in Japanese. The old man listened without changing expression. Then suddenly his lips opened over gold teeth. He threw back his head and laughed like a young man. *"Hai!"*

PART IV

The Cold World

JANUARY–SEPTEMBER 1984
KODIAK, ALASKA

22

SHELIKOF

SHELIKOF STRAIT, LATE JANUARY 1984

A month after Christmas, a panel of wooden Santas still hung by the gangway leading to the Kodiak floats. Pete, on Hank's shoulders, grabbed at them when he passed, but his mittens slipped over the wet board. Kodama, who followed behind, reached up and playfully gripped the child's fingers. Henny and Dawn competed around Hank's legs to be closest to their father. He braced carefully on the center strips of the gangway to leave them room on both sides.

It had turned into a procession down the hill, after a big sendoff lunch at Adele's house. A wet snow left puddles in their tracks and whitened the harbor masts, hulls, and boardwalks below them.

Tom Harris, who had arrived from Chesapeake Bay via Baltimore just that morning, picked his way with a bulging seabag on his shoulder. He was so busy looking right and left at the sights that, with his limp, he nearly lost footing on the slippery treads.

Seth trailed with Jody. He hunched in his thick wool coat with hands in pockets, but he still towered over her. Snow laced his tangle of brown-blond hair. "You'd like her, Jody."

"I'm sure I would."

Seth straightened, puffed out his chest, and grinned when he caught Hank's eye. His face, beginning to line around the mouth and eyes where his scowls usually tightened, had a bright expression not common to him for years. "Her divorce papers still got some months to go."

"You turkey," piped Terry gaily behind them. "Expect us to believe *she* called *you?*"

Seth's husky voice became even deeper. "That's right."

"Come on. When you heard she was free again? After how you've banged our ears forever about your lost Marion?" In answer Seth turned to tousle Terry's cap from his head.

Adele, bringing up the rear of the procession along with Ham and Mo, called out: "I do hope that poor woman knows what's she's getting into, marrying a fisherman after steady life with an accountant."

Seth took it in good humor. "If my Marion liked it with an accountant, ma'am, she'd still be with him."

"Chook chook," clucked Kodama, persisting with Pete on Hank's shoulders. The child regarded him cautiously, pleased with the attention but uncertain of the face. Hank had found the money to fly Kodama back to his family in Japan during the *Puale Bay*'s brief seasonal layup, and had been puzzled by his uneasy refusal to go. "Must see more of American culture," was his excuse. He slept aboard the otherwise-deserted *Puale Bay,* and indeed spent his days walking the few streets of Kodiak. His face became familiar to the clerks at the supermarket and the hardware stores (who finally accepted that he wasn't there to shoplift), where he wandered the aisles frowning over objects and prices without ever touching anything except for the basic groceries that he bought. Once someone reported finding him all the way out at Spruce Cape, miles from town, gazing at the rocks and open water despite an icy rain. He had politely refused a ride and had returned on foot. Whenever Jody had him to dinner, his wistful, gentle concentration on their children made them wonder even more at his decision not to visit home. Jody insisted on his coming along to their seasonal parties, where he remained bashfully quiet although he watched intently. The news that Seth would now captain the *Puale Bay* for a while had seemed to upset him, but only briefly. Now he seemed ready again for sea and the struggle to keep American fishermen in line for Japanese product standards.

The procession reached the floats to join a stream of other crewmen carrying boxes of groceries and bags of gear. The press of their collective feet swayed the floating boards under them. Hank led to the *Jody Dawn,* then waited for Tom to come alongside. He waved toward the bows pressing in from each side of the walk, and explained, "The new season's taking off. Boats ninety to about a hundred and ten feet like my *Jody Dawn*, built to crab with pots, are now geared, you see, for trawl, headed like us around the island to JV for roe pollack until late March or April. Then probably on to cod in the Bering or scratch in the Aleutians for what crab's left. Smaller boats, like those limit seiners over there with max length of fifty-eight feet—"

"Nor single one of those boats ain't big sized," said Tom. "I never seen so many big-sized boats all for fishing."

"Well anyhow, the limit seiners that go for salmon in summer, you see they're now installing longline for black cod out in the Gulf of Alaska. Then see all the way down the line where bigger boats are moored at the cross-pier, that's the hundred-thirty-foot *Puale Bay* I own . . . mostly. She's built specifically to longline in the Gulf and freeze onboard. Seth's going to take her over for the time. And Kodama here as fishing master. They'll probably leave tomorrow."

Tom gazed around. "Lot of boats and people to keep straight all at once." Now that he had put down his seabag his big hands dangled uncomfortably.

"A shame lousy weather held you up in Anchorage for two days, Tom. Jody and I had planned to show you around before we took off. I haven't even had a chance to ask about Cap'n Bart."

Tom reassured him that the old man was fine and sent greetings. It brought a spark to his lean face. "Daddy might even be half relieved to put up for the rest of the season, for all he complained how I'd deserted him, since it's stayed ice back there and oysters scarce anyhow." Tom touched the bow of the *Jody Dawn*, then patted it. "Your boat? Huh. And the other one up there too! We'd thought you was kidding us."

Jody entered the conversation warmly. "I'm sure he lied all over the place, Tom. But we're glad you're here. And we'll be sure to show you around before you go home."

"Go home. Sure."

From the way Tom said it, Hank wondered if his invitation to crew for a limited two-month fishery might have opened larger ideas. The man, having served in Vietnam, had probably seen enough of the world to be restless on a small open boat in Chesapeake Bay losing its oysters.

Adele strode in and took charge. "Now we'll open the champagne, boys. Who's going to do it? Seth! You need to start learning a little finesse for courting a lady."

Hank watched Adele with fond detachment. Inches of red slacks stretched from the ends of her long coat to high galoshes trimmed with fur. Well, that was her style. Had Jones Henry ever appreciated his wife's ability to get things done?

Adele poured from the fizzing bottle while declaring, "Paper cups will have to do. My crystal flutes bought in Paris France are certainly not coming to the dock." She turned to Kodama who stood awkwardly apart. "Mr. Kodama, what do you make of all this?"

The sudden attention flustered Kodama. "Very nice, madam. I liking very nice."

"Then drink, my dear sir!"

Holding their cups of champagne, Seth and Kodama faced each other. Hank had talked to each firmly on the previous day, setting forth their separate jurisdictions on the ship. He had even made them shake hands.

"Okay then, man," ventured Seth, and tipped Kodama's cup with his own.

"So," said Kodama, and poured a drop of his drink into Seth's. *"Gampai!"*

Seth looked startled, then shrugged and returned the gesture. "Gampai yourself, man."

Hank told Ham to rouse the new crewman on the *Jody Dawn* to join them. Ham leapt aboard, pounded on the hatch with a hearty yell, then went inside the cabin and returned. "Jace, he's all passed out, Boss. I don't think he needs no more booze today."

"To safe trips for all of us," said Adele, and raised her cup. "Safe trips, fish, and riches to us all."

Terry, Ham, and Tom clambered over the rail of the *Jody Dawn*. Hank hugged his family each in turn, then even Adele, and once more, Jody. As he stepped aboard his boat Henny ran up and in his deepest voice announced, "I'll toss the lines, Dad." Hank's look at Seth and Mo told them not to interfere.

In the *Jody Dawn*'s wheelhouse Hank breathed the familiar odors of polish, electronics, and lingering fish, started the engine, and enjoyed his boat's throb of power. He watched his young son scamper to throw off fore and aft lines and then the springline, solemnly tossing each to a man on deck.

"Killer wing there, man," declared Terry. "Give it a couple more years and you'll be goin' with us." Henny puffed his chest and grinned.

"And so will I be going," called Dawn.

"Sure, honey, you too."

Hank looked down at his two older children. Sturdy and eager, both. In two more summers, Henny at ten could come aboard and pitch fish or cut bait. And later Dawn, only a year or so younger. It would all come out right. Jody blew him a kiss and he blew it back, then did the same for Dawn who imitated her mother. Other boats were pulling from their slips. Hank waited his turn in the traffic. Mo, destined for the longliner with Seth, called joking instructions to his buddy Ham as water separated them. Everyone waved. The boat passed through the breakwater and Hank tooted his whistle a last time. Snow soon dimmed the sight of those left behind. Clanks on deck and boot thumps overhead told him his guys were battening gear. The boat started an easy rock. It lifted one by one the pressures he'd felt ashore.

Two hours later, the low mounds and markers of Whale Passage sped by as the boat rode with the current. Hank kept the *Jody Dawn* close to the rock bluffs of the northern face where eddies of flood tide kicked least against the bow. Snow showers laid a gauze over the hills of trees ashore. It may have been territory he'd negotiated times by the hundreds, but this afternoon the passage exploded around him fresh and new. Otter heads popped from sheltered pools. White wings glided against the sky. Racing water splashed against a red buoy and pushed it to a slant. The frosty wind blew a life of its own to whine against shrouds, bend an antenna, and kick small waves across the channel. He stretched and did knee bends in the warm wheelhouse without taking his eyes from the water and land. Good to be again on the boat of his design, and headed for action!

Hank checked when he heard a noise on deck. It was Ham, bundled in thick coveralls and a wool cap pulled virtually to the cheeks, jumping with exuberance. He felt it too!

"Yah, *Jody Dawn*," came the accented radio voice of Arne Larsen from the *Northern Queen*. His boat was barely visible astern, flat and gray as cardboard through the snowflakes. "Yah, Hank, I hear it's southwest blowing up de Shelikof like a fuckin' sonofabitch."

"She'll be a cold one, Arne."

They chatted for a while, and Joe Eberhardt joined in. It became a conference of partners on the new joint venture they had formed. Hank watched a whirlpool in the current kick his bow to port with the strength of a battering ram. The boat shuddered. He righted back to course automatically. On the afterdeck Ham gave a whoop, evidently enjoying the action of the Whale as much as Hank did.

Terry bounced up the ladder into the wheelhouse, wiping grease from his hands. Hank motioned him over. "When you line up those rocks to starboard with the end of those rocks to port on Koniuji Island, you should change course to port about twenty-five degrees."

Terry studied the scene, checked it on paper at the chart table, and declared, "Got it."

Hank knew that he had. Terry was a man worth training for the future.

The sky had cleared by the time they left Whale Passage and traversed Kupreanof Strait. Shelikof Strait intersected their course like a T. Thirty miles across the water gleamed the creamy mountain jags of the mainland. The sea between was a field of whitecaps that the wind drove in furrows. Three boats, all approximately *Jody Dawn*'s size, pressed down the Shelikof in the direction Hank was headed. The boats pitched up rhythmically, then slammed down to be half hidden in waves.

"Everything's battened?"

"Ham's thorough. But I've checked anyhow."

Hank looked back at the afterdeck. Ham was shaking the taut chain that secured the big steel otter board portside. "Get him inside before I turn. He's having such a good time there I'm not sure he has the sense to come in by himself."

"He just ain't used to being in charge of anything, Boss. Now that I've told him I'm engineer and he's deck boss, he's got to go over everything again every few minutes. Don't worry. I'll still look over his shoulder."

"You're comfortable with our two new men?"

"Same as you. I've drunk with Jace and even once punched it out with him over I forget what. He's got a lot of mouth, and sometimes hits the booze. That's why he's never been more than a season on any one boat. But nobody complains about his work. I took a chance hiring him while you and Jody were having vacation in Seattle. It's only for two months, so we'll be fine. Your new man Tom from back east, he looks a little seasick right now, but you say he knows his way around boats. We're in good shape." Terry examined the chart and the sounder again, peered at the land on both sides and the water ahead, then said, "I'll go give Ham a hard time for kicks, but don't worry, he's doing good," and left.

The wind and sea caught them broadside when they left the final shelter of mountains on Kodiak Island. The boat rolled to the usual clangs and clicks, but Hank heard no ominous bangs from loose gear. He gradually altered course around Cape Uganik to steady off a few miles from land, then headed southwest into the wind. The bow lifted, then smashed down into churning water. Spray hissed up in sheets and broke against the windows. Hank adjusted his legs automatically to the motion, and turned up the heater a notch.

Ham's voice bellowed from below, then to heavy footsteps Ham himself appeared. He dripped from cap to boots. "Ain't this the right kind of weather, sun and all!" he exulted, then turned businesslike with, "Everything secure, Boss."

"Good. I haven't seen Tom. Is he asleep?"

"Seasick. From practically the time we left the dock, from the minute the boat rocked so you could hardly feel it. Pukin' in a bucket now, out of the wind. I thought he was a fisherman, Boss."

Hank now wondered himself, but said, "Different water, different boats. Give him time."

Terry joined them with a joke about it raining fish from all the water on the windows. They finally faced squarely down the channel. Suddenly, "Oh Jeez, look at that!" exclaimed Terry and Ham together. The sight startled Hank also. He had expected activity, but nothing like that ahead. Through rivulets pouring down the glass they saw that boats packed the horizon.

An hour later, late sun glistened on hulls and masts that surrounded them on every side. Hank needed to steer carefully between them. With the current running windward, large foreign processor ships pulled at their anchor chains and water eddied around the mawlike ramps of their sterns. Smaller boats like his own, unable to anchor in the hundred-fathom water, maneuvered under way with barely a space between them. What would it be like when the fish arrived!

Hank continued to weave the boat south beyond the cone-shaped headland of Cape Karluk. They scanned the national flags that flew beneath the stars and stripes from the foreign buyers while looking for the one with a Japanese red circle on white that would be their own joint-venture buyer. (He'd forgotten its name: Something-*Maru.*) Counting the foreigners became a game. Hank and Terry, on opposite sides of the boat, began to identify and call out their count while Ham told them to go slow as he wrote them down. Before they stopped they had identified ten Japanese and eleven North Korean ships, as well as a half dozen Soviets, and one each from Portugal, West Germany, and Taiwan. They had also begun counting the smaller boats, all of them American, but gave this up after reaching fifty-three and arguing that some had been logged twice.

"That you, Hank?" came the familiar voice of Gus Rosvic over the CB. "I can't seem to shake loose of you, son." Gus had taken a winter break from longlining black cod in the Gulf aboard his *Hinda Bee* to fish roe pollack aboard the larger medium trawler, *Thunder,* which he co-owned. In answer to a question from Hank, "Delivering to the West Germans. You know what they done to us in the War, but at least they're our own kind."

"Best reputation out here is the Soviets, Gus." The second voice was playful. "They aren't slanty-eyed either."

"Mess with Commies? President Reagan calls them Evil Empire, and he should know. And don't tell me about slanty-eyes. Last year, less choice, I started here with a South Korean I see back this time. No damn good on payment, so I left 'em."

"Left 'em pissed, I hear," said another voice.

"That's their business, Luke, but tell you what. Last year after I went over to the Krauts, them Koreans couple of times tried to cut off my gear. Turned course and run right over it. They'd best not do that again."

"The Taiwan boat did that on me. Or it just got in my way, couldn't be sure. It's crowded out here, Gus."

"Just the same."

When it grew dark, lights on all the boats made the water seem a town, albeit one whose lights rose, fell, and dipped.

Hank left Terry in charge of the helm and sought out his Chesapeake Bay friend. Tom was crouched in a sheltered corner of the afterdeck with a bucket beside him. A bare deck bulb reflected on shoulders that were shivering: a man diminished from the clear-eyed waterman at his own tiller on the Chesapeake. "Hey there, man!" said Hank heartily.

Tom looked up with a sheepish smile that accented his cheekbones. "I don't know what. Weather to my boat never done me like this."

Hank kept it easy. "Guess I win the argument for shittier weather than yours. You'll get your legs, don't worry. Come on inside."

"Later, maybe. If I smell some things in there, I'll like to puke again." He pulled a loose wool shirt tighter.

Hank brought a blanket from his own bed and wrapped it around Tom's shoulders. "Once we get working gear you'll just laugh about this."

Tom's inflamed eyes glanced up and then to deck. "If the old man see me now, he'd say told you so."

"Who's going to tell?"

"I'd appreciate that." Tom pulled part of the blanket over his head. "And I appreciate this. I'll make sure not to mess it." He turned to the water. "Just look at them lights. I never seen so many big boats, and all for fishing. Except in pictures. This is some sight. Worth the trip, almost."

"Then I'm glad you came."

A spasm of retching seized Tom. His whole body shook although he held the blanket clear of the bucket. When it was over: "Oh shit," he muttered. "But Hank, I won't let you down when the time comes."

"I'm not worried," assured Hank. But he wondered.

23

OVERLOAD

SHELIKOF STRAIT, LATE JANUARY 1984

The late January wind continued from the southwest, blowing bitter cold, but the sky stayed clear. The fleet that waited for the pollack to arrive quickly sorted itself after a fashion, with fishing boats clustered near the foreign buyer ships to which they would deliver. Hank kept the *Jody Dawn* in sight of the ship sent by the Tsurifunes to receive and process his catch, and close to Joe Eberhardt's *Nestor* and Arne Larsen's *Northern Queen*. All they needed now was the fish.

The screen of the *Jody Dawn*'s color sounder flickered with layers of the yellows and greens that depicted depths of open water rather than creatures. An occasional pip of orange or red would reveal a fish or two swimming past. Sometimes the red became a whole splotch, and whoever was minding the wheelhouse would call Hank to watch. But the red would drift on, with not enough other red behind it to be interesting.

Jody told him by radio that Justin Rider in Seattle had sent him a new contract, thirty pages long on legal-sized paper. She'd studied it as best she could. "It does appear they've separated our house from the rest. You've managed that for us, Hank, thank God. But didn't you say they were going to separate payments for *Jody Dawn* from *Puale Bay?* The language there gets so full of legal words it isn't clear. I think we should have a lawyer read it before you sign anything again."

Hank agreed. Suddenly Terry called his attention to a red mass on the sounder. "Talk about it later, Jody," and he signed off.

Tom Harris remained seasick, to his abject humiliation. Not that he gave up. He appeared at the wheelhouse for his assigned watch, but so weakened—the limp from his war wound had become more pronounced even though he tried to hide it—that Hank ordered him to bed and kept the watch himself. Tom reluctantly went down to the two-bunk cabin he shared with the other new crewman, Jace. A few hours past midnight, when Ham, on watch, went to wake Jace for his relief, he found Tom back on deck bundled in a sleeping bag and blankets. Jace for his part could not be roused beyond a groan and turns in his bunk. The cabin smelled strongly of booze.

Easygoing Ham shrugged at all of it, found an additional blanket for Tom, and with a yawn assumed Jace's watch on top of his own. Being in charge of the entire boat surrounded by lights like a carnival was not unpleasant. He thought of folks back in Idaho and their usual reminders a few weeks ago at Christmas that he was almost thirty and should settle down, and wondered now that Seth was going to make the plunge with this Marion whether it wasn't time for him also, even though no girl he'd met in pickups or even bunked with was good enough to compare to his mom for the long pull. He had pretty well decided it was time when the black sky began to pale. He watched the gradual arrival of the sun, first pinking a haze over the Kodiak mountains, then etching masts and flooding the snow peaks of the mainland with dazzling white. This is all I need, he decided. Just like this.

After waking, Hank checked briskly with Terry who was now on watch, and at breakfast saw a bedraggled Tom sitting inside the doorway for warmth. "Come on, man, this is dumb," he declared. "Get in your bunk for a while."

Tom's red-rimmed eyes looked up at him. "Not in there, Hank. I'm good here."

Ham set a platter of eggs and sausage in front of Hank, who asked routinely, "Jace back asleep after his watch?"

"He didn't exactly take one." Ham explained the situation.

Hank left his platter, and banged open the door to the cabin where Jace was sleeping. Heavy snore. The place reeked of booze. Even, Hank thought with disgust, of piss. No wonder Tom preferred a cold deck! He snapped on the light. Tom's unused upper bunk was bare and neat. An arm in a dirty sleeve dangled from the shadows of the lower bunk. Around it lay a jumble of clothing and boots. Hank shoved aside an open satchel. Glass inside it clinked. He pulled out two pocket flasks of whiskey along with a fifth. His flashlight beam inside the bunk caught a wet chin and a hand clutching a near-empty bottle. Hank pushed Jace's shoulder. "Get up." The man merely rolled his head, muttered a snottish obscenity, then started again to snore.

Hank gathered the bottles and threw them overboard, washed his hands, and returned to his breakfast. He tersely instructed Ham to clear the bunk in a cabin they used for storage. "Then get Tom in there comfortable till he pulls around." Up in the wheelhouse, while he called on the radio to find a boat returning to town, he demanded of Terry, "Where'd you pick up this boozehead?"

"Everybody said he's a good worker, Boss. When I checked him out hangin' around the dock he looked sober." Terry seldom turned apologetic. "I didn't know he'd throw a toot like this. But lots of guys just need a couple hours to sleep it off."

"Hours? When they don't bring their own garbage. This fucker planned for a whole trip! We'll do with one hand less."

"Right. Right. Sorry, Boss."

No boat was going to town. All had committed to wait for the fish.

Hank's anger grew. Sleeping off a drunk was acceptable, but to bring aboard a supply of booze to drink at sea desecrated his boat and reputation! After pacing long enough to control his first impulse he returned to the cabin. The stench disgusted him afresh. He grabbed Jace's shirtfront and yanked him from the bunk. The man merely flopped on the deck. "You! What's-your-name. Outside! Move!"

Ham watched from the door, concerned. "Maybe I'd better just help him move, Boss?"

"He'll move on his fuckin' own." Hank restrained his desire to kick, but placed a foot on the man's rear and prodded him a few inches across the deck. Jace muttered disjointed curses without getting up. He tried to drink from the flask still in his hand, then roused enough to throw the flask toward Hank. The glass shattered on deck.

Hank kicked his buttock once, then caught his breath. "Ham! Grab under one arm and I'll get the other." Jace stayed limp. His legs flopped like those of a puppet on a string when they lifted him. Up close he stank.

Tom Harris, sitting at the hatchway holding his head, stood and pressed against the bulkhead as they dragged Jace past. "I can take him over."

Hank started to refuse, then decided any action would do Tom good. "Yeah, take him. Hold your nose."

When they reached open deck, Hank drew a bucket of water and dashed it over the man's head.

"Boss!" cried Ham. "It's like ice out here."

"On your feet or I'll do it again."

Jace glared up through foggy lids. The water had streaked through smudges on his cheeks from days past. The man's boyish features and long sideburns might have made him handsome with grooming and a less sullen expression, but everything about him appeared ratty. His hair was matted, and long single hairs sprouted from his chin. But he'd found his tongue. "That's . . . bad shit, Captain . . . I got rights." Hank's stare did not change. He drew another bucketful and started to raise it. Slowly Jace wobbled to his feet.

Hank kept his voice cold. "If I'd found a boat to town you'd be on it. You'll get your ass back to town from Karluk. Ham, ready the life raft while I head for the village."

"That's a Klutch place." Jace suddenly straightened and began to shiver. "You can't dump me there. How'll I get back?"

"Your problem." Hank walked away. "Throw your crap together in your bags if you want to keep it."

"Captain! Just let me sleep it off, then I'm okay."

Hank continued inside, but he considered. He'd gripped the man's arm and felt muscle in the bicep. The shithead might indeed be okay sober, and without him they'd be shorthanded. While he thought about it he called over his shoulder, "Tom. You're steady enough to help Ham with the life raft?"

"I'm steady." Hank glanced back. Tom's lean face had taken on color at last. It even wore a kind of grin.

"Skipper!" whined Jace.

Hank entered the galley. He felt angry no more, but agreeably stern. Could that have been admiration in Tom Harris's expression? He decided that, with nothing better to do while they waited for the fish, heading the few miles back toward the native village would be a diversion while he played Jace and judged whether to keep him. No fisherman worth his salt wanted to be dumped. He detached his mug from a hook over the table, filled it from the urn, and climbed to the wheelhouse to change course.

Terry was talking to someone by radio. "Here's Boss now," he said, and handed the mike to Hank.

"Har har," boomed Arne Larsen from the *Northern Queen.* "Hank! You having a little crew trouble?"

Hank frowned at Terry and covered the mike. "What did you tell him? That was our private business."

"Told nothin', Boss. Look at boats all around us. They heard you earlier asking about a ride back to town, and they've got binoculars. Even saw it was booze you threw over since one bottle floated. Somebody else just got on radio and said how he'd once hired Jace but fired him after a couple trips. Said you done right with that bucket of water."

Arne continued his Norwegian laugh. "Back in old country ve tie a fellow like that who drinks booze aboard, tie by the leg and throw him over the side for a minute. Any bastard do that here now, dot's vot I still vould do. Not soft like you, Hank. I see your boys getting ready the life raft. Going to dump him ashore, eh?"

Hank glanced aft from a wheelhouse window. Jace stood shivering alone on deck, his shoulders hunched, while the clumps of boots overhead told Hank that his own orders were being obeyed. This was power! The reminder gave him a rush and made him cautious at the same time. Returning to deck he kept his voice cold, and snapped, "Go inside with a mop and disinfectant. Clean out that cabin of mine you've shitted up. Then swab down yourself. Then we'll see. Move it!" The sobered Jace moved.

Ham called from above that he'd get Jace coffee. He sounded relieved. Hank kept his voice crisp. "You can show him where we store mop and soogee. Coffee's his own affair."

He decided still to cruise in the direction of Karluk in case the business went wrong, but with a gesture he stopped Ham's work on the life raft. "Better check out gear with our Chesapeake Bay greenhorn," he called with a wink at Tom. "He's been too busy puking to tell a trawl door from a shovel."

Tom laughed. Good sign.

Suddenly they heard shots fired, then shouts delivered in a high-pitched Asian scream. It was coming from one of the South Korean mother ships. Crews began to line the rails of all the boats around them. Hank grabbed binoculars. A trawler of about their own 108-foot length pitched beneath the 350-foot ship. A man on the bridge of the trawler held a rifle, while his crew around him yelled and waved fists. It was Gus Rosvic.

"Har har," continued Arne over the CB. "I vatch it all. This fellow from Anacortes on *Thunder*, forget his name, must have high blood pressure. The Korean ran over his line, and the fellow shot at the ship."

Hank quickly tried to communicate. "*Thunder*, fishing vessel *Thunder*, Gus! Read me! Over!"

A few moments later Gus's voice said calmly, "That you, Hank? Don't worry. I just shot high to their wheelhouse. Nobody hurt unless one of 'em was hanging from the ceiling like a monkey. Buggers overrun my gear again on purpose."

Hank flashed on his own incident in the Bering Sea years before, when Seth in fury over gear being overrun fired at a Japanese ship, bringing down the wrath of the State Department.

"Gus! Now get your ass out of there."

"Well, Hank, mebbe to please you."

Moments later there were more shouts. The Korean crew had begun to throw garbage at the *Thunder*.

"Now see that?" Gus exclaimed. "You know them fellows were up to no good."

"Gus, *move!*"

All at once boats around them began to blow whistles. "Boss . . . Boss!" called Terry beside him in the wheelhouse. "Sounder's going red all over the place!"

Indeed, the screen displayed more red than any other color. It passed in big blotches at depths below a hundred fathoms. Hank had never seen so much solid red on a sounder screen. He quickly checked his position relative to the boats around him.

"Yah, Hank," came Arne Larsen's voice over the CB. "You see vot I see? Or is it broke, my machine?"

"Red here too, Arne. Red red red."

Joe Eberhardt's voice joined from the *Nestor*. "Those fuckers are coming like everybody said they would. And looks like they're holding to the bottom, swimming deep."

"Vait, vait," said Arne. "Now it's a mess of red moving up to midwater. Takes less cable and weights for pelagic. I think I try those fish. Good-bye."

Indeed, the red now moving past them with the current had risen to a higher position in the water column. Hank told Terry to start Ham and Tom laying out the trawl gear. "I'm not leaving up here now, so you look in on what's-his-name, the drunk. No time now to dump him ashore. You be the judge. He's not going on my deck boozed even if we have to lock him in the cabin."

"Gotcha." And Terry was off.

Hank cruised among the fleet. Not as crowded as he'd expected since boats had fanned out over the thirty-mile expanse of the Shelikof to gain space. He headed into the current and wind and considered what Arne had said. Catching a midwater school would use shorter cable with less drag on the engine.

He glanced aft. Tom was helping Ham at the starboard rail and seemed to be doing all right. After attaching the net line, they released the chain that secured the trawl door tightly against the side. The heavy steel flat bumped free at the boat's hull, ready to be dropped into the water. When Ham pointed, Tom nodded his understanding and went portside to do the same on the other door. Together the two—a crewman short, but they managed—dragged the heavy trawl bag and chafing gear astern and readied it for launch. Ham's directions appeared to be direct and clear, while Tom responded with quick intelligence and a ready back. Hank felt reassured. Tom knew his way around work. And, nice to see in a guy who'd been so guarded back in Maryland, he now seemed eager and lively. Even his war-wound limp had smoothed under the drive of jobs with purpose.

Other boats around them cruised for location. Whistles blew to signal nets being dropped. The red blotches on the color sounder drifted on either side of the *Jody Dawn* at varying depths like targets at a range. On the busy surface, milky swirls that rode the swells signaled fish sperm below. Hank felt his own excitement rise. Just wait for the right blob of red. Finally a bolus of it approached them, directly centered. "Stand by," he announced over the deck speaker.

When next he glanced back, all four of his crew stood at the ready. Jace wore clean coveralls over what appeared to be his drunk clothes, and a clean cap anchored hair still in a tangle. He seemed alert. Terry looked up, gestured toward Jace, and fingered an okay.

Hank accelerated the boat and pulled the whistle. Over went the end of
the trawl bag. Prop wash swirled around the attached red plastic floats. A
puff of net stayed above water briefly, then sank. Hank adjusted to a
steady slow speed through the oncoming swells. His boat's forward
motion against the friction of net already in the water pulled the rest of
the net across deck and overboard. At Hank's signal his men released the
trawl doors and they splashed into the water. Down, down—the heavy
steel doors weighted the net. They were attached to parallel cables that
spun out from their drums on deck. Ham called out fathom markers on
the cables as they clattered by.

Hank kept the images below surface in his mind. The boat's forward
motion should by now have activated the doors to paravane out like sails
that would be pulling open the mouth of the net. If his adjustments were
correct, the mouth would engulf the school of fish and entrap it.

No drag he'd ever made had lasted less than an hour, so he continued to
tow while waiting for another mass of red on the sounder. At last he
radioed the Tsurifune processor that he was hauling in. "Must wait,"
came the reply. "Going presently first to fishing vessel *Northern Queen*.
You must waiting please." Hank decided to continue his tow since Arne
had hauled in ahead of him.

"Sonofabitch!" exclaimed Arne a while later over the radio. "Bring up
bagful of fish, send it offur to fuckin' Japs, dey call back fish is too little.
Jap machines set for bigger fish. Dey sample a few, say not enough eggs to
do it all by hand, goddamn bastards say dey are not going to buy, throw
fish back."

Hank hauled in at once. The fish that bulged against the trawl bag
measured only inches when he had expected lengths over a foot. Only Jace
of the four on deck did not appear astonished. "I been here last year," he
called up. "The big fish they want go along the bottom. Didn't nobody
tell you?" Nor did you, thought Hank, furious.

Instead of detaching the bag to a delivery skiff as planned, Hank had his
men ease it up the stern ramp until they could reach the release cord at
bag end. "Open it!" he called down, sickened by the waste.

At least Jace was the one who insisted on easing himself down the slip-
pery ramp, gripping fingers for support into mesh tightened against fish.
He now wore oilskins with a fresh shirt showing beneath, and from
Terry's report had vigorously cleaned himself and the room during the

time of the tow. He leaned over the swirling water, grappled for the cord, then tugged and tugged until the clamp snapped to release the circular drawstring. The end of the net opened. Fish gushed back into the sea. They floated dead, a carpet of dull silver.

Jace gripped his way back up the ramp with fingers in now-loose mesh and kicked his boot into the bag to dislodge fish that had stuck against the sides. Then, as they watched, he clung to the web, lowered his head, and vomited over and over. Ham slipped down the ramp to grip his arm, but it did not appear necessary.

Terry began to laugh. Tom, at first startled, joined in. Ham turned but kept his grip on the vomiting man. His large, open face was serious. "You guys sure pick some funny things to think is funny."

Hank waited until the sobered drunk had pulled himself back to deck and could look up through watery eyes to signal he was safe, then returned to the images on the color sounder. The sight of wasted fish that now bobbed around his hull appalled him, but he put it out of mind.

On deck under Ham's direction Tom and Jace lowered the net back into the water to clean it, then prepared to set again. In the wheelhouse the blotches of red continued to pass at differing depths and concentrations. Hank decided to bide his time for a perfect bottom mass of fish.

Terry joined him in the wheelhouse. "You saw Jace could work. Think you might keep him now, Boss?"

Hank saw that Terry's hiring ability was on the line. "I'll do it for *you*," he declared, feeling expansive. "But don't bother telling him yet."

"Good idea! Let him sweat. Thanks. Jace is the one of us who's done the Shelikof roe before. That's why I took him on."

"Then if he knows anything it's time to hear it. Not after we've made the mistakes."

Terry brought Jace to the wheelhouse. He was still a mess, bleary-eyed although he now poked up his shoulders. "So we shouldn't fish the mid-water schools?" Hank asked sternly. "What else do you know?"

"Well, Captain . . ." Jace looked around, still unsure but suddenly cocky. "That's the main thing for now. But there's plenty I know since I'm the only one here's done Shelikof roe before. You still going to put me ashore in that Klutch place?" It sounded more like a challenge than a plea.

Hank allowed a grave silence before saying, "You're on probation. Terry, what's his cabin look like now?"

"Swabbed out, Boss. Everything neat as a whore's buttons."

"Then grab yourself some coffee or something, Jace. We'll be setting again soon."

The man didn't move. "You know, Captain, since I'm the one knows most about the fishing here, I oughtta be deck boss. Don't you think?"

Hank controlled an explosion. Terry understood and hustled the man below.

Suddenly the red masses that crawled across the sounder screen turned solid red in a swath from the seafloor to several fathoms above. Shouts and whistles sounded from other boats. Above water, the surface of the long, wind-driven waves popped and boiled. Birds swooped and squawked overhead, diving into the boils and ascending with fish in their beaks. The air coming through the windows smelled of churning brine.

"On deck!" Hank shouted through the speaker.

Within minutes they had floated the trawl bag astern again and the steel doors pulled it below the surface. The depth sounder showed a curve that, while Hank watched and maneuvered among the boats, descended from 130 fathoms to 146 before leveling off. Hank calculated triple the depth for his cable, roughly 450 fathoms or 2,700 feet, more than half a mile.

Boots hit the metal stairway and Jace appeared in the wheelhouse door. "Skipper! I remember something else. Don't set clear to the bottom when it's solid fish down there. If it's too many you won't get your net back up."

Hank had heard the tales but judged them barroom yarns. Jace sounded like he knew. By now his own net would be approaching bottom. No time to consider. He accelerated the boat to make the trawl doors paravane upward and barked "Hauling in!" through the speaker.

Terry appeared, breathless. "Boss! We just set her."

"Taking a chance." He could feel the engine strain. They couldn't gain the speed he'd expected. Maybe they'd already snagged or overweighted the trawl, and pressure might snap the cables. "Off the deck!" he shouted.

He had kept the wheelhouse radios open on CB for his partners and on VHF for the fleet. The fleet band, which had droned with long time-killing conversations, now crackled with short comments but little else. "Guys," volunteered Hank over CB, "better watch out going straight down into the deep fish."

"Anybody's fished here before knows that's a fact," said a voice.

"Oh, Jesus Christ," came back Joe Eberhardt's voice. "Too late. It's like I'm anchored dead to the bottom. I'm yanked like a dog whenever I try to move." Arne Larsen answered with a steady stream of curses.

Simultaneously the wind accelerated, driving the steady waves higher straight into their bow.

Hank's orders turned precise. "Terry. You by one winch, Ham by the other, nobody else on deck. If those cables snap it's whiplash, so stay ducked behind the drums except when I call. I'll cut speed in spurts to give cable slack, then you two wheel in all you can for the seconds I give you before I throttle again. And repeat—Tom and Jace off deck."

During the next hour he gained back cable fathom by fathom. When he slowed, the waves hitting his front drove the boat back so that he needed to guard against tangling cable in the propeller. At length he knew that he had kept control and that as long as he kept moving, whatever his trawl bag held would not sink to the bottom. Arne, between curses, appeared to have done the same. Joe's trawl remained stuck. "When I try to reel in cable I can draw up my safety slack but it pulls me back with it. Any pressure drags down my stern. Been in worse. I'll just keep nudging her."

A commotion on the VHF made Hank look to starboard. A quarter mile away, a boat that he didn't know, shorter and narrower than the broad-beamed Bering Sea crabbers he and his partners rode, had tilted down at the stern. Whenever a wave washed the bow higher more sea gushed up the afterdeck. Water sluiced around men frantically sawing the cables. Didn't they have axes? The cables were like a taut leash that yielded slack then jerked up tight. If such cables snapped under the pressure they'd cut the men in half, but if they held they'd pull the boat under. He read the name with binoculars. "*Skagee* over there," he radioed on the open band. "Slack your winches. Throw off the damn cables. Give 'em up, for Chrissake!"

"They can't," came a voice from another boat. "Their winches is jammed."

A foam-cresting wave higher than the rest reared toward the imperiled boat. It raised the boat's bow, the deck slanted nearly vertical, and the men dropped into the water. Somebody on the emergency channel was calling the Coast Guard Air Base in Kodiak. But even with quick response the Coastie chopper might not reach the men before winter seas froze them. Hank hesitated, thought of his obligations, then dismissed thought.

His own boat was out of danger now, and, from the showdown with Jace, their life raft was probably the only one already half launched. He grabbed his survival suit from its rack and began to pull it on while he shouted orders out the window to lower the life raft.

Terry scampered to the wheelhouse. Hank told him to take over, hold way into the wind, and slowly haul the trawl bag up to the stern after the raft was launched.

"No, Boss, I'm the one should go."

"No, I've handled the raft more than you."

"But that time when Jones Henry died on you wasn't good."

"I learned, I learned." By now Hank was zipping up the front of the foam rubber suit.

"But you need another guy with you, Boss. That's me."

"Need you here."

Within minutes Hank had stomped to deck encased to the chin in the clumsy survival suit. The raft was already inflated and bouncing by the rail. Ham, aboard, had started the engine. He wore neither survival suit nor even float jacket. Hank ordered him out while Ham protested he'd be fine. Indeed, the ballooning bow of the rubber raft tipped upward with only a man in the stern, but: "No time. By time you suit up they'll drown. Out, Ham. Go!"

Alone in the raft, Hank cast off the line Ham held, and the flat-bottomed craft bounced free. He settled on his haunches as far toward the center as possible with hand on the tiller, and steered around Arne's boat blocking the way, gauging the swells. Cold water slapped his face, but he felt in control except that he kept losing sight of his target. Arms and shouts from Arne's deck above him pointed the direction. He dismissed the memory of the Jones Henry's loss by his side in the same life raft a year and a half before. This time there would be no deaths.

The *Skagee* had already submerged halfway. Its bow pointed upward like the sinking *Titanic*'s. Hank made out single figures holding to the now-vertical rail on opposite sides. He chose first the man closest, and eased the raft against the hull as best he dared without creating new instability. The man coughed and struggled. Water rolled over his head. Hank could not safely leave the tiller. Should have waited for Ham! he realized. He maneuvered to grip one of the man's arms and lock it over the inflated side with his knee. Bit by bit the man slowly bellied aboard. Hank recognized the guy, a part-native named Emmitt. With Emmitt in the center the raft was more level. Up close he couldn't see the opposite side of the bow.

"How many are you?"

Emmitt didn't hear or chose not to. He had collapsed. Hank realized that he himself needed to be brutal. He kicked out at the man with one foot while he steered. *"How many?"*

"Three."

On the other side, still clinging to the upthrust bow, was only one. It was his former crewman Oddmund! Odds, his eyes groggy-lidded, gripped the plunging rail with a single hand, riding up then under the water with the wreck's motion. His other hand held something below the surface. He tipped his head toward the hand submerged, and tried to speak but made only weak sounds.

"Grab what he's holding!" Hank commanded, and nudged Emmitt again with his boot.

Emmitt weakly snaked one arm, and then the other, over the side, leaned into the water, and clutched onto the neck of a shirt. "Oh Jesus," he cried, and started to pull. A head, with eyes closed, emerged. "It's Mikey."

"Hold him tight," Hank ordered. With the boat balanced he grabbed Odds's now-free arm and helped him wriggle into the raft. Odds crawled at once beside his shipmate. Both were barely able to move, but together they grunted and pulled the limp, dripping figure slowly over the raft side.

The figure's head rolled loosely. Slimy water oozed from his open mouth. His lips were blue.

"You had another guy?" Hank cried.

"Lost hold," mumbled Odds. "Don't know."

Hank demanded if either knew CPR, and when they shook their heads, ordered Odds to the tiller. "Keep us away from your hull, steer toward the closest boat without getting in a trough." He crawled alongside Emmitt, showed him how to press the man's chest on command, cleared a finger through the man's mouth, and without thinking of it further bent his own mouth to the cold blue lips.

When he paused at intervals to spit sour fluid or to instruct, Hank could glance and hear activity around him from another life raft and a boat, as well as a throbbing overhead. "Coast Guard chopper's coming down," somebody called.

"No, she's lowering a basket," said another.

"Fourth man somewhere," called Hank.

"Our boat picked up one."

"He's okay?"

"Body."

Time moved in a haze, but within minutes or hours the three survivors were drawn up one by one into the chopper: first the one unconscious, the last one Odds with Hank's assistance.

Hank retched and spat. Voices called to him. People wanted to pull him aboard their boats. He waved them aside, and headed back over the swells toward his *Jody Dawn*. He began to shiver, then sob, while the cold spray drenched him clean.

24

ICE

SHELIKOF STRAIT, FEBRUARY 1984

A frigid southwest wind continued steadily. Only half the *Skagee*'s crew had survived. Despite Hank's effort at resuscitation Michael Tulganuk never breathed again, nor did the man picked up by another skiff. The boat itself sank before it could be towed, to create a new obstruction to trawls dragging the Shelikof grounds.

The experience left Hank quiet. The sour, acrid, awful taste around the dead man's lips lingered in his imagination long after he'd washed and gargled enough to clean out a dozen mouths. Death had passed through that man's body and he'd felt it, felt it! after sensing the return of breath only moments before. Radio messages from the fleet, and even from Odds's wife and then Odds himself when released from the Kodiak hospital, made him out a hero, but it gave him no comfort. As with Jones Henry in the life raft, he'd failed to save.

The most sobering call came from Jody. They said little, just talked around it. "Take care. I love you," she said in conclusion, then added, "Your kids love you too."

Several first-timers to the roe fishery had ignored the barroom tales of trawl bags so plugged they could not be lifted. Joe Eberhardt barely escaped a disaster like that of the *Skagee* because his *Nestor* was a bigger boat with a stronger engine. It had taken him hours of maneuvering, however, to coax his overplugged trawl bag free of the bottom, while probably his best piece of luck had been a rip in the mesh that allowed some of the fish to escape and lighten the load. Two other boats of lesser capacity—also crewed by novices to the grounds—survived by cutting their cables to sacrifice nets, lines, cables, and trawl doors. All this gear now lodged on the bottom, snags that waited to rip or entangle other nets and lines.

Quickly Hank straightened the kinks in his fishing pattern. His routine wheelhouse challenge in trawling—to hold in mind a picture of unseen fish and opened net in motion, while above surface to tune both speed and the cables whose length determined the net's position—was complicated here by the storming abundance of fish. It was necessary to avoid setting on the solid strips of red when they filled the color screen, to act with trigger response or risk losing gear. He soon became adept at finding gaps or weak spots in the schools where he could slip in his net without engaging the full mass of fish. Arne and Joe learned to do the same. It was a whole different kind of fishing. Never before had they worked to avoid the thick of a potential harvest.

On the crew's part the routine was less pressured but steady. Although the fish they caught never came aboard but were transported by the bulging bagful directly to the joint-venture processor, the tows lasted only a short time. It required a steady shift of trawl bags, and consequent adjustment of supporting tackle. Each emptied bag towed back from the processor needed inspection. Rips and tears in the web were inevitable since vessels dragged nets close together.

Jace obviously knew his way around a deck and into the specialized Shelikof fishery. He even mended web faster and into cleaner meshes than Terry or Ham. Between sets he volunteered—although with an elaborate concern close to condescension—to coach Tom, whose fishing experience had seldom included nets. At least he now sensed Hank's intolerance of bullshit and had stopped pressing to become deck boss.

The deck routine involved a minimum of mess since fish did not come aboard, while steady netfuls clocked off the dollars. "But no fun a-*tall* when you never touch what you catch," grumped Terry, who seldom complained. Ham echoed with "Yeah." Tom Harris remained too fascinated by the sea's abundance and with learning new skills to be concerned. What most bothered all of them except Jace was the mass of gutted carcasses that soon floated everywhere. Wind dispersed only partially the stench of decay. "You don't waste food like that," Hank muttered. "What's wrong with those people?"

One day the net brought in a high tangle of line around a battered wire pot, evidently from king crabbing days at least five years before. They needed to bring it on deck to clear the net. Everyone gathered. The thing dripped slime and sea growth. Small creatures slithered from within. Big whitened shells inside attested to crabs caught that never escaped since the pot, after being lost, had evidently continued to fish.

A lump of black mud in the pot stirred, and out crawled a king crab. Its carapace, luminously purple, was as wide as a dessert plate. The thick claws on its meaty legs snapped sluggishly. Ham ran for his camera. Tom Harris sucked in his breath and began to mutter that all the tales were true and he'd never believed it. Terry knelt to watch its movements with a kind of reverence, and murmured, "Oh, wasn't that the days!" Hank stared with the rest. The creature had the beauty of things lost. The thousands of these we caught, he mused. All the years before they disappeared, whether overfished or moved off by Nature.

"The cookpot for you, baby." Jace started to grab the tubelike legs.

Terry gripped his arm with a strength that nearly threw Jace off balance. "Hurt him and you go in the pot too."

Jace turned indignantly to Hank, but Hank had leaned down to the crab to croon, "Thanks for calling. Go back home when it suits you. Meanwhile, we'll just enjoy your pretty face."

On a relatively calm afternoon Hank lowered the life raft again and, with Terry, motored over to the Japanese processor ship. The captain received them politely, but asked with concern, "Have not stopped fishing?"

"No, no," assured Hank. "Crew still fishing fishing."

The vessel, more than twice the length of their own, had the usual metallic and carbolic smells of a fish factory. Nothing aboard was unusual for a floating processor. A conveyor belt on the enclosed center deck carried fish from a delivery bin to a table lined by workers. Another belt transported the finished product to containers where others packed it for freezing. But the waste was startling. A man in rubber coveralls stood in the delivery bin up to his thighs. His hands flew, throwing female pollack onto the belt but tossing males to deck. With impersonal efficiency the men at the table slit open the females bulging with egg sacks, cut out the pink flopping planks of roe, then threw down the remaining bodies. Another worker with a pressure hose flushed the mass of females—their guts tumbled from their bellies—through the scuppers along with the discarded whole males.

"That's good fish," Hank told the captain. He made a gesture of eating. "Food. Food. No good to throw away."

The captain shrugged. "Eggs precious. Porrack-fish cheap."

Hank felt a flare of resentment. He was being hired to waste the fish of his country after fighting to save them, in order to pump up a Japanese luxury market.

Back aboard his own boat, Hank groused over the radio with fellow Americans. "We don't need another damn fish law," he said, "but I'd endorse one to stop that waste."

The comment of one voice spoke for the majority. "Too bad. Those fish are stormin' in like raindrops and their meat's not worth shit compared to the eggs. Plenty more where they came from."

"All the foreigners waste our fish," grumbled the voice of Gus Rosvic. "Why not? It ain't their own."

"Heyyy, Gus," said another voice. "Who you plan to shoot today?"

"Why, I suppose any fellow runs over my gear, Luke. You feeling brave?" Luke laughed.

Somebody else noted that there was talk back in Kodiak of setting up a shore plant to process the pollack carcasses into fish paste for *surimi*. "But that's Jap food and the Japs are making enough paste of their own in other places, so people say no way they'll buy ours."

From Luke, "One problem for the foreigners, in case you don't know it, is something I read in *National Fisherman*. Our dollar's strong the way it should be. So Japs and Europeans can't afford to buy our stuff anyhow."

"Don't let 'em suck you in, Hank," added Gus. "They'll always have their excuse."

"So just grab your share, man," concluded the first voice, "and stop bitching."

Spawning pollack continued to thicken the water. Sometimes the surface boiled and swirled from the intensity of the fish driving below. They migrated and the boats followed, up the wide Shelikof Strait hemmed by mainland mountains to the west and the high wooded foothills of Kodiak Island to the east.

The snow peaks on the mainland varied from volcanic cones still puffing seventy years after their last eruption, to canyons and sheer faces where centuries of weather had scooped out the rock. Each man responded to them differently. They held Terry's gaze when he wasn't working. "Gotten to be almost friends, those hills, always there," he mused. Tom Harris regarded them with simple wonder. "On Chesapeake it's nice enough flat which lets you see good if the weather's clear," he assured himself, "But this! Oh my." Ham's judgment was indifferent: "They're real pretty, I guess." And from Jace, "Too cold for this puppy, thanks." Hank's eye traveled the ridges often. They had a terrible beauty that had joined itself to his own history more than once, and he never tired of watching them.

Whatever demons that had been stirred in Hank by the *Skagee* rescue and deaths receded under the routines of fishing. The fleet now worked its nets abeam the very bay, Puale, where he'd married Jody when his boat and Jones Henry's had rushed for shelter from an ice storm. He gazed at the half-hidden opening in the mountains that led into Puale Bay: an uneasy anchorage that offered rocky bottom and only limited protection from gales along a hostile coast.

What would it be like, he daydreamed, to own several fishing boats all churning out a percentage into his pocket? The Japanese could do this for him and no others. Now that he'd straightened it out with the Tsurifune team, he knew what to expect. They just needed to be faced down now and then. He'd make money for all kinds of independence. Buy Jody anything she wanted, send the kids to any school, impress Dad and make him proud. The Japanese were good people after all. He'd absorbed their culture, enjoyed their hospitality, and felt comfortable with them. Liked them!

Hank talked daily to Seth who was aboard the *Puale Bay,* fishing black cod in the gulf. Since the start of the new black cod season the ship had delivered ashore in Kodiak rather than to a Japanese freezer ship. It apparently made for a happier crew all around since they no longer put in months at sea without a break. "Pulling fish, pulling fish," was Seth's usual report. The prospect of marriage had made him more relaxed, even talkative, than he'd been for years past. "Shitty kind of weather you'd expect for winters here. Guys at the rail stay wet all the time."

Eventually Hank broached the subject of Kodama, cautiously, since they were on the air for anybody to hear. "Could be worse," Seth said. "Since our understanding. Kodo tried his ordering-about shit with me first day out, and I yelled him off my bridge. Shook him up. Funny how Japs fold when you yell at them. Kodo gets it now. He runs the fish pack is all. Totals up the catch log and delivers it. The rest is mine. And Mo's my man for deck boss. That's what we settled."

Seth and Kodama had also reached another understanding. "I mean," Seth continued, "what's the use being a fisherman if you never get, like . . .

wet? Some people, it's just the money, but for me, I want the buzz. And Kodo, he's a person anyhow wants to be in charge. Turns out he can handle a boat. He can ease up to a marker buoy with us pitching all-hell, then hold the side against the line coming in, all that. So each day, maybe twice, he goes to wheelhouse and me to deck. We switch places."

"Makes sense. Good!"

"I guess I've got to admit it," Seth continued. "Ol' Kodo ain't so bad. Get this. He says, once we get ashore, he'll teach me judo. I said let's start now, man, but he says too dangerous on a boat jumpin' the way we are out here."

Hank smiled to himself at the drubbing in store for Seth when they reached a mat. "You'll enjoy it."

"I just hope I don't hurt him if we get tangled. I'm a lot bigger."

"He'll manage."

February wore on, mostly in bitter cold. Southwest winds continued to prevail, building steady swells from the open Pacific Ocean. The wave pattern from crest to crest made for rough pitching aboard former Bering Sea crabbers with lengths more than a hundred feet like *Jody Dawn*. The former shrimpers from Kodiak fared better since their length, in the seventy–eighty-foot range, fitted the period of the swells. In compensation, the larger boats could stay longer on the grounds before refueling from their mother ships.

One bright afternoon, the wind had calmed to little more than puffs, and swells had leveled out. The temperature held frigid, but sun sparkled on choppy water with an intensity that required sunglasses. The tow was under control. Tom came to the warm wheelhouse, as he often did between jobs, to admire the scenery. He handed Hank a mug of fresh coffee, and pointed to the holder with spare binoculars. "You mind, Boss?"

"Help yourself." Tom had adopted Terry's and Ham's term rather than calling him by name. Hank did not object. While he had never told his crewmen to call him "Boss"—it had just happened—he'd spent enough time as a navy officer to be comfortable with an automatic recognition of authority. It kept things clear when commands became necessary.

Tom pointed to the charts, asked permission again, and unfolded the one for Shelikof Strait. He had set himself the task of recognizing all the bays and mountains within sight. He seldom spoke more than a few words at a time, but his eyes were always alert. Hank knew that Tom had seen parts of the world even though he'd clamped shut at mention of his Vietnam service, but the man's wonder seemed that of one who'd never left his own backyard. Tom now focused on the mountains ridging the mainland a few miles away. They rose like white buttresses, their shadows blue, rock edges jutting through the snow as precise as etched lines. "Looks just like vanilla ice cream," Tom volunteered. "It's honey syrup in Alaska, everything, bad weather and all."

Two large birds glided through the air like children's kites, holding a steady course, then changing with a flip. "Oh my soul," Tom breathed. "So those are eagles. Look how easy they fly!" Hank watched him peer at the birds with all his body, his large, capable hands clutching the glasses like a precious object, his mouth opened in an excitement that sent creases along his cheeks. Tom's voice turned husky. "Wish every day for the rest of my life I could be here, like this."

"Then stay here, Tom."

"You think it's possible?" Suddenly Tom became excited. "When I was a kid going to be drafted and joined the Marines," he started, "I didn't look to right nor left. Never left camp down to Quantico. Thought home was the only place worth knowing. Got shipped to that terrible jungle and knowed soon enough I had no use for nothing but back home. Thought, when . . ." He looked away. "When certain things happened over there, thought I'd never see home again. Then there was hospital, and discharge. Done my duty and gone straight home, neither night spent nowhere's else." He faced Hank again. "Only then, when I got back and closed the door, went back to oyster and crab with Daddy, did I realize that I'd been around the world but never looked out the window."

Hank nodded, but had nothing to say. Tom just stood, and the words continued to pour.

"Then that day you come out tonging with us on the bay, I saw there could be some right kind of people from places I'd wondered about all along, like Alaska. Saw how I'd let it all pass me by. When you called, Hank, and said come up for a time to work on your boat, there was never a thing could have stopped me. I went straight to pack. Daddy saw it and knew. He didn't try no more to stop me than to kick at the moon, even though he knew he couldn't fish his boat no more alone. Said good-bye even sadder than when he saw me off to war, I think." Tom turned away quickly, with tears in his eyes. "I think he knowed I wouldn't come back more except to visit."

Hank was moved himself. The invitation had been for merely the two or three months of roe pollack, a return gesture for hospitality. But, he

decided, I'll find a place for Tom on one of my boats even if I put somebody else ashore.

One day when Seth called, his tone had changed. "Yeah, pulling fish
pulling fish like always," he uttered, then asked sharply, "You ever take
the time to count what comes aboard here fish by fish?" When Hank
asked if there was a problem, Seth declared, "Better not be!"

On the following day Seth's voice had darkened further. "Your buddy.
Not naming names. You looked him over before you brought him aboard,
didn't you?"

"Assuming you mean somebody good with judo? Yes."

"That ain't the only thing some people might be good with. Not saying
anything more till we get ashore to deliver."

The restrictions of open radio, even on their privately arranged frequency, kept Hank from questioning him more. He hoped that Seth and
Kodama had merely locked horns again.

A few days later, Jody spoke to him from Kodiak. Her tone troubled
Hank at once. "Last night Seth brought the ship in town to deliver. He
has something on his mind."

Hank tried to sound casual. "More than on his mind, I guess, if
Kodama gave him a judo lesson."

"Well, I wish it was a joke. There's a tender coming out there this afternoon." She named its skipper, an old friend. "He's agreed to put me on
the factory ship you're delivering to if they can't find your boat."

Hank tried to dissuade her because of the rough water. "If Seth and
somebody had a tiff, let's just talk about it, and if anybody overhears that's
tough." But the thought of seeing Jody . . . And when did Jody mind
rough water?

The tender delivered her to the side of the *Jody Dawn*. The rails of the
two boats, riding different parts of the same surge, rose and fell in opposing directions. Hank called for Jody to stay while he negotiated the rails to
join her on the tender, but instead she took a bold leap and landed in his
arms laughing. Hank hugged her with relief while the men on both vessels, standing by, cheered.

Terry called from the wheelhouse. "Boss, the captain of the *Maru* we
deliver to just called on radio. Said something like, 'Captain and Madam
Captain please do honor come to dinner.' That's the funny way he said it.
I guess they were watching just now when Jody jumped aboard."

Hank turned to Jody. "Probably serve us fancy Japanese food. When they do hospitality they really do it. Put you in a float suit for the trip over." She shook her head so firmly that he called back to Terry. "Say thanks and some other time. Say weather's too rough and Madam Captain's tired."

Soon after, Terry reported that the captain said they'd lift madam in a basket very safely. Hank called up another refusal.

In his cabin, while she dried off, Jody came to the point at once. "Seth's found out something beyond what he thinks he can handle." He had followed Hank's advice from Baltimore to check everything, and had begun to watch Kodama's catch reports. He'd enlisted Mo, who as deck boss was on site most of the time, and they took turns secretly counting every fish that came aboard. Kodama's log at the end of the day came short of their count by more than three hundred fish. The next day it was the same. Seth then slipped into the freezer, and counted the fish tray by tray. There were at least five thousand pounds of fish more than the catch log showed. "Did you ever do that kind of checking, Hank?"

Hank forced himself to remain calm. "I never needed to. There's been some mistake."

"Seth then confronted Kodama. Your Japanese friend pretended not to understand English all of a sudden."

"He got flustered. You know how Seth can come at you."

"Listen to me, Hank. Your friend finally broke down and started beating himself on the head. Then, Seth said, he began to wail and grind his teeth like one of those Kabuki actors you've told me about. Seth said that for a minute he was scared for his own safety. You know that's not like Seth."

Hank turned away. Swede's warning! He should have pursued doubts of Kodama himself. "Sonofabitch! Where's Kodama now?"

"Still shut in his cabin when I left. After Seth told me all this I went down to talk to him, although I had no idea what I'd say. If he's been cheating you all this time, what *could* I say? But not even a sound when I spoke and knocked on the door."

Seth had read of disgraced Japanese committing hari-kiri, so they decided finally to break the lock. Kodama was sitting motionless with his head in his hands.

Hank sat on the bunk and rubbed his own head. "I brought him over as my friend. I trusted him. He'd look me in the eye." He felt desolate, but tried to think it through. "Kodama wouldn't have done it alone."

"I don't think so either."

"Two months ago in Anchorage old man Tsurifune looked at me straight and said they had no part in the cheating I'd heard about. I trusted him. I've thought they were all good people. I've defended them. Bastards!"

Jody's hand kneaded his tense shoulder. "I know, I know."

"What am I going to do? They have me."

Jody sat beside him. Neither spoke for a while.

"If he's doing this to me he's doing it all over. He's screwing Tolly. And both our crews. He's trying to screw all the Americans trying to fish quota—Gus, everybody. Now that I know, I'm part of it."

"I think we both know what you have to do, Hank."

"If I blow the whistle on Tsurifune . . . That could mean the end of owning *Puale Bay* . . . or any other big longliner in the future. And he still has my *Jody Dawn* that we're aboard right here. Look, now I think about it, there's probably some mistake. Seth's a damn hothead."

Jody said nothing.

"Where could I ever find money somewhere else to buy back my *Jody Dawn?* At best I haven't paid off half to the bank, since we had only two good crab years before crab went bust."

At last she said quietly, "We'll have to manage."

"Oh, shit."

Terry knocked on the door. "That tug they call a Kawasaki boat that takes our fish to the *Maru?* It's just come over. The guy aboard, I think he's the first mate, says it's urgent you come over, Boss."

Hank started out. "I'll tell the guy to go to hell myself. I'm not talking to any damn Japs tonight."

Jody restrained him. "See what they have to say."

Hank slipped into float coveralls for the ride over. He said nothing to the mate beyond an acknowledgment. At the high hull of the ship he refused the lowered basket in favor of a jump to the Jacob's ladder and a long climb. The captain stood on deck with a smiling bow. He expressed sorrow that madam could not come, and asked Hank please to come to the wardroom for friendly dinner.

Hank knew that he was breaking all rules of Japanese etiquette, but he said curtly, "No dinner, no beer, no sake. Just tell me what's urgent, please."

The captain led the way to the ship's radio room, and snapped a command to the man on duty. The radioman immediately punched signals, spoke in Japanese, then handed Hank a phone. "Special new technology," said the captain, and pulled out a chair for Hank. "Japan. Special secure call, all private. You shall hear Director Tsurifune in self, perhaps! Please." He waved the radioman out of the room and left himself.

Instead, it was the smooth voice of Tsurifune the younger. "Hank! How are you? Is it raining? Rough weather there, eh?"

"What's up, Mike? Let's get to the point."

"Well then, Hank. Father and I have heard disturbing news. It probably comes with having subordinate O'Malley in charge of your vessel. The man seems to have a strange notion. You and I can have a chuckle over this once it's explained."

"Explain it, then."

"This subordinate has a fantasy, that our man Kodama was not reporting all fish that came aboard. This is of course a distressing accusation."

"Cut the bullshit, Mike. We caught you underlogging, and cheating us."

There was enough of a pause that Hank thought they had been disconnected. "Well now, Hank. If there was any misunderstanding, we'll certainly make it up to you. After all, friends stick together. In order to keep everybody happy, Father and I've instructed our man Kodama to return home to enjoy his family for a while. Coming to replace is an excellent production master, Mr. Hoshi Tamukai, former high-seas fisherman, very honest and capable. If this Kodama has made error, we surely regret and will see that you don't lose by it. So let's just have a friendly laugh over misunderstanding, and keep producing."

The radio room was hot. Hank still wore his float coveralls. He stood and peeled down the thick arms while collecting his thoughts. Buy the lie? he debated with himself. Because lie it was, he was now certain.

"Are you still there, Hank?"

"Just wondering, Mike, what threat you or your dad made to poor Kodama, to force a man with that much honor to cheat. We have proof he cheated, and I'm convinced he didn't do it on his own. And if—"

"All right, Hank. We'll make you glad that you've forgotten this foolishness. To apologize for misunderstanding among friends—friends who take care of each other, Hank—we'll be foolishly generous and credit you double profit for all sablefish since you began to fish for us and until the debt on your vessel *Jody Dawn* is paid."

"And if you're doing it to me, you're cheating every other American you've made deals with, and by default other American fishermen out there competing against you."

"Did you hear me, Hank? Double profit. And, Father will question my generosity, but . . . forty thousand dollars more against your debt to us, registered at once to our Seattle bank. I think we shall also give your overzealous subordinate O'Malley, say, five thousand dollars cash to help him realize the mistake he's made. You have a great future with us, Hank. Produce well, and one day you'll own longline vessel *Puale Bay*, then another, then vessels vessels and be rich!"

Hank was sweating. He mopped his sleeve over his face again and again.

"As long as we're having a laugh over it, Hank, let me outline what would happen if Father suddenly decided that you were a poor producer and not a friend. Our bank would be forced to call in everything. For the sake of argument, let's consider your vessel *Jody Dawn*. The shipyard price was what? One million five hundred ninety dollars I believe. Through hard work, which all admire, you'd paid off, say, thirty-seven, percent plus interest to the bank that loaned you the money before we assumed the loan. Since then, through earnings with us, we'll say that you've paid another ten percent, give or take after accumulated interest. Do you follow, Hank?"

"I follow."

"Unfortunately, since the collapse of king crab, and consider also aging, this vessel is no longer worth as much as your bank paid for it. Many such vessels are rusting idle and worthless. If we were forced to foreclose and auction the vessel, it would go for less. Let's be optimistic and say that with good luck we'd realize one million one hundred thousand. Our fifty-three percent ownership would still come from purchase price on which we assumed the loan, not auction price. Let me calculate here. We'd need to claim eight hundred forty-three thousand, plus a few more for interest, leaving you about two hundred fifty thousand of the nearly seven hundred fifty you've invested. Enough still to buy a nice, little boat, I expect."

Hank closed his eyes and swayed in the heat.

"But, suppose the vessel brought merely nine hundred thousand at auction—disaster! Then you would only receive back, oh dear, let me check that again to make sure. Yes, you'd receive back only fifty-eight thousand dollars, at personal loss to you—let's not even talk about it please, too distressing. All those years of work. Surely not enough to buy a new vessel much beyond a rowboat, eh? And remember, it might take a year or two even to reach auction before you received a penny, while meantime you'd have no vessel to earn with. And then there's your home, your castle, as Americans like to put it."

"Wait! Our agreement took my house off the table."

"A gentleman's agreement among friends until signed by both parties. But when friends are no longer friends . . ."

"Your father had that lawyer Rider draw up a changed contract!"

"And he did. But when did you sign it? You had so many changes and questions on the copy we sent, that some lawyer of yours returned it. Such changes have taken long long to consider."

"Now I see that you wrote it wrong the first time on purpose."

After a pause Mike said, "Well, Hank, we're only being theoretical, so let's stop. Have a good night's sleep, and keep producing. It will all be fine among friends. Father sends cordial wishes, and looks forward to the occasion soon when we'll bring you back to Japan, perhaps with your beautiful wife."

When Hank emerged from the radio room where the captain had left him alone, the captain offered him warm sake and he accepted it. He allowed himself to be returned to the Kawasaki boat by basket, and jumped clumsily rail to rail back on his own boat. Back in the cabin he told Jody about the house, and wept on her lap. She patted his head.

By next morning he had pulled himself outwardly together. But he snapped and was irritable all day. When one of the tow lines tangled, he started berating Tom and Jace in the worst fashion of a screaming skipper. Tom looked up, startled. Jace scowled, and muttered that he knew the sort. The tender was to pick Jody back up late in the day. She watched Hank, worried, and wondered if she should go. They were eating glumly in the galley, when Terry on watch called down.

"Look astern, Boss. Skipper Lars radioed over, and so did Skipper Gus. Think you'd better look."

Hank hurried to the wheelhouse. Layers of haze hung around the mainland peaks to starboard and had obliterated the lower Kodiak hills to port. The thickest haze moved slowly upward. He checked his barometer. It fell as he watched. Nothing in the morning forecast had predicted different weather. But such wind as now breezed outside had altered direction. A change was in motion. "We're hauling in," he barked over the speaker.

Tom was the first to reach deck and had begun to undog the windlass by the time that the others appeared.

Hank radioed his partners. "Yah," said Lars, "that kind of fog here means maybe going to blow norderly. Rain for sure. But she's below freezing. If it's snow ve got no problem. Anyhow, I think I haul in too. See what happens." Joe Eberhardt said he was doing the same.

"I know the signs," said Gus when Hank called him. "It's ice coming sure. We've chopped lines and we're heading for a lee. Geographic Bay's best shelter but too far away unless she holds off. Take care yourself, Hank."

The tender that was to have picked up Jody was now delivering supplies miles from the *Jody Dawn,* and the captain decided to race for shelter while he could. "Sorry," he radioed. Jody sent an apologetic message via the cannery office to the friend who had picked up the kids from school, supposedly for just dinner with her own children. Then she went below to fix a meal before the storm broke, since Ham the cook would be staying busy on deck.

For days the wind and waves had come from the southern end of Shelikof Strait, where the sun still shone through a clear sky. Within an hour the wind shifted to blow nearly a reverse course. Gray clouds black in their deepest part moved from the north, covering everything in their wake. They slowly obliterated the highest of the snow peaks, although those to the south still glowed. The wind increased with the same dark thrust. It had raced around the compass blowing harder by the minute. The water began to build in long swells.

Hank had set his tow heading into then-prevailing wind and current. He now was committed to the same direction for haul-in while the altered forces pushed him from behind. The newly rising swells built higher, glistening dark green in the center. They chased the boat, surged up the stern ramp, splashed in the air, and blew over the men.

"Area Four-B," came a voice on the emergency channel. "Northwest gale warning from west sides Afognak and Kodiak Islands to the Shumagins including entire Shelikof Strait. Freezing winds predicted up to fifty knots. Small vessel alert. Icing may occur. It is recommended that all vessels in Shelikof Strait move to shelter."

"Fuckin' late warning," said Joe Eberhardt over the CB. "She's on us."

Waves suddenly started to race down the strait. Their tops dissolved into foam that blew off in strips of scud. A discharge of dead fish from the Japanese mother ship, which had floated away from them an hour before, now overtook them like a wall and started to wash up the ramp onto deck. Tom and Jace shoveled them back over the rail. Some of the fish hovered in the air and then blew back to deck. Hank saw in a glance that Tom managed two shovelfuls to the sobered drunk's one although the latter kept at it with an even pace.

Terry shouted up the cable markings as the warps wound in. He raised his face and the wind blew away his cap. The *Jody Dawn* still had a quarter mile of gear in the water. Hank altered course as much as he dared toward the mainland, but other boats were also hauling in while trying to do the same. Tangled lines would bind them all. Since wind and sea built in the same direction, however, the twin forces on boats with a tow pushed them down the waterway in a collective line.

A massive gust of spray plumed up the ramp. It dispersed against the cabin with a tinkle. "Oh shit, she's comin' ice," said a radio voice. As Hank watched, small crystals began to join in midair and hit the cabin. A shaft of sun sparkled the ice into rainbow colors. The rigging began to thicken, then the rails. Back on deck Ham slid, fell, and scrambled back up. "Watch your footing!" Hank shouted needlessly into the speaker. All the men now gripped handholds as they moved. Using gaffs as clubs they hit at the ice. Shards blew free from the wires. Some pieces scattered to sea, but others attached to the boat elsewhere.

At last the trawl doors surfaced and each bumped up the hull to its side of the boat. Ham and Tom skidded over deck to secure the one, and Terry with Jace the other. Spray lodged and glistened thickly on the flat metal and its chains even as they worked.

Their fat bag of fish now floated astern. As soon as it hit air the meshes began to whiten. "Terry!" Hank called over the speaker. "Attach a marker buoy if you can, but send it free. Now!" Terry waved assent. Soon Ham and Tom were sliding aft, each holding a buoy. Tom lashed one buoy to the bag's ground line. Ham threw the other, attached to an anchor, into the mesh. When they unshackled the bag it floated free. Dead gutted fish washed around it and froze to the sides. Quickly the part of the bag above surface became a white glazed hump.

With the boat freed of its tow Hank was able to set a course and maneuver around other vessels. "Everybody off deck," he commanded over the speaker as the boat heeled and entered a more violent pattern of motion. Jody called out that they'd better eat while they could so come get it, and brought him hamburgers in buns.

Hank chewed while he checked the chart, and tried to be casual. "What do you know. Puale Bay's the closest shelter."

"Not again!" she joked, and took his arm. But her grip was tight. The place reminded both of the decision they needed to face.

Hank broadcasted the destination to his partners and whoever else might be listening. "I've been in before. Follow me if anybody wants. Poor anchorage and maybe willies, unstable rocky bottom, but it's what we can reach. I remember a shelter from northers. I'm heading now toward that headland, Cape Aklek. It's covered with cloud where I sit, but you'll see it's a protrusion on radar."

The course took him across the swells. They lifted the boat and thumped it down, causing cascades of spray across the starboard rail. In seconds the spray had turned to ice.

Hank had faced extreme icing only twice before but enough to remember crew fatigue, and he called up Terry. "Pair off in two separate shifts to chip ice. Relieve each other every twenty minutes. But those gaffs won't do it. We've got axes in the engine room."

"Already brought 'em up."

"Tell Tom out there to hold on to something. He might not know."

"He's not the one worries me. It's Jace crawled into his bunk and says he won't come out till he sees dry land."

Hank swore to himself, and wondered how far he could act without committing a crime. He hoped that words would do it, and hardened his voice for emphasis. "Tell him I'll kick into his goddamn bones if I need to come down. I'll see that he never gets another berth anywhere. And ashore, he goes to court for mutiny."

Terry left slowly, impressed, trying to keep straight all parts of the message.

"Mutiny, that'll be a good one to try," said Jody, keeping it light. "Maybe I should talk to him."

"Just stay here with me!" Suddenly he was afraid for her. What if harm came to Jody? Or if they both went down and left three children ashore? The anger and uncertainty over the Tsurifune contract passed through his mind and out again. A relief, at least, to have an excuse to forget it for a while. He returned to his main concern.

Ice had begun to glaze the water. As the bow pushed through it an ominous sound arose like the crackling of glass. He drove with full power but they moved with increasing slowness. The smaller boats made way with even greater difficulty. Many had headed for the mother ships and were nestled around them like birds.

They passed Gus Rosvic's smaller *Thunder*. It had already begun to linger sluggishly to starboard on each roll while the crew beat on the ice with little effect. Hank stopped, backed the *Jody Dawn* into waves that pitched him high, and came alongside to windward. "Gus! Follow in my lee," he radioed. "Too bad you're driving that kiddie cart."

"Well, Hank," came the calm reply, "it's nice to know that tub of yours is good for something. I guess we'll take you up on that."

Terry appeared. He was bundled in thermal coveralls and oilskins. "It's funny, Boss. I didn't need to tell Jace those things. Tom, he went in, and come out of the cabin holding Jace by the collar like a dog or cat. Jace blubberin' he's got rights and he don't want to die, and Tom all quiet telling him to pull it together."

Hank was relieved but kept his voice even. "Make sure he does his share. Time to start chopping."

Terry waved his arm in good cheer. "Goin' out."

Their passage went slower and slower. Visibility closed down to a circle only a few feet around, and Hank needed to rely on radar. His lee was helping Gus Rosvic's crew cope with their ice. A big sheet dislodged and slipped off of the side it had been keeping unbalanced, and Gus's boat stabilized. They passed other boats in trouble. One joined the convoy in Gus's lee.

Suddenly cries rose from Hank's own boat. He tensed and looked back to see a prone figure on deck. At least not overboard. "Boss!" called Ham up the stairs. "Jace is hurt."

"A fuckup besides everything else," Hank muttered. Jody left to see what she could do. "Stay off deck," he called after her.

Jace's wails and curses echoed from the galley when they carried him in. "Big chunk of ice banged off on his leg," Terry reported. "It's already swelling or punched out or something. What do we do, Boss? I've sent Ham and Tom back out ahead of their time to keep chopping."

"Give him a damn rag to chew on. Wait. Take the helm." He fetched the boat's emergency kit from a locked drawer in his cabin. Indeed, when he hurried down to look, the man's leg beneath clothes and oilskins had a protrusion like a bone. Jody had propped his head with a pillow. She looked up anxiously. "Hang in there," Hank muttered, now concerned.

"Oh Jesus, Jesus! Do something! I'm gonna die!"

Hank opened the morphine container, glanced through the directions and cautions, called for water, and put one of the pills in the man's mouth. "Swallow now, you'll be okay." He decided to leave Jace on the galley deck rather than carry him to a bunk and risk his falling out if the boat rolled. (Better access to escape if ice sank them; don't think about it.)

Jody pulled blankets from bunks in the nearest cabin and wrapped them around Jace, then braced the leg with pillows, while Hank pondered what to do next. "Jody. You've got to steer us in, while I go on deck with Terry in this guy's place." She nodded.

"Don't leave me!" screamed Jace when they left.

It was already past time for Ham and Tom to come in for relief, but they remained on deck chopping ice. In the wheelhouse Hank checked radar and showed Jody the course. At least three miles farther before they could hope for shelter, and their speed had become a crawl. He pulled out thermals from his cabin and put them on. "Just keep that course, honey," he said, trying to be casual.

She gripped his arms and looked up into his face. "Be careful out there. I love you. And everything's going to be all right even if we leave the Japanese, however we do it."

He hugged her, then left quickly. Below in the galley he stepped around Jace—who watched him accusingly and whimpered as the drug took effect—and, with Terry, opened the door to the open deck.

Water hit his face like needles. He gasped at the cold after wheelhouse warmth, started toward the bundled figures of Ham and Tom, slipped, and fell. The tread on his boots gripped nothing. When he grabbed for support his gloves slicked on every handhold. Pull it together, he told himself, and prepared to joke about the fall if anybody had seen.

The ice was building highest to starboard where the wind and water hit broadside. Uneven weight had begun to slant the deck toward the water, so that a careless move could slide a man overboard. By the time Hank reached the others, shuffling now with bent knees to lower his center of gravity, he felt already winded. Ham and Tom both sweated with faces flushed and eyes watering. Ice drops hung from their eyebrows. He could see their fatigue after only minutes, already worse than that caused by normal rough hours on deck.

When Hank reached for the ax in Tom's hand, Tom insisted, "I'm still good out here, Boss—Hank. I'm good."

"No. It's a long haul. Take your rest."

"Been thinking, Boss," panted Ham. "Drive short big-head nails in our soles to grip this ice."

"Good idea. Go do it. Both of you." Ham asked about Jace. "We'll make shelter, then call Coast Guard. Leave him where he is. Save your energy for this. Go."

Ice had smoothed but enlarged every object. The coated metal glowed darkly under deck lights. Terry and he agreed on separate places to chop. Alone, he hadn't expected to feel at once so vulnerable. Bulky shapes enclosed him as never before when he was looking down from a heated wheelhouse. A strange cottony wet in the air penetrated his nostrils and mouth with the substance of smoke. The slick underfoot required uncertain balances. A sea crashed over the rail against his back. It sent a shatter of pellets that clung everywhere, dripped for an instant, then froze, adding new ice.

He wrapped one leg around a support rail and pounded on one of the drumheads where ice had accumulated like a frozen waterfall. Down went the ax edge but it glanced off, nearly cutting him. Ice already firm. He drove harder and penetrated to metal, then drove into another point inches away and twisted. Off fell a chunk. It tried to bond to the slick deck even as he kicked it overboard. New ice had meanwhile formed on the flat ax head and the top of his gloves.

Drops pinged against his oilskins and attached. The sleeves had turned so stiff that they crackled when he swung. A few more strokes, and he was short of breath while sweat poured over his face and froze.

He stopped panting to look for the next place to attack, and felt the silence. Ice coating the shrouds had dampened even the sound of the wind, which now blew at a steady shriek that sounded distant. Even the smash of his ax was muffled. Out over the dark water, inside the circle of visibility, white birds swooped, carelessly at home. He shuddered. Only he intruded and, washed overboard, the silence would suck him in. Suddenly it hit him. My life is short and threatened, he thought. But whatever I decide makes no difference here: all this continues on. In twenty years who's going to care what I do about a few catch reports? I need to chip ice here to survive Nature, but then I need to survive in my own world of men.

He called for Terry to help with ice on the hatch, and gladly watched the solidly real yellow–oilskinned figure duck-walk toward him. With action he'd no need to think. "You at one side, me at the other, maybe we can cut loose a big one." They chopped energetically and dislodged a long heavy slab. Upended over the rail, it hit the water with a splash that sent up new spray to freeze on their faces.

When the relief shift reappeared after the agreed-upon twenty minutes, Hank took a few more swipes to prove he was okay, then gladly handed Tom the ax. He was panting and dizzy.

Back in the warm galley he slumped, a man once easy with multihour shifts horsing thousand-pound crab pots, now with hands shaking. Despite the heat close to the stove he still felt the ice in his lungs. And by his own decree he'd soon be back out in it. With an effort he picked up the nails and hammer left by Ham on the table, and raised one of his boots.

Jace, blanketed on deck, watched him with glassy, sullen eyes. "You don't care nothing for a fellow human being. Leave me to die is all you care. Think I don't hurt? Goin' to tell the newspapers." He began to whimper. Hank gave him another morphine pill and offered him a candy bar, but said nothing. He himself chewed candy, hoping for energy, then climbed to the wheelhouse for a quick check on Jody and a forced joke to reassure her, before going back into the ice.

At last they reached the safety of Puale Bay. It had already turned a black dark at four in the afternoon so that only radar told Hank where they were. Gus thanked him with a barrage of insults, and Hank, holding tight to support his shaking fatigue, bantered back. Then he picked his way, referring to charts, *Coast Pilot*, and memory, to the uneasy shelter against northwesterlies that he remembered from a decade before.

By now he had radioed the Coast Guard Air Station to report his injured man. "Is life in danger?" was the first question.

"A compound fracture, I think. The guy's in real pain."

"We can't risk a chopper in this kind of storm unless it's life-threat. Our vessels are on site in your vicinity but we've got boats sinking. Maybe later you can rendezvous with one. Meanwhile, connect you with a doc for advice."

Hank had planned to reach shelter and anchor, but the anchor windlass on the bow had become a solid sculpture. Ludicrously, gutted fish were embedded in the glaze. It would take pounding to free it to the gears, energy none of them had left, so he decided to set watches for the night. Jody said without hesitation, "You guys sleep. I've got it." Gus Rosvic's boat hovered nearby, kept underway also with a frozen anchor.

First, Hank splinted Jace's leg, coached by radio from the Kodiak hospital. Jody tried to soothe Jace with his head in her lap, while Jace let them know, moving in and out of his pain, that none of them cared a fuck what happened to a shipmate. The fatigued Tom chose to sit with him all night.

At two in the morning with the storm still roaring, they left sleep and shelter to meet a Coast Guard cutter back at the mouth of the bay. On the way, a gusting williwaw tore at the boat and heeled it thirty degrees. At least the sudden maverick wind knocked loose some ice. They transferred Jace, who cursed them and screamed at each jiggle of the stretcher.

Jody stood with Hank on deck. The wind wailed across mountaintops above them. She took his arm. "Our biggest decisions seem to come in this wild place. Are you ready to face it?"

"We could let it ride for a few more days," he ventured.

"The more you do that the more you're part of it."

"I know. I know." He knew that pretending it didn't exist cheated the entire fishing community that he'd made his own. My dad with his talk of honor, he wondered. Had he ever faced such a decision? "We may be hurt."

"I'll live with you either way, Hank."

Without pondering it further Hank climbed aboard the Coast Guard ship, asked for the officer in charge of fishing boat inspection, and reported possible logging irregularities aboard the Japanese black cod fleet, including his own jointly held longliner in the gulf. When he returned, he and Jody hugged each other silently.

"Poor Jace," said Ham while they returned to shelter. "He don't have many friends, he once told me."

Terry shrugged. "Wonder why."

Tom laughed with uncharacteristic harsh energy. "There's always one like him. Chesapeake Bay, anywhere's, even . . ." He paused, then said it. "Even 'Nam especially. Fellow who works real hard when it suits him. Maybe even knows things, but not how much as he thinks. And the world's always against him."

"Then why'd you lose your sleep over him?" asked Terry.

"Because I was the one kicked him back on deck where he got hurt. But I've seen 'em before. Even how they's the ones always gets hurt."

By the time they returned to shelter their fatigue had lifted. Even though it was now three in the morning they decided to free the anchor windlass. Jody cheered them on from the wheelhouse window. Walking firmly in nailed boots they all slipped around to the bow together, Hank among them, and with shouts almost gleeful pounded the ice until piece by piece it broke apart.

The anchor rattled down. Hank flipped on the anchor lights, then hailed the watch on Gus Rosvic's boat. Gus woke, and brought the *Thunder* to tie alongside. Both crews gathered in the *Jody Dawn*'s galley. They were all sleepy but too charged and bonded by their experience to disperse.

Hank, with action taken, felt both relaxed and numb. The decision had passed to others. He put his arm around Jody's waist and she squeezed his hand.

"Too bad we didn't each give ol' Jace a good-bye kiss and drink his breath," sighed Terry. "I could sure use one."

Ham went into the cabin left by Jace and came back grinning with a pint of whiskey. "When I packed together his things, this fell out. Must've forgot he had it."

"Yaaay!" cried Terry. "You old thief."

"No. He'd've drunk it if I'd told him. And with that pain stuff Boss gave him, it might have made him sick."

After a silence Tom ventured, "Wouldn't hurt us now."

"Sure wouldn't," said Zack of the *Thunder.*

Jody laughed as both crews turned to their skippers. The two had strict rules against booze on board. Hank and Gus exchanged looks. Gus's lined face remained set, but his eyebrow flicked and he made no objection. "Well," Hank reasoned aloud, keeping it serious, "A pint among this bunch . . ." He turned to Ham. "You found it. Take your swig, then pass it around."

The whiskey wasn't best quality, but it warmed and comforted. An hour later, with the bottle emptied, both crews were back in their bunks asleep.

25

FISH HOLD

SHELIKOF STRAIT, FEBRUARY 1984

"Well, now," bantered Gus Rosvic next afternoon by radio. "I can't say much about a man needs to bring his wife along to teach him how to fish." The two boats had separated after Gus's men freed their windlass, and now both crews knocked off the remaining ice from the storm.

"Too bad," Hank replied. "Jody here says you'd know twice as much today if you'd ever brought your lady along." Jody beside him in the wheelhouse raised an eyebrow and handed him a piece of an apple she was slicing.

Outside the wind still blew, and occasionally it screamed down the mountains in sudden williwaws. Several other boats had also entered the bay. With erratic winds, and a rocky bottom an anchor could slip on, each needed to maintain a wide swinging circle from the others, but they were safe at anchor as long as their watches stayed alert.

All radio talk had been sober on the morning after the Coast Guard reported three boats rolled over, top-heavy with ice, and two men lost on one of them. More vessels would probably have gone down if they had not crowded into the lees of the large mother ships, as did Hank's fishing partners Joe and Lars. When Hank and Gus received news of the disasters they gave it the gravity it deserved, but hours had now passed; it might be days before fishing could safely resume, and their CB talk had turned casual.

"Well, Hank," Gus continued, "I've got no problem with all your lady teaches you. Hello, Jody, if you're listening. But I never did get straight who else gives you the word. Jody! Tell the old man maybe he'd better look over his buddies in Tokyo and figure where their knives is hid. I've got sources in some back-door places and they ain't always accurate, but . . . Seems two years ago—that's how long it takes the bureaucrats in Washington to get their minds together—two years ago the Coast Guard boarded a Jap trawler in the Bering and found some papers they'd hid. All of it written in Jap, if you know what I mean. I guess that way they figured nobody would notice."

Hank tensed, but said mildly, "That's their language, Gus. How else would they write it?"

"See what I mean, Hank? You can't help being on their side, son. Now Jody or me, we'd have found somebody in two days to translate them papers and find what they said. Two years later our bureaucrats, they're still figuring it out."

"Planning another Pearl Harbor, were they?" said an easy third voice. It showed that others at anchor were listening.

"Just as sneaky, Ralph! I heard it was instructions clear as a Boy Scout handbook, a do-it-yourself on how to trick the observers and inspectors, so to catch and hide twice what they reported."

"Sorry to hear that," said Ralph. "I've done pretty good with Japs. They bargain slick but keep their word."

"Ah so ah so," mocked another voice. "Fu Manchu velly smart, watch out."

Jody looked at Hank's face in turmoil, and took the microphone from his hand. "Gus, you rumormonger! I'll bet if the man in the moon whispered in your ear that foreigners had six toes you'd call it around."

"Now Jody, it's just what I heard."

Three days later the Shelikof roe pollack fishery resumed in such glowing clear weather that ice became a nightmare forgotten. A tender returned Jody to town at last. She and Hank had talked around and around his declaration to the Coast Guard. At the pace that bureaucrats acted—Gus was right on that—any consequence would probably be long down the road. Having taken action, Hank's anger subsided to a calm burn. What to do about Kodama? What to tell Seth? How to face old Tsurifune and son after their treachery? It had been difficult to reach anyone by radio since the closed-in mountains blocked clear reception (although boat talk somewhere off Hawaii came in clear). Seth had not answered Hank's static-laced calls to the ship. Swede was away in Seattle, and John Gains was in Japan. Hank might have tried to reach others for news, but he wanted to keep his concerns private.

Back in town, when the tender Jody rode passed the cannery piers, Jody saw the *Puale Bay* still moored at Pacific Future. After thanking her host when they moored two canneries down the line, she walked to it and climbed aboard. The ship was deserted except for a uniformed marshal who sat in the galley with a civilian poring over papers. "You'll have to get off, ma'am. Can't talk, I'm sorry," he said.

Tensely Jody hurried across the pier, through the processing lines, and upstairs to the desks. She passed John Gains coming from his private office. He carried a heavy taped box in his arms. Sweat plastered his loose black hair. "Thought you were in Japan," she said.

"Back last night." He appeared uneasy and looked away. "Hold that gate for me? Thanks." She started to ask questions but he was gone.

Swede's office was adjacent to Gains's, each protected from casual visitors by a roomful of desks occupied by a manager and several clerks. A suitcase blocked half of Swede's doorway as if it had just been dropped. Swede stood by his desk leafing intently through a handful of papers. He looked up and motioned her in. "Just got here. What the hell's happened?"

The office manager trailed in, a nervous clerk type who declared, thank God the people in charge had finally come back. "Now you can deal with those government men who came yesterday and took over the *Puale Bay* out there!" He said that for two days he'd been fielding instructions from Japan, some for actions beyond his authority. Shoji Tsurifune had called personally to order the *Puale Bay* kept in port until Kodama's replacement arrived, and had authorized Kodama's immediate return to Japan.

" 'Whether the fellow wants to come or not!' is how he put it about Kodama," said the manager. "But that poor guy didn't object. He's barely eaten or spoken, just sits back here in the storage room with his bags packed. No plane seat was available until this afternoon. Then this morning when I opened up, Mr. Gains's office was locked and somebody bumping around inside. I called security, but it was Mr. Gains himself. He was supposed to be in Hokkaido for another week."

In addition, the manager continued, a Seattle bank had been calling to speak to Hank. Also today two registered letters with signatures required had arrived for Henry and Judith Crawford.

"Where's Seth O'Malley?" asked Jody.

The manager didn't know. "Last I saw him yesterday he was cussing so loud around the ladies in the office I told him take it outside, and he left, but I didn't mean for him to disappear. That was after the marshals went down to the ship, though they wouldn't tell me anything."

Jody accepted the letters and opened them while Swede eased out the office manager and closed the door. Both letters were from the Seattle bank with which Hank had contracted to the Japanese. One gave notice of foreclosure on their house, the other of repossessing the *Jody Dawn*.

For the first time since she had left on the tender to tell Hank of Seth's accusation, Jody was frightened. She told Swede all that had happened.

He was silent for a while, then muttered, "This is the other side of the Tsurifunes." He paced the office, then sat at his desk. "We might have patched this up somehow if Hank had held his fire. I'd been trying to warn him."

"We decided together," said Jody firmly. "We decided to stay honest."

Swede opened the drawer that was known to contain a bottle, considered, then closed it again. "You two never learned to maneuver. When you put the Federals onto something, they'll either ignore you or tear you apart. Unfortunately, the Commerce Department's suddenly gunning for proof of foreign cheats. Fishermen are pushing their congressmen to end the foreign quotas and Commerce needs ammunition. State Department won't get tough on quota negotiations without ammunition. Hank's set off firecrackers at the least, maybe a bomb."

Swede had only just arrived from the Seattle-Anchorage flight. When he heard that John Gains was back, he went out to find him. One of the clerks said that Mr. Gains had left with three or four big boxes he'd packed and carried out by himself, and his station wagon was gone.

Jody decided to see Kodama even though his betrayal had injured them. She found him in a back storage room, seated in the center on a straight-backed chair surrounded by his luggage. His tightly clasped hands rested on legs parallel in front of him. His eyes in a face turned lean looked sternly ahead at nothing. "Why did you do it?" she demanded.

"Having duty, madam."

"And what does it get you back in Japan? A medal?"

"No, Madam."

"Oh, Kodama. Hank trusted you!"

His mouth worked but he said nothing.

She thought of his shy pleasure at each new thing American however small, and his fond gentleness toward Pete. "Have you eaten?" she asked less sharply.

"Not necessary."

"Come on. We'll go get a hamburger."

He shook his head and continued to stare.

"What can I bring you, then?"

Kodama shook his head again.

She strode around to face him, so that his eyes had no choice but to focus on her. "Tell me straight. Did somebody force you to change the catch logs, or was it your own idea?"

His expression of raw anguish startled her, but all he repeated was, "Having duty, madam."

Jody left him, shaken herself.

She phoned Madge. Her friend said, "Oh, your kids are fine. They've gone with mine to Jebby Stevens's birthday party so they wouldn't welcome your coming for them yet. Make it for dinner, just meatloaf, and tell us all about the storm." Jody agreed with lively cheer, even though she wanted with sudden desperation to hold her children one by one.

When she returned to the open area of desks, Swede was speaking to three clerks in a low voice. The women were tense. The adjacent door to John Gains's office stood open, guarded now by a uniformed policeman. Inside, the office manager nervously watched two men open file cabinets.

"What kind of boxes?" she heard Swede say.

"Heavy, I think," said the woman addressed. "They weighted his arms down straight, that's all I saw. And no, he didn't say where he was going. Is something going to happen to us?"

Swede reassured her. Back with Jody he muttered, "It's happening fast. Court order just came from Anchorage. Gives them access to all catch records of Tsurifune Suisan. Gains keeps a locked file that I never see. It's not locked now, and there's nothing in it but old law books. Did you see Gains head off?"

"Yes, but no idea where. He doesn't consult you then?"

"I run the plant. Gains plays their games in Japan. Some days we don't even pass each other."

Jody went out and brought back for Kodama two hamburgers, a chocolate milk shake, and popcorn, all things she remembered he liked. Back in
the room she arranged them on a table, and told him to come eat.

"No, madam." He continued to stare ahead, but tears welled in his eyes.

Jody took his head in her hands and hugged him, then left him alone.

Back in the offices a grim, overweight man Jody had never met sat at
Swede's desk. He was conducting two phone conversations alternately,
and appeared to be relaying messages from one party to another while
scribbling on a notepad. It was Justin Rider, Swede told her, counsel for
Tsurifune Suisan, just arrived from Seattle. "You might do well to stay out
of his way, Jody," Swede suggested.

"Why?"

"From his clients' viewpoint, Hank started all this fracas around us."

"I'll settle that!" She waited, in his sight. The man sweated enough to
keep wiping his face, but he exuded an unflustered energy that was com-
manding. When he put down the phones she stepped up to speak.

He rose with his notes and brushed past her with, "Who are you?
Excuse me." Moments later she heard his voice raised in John Gains's
office, where agents were still looking through files.

When Rider returned to Swede's office Jody introduced herself. He
studied her, then said, "Yes. I'll be dealing with you and your husband
later. I suggest you read your contract. Now please excuse me." Without
ceremony he motioned her out the door and closed it.

She accompanied Swede when he drove Kodama to the airport. Kodama
walked straight and insisted on carrying all his own baggage. The food she
had brought remained untouched. Jody pitied him. "Your wife and children will be glad to see you, I'll bet," she said to make conversation.

"Yes, madam," he replied from the backseat.

"Now, you have a son, how old? Bet you're proud of him."

After a long pause, "Son will now see father in disgrace."

At the airport Kodama stood holding his bags while Swede checked
him in. His stance was so rigid that he might have been carved of wood.
Jody could find nothing further to say, but she waited beside him in case
it gave him comfort. She herself had begun to tremble. What had been
unleashed? When the time came for parting she hugged him again, and
murmured: "Take care. I think it wasn't your fault." Kodama's body
remained stiff but he bowed his head.

As she and Swede left the terminal, she noticed John Gains coming briskly from the shipping entrance. He saw her and hurried back through the door.

Jody's next day passed in a nightmare of legal issues. Henry Sollers, the lawyer Swede had arranged for her to see who had examined and faulted the new Tsurifune contract, said he'd now need to study the original contract. When Hank told her where to find his copy and Sollers had studied it, he said, "Your husband didn't do much to protect his back. Whoever wrote this one tied you coming and going."

Another lawyer found her who represented Jason Shub, "crewman lately aboard the trawler *Jody Dawn* in Shelikof Strait." His client had filed a claim for medical bills, plus $250,000 in damages for willful negligence that led to his life-threatening injury. Jody told him brusquely that the boat was insured by the Tsurifune company, while she wondered to herself what kind of help they could now expect.

"But the negligence part," said the lawyer (and he seemed to enjoy saying it), "is against Henry Crawford personally. My client suffered abuse from Mr. Crawford, and this abuse so upset Mr. Shub that he was unable to concentrate on his duties, which led directly to his injury. And the abuse continued into callous neglect while my client lay helpless in agony."

"That's bullshit!" Jody exploded. "The mealy little bastard hid in his bunk during a crisis. We needed to turn to to save our lives, and he was hauled out to do his share. Then we nursed the whining piece of shit the best we could."

The lawyer smiled. "We see where the atmosphere of abuse comes from." He handed her papers.

Jody's indignation served no better with Justin Rider. "I don't know what you hoped to gain," he told her, "by starting a witch hunt against all Japanese. But it's clear that Director Tsurifune misplaced trust in your husband. I might add that your husband deeply overstepped his bounds with the director in Anchorage two months ago. I was shocked, and the director's son was offended. It was only through the director's generous nature that we didn't close the book on your husband that night."

Jody stared at him with the coldness that she felt. "You'd already been cheating him, and it didn't stop you."

"Watch your accusations, young woman. Your husband has acted on hearsay, not proof, and there's such a thing as slander. After we've proven

our innocence, be grateful if you get out of this with only a few losses and
a reputation for incompetence in the fishery. Your husband has been what
we term a poor producer."

And what proof do we have? Jody wondered. But she narrowed her eyes
and stormed ahead. "Hank a poor producer? Only because you doctored
his catch logs! Ask anybody what kind of fisherman Hank is. Ask even John
Gains right here in the office. He once crewed for Hank. Go ask him now!"

"I'd need to go all the way to Japan to do that."

"No. I just saw him here yesterday, with a box."

"You'll find that he flew out last night."

And with boxes, Jody realized. Probably with the documents that might
have proved cheating. And with poor Kodama on the same flight, the only
true witness to what had been done.

"I'm sorry to say it, Mrs. Crawford, but you need to look for a new res-
idence. Mr. Tsurifune doesn't want to be unfair, so he's instructed me to
give you an entire week to move from the property our bank holds. We're
now examining our roster to find captains for both our fishing vessels
Puale Bay and *Jody Dawn.* Your husband can expect to be relieved out
there in a day or two. I'm sorry for you, but these are things that your husband should have considered before trying to betray someone as important and respected as Director Kiyoshi Tsurifune."

Radio reception was clear when she reached Hank. All that she wanted
to say was private, but she had no choice except to tell it on open band.
"Jesus," was all he could mutter, and then, humbly, "I'm sorry for what
I've done to you."

By now Jody had pulled herself together. "Unfortunately Adele's sublet
her house for the winter so we can't go there to catch our breath. But I've
found one of the Aleutian Homes houses on the hill that'll take just a six-
month lease."

"Those run-down dumps that should have been torn down ten years ago?"

"Don't exaggerate. This one has enough rooms if Henny and Pete double up. And the price for Kodiak could be worse."

"But my boat. My boat."

She found Seth at last, drinking with Mo midday at Tony's with only
two or three habitués at the bar and the jukebox blaring. He scowled at her
as if preparing to leap from his stool to begin a fight. Mo rose respectfully.

"What can you prove about this?" she demanded.

"What I counted is what."

"Papers? Did you keep any papers?"

"Mo's and my fish-counts we kept. And yeah, I slid one of Kodo's crooked counts in my pocket before Kodo took all the rest up to the office. Did you know those damn marshals came down and told us to pack up in ten minutes? And it was *papers* they were looking for. If they'd known what I had, they'd have waved their badges and taken it."

"Wait till Boss hears," rumbled Mo. "No time even to grab our oilskins from deck. Nobody better steal them."

Seth kept a two-room apartment in town, where he and Mo now stayed. The rest of the crew were waiting idle in the cannery bunkhouse. "Right beside the Viet and Mex fish-plant workers," said Seth. "Take it or leave it, all their stuff."

Mo threw out his large hands. "What do we do now, Jody? It's no good stuck ashore like this with no boat. Look now, all afternoon ahead and then there's night, and I've already had all to drink I want."

Jody had no answer except to make them come with her for something to eat. After a glum meal of burgers and fries they were drawn to the pier where the *Puale Bay* lay tied and embargoed. They stared for a while. "Heck with this!" Mo declared, and climbed down to collect their oilskins from pegs in the covered gear alley.

Mo was coming back up when the wheelhouse door flew open and a voice demanded, "Hey, where you going with those?" Mo turned belligerently, and the voice continued, "That Mo? What the hell, man!" It was Tolly Smith, gold earring and all. He followed to the top of the pier.

It turned out that the Tsurifune people had instructed Tolly to bring in the smaller boat he fished for them, and had just told him that he was to captain the *Puale Bay*. "Wow, this setup!" Tolly exclaimed, waving an arm. "Leaves that tub they put me up in back to nowhere. What happened, Jody? Hank get tired of doing black cod? Great opportunity for me. Jennie really got excited when she heard. Ownership and all."

Jody told him what had happened.

"Oh shit," said Tolly. "They've already had me sign papers. Nobody told me any of this."

Jody exclaimed in anger. She strode across the pier and up the stairs to the company office and unlatched the gate that led into the offices as she'd always done routinely to call on Swede. The clerk who controlled the gate hurried over, embarrassed. "Jody, I'm real sorry. Mr. Rider says you're not allowed in."

"Call Swede out for me, Dolores."

"He's gone back down to Seattle."

Jody almost gasped. Her support had deserted. Instead she demanded, "Where's Rider?" Dolores indicated the closed door of an office. "Not your fault," Jody muttered, and brushed past to throw open the door.

There sat Justin Rider. He half rose, startled, then said sourly, "You're intruding, Mrs. Crawford. Kindly leave."

A Japanese man was pacing by the window that overlooked the piers. He turned to look at her. He was tall, still young, with black hair that fell in laps over a high forehead. His trim dark suit looked out of place in a Kodiak fish plant.

"Cheap trick," said Jody. "Playing one good man against another. It'll catch up with you."

"Get out, please. I've said it nicely."

"You sit on your fat ass while real men do work and think you'll jerk them around?"

Rider reached for the intercom. "Get security up here."

"So you're Hank Crawford's wife?" asked the Japanese smoothly. "You don't do a good job of controlling him, I'm afraid. Sorry to have to tell you. Your husband has embarrassed us greatly, and I fear that he's broken a faith of friendship and hospitality. All such things come with consequence."

"Who are you?" Jody demanded.

The security guard, whom Jody knew, came to the door. Rider told him to escort the lady out. The guard touched her elbow and said in a low voice, "It's my job, Jody. Sorry."

Jody brushed him off and advanced toward the Japanese. "Are you Tsurifune?" He acknowledged. "What have you done to poor Kodama? He wasn't the one who cooked this up, was he? You were scheming all along when you took Hank over there and gave him parties."

Shoji Tsurifune bowed with a polite smile. "Excuse me, but I don't argue with wives."

Jody's explosion did her no good. Joe the security guard anxiously escorted her out while apologizing under his voice.

She explained to the children that they were moving to a new place for a while. Its location in town nearer their friends overrode any feelings they had over leaving home. But the accumulation of their possessions! With a heavy heart Jody found warehouse space to rent. Then came a new blow. When she went to the bank to draw out money for rentals on the house and storage space she learned that their main account—tied to Tsurifune's bank in Seattle—had been frozen. Only a small personal savings account remained open. Thank heaven she had a job, she realized. But her pay simply covered existing bills and was no help in the sudden emergency, since Hank's earnings had all been tied into the Tsurifune contract.

The Tsurifune people hired a substitute captain and crew for the *Jody Dawn,* former Bering Sea crabbers recruited at the Seattle Fishermen's Terminal, who were glad to be back at sea and didn't question the reason.

Hank's misfortune soon became known throughout the fleet, without the details that might have gained him more sympathy. "What you get for signing in too cozy with the Japs," said one radio voice to Gus Rosvic out in the Shelikof. Gus for once was worried rather than judgmental. "That boy Hank's honest, whatever fool thing he's done. Somebody's gone out to get him and it ain't good for any of us."

Arne Larsen and Joe Eberhardt both secretly believed that Hank had made so many deals with the Japanese that his leaving was some kind of ploy. They continued to fish and deliver to the Tsurifune processor, and soon became again so immersed in setting trawl on tricky masses of pollack during dangerous weather that they forgot his absence. They even helped advise the new skipper of the *Jody Dawn.*

Tolly stoutly refused to take over the *Puale Bay* for all of two days. Then Justin Rider sat him down and outlined the consequences if he reneged on the contract he'd just signed. Within a week, government agents had relinquished hold on the longliner after failing to find evidence of log tampering, and the *Puale Bay* headed back to fish black cod in the Gulf of Alaska. It carried new captain Roland "Tolly" Smith, new processing master Hoshi Tamukai, and all the former crew except for Seth O'Malley and Thaddeus "Mo" Wheeler. The company had officially fired the latter two for "inadequate production" before they'd had a chance to quit.

Fishery agents with their subpoenas had also been unable to find incriminating documents in the offices of Pacific Future. After Rider flew to Washington and called on friends in the State and Commerce Departments to explain the actions that a disgruntled fisherman had taken to hide his own mediocre performance, the company was allowed to resume business. Suspicions still lingered over the Tsurifune alliances. The door

that Hank opened would not close again that easily. He'd indeed damaged them—but the suspicions slipped back in a file alongside other
ongoing investigations.

Hank, Terry, Ham, and Tom returned to Kodiak aboard a tender. They
chose to huddle in their oilskins on open deck despite a raw, cold rain and
a hospitable warm galley open to them. They brooded together as they
watched the bare brown hills along the narrows that led back to town.
Jody met them with the children and with Seth and Mo. They all drove
over the potholed, frozen road to the house. Jody's lawyer had at least
gained her an extra week to vacate. Boxes and clothing lined the living
room wall, ready for storage, but chairs were still arranged by the big picture window. Hank soon fired stoves to heat the place. Jody herded the
children into their bedrooms to do homework, then plumped a bottle of
scotch on the table by the chairs, and left them alone while she started to
peel onions in the kitchen.

"I've got to weather this alone," said Hank after they'd all taken a drink.
"You guys—it makes me sick to say it—you don't have a boat with me
anymore." He turned to Tom. "Bunk here with us wherever we light,
until you decide what to do. You'll eventually get paid, and enough to
make your trip worthwhile, I think. The bastards have to settle with me
whatever their tricks. We'll find your airfare back to Baltimore, then send
you your check when they settle."

"Don't you worry about me," said Tom. "I ain't leaving. Not yet."

Seth cleared his throat. "I brought this on. I've got—"

"No you didn't," said Hank. "You found out things I should have seen."

"Let me finish, will you? I've got savings since I didn't throw anything
in with the Japs. Don't nobody here need to worry about ready money,
and that includes you and Jody."

"Hell, Boss, we've all got savings," said Terry. "Just say it if you need
anything."

"Yeah, Boss," chimed Mo and Ham together.

They sat in the gathering twilight and stared through the window at
trees and gray mist. Occasionally the mist scattered to reveal lights along
the town's cannery piers miles away over the water. Tom remarked that it
was sure beautiful, just like everything else in Alaska.

And it's being taken from me, thought Hank in despair. He'd asked
Jody about Swede, the one person who might provide some guidance.
Even Swede had peeled away from the loser and escaped to Seattle.

Someone knocked on the door. It was John Gains. He wore no hat, and his thick black hair was matted against his forehead by the rain. When Jody opened the door he stood there until she urged him in. His expression was both wary and troubled. The men by the window fell silent.

"Thought you were in Japan," said Jody. "Give me your coat."

"I didn't come to stay. I just . . ." He turned his back to Hank and the men, and held out an envelope. "Just take this," he muttered. "No questions. It's terrible what's happened." He left quickly, even though Jody called after him to come back and dry off.

Jody slipped the envelope behind cans of flour and rice on the kitchen shelf. Worry about it later, she decided.

She fixed hamburgers rather than the steaks she'd normally have served for a homecoming from the sea. After that they drank some more, all together put the children to bed—the bachelors Terry and Tom with wistful hugs that lingered—and drank further. Everyone became cheerful, occasionally boisterous. At last Hank dragged out mattresses and futons, and those without beds curled by the fireplace for the night.

The envelope that John Gains had slipped to Jody contained thirteen crisp hundred-dollar bills. She and Hank both regarded the bills, even, it seemed, caressed them.

"That's his guilt for sliding all the incriminating documents off to Japan before the Feds arrived," said Hank. Jody resealed the envelope and next day returned it to the office with no comment.

The following days took sorting out. Seth, Terry, Mo, and Ham conferred and pooled resources, then ceremoniously offered Hank and Jody enough money to pay off the home mortgage. Jody was moved, and might have accepted, with Hank remaining silent, had not the lawyer advising them said that the three properties of the contract—house, *Jody Dawn*, and *Puale Bay*—were tied together as a unit. Only after all had been redeemed could they be separated, except with the consent of both parties. Hank could barely speak in front of Jody for his carelessness in signing such a document, but she did nothing to rub it in.

Her acceptance of the situation became pragmatic: how best to survive it. She dressed well, went to the fishery office, and this time waited outside the gated rail along with two plant workers until the lawyer Rider consented to see her. He had now taken over a back office with new private phone lines. When she made a personal appeal that the contract be modified to separate the properties, Rider merely said, "It doesn't work that way. You've put the Tsurifune reputation on the line; they're doing what's needed to survive it, and I can't help you."

When she left, John Gains in the adjacent office rose from his desk. His expression was as troubled as when he'd offered the envelope. Jody paused long enough to say, "It's out of your control, isn't it?" He nodded, and she hurried away.

Nipping at them like an ill-tempered terrier was the lawsuit of Jason Shub. Hank's insurance would cover the medical portion without question, but the $250,000 portion for willful negligence and brutality would be Hank's alone if proven. It meant hiring the services of yet another lawyer. Hank became furious whenever he thought of it. "If I'm blamed, sorry I didn't boot his gut into his spine the way he deserved!" The lawyer told him not to worry, since there were witnesses to prove it was a mere frivolous charge, and presented Hank with his first bill for five hundred dollars' advance.

The Tsurifune push for retribution and self-justification continued a relentless course. When Hank applied for a modest loan at the bank where his accounts were frozen they told him he was now listed as a credit risk. They added that this information was available to other banks that might inquire.

After the two weeks' grace, Hank and Jody were forced to move from their house. An agent for the company at least waited discreetly until Hank and his former crewmen had trucked out the last piece of furniture. Jody, although Hank told her bitterly not to, swept each room before leaving.

"I'd have pissed on each fuckin' floor," muttered Seth.

Jody took a final look at the house, standing in rain beside the station wagon. She'd told Hank and his guys to go on ahead with the final truck-load to spare him. He'd kept feverishly busy so not to think, she knew. Inside the wagon Dawn wailed dramatically, now that she understood the situation, while she squeezed the dog Rusty's neck. Henny, wide-eyed and silent, pressed his face against the window toward the house. Young Pete held one of the cats lightly and leafed through a picture book, unconcerned. Well, house, she thought. I didn't like moving this far from town so at times I almost hated you. But my children learned to run safely here. Hank helped build you; I see his hand in you everywhere, and now I'm sorry to go.

The new quarters were depressing. Hank was right. The houses had been constructed expediently during World War II, and now decades later they needed patching and repair. A narrow porch looking over other tract houses was a poor substitute for Hank's beloved picture window facing water. At least the kids could walk to school and didn't need to be chauffered everywhere. The two cats settled in at once to roam and sniff things new. Only the dog and Hank could not adjust. Rusty, used to roaming without a leash, now mourned in a corner. Hank mourned almost in the same manner, and seldom left the dark living room except to confer with lawyers. Downtown he skirted the waterfront that had been his turf.

Hank might have swallowed pride and looked to crew on somebody else's boat, but he needed to stay close to handle legal problems. His men remained faithful in spirit, but one by one they found berths. Even Tom was hired, to his unconcealed wonder at the way opportunity opened.

"Come on, Boss. Down to Solly's for a brew," urged any of his old crew when they came to town. Hank found excuses each time not to go. He brooded. Even Swede had deserted the sinking ship and stayed in Seattle.

Jody would have worried less about him if he'd turned testy and vented his anger. But, although Hank continued to walk straight, his voice lost its energy. He was gentle but distant with the children rather than giving them his usual warmth and vigor. Each new expense depressed him further. "What about your father?" she suggested cautiously when another lawyer's bill arrived. "Just a temporary loan."

Hank thought of the way he'd defended his career against his dad's admonitions a few months before. "Out of the question."

Then one evening he hurried in late for dinner but purposefully. "Just keep eating without me," he said, and kissed her, then dressed in some of his oldest clothes. "Don't wait up," he called as he left. "I've got a night job."

"Doing what? Where?"

"See you in the morning."

He reported to a new fish plant opened by the native corporation, punched the time clock, and checked in with the foreman. Soon he stood waist-deep in fish and frigid water, encased in heavy rubber waders, in the hold of a boat that had delivered groundfish. Oddmund, whom he'd suddenly pulled himself together to approach that afternoon, had reluctantly seen to it that he was hired while saying gravely, "Boss, you needn't ought to have to do this. It's crummy work nobody else wants. But you're not native. My people couldn't hire you to a better job even if we had one."

"Just work with overtime pay for night shift is fine."

He shared the hold with a taciturn native teenager who found excuses to rest against a bulkhead every few minutes. Dead fish swirled around them in water encrusted with odorous icy brown sludge. Other brown ice fell over their heads from above. It dribbled under the collar of his cannery-issue oilskin jacket. The job required wading back and forth through the hold pushing wide wooden paddles, to corral the fish toward a thick suction hose. It was clammy, cold work until his body heat took over.

When portions of the hold had been sucked clear, Hank gave up waiting for the teenager to help and gripped the thick slimy hose against his chest with both arms to haul it to another spot. If the kid had been a crewman under me, he thought without heat, I'd have barked him into shape or dumped his ass back on the pier in minutes.

After two hours the hold was clear enough for him to scoop up fish with a shovel and dump them in front of the suction hose. At last the big hose could be raised. For the next hour, with smaller hoses, they scrubbed slime from the bulkheads, then scrubbed again with nostril-burning disinfectant, then tackled the deck boards, and finally, the steel deck itself. At last the foreman in clean coveralls climbed down, shone a flashlight into every corner, and passed on the job.

The time came to wash themselves off outside the hold, when usually partners directed the hose on each other, but the kid just wandered off dripping gurry. Hank went for a coffee break and doughnuts, then suggested diplomatically to the foreman that he could handle cleaning holds by himself. The foreman understood. "Son of one of our directors," he shrugged. When Hank entered the hold of the next boat the kid was slowly pushing a broom through an area not particularly dirty.

Hank shivered afresh in the frigid slurry before exertion warmed him. But he began to sing to himself, and he developed a rhythm.

Ten hours later in pale morning light he punched out and walked slowly up the hill to the house. He ached and stank. He also felt at peace. He was a man again, working.

Next night he punched in, and continued.

26

DAYLIGHT

KODIAK, MARCH–APRIL 1984

Hank, during his first youthful batting-around days in Kodiak, had sometimes been short enough of money to miss a meal. Back then he'd come from the East Coast for adventure, all experiences qualified, and being broke had been almost fun. Now his empire had crumbled while his responsibilities remained. Lawyers' bills mounted, but he saw no way out of the Tsurifune mess without defending himself. He remained in a tense limbo, unable to do more than survive from day to day.

Adding to the darkness for Hank was the desertion of Swede Scorden. Swede had conveniently disappeared to Seattle just as Justin Rider had arrived to cut and slash. When Swede returned at last to resume running the plant, Hank waited to hear from him but was reluctant to call. No call came. When once Hank encountered him in the square, Swede was gruffly distant and eased away before anything could be said.

Hank also chafed over the lawyer, Henry Sollers, whom Swede had recommended to Jody before his defection, to examine the faulty second contract. Sollers was lean and focused, but Hank suspected him of being more interested in sport fishing than commercial. Based in Anchorage, he came weekly to his Kodiak suboffice and had a partner in Seattle. At a fee of one hundred dollars an hour for each portion of time spent at any of the offices, Sollers continued to try breaking into the original Tsurifune contract in order to separate the house and *Jody Dawn*

from the cripplingly priced *Puale Bay,* or to find some other compromise. "That Justin Rider's a hard ticket," he declared with a professional
appreciation that Hank resented. "He, or his clients, aren't budging an
inch."

Meanwhile, Oddmund, who owed his own life and that of another
native crewman to Hank's rescue, hinted that the native corporation
might find a way to take over the remaining bank loan on the *Jody Dawn*
if this liability could be separated from the others. But nothing budged,
while expenses continued.

Eventually Hank's night duties at the cannery expanded, per Oddmund's intervention, to include jobs freeze-packing and simple mechanics
when there were no holds to be cleaned. The shift provided his steady
income although, with his will and energy revived, he also now found
daytime work. Lost sleep meant less than making money to cover legal
fees, and keeping busy. While nobody could bail him out of his troubles,
friends, even casual ones, helped in ways he could accept. He realized that
he indeed was part of a community. He also found that the work skills all
fishermen needed to teach themselves in order to survive away from land,
as well as the skills he'd acquired building his home, had equipped him to
handle nearly any job he was offered.

When late-winter weather permitted, a builder friend hired him intermittently to lay foundations and do simple carpentry. He turned down
another offer to clerk in the supermarket. That job alone, even though it
meant staying dry and warm, seemed to him a loss of pride, to wait on
people he knew. And a friend at one of the boatyards—the one that had
repaired the *Jody Dawn*—took him on part-time to weld and to power-
scrape rust from hulls.

During the two months that passed, physical work helped him forget
his anger for hours at a time. His bleakest despair left him, although not
the sadness nor the guilt toward Jody.

Jody for her part found extra work grading high school papers at night.
She never spoke of the way he'd lost their house. They heard, but tried to
forget, that assessors had evaluated the house and land. The auction was
delayed only pending better weather, when the long potholed road to the
house would not be made more treacherous by ice.

A judge finally dismissed as frivolous Jason Shub's lawsuit against
Hank, but not without time-consuming testimony and confrontation.

The Kodiak lawyer had predicted this, but his fee for success was more than two thousand dollars (which he claimed was giving them a break). The bill consumed what Hank had earned at the cannery.

Adele Henry stayed in San Diego since her house was occupied, but she phoned regularly and made it clear that she missed the children. Jody told her some details of their situation and Adele assured Hank that Jones's boat was at his disposal.

The limit seiner *Adele H* was indeed Hank's potential escape if he could free himself of legal tangles and accept the loss of his larger *Jody Dawn*. While Jody had captained the boat for salmon during the two previous summers, and Adele had once let a pickup crew work it intermittently with cod pots, the boat now lay idle at the pier pending routine maintenance for the next summer's salmon runs.

But all plans remained in limbo. Somehow the unimaginable became routine. "It's nice having you around every day," Jody soothed. "The kids have gotten to recognize your face." Hank knew this to be true. At times he could disentangle it from what was happening and enjoy his family in gaps of time between work and sleep.

When the Shelikof roe pollack season ended in April the local boats returned to town. Hank watched them steam down the narrows from the hillside construction site where he was laying cinder blocks one afternoon. The converted crabbers of Arne Larsen and Joe Eberhardt would have gone home to Seattle. But there was Gus Rosvic's smaller *Thunder*, and many other local boats he recognized.

Suddenly, in the distance through mist and shoreline spruce, there came his *Jody Dawn*. Before other details became clear he recognized her lines and the silhouetted extra antenna he'd added. His throat tightened. How she could cut through the water! As she neared he cupped hands around his eyes to see whether she'd been cared for properly. Scuffed, of course, from heavy weather. Needed paint. His hands ached to do it. But— strange line of letters on her bow. They'd changed her name, with a new letter over each of the letters of "Jody Dawn," to *Amer Vict!* He checked the boat's details, then checked again. Yes. His *Jody Dawn!* (And what kind of sappy name? He remembered Tsurifune once suggesting "*American Victory.*") The new outrage rekindled all his anger.

"Would you want them to keep your old name?" asked practical Jody.

"I don't know what I want, except to have her back."

The lawyer Sollers phoned from Anchorage. "You're not going to like this, but I might as well tell you straight." The Tsurifunes had sold the *Jody Dawn*. The Japanese company remained adamant about also selling the house. "Then you'll have a settlement, and I expect we'll get you back a few thousand dollars. Our hands are tied because of the wording of your signed contract."

Hank handed Jody the phone and left the house.

Past midnight, having finished cleaning a ship's hold at the cannery with an intensity that broke two long scrubbing brushes, he punched out and trotted the half mile to the docks to find the *Jody Dawn*. The boat's noble bow rose in its graceful arc as always, but she was no longer his to climb aboard. He walked her length along the pier, touched her hull, smelled her odors. His hand rested on welds he'd soldered himself. The boat's new name had been painted crudely on a swath of white paint that covered only lightly the letters for "Jody Dawn." He resisted tearing at them, and forced himself to walk away.

He knew where to find the *Adele H* at an adjacent float among the sein-ers. It occupied the same slip as in the days of Jones Henry: the slip where Jones had thrown his great boat-christening bash and from which Adele gave his ashes their final send-off. Her bow rose less grandly than that of the *Jody Dawn,* and quarters were cramped in comparison, but her design had the feel of being at one with the water.

How often, Hank thought, have I told myself that all I wanted as a fish-erman was to stay with a boat this size? Jones had once tried a larger craft, then faced the fact that his ambition was limited and he had no taste for Bering Sea dangers in million-dollar vessels, and returned to fishing around Kodiak. His one later venture away from the island, in a different boat, had killed him.

Hank climbed aboard. The cabin and wheelhouse were padlocked, but he walked the open deck. She wasn't a boat sized for ambition in far places where greatest opportunity lay; she'd been built to make a steady living in water sometimes rough but close to land and all its supports. Hadn't Jody, and he himself, fished well in her?

But his *Jody Dawn!* He'd designed and nursed her to completion him-self. None other should have her. It was the vessel of his earned experi-ence, of his hopes and ambition. He returned to the float where *Jody*

Dawn lay moored, sat on the pier with his back pressed against the boat's hull, and held his face in his hands.

A flashlight beam shone. "Hank? Now what the hell, son!"

Hank jumped to his feet, embarrassed to be discovered. It was Gus Rosvic, who explained, "I just happened to be taking a piss call from my deck and saw somebody snooping on the *Adele H.* You don't look good. Come on back to my cabin."

Hank followed, swiping a hand over his face in the dark to clear it.

Gus had already closed down the jointly owned trawler *Thunder* to return to his seiner *Hinda Bee* and prepare for longlining black cod. The *Hinda* and *Adele H* duplicated each other enough in size and layout that Hank felt comfortable at once in its galley.

"Too late for coffee by my book," drawled Gus. "But, now, a little medicine in port won't hurt nothing." He produced a fifth of bourbon from his cabin, opened it, banged down two glasses, and passed Hank the bottle. "You young fellows fancy scotch like its the second coming, but the stuff tastes namby-pam to old-timers like me. Now tell me what's happened. Start by why you smell like a bin of dead fish this late at night. Jody didn't finally get smart and throw you out, did she?"

Hank had recovered enough to make a joke of his account, and to tell it with a shrug, although Gus listened with grave attention. The whiskey sent relaxing fingers through his body, and he was grateful for Gus's easy reality, but he decided quickly not to accuse the Japanese of cheating and start a drumroll among the anti-Jap forces. No reason, he thought as he gained back perspective, to hurt those innocent in Japan who had treated him well. Let the government sort it out. His own fight was with the Tsurifune team, and what if they were the only cheats?

When Hank had finished, Gus said, "Well, that's too bad. Now what do you plan to do? Become a star fish-plant worker?"

"Up to this point I've stayed close to town hoping for some way to get back my *Jody Dawn.*" The immensity of his loss rolled back over him.

"I know, I know. Nothing worse than to lose your boat." After a silence, he added, "Except maybe lose your Jody. Some I know, they'd give up the old lady first. You ain't that dumb?"

Hank shook his head.

"Since I caught you snooping around Jones Henry's seiner, you may not have gone completely daft. That loud wife of Jones's has already made conversion for halibut longline, hasn't she? Needs smaller hooks for black cod, but you should be an expert on that by now. And you should've got used to it by now, to run a boat that's had women crawled all over it. The boat ain't turned over yet so she probably won't. Though it's a shame to see such a fine old superstition gone wrong."

Gus drank a single shot of whiskey neat, then pushed away the glass. Hank had diluted his drink with water. He poured himself another.

"Time you stopped fooling around with one foot on both sides, Hank. Get with the rest of us here in your own country. Go convert Jones Henry's old boat, get out there and fish her for black cod *against* the foreigners for a change, and stop feeling sorry for yourself."

Hank listened to words that he suddenly wanted to hear.

"Maybe you've been with your banzai friends over there so long," Gus continued calmly, "that maybe you don't know this is the year we've all decided to push the black cod so hard we'll catch the whole quota, and settle this argument about giving fish away to foreigners. Last year we tried and didn't make it. Didn't come close. What's got us fired up this year is, our own government says we can't do it. Fellows here now, who never thought of converting their seiners and such to longline for other than halibut, they don't think much of a government tells them there's something they can't do."

Three refills for Hank later, around 2 AM, he shook Gus's hand—pumped it until Gus asked if he planned to give it back—and wove home. He stopped on the hill to Aleutian Homes long enough to look down over the darkened town and harbor, and thought with a rush: it's still my time. And wherever I live here, this is my place. In answer, clouds blew free to clear a nearly full moon. The silver light etched rooftops, masts, and sea ripples. "Hey there, my place!" he shouted. After a silence it seemed right to shout again and wave his arms besides.

Next day, diplomatically through Oddmund, Hank quit the cannery and put behind him the penance of cleaning fish holds. He kept such daytime work as friends provided, and in between started reconverting the *Adele H* to longline. The boatyard friend who had hired him part-time allowed him free space for the work. To his gratification, a local banker said, "Sure, Hank, your credit's good again now we see where you're headed. Everybody knows you deliver," so that he had the funds to buy gear as well as to cover some home expenses.

He saw Swede again while ordering hooks. The man's detachment appeared so great that Hank turned away. Yet, then, Swede walked down the aisle beside him and without stopping muttered, "Stay in town a while longer, Crawford."

One by one his old crew reassembled around him enthusiastically. First came Seth with "It's about damn time," then Terry with a joke, then Mo and Ham tumbling over each other together while their latest girlfriends kept a distance. Hank hesitated to contact Tom, who had found a secure enough berth to have rented his own room in town. One late afternoon Tom approached the boatyard, stood with hands in pockets watching the *Adele H* and the others working over her, and finally said to Hank, "Guess you're filled up, Boss."

"Except for *your* berth waiting if you want it."

"Oh, I do!" Tom leapt aboard and pitched in at once.

The new atmosphere also brightened Jody and the children. As April drew to a close and daylight savings began, the afternoon light lengthened further every day. It left less dark time to brood and made the Tsurifune business seem less overpowering, even though nothing there had been mitigated. Hank learned to pass his *Jody Dawn* in harbor, obscenely renamed and idle, with only sorrow in place of devastation.

The sorrow increased when he and Jody read the auction notice for their home. Jody went to the cannery office for one more appeal. Rider the lawyer had returned to Seattle and Swede reoccupied his old office. No one seemed willing to talk. John Gains, it seemed to her, elaborately failed to notice her from his open doorway. Swede, their once-dependable friend for all seasons, came from his closed office at last. "It's in the hands of the bank," he said curtly. "I hope you and Hank are weathering this."

Jody turned cold. "We've managed."

"That lawyer Sollers I recommended—has he helped you?"

"Prompt with bad news and his bills, if that's what you mean. Not much else."

Swede hesitated, then suggested that it would be good for Hank to stay in town. "No harm for him to keep on with odd jobs. Just hold off on the *Adele H* for a while." Jody realized that he had followed their activities, but she remained cold. Swede quickly terminated the conversation.

Only the pending auction kept Hank from going to sea, so that he could be with Jody. On the day before, he took her to lunch on the side of town farthest from the road to the home he'd built. They spoke little, but he felt that their thoughts were the same.

"Excuse me," said a voice. They both looked up. It was John Gains, suited soberly as usual. "Hank," he said. "Go out to the red pickup for a minute. Excuse me, Jody." And he left.

Swede was in the truck. When Hank approached he pushed open the passenger door and motioned Hank in. Gains was already driving away in another vehicle.

"What's this?" Hank demanded. "Trailing me?"

"Don't think it's been easy finding you alone, Crawford." Swede handed him a thick envelope. "Take this to Sollers right away. He's waiting. You haven't been here with anybody but your wife today. Scoot."

"Ha," said the lawyer when Hank delivered the envelope. "Now I have work to do, so please leave."

Before the day had ended, the auction notices were taken down. In the evening, at the rental house, someone knocked on the door. Hank opened it in time to see a car drive away. A note fluttered to his feet. It read:

> *You've got your house back, Crawford. Don't ever sign anything again without two independent lawyers. You're not smart enough.*

Sollers phoned soon after. "You have friends in high places," he said. "The papers you delivered to me today were enough to convince certain parties in Seattle that they might get reasonable. The lien on your house is lifted and back home you can go. Stop in here tomorrow for the keys. No. Can't tell you more tonight."

The news was too great for noisy rejoicing. Hank sat by Jody in the temporary living room, and together they watched their children frown over homework.

Next morning Sollers would say little to answer Hank's questions. "Right now," he warned, "the best favor you can do anybody who might have helped you is to say nothing. Some careers are walking a delicate balance, and some people in Seattle and Tokyo, I believe, are pissed as hell." He handed Hank a note. "You're to read this, then tear it up and throw it in that wastebasket there."

The note, in a scrawl that Hank now assumed was Swede's although they had never exchanged letters, read:

> *Go fishing now, Crawford. If your* Jody Dawn *is lost, get over it and be glad you can start again with Jones Henry's old boat. Some fools aren't so lucky. Have your glory dreams another way until you learn to read a contract.*

"I want to keep this," said Hank. "Like to show it to my wife. I'll guard it."

"Wastebasket, sir."

27

EPILOGUE: SONS

ANCHORAGE, SEPTEMBER 1984

More fishermen than usual left their boats for the occasion. They crowded into narrow chairs and stood along the sides of the meeting rooms in the Anchorage hotel that hosted the September sessions of the North Pacific Fishery Management Council. Many had wives elsewhere in town shopping, since they'd be off to Hawaii as soon as Council adjourned. For the first time in years, wool shirts with shoulders bulging against them were as much in evidence as trim dark suits.

And there were grins. As one of Nels Tormulsen's longline crew put it, "We just want to fuckin' hear it for ourselves."

Dr. Lester Kronman of the Scientific Committee took it in stride without losing his dignity. He paid off a bet forced on him the year before by a then-indignant spokesman for the longline fishermen. "Conceded. I didn't think you could do it, so it was reasonable for me to vote negative." But he added, "Now that you've won, see that you don't waste the resource."

The spokesman pocketed Kronman's twenty dollars with a grin and answered in kind. "We will embrace the resource, sir."

The victory was complete and spectacular. American fishermen had rallied together, concentrated forces, and harvested the entire 6.7 million-pound black cod optimum yield in the western Gulf of Alaska. Only the year before, their catch had been less than a quarter of that. It left nothing for the Japanese, who had hoped that by agreeing to wait until early October there would still be tons of fish for them to catch.

Hank came to the Council dressed in jeans and a plaid shirt like the fisherman he again considered himself. He stayed at a cheaper hotel near the large one where the meetings were held, since most of what he earned continued to pay debts and lawyers' fees.

While recovering aboard the *Adele H,* he had driven his crew and himself relentlessly. He'd needed the money, but above all he craved satisfaction against the Tsurifune clan. In Kodiak he'd brought his deliveries to any of the eager Japanese buyers but Tsurifune.

"Don't you guys ever rest?" Tom Harris had asked in admiration. But the Chesapeake Bay transplant had come to enjoy the challenge and he'd kept up.

Terry would look Tom over through eyes bleary from lack of sleep. "Anybody keeps at this, *like* this, is nuts. If I never see another slippery black fish, I'll . . ." He'd shrug and continue to coil. "Your turn to ice the buggers."

The wind had sometimes blown for days, with nearly as much force as the solid waves that hit them. Both wind and water had slammed them off balance as they moved. Without Hank's drive they would often have quitted the deck.

Inevitably Hank sometimes needed to fish his boat close to the *Puale Bay,* late of his command, since they shared the same grounds. At 130 feet it was a monster compared to the 58-foot *Adele H.* Hank was glad to be free of it, he told himself, even though some of his debt remained tied to its fortunes. Tolly Smith remained captain. The two friends, now wary of each other, communicated only if the gear of one threatened that of the other.

Tolly had no choice but to take over from me, Hank told himself, but he still resented it. Tolly on his part knew that he had compromised himself. It troubled him, but he rationalized: I'm not taking anything from Hank that Tsurifune would have given back. His Jennie could now count on the full bank account that she deserved.

The announcement to boats on the water that the black cod quota was filled for the year had set off a storm of horns and whistles. While Hank duly grinned at his men's firecrackers and yells to other boats, the victory left him only tired and thoughtful.

The victory turned embarrassing when he brought in the *Adele H* for its final delivery. Strangers waited around the pier along with people he knew from the fishing magazines and local papers. The strangers turned out to be reporters from Anchorage and Seattle. They converged on him when somebody said he had defected from the Japanese.

"Not quite that way," he hedged.

Adele Henry arrived with a bottle of champagne and glasses. She threw her arms around him. "Daddy would be so proud that his boat helped do this. At last we've driven the foreigners from our shores!"

A photographer posed Adele with Hank despite his reluctance. People later attributed the absence of Hank's famous grin in the photo to his seriousness on such an occasion. The caption, when it was printed in a Seattle paper, read: "Kodiak beats foreign fishers, hits the bubbly."

In Anchorage between Council sessions, Hank called on Sollers to tie up loose ends. He learned that the *Jody Dawn*, rechristened *American Victory*, was now tendering fish to a Tsurifune cannery off Adak in the Aleutians. "That's a waste," he exclaimed. "She should be *catching* fish out there, not taking other peoples' catch!" But he knew the waste: that he was not aboard her.

Sollers's advice was practical. "That's not your boat anymore. Suggest you forget it. Sign these papers and get on with your life."

The sale of the *Jody Dawn*, after all settlements, would eventually provide him with enough money to pay his debts at last and to buy the *Adele H* from Adele Henry if he chose. Lost to him, however, was nearly $400,000 in boat payments and interest, the earnings of six years' hard fishing. Most of that had come from the two seasons of now-vanished king crab wealth that might never again be duplicated for another try at big prosperity.

Hank was unsure how deeply lay his debt to Swede and John. Clearly they'd pulled something, or the Tsurifune forces would not have released his house. Jody had seen Gains rush from the Kodiak office with a box, then recognized him at the airport cargo office, all this just the day before federal agents came to search the office. She and Hank surmised that he'd escorted incriminating papers back to Tokyo. Had Gains then called in a favor? Or had he saved out some papers and given them up for Hank's sake? Their concern increased when the news came that Gains had been fired. Had his involvement with Hank been responsible?

"John always seemed to me such a jerk," mused Hank. "Always so buttoned down, even fussy, and sucking up everywhere. The guy started to piss me off almost from the day I hired him in my crew. He worked hard enough, but I was glad when he left to start climbing the office ladder. You know how I used to call him Asshole John? Yet this isn't the first time he's gone to bat for me. Remember during crab days in the Bering, when Seth took a shot at the Japanese trawler that scraped over our pots? State Department was out to crucify me, and, according to Swede, John softened the Japanese to intercede with State. Then when Jones Henry and I were in the life raft, and Swede was the only one willing to drive a chopper in that storm to save us, it was John who volunteer-crewed."

"Sometimes you don't judge people that well, do you?" Jody said mildly. She had settled into enjoying the home they'd almost lost, and, while vowing to herself that this didn't end it, had gracefully relinquished her summer captaincy for salmon on the *Adele H* so that he could work the only boat available to him. "And I'll say it again," she continued. "Kodama might have doctored his reports, but it wasn't his idea, and he was suffering for it when I put him on the plane. I wish you'd at least call Japan to see how he is. If I did it they might make the wrong inference."

Hank had remained adamant. "He was part of their package."

Between Council sessions that mattered to him, Hank wandered the hotel lobby and meeting rooms. He felt detached and depressed, although he forced himself to liven whenever people greeted him.

"Here he is," said Gus Rosvic, and pulled him into a conversation with other longline skippers who had come from the black cod grounds. They were now gathering their forces to pressure the Council to ban even American boats from using trawls, pots, and gill nets to catch black cod. Only longliners. "I could run a junkyard with the ghost gear I've pulled up," Gus asserted. "Cut every bit of it by draggers."

"Gus, you ol' firecracker," joked one of the younger captains. "You used to blame every bit of that on the big Jap longliners."

"True enough, Luke. Those Jap buzzards laid their lines thick as cable and dumped it around like spiderweb. That's true enough—but not the whole truth." Gus's shrewd eyes surrounded by sun wrinkles peered around from under his cap. Hank marveled at how occasion could change Gus from mellow old-timer to an adversary almost vicious. "Mebbe we've won that fight, Luke, though don't trust the State Department boys in D.C. not to find some way around it. But if it ain't one kind of raider out there, it's another. Now we've got to settle things with our own." He turned to Hank. "Time you saw that, son. Got to fight for every little bit of what's yours."

"I hear you." Hank knew that turf fights and rivalries lay ahead. If the Council allowed all gear types to continue on the black cod grounds, longlines would snag gill nets and snap off on pots, and trawls would shred everything in their path while ripping open their meshes on pots and the anchors of other gear. Each fight in the fishing game now led to the next. It had once seemed so simple.

Shoji Tsurifune entered the lobby from a taxi. He held only a briefcase, although another Japanese behind him carried suitcases in his hands and under his arms. As always Mike's hair was sleek and his dark suit impeccable. When he saw Hank walking toward him his face assumed a cordial expression. "Well, Hank," he said calmly, "I see you've survived the evil little yellow men."

Hank had planned to be contained about it, but Mike's smoothness irritated him at once. "Come off it, Mike. Don't pull guilt on me. A Harvard man? You're enough American to answer for yourself, not hide behind being Japanese. You simply tried to trick me. That's universal with some people wherever they come from."

"You're talking nonsense, Hank. But you surely succeeded in doing us mischief."

"And you knew how to screw me."

"If you corner a dragon, don't whine if the dragon defends himself."

"At least the reptile part's right. You took my boat. I won't forget."

"Your debt-laden vessel in which we'd invested a fortune. Father and I were saving what we could from wreckage."

"I'd trusted at least your dad. Is he here now, or back in Tokyo hatching new schemes?"

Shoji's lip twitched. It appeared to be a disturbing question. "Here later, perhaps."

"And I don't know all of what you did to my man Kodama, but you hurt him."

Shoji sighed, waved the man beside him with suitcases toward the check-in desk, and turned back calmly. "Hank, Hank, this fellow wasn't

'your man,' as you call it. Mr. Kodama is a Japanese employee who under-
stands his position."

"He's a hell of a fine fisherman."

"Tsurifune company has many superb fishermen. They are all unemployed because you Americans have closed your waters. Even more now
shall be unemployed."

"And you've screwed your man John Gains too, I hear."

"I'm afraid being our man was John's illusion. He surely tried to ingra-
tiate himself. An efficient, energetic fellow. How much Japanese did you
ever learn to be with us, Hank? But our watchmen reported more than
once that while John worked late in his office, commendable, he'd be seen
examining off-limits files. At last we decided to distrust him."

Hank wondered about Swede, who probably knew more company
secrets than Gains, but ventured instead, "I guess every business has its
secrets."

"Shall we change the subject? In spite of everything, Father wishes you
well."

"Did he instruct Kodama to cheat on my catches?"

"I don't believe that you understand survival, Hank."

"Survival's what hooked me in with you."

"Not greed to get your share and more?" Shoji smiled, but his face was
not pleasant.

Hank paused long enough to consider. "No. Just my share."

"A buccaneer's share, if you'll permit me. You Americans are hoarders,
you know. The fruits of the ocean should be there for those who need
it, not—"

"Those who need, hell. You mean for those like yourself, who raped it
before we stopped you. Who've already fished out their own waters."

"Look to yourselves also for greed, Hank. Do you think that American
competitiveness, and the technology you love so to keep improving, will
keep you from overfishing now that you have the opportunity?" Mike
closed his eyes and retained his dignity. "You have all, so you can take all.
This is the understandable way of the world."

"We have our own mouths to feed like everybody else." Hank stopped
himself. Their argument was backing into truths on both sides and could
have no answer. "Greet your dad back for me. In spite of what I feel, I
hope he's well?"

"Oh, genki, genki. Father did enjoy you. He'll be glad to hear that you've survived."

They found nothing further to say. After a silence they exchanged courtesies halfway between an American nod and a Japanese bow, then parted in opposite directions.

Hank had advanced toward the elevator only a few steps before John Gains stopped him to shake hands. John still wore the same kind of dark suit and sober tie as Shoji Tsurifune, and his black hair had the same sleekness. What do I owe him? Hank wondered, and took the proffered hand.

"Now, Hank," Gains began without preamble, "I suppose, since I saw you with the Rosvic crowd, that you're committed to longline for sablefish. But I hope you're not working to ban trawls. You've trawled, so you know a net can be tuned to fish clean. And you'd know, for example, that trawl doesn't take the horrendous toll on seabirds that longline hooks do. Soon environmentalists are going to be all over longliners on that. And trawl has other advantages. The two groups of us should be joining forces to ban pots and gill nets from the black cod fishery, not fighting each other."

"Hello yourself, John, and what's it to you?"

"You should have my card. Here. I now represent the United Trawlers Association."

"*That's* a quick jump from the Japanese pocket!"

"Indeed." Gains continued unfazed. "I saw you talking to Shoji there. Sharp fellow. We've remained friends, but the company didn't have room for my personal growth anymore. So, best to give notice, though the director himself tried to keep me. It wasn't hard with my experience to find a new place up the line."

"I was afraid they'd dumped you. Glad it's different."

"Thanks for your good wishes, but it was a matter of business."

Hank hesitated, then continued, "If you're still on such good terms, do you ever see the old man? What's he up to?"

"The director? I hear he's in New York now, they say to sell some of those gosh-awful paintings."

Hank frowned. "He loved those paintings."

"And was smart enough to invest in ones that accrued in value, I hear. Frankly, they all looked like a joke to me, although I took the time to learn about them. Now I believe he's trying to raise enough on them to save the family company."

Hank glanced toward the spot where he'd quitted Mike Tsurifune. "They're in that kind of trouble?"

"Unpopular American lawyers who fight Americans for foreign fishing rights don't come cheap. I've seen some of their bills. Too bad." He gave a thin smile. "Don't worry, Hank. They'll probably weather your turning them in. Just don't expect them to trust you again. Of course, if you have what they want, they'll do business."

"Whatever you did for me, John . . . I appreciate it."

Gains's driving energy eased. "Just old crewmates, Hank," he said quietly. "I'm sorry I couldn't have saved your boat. And you can thank your fellow Seth for having pocketed one of their documents besides what I might have . . . contributed."

"And Swede?"

John told him that Swede had also been fired. Since Swede had made nothing of it, few people knew. John became even quieter. "I used to turn up my nose at him a bit because he didn't try to get any further ahead. And the drinking. I'm afraid he reminded me of my father. I might have told you Dad was a plumber, but I'm sure I didn't mention the booze. I've struggled uphill all the way. It's made me devalue people who don't need to fight. Or don't appear to. Swede's a straight arrow."

"So are you, John."

Gains shrugged, although he seemed gratified, and his brisk manner returned. "Catch you for a drink later, Hank. I'll try to convince you that trawling for black cod is good."

"I'll try to be convinced."

That evening he talked with Jody in Kodiak. In their fatter times she might have been with him in the big city during Council, even preparing for a jaunt to Hawaii. Tonight she sat again in their living room overlooking the water while Dawn and Henny bent over homework, each at a separate table. But she sounded content.

"I've got to do something for Swede," he said.

"Yes! But I think you also need to call Kodama. You didn't see his devastation." Hank was silent.

During the ensuing day of Council affairs, it became official that the Japanese had lost their black cod quota for good, since Americans had proven they could catch it all. The Japanese through their lawyers managed, however, to gain a recommendation for extra Bering Sea pollack and true-cod allotments, as partial compensation for the loss. The Council in this case made a practical concession. There might otherwise have been a lawsuit from the more militant segment of the Japanese fishing industry, charging that the U.S. broke long-term commitments.

All right, Hank decided, and called Kodama. He reached him at the Tsurifune office since Kodama had no phone at his home. The conversation was both reassuring and unsatisfactory.

"Busy," said Kodama brusquely. "Many problems in company for keeping busy."

"Are you able to talk?"

"Of course."

At least, Hank decided, guilt had not crushed the guy as Jody had feared. "Are things okay with you?" he asked.

"Of course."

Hank went straight to his question on the expensive call. "Kodama-san. Did they force you to change my catch reports?"

After a pause: "Company policy important."

"That's not my point."

"Hank-san," said Kodama quietly, using Hank's given name for the first and only time, "all things not the point." His voice had suddenly lost its vitality.

Hank felt a surge of affection and sadness, but he could find no words for comfort. "Hit 'em hard at the Judo-kan, buddy," he said lamely in parting.

"*Kodo*-kan," Kodama corrected, but without his signature snap. "Hai. Of course."

When Hank reported the conversation later to Jody, he admitted that he was glad he'd called. From the phone booth in the hotel lobby where he was speaking, he at last saw Swede. His friend wandered the corridor like an old bear, scowling, even hunched. Hank started out toward him.

Shoji Tsurifune eased into his way. "Father wishes to speak you," he said curtly. "Please follow to his room."

"I didn't know he was here."

Mike made no answer. He led the way to the elevator without speaking further, and conducted Hank to the room. Inside, Director Tsurifune sat behind a table. A lamp cast a glare on his bald head and created dark shadows on his face. Hank remembered him at a similar table in the same hotel only months before, seated like an icon but with his wrinkled face full of vital authority and humor. Since then the director had aged. His back remained straight—even straighter than before—but his face was now a rigid mask. "Thank you to come, Mr. Crawford," he said, and gestured toward a chair.

"Sir." Hank sat, but did not relax.

The director then glared up at his son and nodded.

Shoji Tsurifune remained standing. His voice was precise, without the usual bright mannerisms. "My father wishes to tell you, Hank, that he is dishonored. His son did not consult or tell him of altered catch reports in the fishery. Also, Father did not know that I withheld your home after he had agreed to remove it from lien. Further, as regards your vessel, *Jody Dawn*—"

The director interrupted sharply in Japanese.

"Father tells me to add regrets, that you and wife were forced to move from your home. He knows this caused you surely pain and disruption."

Hank inclined his head gravely. It made less difference now that it was over, but he knew that he'd wanted the old man to be innocent.

"Further, then, as regards your vessel, *Jody Dawn*—Father is shamed that his son refused negotiation which might have allowed repossession of your vessel, a concession which also might have been promised you. However, he accepts full guilt because he is director, and he failed to be alert to the affairs of his company." Shoji had been speaking coolly, but now his voice faltered. "Therefore, on behalf of the company that bears my father's name, and his father's . . . and mine . . . we . . . beg forgiveness."

During Shoji's speech the director's eyes burned into Hank's with a red-rimmed Kabuki intensity.

Hank felt a stir of excitement. With Oddmund's offer from the native corporation . . . "Then, sir, there's a way for me to buy back my boat if I find the money?"

Slowly the director shook his head. "Vessel has been sold." He picked his words in a low voice. "I cannot to make return of your vessel."

"We're a small company, Hank," added Shoji, his self-control regained. "Not Taiyo or Marubini. Loss of Alaska fish is ruin unless we find ways. Thus the catch log. Thus taking profit on your boat when such procedure observed letter of original contract."

The director held up his hand. "Do not shame us further with excuse!"

Hank prepared to make a small speech of forgiveness in the director's formal Japanese style. All done was done, and from the old director's appearance, Hank believed him. They'd made nothing of his own betrayal of them. Both had accepted their fault. It was honor of sorts. But first he said, "I accept what's happened. But I want this of you." He turned to Shoji, whose face had become nearly as masklike as his father's. "Mr. Yuk-ihiro Kodama has also been shamed by what you made him do. Promise that you'll keep him fishing master on one of your vessels but that you'll never again require him to cheat."

"Hank, the man's a mere worker."

The old man spoke angrily in Japanese.

Shoji sighed. "Agreed, Hank. So long as the company exists with fishing vessels."

Hank regarded him evenly. "Is this one I can trust you on?"

Shoji's voice chilled. "Yes, Hank."

The director spoke to his son again in Japanese. He rose with a deter-mined expression but his appearance startled Hank. How frail his body appeared! Shoji began to argue urgently. He had lost his cool veneer. The director was clearly back in charge.

Shoji turned to Hank and his tone became distant. "My father is now acting as if we are still in the wealthy days and I have continued to advise no. But I'll obey him." He went into another room and returned with a long picture mounted behind Plexiglass. "Father decides this to be yours."

The picture consisted of dimly-colored cross-hatches placed ingeniously at different intersecting angles.

"From what you've told me, Hank, I don't expect you'll appreciate such a work. The artist is Jasper Johns, and the work has its price. Greater value with time, probably, so I suggest that you don't run off and sell it right away. Its title is Usuyuki from a famous Kabuki drama, since Father remembered that you liked Kabuki screen print, thirty colors."

Where, thought Hank with wild humor, could you find Kabuki or any-thing else but pick-up sticks in such a picture? Yet, the work had a strange appeal. He bowed to the director. "I can't accept it, sir. It's nice. Interest-ing . . . Beautiful, I guess. But not my—"

"It's now settled," Shoji continued. "Attorney Rider has already been told to draw up papers which transfer ownership. You own a property that I suggest you place in the hotel safe until you take it home."

"No. I really—"

"Stop," said the director in a voice suddenly strong. "You must take it as gift, Mr. Crawford." He held out a hand that trembled. "Stay survived, Mr. Crawford. Now you must take artwork, please, and go. I am tired."

When Hank phoned Jody to tell her what had happened, she said with light gravity, "Oh, you boys and your honor. If you'd only think to do it right at the beginning, think of all the thrashing around you'd save yourselves. I hope you damn well put the thing in a safe?"

Hank at last found Swede outside a meeting room where testimony was droning on. He approached him boldly. "Still afraid to be seen with me?"

"Who wouldn't be, Crawford?" said Swede in surprising good humor. "How's it feel to have your tail trimmed back?"

"Some of it I'll never forgive, but I'm getting over it. In part, thanks to you, I believe. And now you've been shafted."

"I'll manage." Swede gestured toward the meeting room. "They're held up in there on habitat, and everybody's got to have his say. A Coast Guard friend whispered to me that later today there might be a surprise topic to interest you and me both, so we'll stay close. But I'm dry."

Swede's returned to booze? Hank worried, but exclaimed that he'd buy, glad that they were talking again. They went to an open café area within sight of the corridor that led to the meeting room's doors. He was relieved when Swede ordered lemonade, and did the same.

Swede sipped his drink. "Can't forgive when all's fair in war?" His hair, now nearly white but still full, was less shaggy than usual, probably from a rare pre-Council barber visit. "Some small and mid-sized Japanese fishing companies are going under. They couldn't all diversify like the giants. The Tsurifunes are survivors, though."

Suddenly the doors of the meeting room banged open and people streamed out to form knots in the corridor. One group of several Japanese, Shoji Tsurifune among them, circled Justin Rider. All their expressions were intense. A group of Americans clustered near a reporter who scribbled notes while he talked to a Coast Guard officer.

"I expect that we missed it after all," said Swede.

Nels Tormulsen of the Seattle halibut schooner fleet strode past and stopped, his lean face suppressing a grin. "Finally! We've caught 'em!" He circled his arm toward the bartender for drinks. "You men missed what they'll talk about for the rest of the year."

Three scotches arrived. Swede pushed away the glassful placed in front of him and asked what had happened.

"The Japs are finally caught is what!" Nels waved a printed statement. "Read this!" He waved it again toward a group of fellow halibut fishermen from Seattle who cheered, then handed it to Hank.

The statement, signed by the National Marine Fisheries Service, informed the Council of documents proving a conspiracy among certain Japanese fishing organizations since at least 1980. The documents had been seized from the Japanese stern trawler *Hamazen Maru* Number 35 in November 1982 and subsequently also from the Japanese longliner *Eikyu Maru* Number 82 in March 1983.

Hank skimmed the statement. It declared in part:

> *The documents appear to include instructions, plans, and policies which outline, implement, and direct organized schemes aimed at manipulating observer coverage and the "best blend" determination of catch. The documents also reveal an effort by Japanese vessels to evade and thereby defeat our at-sea enforcement . . . According to the translated documents, tactics included purposeful reductions in catch . . .*

Another fisherman came up, and Nels eased the statement from Hank's hands to show it to him. Usually a deliberate drinker who took his time over a glass, Nels finished his scotch in rapid gulps. "The chairman's called a half-hour recess to clear the air. Too many of us started talking at once. Everybody says, cut *all* Jap allocations, not just black cod, zap, now! *Every*body!" He toyed with Swede's rejected glass of scotch, then pushed it toward Hank. "Going back in. This is too good to miss a minute. The question I want answered is, why'd it take the damn bureaucrats two years to speak up from when they caught the first cheater?"

"I expect," said Swede in his calm, dry voice, "that they first needed to translate, and then to decide how to handle it. After all, Japan's a military ally. Fish isn't the world's only priority."

"While for two years they stole our fish from under us and we didn't have to let them?" Nels voice hardened. "I forgot. You work for them."

"Swede watches the whole picture," Hank interjected quickly. "None of it's simple. Thanks for the drink."

Nels joined his buddies, and Hank watched again the knot of Japanese. They seemed smaller than ever—vulnerable even: short men, all dressed like funeral directors. Shoji's head rose above the others. His face was tense and pale.

"What's going to happen now, Swede?"

"Small companies could go under. Tsurifune? Middle-sized. Nobody turned them in except you. The documents that prove they scammed are safe somewhere in Japan, except for a few slipped from a box that there's now no reason to show anybody."

"You seem pretty understanding. No grudges?"

"For saving their own skins? I found them honest except for this. The Harvard boy learned the American way too well, then pushed it where he could. Maybe not again. As best I can tell, and I've watched from inside, they weren't part of the conspiracy your happy friend's jumping over. Shoji was merely picking off a dumb American who didn't read his contract."

"Thanks for that. But they dumped you. What'll you do?"

"I was getting tired of little Japs looking over my shoulder. Mary and I get along best when I'm away, but I'll find something in Seattle to keep me out of the house."

Before the Council members ended their session, they voted unanimously to recommend "that the Department of State not allocate any more fish to Japan to catch off Alaska."

Hank flew back to Kodiak holding the picture wrapped in newspapers. He had never owned anything valuable that was smaller than a boat. What was he to do with it? he wondered. Rent some kind of big safe to keep it in?

"All right to sit with you, Hank?" It was Oddmund. His native causes at Council had kept him in different hearings than Hank so they had only nodded in passing. Odds offered to make more room by taking Hank's bulky flat package to a luggage compartment, but Hank refused; Odds then asked about his one-trip shipmate, Kodama.

"Back in Japan with his family, doing fine," said Hank, and elaborated no further. He wondered what Kodama would say now about the white man's oppression that the two had so belabored.

Odds gravely reiterated his debt to Hank for saving his life. By now Hank accepted that this would happen again and again, and he'd developed a

gentle rejoinder to keep it as brief as possible. "But Hank," Odds continued earnestly, "if you ever need—"

"Still lend me the money to buy back my *Jody Dawn?*" said Hank, half
teasing.

"We'd find a way."

The response gave Hank a surge of excitement. Maybe not over yet,
after all! But he followed with a more immediate idea. During his time
slinging fish at the new native plant only months before, which had
enabled him to pull himself together, the place had been managed loosely.
"Tell you what to do for me, Odds." Before the flight landed, Hank had
brokered the job of plant manager for Swede Scorden if Swede wanted it,
and had made Odds eager to have a man of such caliber.

When he stepped off the plane in late afternoon it was already dark. A
cold, clear wind hit his face. Summer had ended, along with its fogs and
occasional warm, calm days at sea. The time of steady storms and long
nights was moving back in. By taking over the *Adele H* as his own, he'd be
back on a boat of modest size, almost back where he'd started.

Jody and the children met him. They crowded Odds into the station
wagon also and drove him home, waved to his wife at the door, then
headed along the flats to their own home. The children each had things to
tell him. Pete had learned a song that he sang twice. Henny had become
eligible for junior basketball, and Dawn had a new favorite horse.

Jody shook her head when she saw the picture. "Which end's supposed
to be up? Well, it's interesting. Has a kind of glow. I suppose we could
hang it on a wall somewhere. But vertical or horizontal?"

With Jody in charge of the art and taking its possession casually, Hank
was able to forget his worry. He needed to rig the *Adele H* for a winter
fishery and earn a living for his crew and himself. Halibut and black cod
were through for the season, but the big steel-framed pots formerly used
to catch king crabs were being rigged to catch newly abundant true cod
around the island. It was a fishery with a fraction of king crab's drive and
income, although it would provide a living on the water.

"If I should buy Jones Henry's boat from Adele," he asked Jody cautiously, "do you think she'd be offended if I changed its name?" Jody
agreed to ask.

Seth had flown to California after quietly passing to Swede the single
incriminating document he'd salvaged from the *Puale Bay.* "Wish me

luck," he said expansively to Mo and Terry, covering his unease. Meeting him, he hoped, was the divorced Marion who had once jilted him. "At least he's got a maybe there," said Terry wistfully, waving him off.

While waiting around to fish again, Mo and Ham reveled in idleness. Since they had no boat on which to sleep, each moved in with his girlfriend. At nights after the girls finished work at the supermarket, they became a noisy foursome in town. Terry and Tom Harris took over Seth's rooms while he was away. Although their restless natures came from different causes, they both found work and welcomed it to keep busy, even in the barnlike, unheated shed where they loudly welded and netted cod traps with other fishermen on the beach. For Tom it was one more Alaskan adventure.

Tom remained unsure of his course. Oyster season had begun again in Chesapeake Bay. Part of him missed it. But he feared that if he went back, even calling it a mere visit, he'd end up committed to shaft tongs with his dad and be stuck again. A phone call home left him relieved and sad. Captain Bart, deaf enough to use the phone seldom, shouted "That you, Tom? Time for arster and I bet you miss it, son." His mother took over the conversation with her calm practicality. "If you're content for once, you stay there, Tom. He'll be all right." The captain still went most mornings to Miss Ruby's, and now even rode out occasionally with Captain Billy. "Those two old goats," said his mother. "They've decided they can stand each other again. Gets him out from under my feet some days, thank goodness. There's a man still don't belong in a house." Tom was grateful to end the call with a laugh.

Seth phoned Hank from San Diego. He had decided to stay south for the winter. "Now that I've grandfathered myself into fishing black cod, I need a break from shitty weather."

"At least one of us has sense," Hank joked. He asked about the elusive Marion.

"Things not going bad, not bad," was all Seth would say.

Fishing with pots required less crew than longlining, and Seth's withdrawal made it feasible for Hank to keep Tom aboard. The others gathered at the boat and began converting gear from longline to pot-launch. Jones Henry's old king crab pots stood in a high square stack among others on open ground. Weather had faded the pink plastic buoys inside each but they remained firm. The straps and lines needed to be tested and some renewed. It was a week's steady work.

One day Hank, working over the stack with the rest, looked across the harbor. There into port glided his *Jody Dawn*. The hated letters for *American Victory* were now cleanly spelled out, with no trace beneath of the boat's christened name. Dark-brown rust spots pocked her black hull and white superstructure, and honey-brown rust streaked the mast. Black exhaust astern showed that the engine was burning oil. The sight gave him a wave of sick anger.

His malaise stayed for the rest of the day. "Watch the fuck there, line's expensive!" he barked when Tom inadvertently cut a strap too short and needed to toss it. The dark mood followed him home where he growled at Pete for pummeling him too hard in play, and then at Dawn for talking too much.

"Snap out of this," said Jody after the children had gone to bed.

He told her what he had seen. "The boat I put together myself, and now some careless asshole is killing her!"

"Oh, fishermen and their damn boat mistresses! Since you can't change this, Hank, get over it." He acknowledged gloomily, and apologized. "Speaking of boats and their lady names," Jody continued, "Adele phoned today and I asked her. She laughed and said, 'Sure, tell him to put some other floozy's name there in place of mine.' She went on to say that 'Poor Daddy, rest his soul' would be so pleased you're taking over his boat he'd forgive you. Make of that what you want. But Hank, I'm tired of being a name on a boat myself, so no more Jody-boats, please. Keep your wife and boat separate."

"Then what about Dawn? Or Danielle? She'd like that."

"Why not the 'Henny-Pete'? Or the 'Jones Henry'? Or maybe just the 'Hank'?" she asked wickedly.

"Be serious."

On the night before departure, Jody prepared a big steak dinner for them all. There was plenty of beer, and red wine for those who wanted it. Terry and Tom brought sleeping bags and planned to stay over. Mo and Ham arrived with their girlfriends, and lustily declared their intentions back in town on this big final night, while the girls held their men's muscular arms and giggled. It became a noisy, happy occasion, in the house they all once thought had been lost.

Jokes were many about the long Japanese picture on the wall. Jody had decided to hang it vertically. Everybody had an opinion. Word had passed around that it was valuable although nobody knew the degree. Terry declared he could do the same job with a box of dry macaroni for three bucks. Mo said he could do it even better running his toes through mud. It became a contest to see who could duplicate the picture best with what.

The children liked the game especially. Young Pete caught the spirit and started laughing with such noisy glee that Jody needed to calm him down. "I see a princess in it," announced Dawn. "Then you're even nuttier than I thought," said Henny. "It's just a lot of little lines."

Yet, thought Hank as the blaze from logs in the fireplace flickered a remarkable life into the picture, he liked it more and more. Maybe it did have some of the orderly slam-bang of Kabuki. He wished that the thing wasn't valuable.

The phone rang and Jody answered it, then soberly touched Hank's arm and told him to take the call in their bedroom.

It was Swede Scorden. His dry voice was level and quiet. "I just thought you might want to know. The old director went back home to Japan and shot himself."

"Why would he do that?" gasped Hank, knowing why even as he hoped he was wrong.

"Old-fashioned Japanese honor, I'd expect. The word is, he did it with some ceremony." Hank struggled for words. He felt that he himself was responsible. Swede must have sensed it. "You only reported facts, Crawford. Like Harry Truman's 'buck stops here.' Whether the old man knew what was happening in his company or not, he took responsibility. The kind of honor you don't find around much anymore, in Japan or anywhere else."

"What of Shoji? Did you hear anything about him?"

"I wouldn't speculate. The old man may now be the ancestor he'll need to answer to."

Hank, drained of party spirit, returned to the living room. The Japanese picture seemed to flash at him reproachfully with the flickers from the fireplace. He held up his hand to make an announcement. Jody took his arm and said quietly, "Don't. Nobody else here would understand." On impulse, Hank returned to the bedroom and phoned Baltimore.

"Dear!" said his mother. "It's two in the morning. Is somebody sick?"

"Nothing. Just wondered how you and Dad were."

On another line the elder Crawford declared heartily, "Just fine and asleep until you called. Hi. What's up?"

Hank made a joke of it. "Just wanted to hear your voices, honorable parents."

But, after he'd put down the phone . . . The old director, vital Mr. T. . . .

Next morning, as Hank and his crew readied to go fishing, the air was clean and cold. Hank laid out charts. He and Terry studied them. It would be new fishing for both, starting almost from scratch to find their grounds. Although storms and ice would remain as threatening as ever, they'd seldom need to go beyond the sight of Kodiak Island's mountains, never into such far wilds as the Bering Sea. (And, staying local, he could leave all the Anchorage fish politicking behind!) Hank felt a stir of adventure. He was reentering the turf where he'd started under Jones Henry, exploring for species not abundant in Jones's time but covering the same grounds. Maybe, he thought, to acknowledge the new start, he'd rename the *Adele H* something like "Sea Raider" when he could get to it.

Hank's family saw them off. He held Jody, smelled her scent, and lingered. "You're not going to the Bering Sea this time," she said gently. "I'll see you for dinner Saturday."

Henny and Dawn vied with each other to cast off the boat's lines. He needed to intervene to direct one forward and the other aft. Each handled the rope well. Both had the feel. Eventually he'd take them to sea with him, in summer calm. Soon! Would Pete follow suit? So far he'd shown no interest. But Henny and Dawn were becoming sea-babies, both teaching themselves the names of gear and arguing over relative merits of nets and lines. Suddenly he realized. He didn't have the option to abandon fish politics and merely fish. He'd need to do all he could to ensure that the water retained abundant life for his children to harvest.

The children waved, Pete jumping up and down, Henny with the solemnity of the departure as his eyes already followed the boat wistfully, Dawn calling him a last instruction to please bring her back a shell from the ocean for show-and-tell. And Jody. As lithe and sassy-postured as the day they'd met. Hair back in the same ponytail, mouth wide in that smile that stretched to the cheeks.

He headed for the narrows toward Marmot Bay, squinting into the sun. Terry, Mo, and Ham crowded gaily into the wheelhouse to watch and visit as in former days before the big longliner. When Tom came up the stairs they quieted and nudged each other. Tom swung a pair of his socks tightly knotted. Hank watched, interested. It was their way of initiating him into full crew status, but would Tom understand?

He turned back to the harbor once more to see his family. There moored nearby was his former *Jody Dawn*. He watched it all grow smaller with distance, then forced himself to look ahead.